The ASBO Effect

By Ray Coleman

Published in 2009 by New Generation Publishing

Copyright © Ray Coleman

First Edition

Chapter 1
New Horizons Park.

It could have been one of Nature's diversions, a clever little trick played by evolution, or perhaps a brainstorm release of soothing narcotics. But no, not for Karen, Karen believed in love and she was in love. Again. Oh yes, she had problems, but negative thoughts were receding as her world once more emerging from the shadows, seemed a happy place in which to live. She lived, with the help of benefits, in a housing association block which thrust a stack of towering concrete high above the neighbourhood, and it was towards this unsightly landmark that Karen negotiated her rusting Metro. Her meagre wages had been wisely spent on securing another week's supply of supermarket offers. These nestled reassuringly in the boot.

She drove into the parking area, reversing her car with confident use of the mirror and turned off the engine. She adjusted the mirror to check her appearance and was pleased with what she saw. Not bad for an attractive brunette approaching forty. She looked pretty, beautiful even, beautiful for Mike her lover. An abandoned vehicle stripped of all useful parts and filled with fragments of busted glass went unnoticed. This was nothing unusual. Vandalism, casual litter and obscene graffiti were a regular feature of New Horizons Park, but today, the Autumn sunshine was something special, it's delicate rays adding a certain lustre to the housing estate, warming Karen, giving her hope, making her feel positive.

Matt, her youngest teenage son, came out to help and they began unloading the boot. 'Where's Ben?' Karen asked, showing some annoyance.

'Oh I couldn't drag him away from his playstation' Matt replied with hopeless resignation. 'And he knows the lift isn't working.'

'You've had something to eat?' Karen asked, checking earlier instructions.

'I microwaved the curry, like you said, but Ben's already opened the tin of beans.'

'They were for tomorrow's breakfast. I can't take much more of Ben, he puts so much pressure on us all. What is it with him?' A nervous tic had developed around Matt's left eye and it began winking furiously. Karen felt a surge of motherly love, 'No racing up the stairwell Matt, you know I can't keep up with you.'

Grime and graffiti smothered the stairwell and in this conduit of nightmares, old fears and misgivings were amplified by echoing footsteps. Where had she gone wrong with Ben? Had she really been such a bad parent? She had tried to set standards, house rules, boundaries, regular meals, all those things which feature in the guideline jargon of good parenting, but with Ben she had failed miserably and her love for him had counted for nothing. Ben could only express hatred for his mother and showed her no respect whatsoever.

They entered the flat and Ben, hunching forward on the edge of the settee, gave no welcome, no recognition even of their presence. An empty tin lay discarded on the floor, an empty plate hung over the arms of the settee as if about to launch itself into space and a messy fork burrowed it's way between the folds of the upholstery. Ben's fingers jerked at the playstation producing a series of loud explosions and flashes of light. His face twisted with satisfaction as each hit graphically exploded on the TV screen.

'Ben for goodness sake turn off that awful noise and look at the mess your making, someone always has to clean up after you.' Karen shouted across the room.

'How can Matt concentrate on his homework with that racket going on?' Ben ignoring his mother, turned up the volume, and the optimism which during the day had stiffened her resolve, began to fade. How could she deal with her wayward son, his aggression, his refusal to co-operate, his bullying and his spite? All her efforts to hold the family together were being gradually undermined. She had found a new love in her life, but reawakened hopes and dreams were not enough to mend the hurt she felt. Ben had broken her heart.

Matt arranged his school books on the table and began making notes. He was tall for his fifteen years, a gangling youth who had suddenly outgrown his strength. However, a warm personality and an intelligent face made him easily recognisable as his mother's son. He loved her and had an earnest desire to help her escape the squalor of New Horizons Park, which during his formative years, had developed an unsavoury reputation. It had become a no go area for both law abiding citizens and law enforcement officers. Driven by love for his mother and steel determination, Matt was able to lower a shutter against the noisy intrusion of Ben's war games, and as the revelations of science opened before him, he escaped into the world of knowledge and reason.

Karen, tired of confrontation, retreated into the kitchen and began unloading their provisions. Battery eggs, battery chicken, intensively farmed bacon and other cheap perishables were hastily stowed in the fridge and as she struggled with faulty catches on the shoddy arrangement of kitchen cupboards, her trembling fingers betrayed a lack of control. Matt had thoughtfully done most of the day's washing up leaving cups, plates and utensils on the drainer. She reached for the drying up cloth and paused to look out over New Horizons Park. The kitchen window presented an elevated yet narrow view over the city and Karen, ignoring the damp penetration around its frame, gazed at the distant skyline.

The original planning of New Horizons Park envisaged a high rise complex offering a fresh approach to communal living. Even so, land costs had been the chief consideration. The projected vision on paper, conjoured by insular bureaucracy, had not materialised, and now the accomodation presented nothing more than a depository for disfunctional humanity. It had become a parking lot for those whose lives had been fragmented by the breakdown of family life, those unable to take responsibility for themselves, those with low self esteem, those with low expectations and little hope. Obscure laws, rules and regulations increased the tensions, as New Horizons park degenerated into an appalling conglomerate of truancy, theft, alcohol abuse, domestic violence and drug trafficking. It had been a favourite stomping ground for social workers, probation officers and the like, a rich source of subject matter for their endless meetings and written reports, but the futility of it all had silenced their bleating. Gang culture reigned, and a group of hoodies led by a teenager with above average intelligence, terrorised all those foolhardy enough to venture out of doors after dark. They organised violence on the football terraces, vandalised property, trashed cars and experimented with drugs. Their leader had declared war on society and Karen was well acquainted with his activities. His name was Ben Mackay. Ben Mackay, her once much loved, eldest son. The skyline melted in tears and she wiped them away with the drying up cloth. It was no use dreaming, no use staring out on the promised land.

Then for a moment there was silence and as Karen opened the door to investigate a thankful reprieve, a new crisis unfolded. Katrina her daughter, had drawn the plug on Ben's playstation and was screaming at him. ' Ben, What have you done with my mobile, you've nicked it haven't you? You absolute pig!'

'Shut your noise, I haven't seen your mobile, I've got a mobile. You're always losing stuff.'

'You're a natural liar and a pig! I know you've been through my things again and it *was* you who stole my money. The money I earned in the school holidays, I just hate you!'

'Please' Karen interceded, 'Please stop shouting and please stop using such awful language. Ben give her back her mobile.'

Matt rose from the table seething with anger and frustration. 'Take a good look at yourself Ben, always acting like a moron. You ate the beans when you knew mum wanted them for breakfast tomorrow. You knew the lift wasn't working but you made her struggle up the stairs, and now you're stealing from your own family to buy drugs. Give Kat back her mobile.'

'What *you* gonna do about it mummy's boy? Mum needs this, mum needs that, I don't care what mum needs. We all know what she really wants and if I want stupid beans, I'll have stupid beans.'

Matt remained standing. 'Ben you're a mess, a complete mess. Why don't you get yourself a job, help mum out a bit instead of trying to make life impossible for her, for all of us?'

Ben leant back in a nonchalant mood, he stretched his athletic frame, hands behind his head. A year older than Matt, he was undeniably handsome, but his blonde hair and rugged features now revealed a mean streak. 'Well isn't mum making life difficult for *us* now she's got a new boyfriend? She's all over him, thinks he's cool when he's just another fuckin idiot.'

Matt struck back. 'Mike's a good bloke, he's helping me with my GCSE's'

'Mike's just another DIY merchant. Thinks he knows everything. Anyone can see he's only after one thing. Anyway, who needs GCSE's?'

'I do,' Matt said, 'And I want my A levels. I'm not ending up like you, expelled from school with us living from hand to mouth in a dump like this, worrying whether we can afford to eat beans or a takeaway. Matter of fact I've decided I want to be a forensic scientist.'

'What a cop! Lot of use they are. What can they do, they're never around? All they do is put on a show with fancy uniforms, riding around in brand new squad cars and helicopters and stuff. Only yesterday they were down Cumber road. I counted twenty two police guys, six squad cars, two big vans and a couple of motorbikes, just in case. And what were they doing? They were playing with their latest toy, Automatic Number Plate Recognition. They caught three people driving without car insurance!'

'They do catch criminals, they caught you didn't they? Gave you an ASBO, bringing shame on the whole family. Either way I'm interested in it, I like science and Mike says I can get work experience.'

'He's nothing to do with the cops is he?' Ben queried with alarm.

'No he's a joiner, got his own business, makes oak furniture.'

Karen felt a curious surge of pins and needles, her cheeks were numb, her mouth went dry and her legs trembled. Confrontation between her sons set her apart, shut her out of their lives, leaving her in isolation. This place, the sanctuary she had tried to make a home, had become a crucible of hate. Her needs, her opinions, her feelings, were of no account. She screamed in desperation. 'God! I can't take much more of this. Ben, you've no respect, no consideration, always out for youself, always on the take, everything's all about *you*. What have you done with Kat's mobile?

'All you think about is Mike, you're fancy man'

'How could you say that! I've worked my fingers to the bone to keep this family together with absolutely no help from you're father. Mike's the best thing that's happened to me for a long time, he's loving and caring and without him there's no way we could keep a car on the road or enjoy a few extras.'

'Your last boy friend was the best thing that's happened to you,' Ben sneered, 'That was till he left you, just like Dad. They didn't want you in their lives and neither do I. I've got friends. I can go it alone.'

'You're father was a waster and a drunk, insanely jealous and violent. Do you want to end up like him? If only you *could* move out, if only you *could* go it alone, well that would be just fine, better for all of us. But we both know that going it alone for you means messing with drugs. I know those young thugs you meet up with, those hoodies in the amusement arcade, they're all a bunch of crooks.'

'It's no use mum.' Katrina said, calmly interrupting her mother's mounting tirade. 'I know Ben hates us all. I'm not afraid of him. I'm going to call the police.'

'No Kat, not the police, taking statements, social workers and mountains of paperwork,' Karen warned, nervously twisting the locks of her hair. 'That wouldn't help Matt or any of us. Mike's on his way over, perhaps he can get through to Ben'

'Oh yes, wonderful Mike. Taking us all under his wing is he?' Ben said, his voice loaded with sarcasm.

'Well he's a big strong guy and I think you're scared of him. You know you can't treat him the way you treat us.' Katrina said, offering support for her mother.

Mike left his van in a small shopping precinct, preferring to walk the remaining half mile to New Horizons Park. On two occasions he had risked parking near Karen's Metro and each time the rear doors had been forced and valuable tools had been stolen. He had reported the thefts, but there was no crime busting response from the police, no enquiries, no finger printing, only a warning against such foolhardiness and a reminder that he had failed to record the serial numbers.

Mike and Karen made an unlikely pair. She stood, in moderately high heels, slightly taller than Mike's five feet nine, and her slender figure and long beautiful hair were in direct contrast to his heavy muscular frame and balding head. In his youth Mike had played rugby league and was something of a legend in rugby league circles, a player's player, a tireless powerhouse of aggression, who led his forwards from the front. He had never been a good looker and at forty five, the results of his sporting activities were very much in evidence. His face bore the battle scars and his generous nose had been rearranged many times. However, Mike was a true gentleman, gentle to the women in his life, honest and trustworthy and Karen felt completely safe with him.

Eight years previously Mike had lost his wife Sheila, in mysterious circumstances. She was a Botanist and Mike had loved her dearly, but one day, she literally walked out on him. Their daughter Sarah, was taking a gap year from Liverpool University and Josh, their teenage son, was on a surfing holiday with friends. For the first time in their married life, Mike and Sheila had escaped family pressures by taking an adventure holiday, treking in the Himalayan foothills. Their guide had been very clear about the dangers of their environment but Sheila had broken the rules. In her search for exotic flora, she had wandered from the main group and was never seen again. Numerous enquiries and expensive search expeditions had yielded not a single clue, leaving Mike unable to grieve her loss. He dealt with the tragedy by throwing his energy into his craft, developing his joinery skills to the level of a cabinet maker. He made distinctive oak furniture, hand carved and beautifully finished. His designs, which had a medievil feel about them, soon attracted attention. Trade exhibitions followed, then a very select clientele. Mike resisted the pressure to expand, to think in terms of mass production, he just quietly worked at his bench, absorbed in the intricacies of his craft. Josh, his apprenticed son worked with him and Mike was entirely at ease with himself and the world around him, but at times he felt lonely. He needed a woman in his life

Then one day Mike met Karen, or rather he became aware of her, busily working the till on a supermarket checkout. He became so aware of her, that instead of shopping once a week as was his custom, he shopped twice a week, making sure that Karen was on the till. Karen greeted each customer with a welcome smile and a bit of friendly chat which Mike regarded as something special. After a few weeks Karen realised that this pugnacious looking character was in fact a very regular customer, though she was at a loss to understand why he made so many visits in order to make so few purchases. Karen had always judged men by their outward appearance, they had to be taller than herself and good looking, but the warmth and physical presence of this man gradually began to envelope her. She truly expected something might happen between them and gradually her smiles melted into special smiles and her chat became brief conversation. A faint heart was beyond Mike's comprehension and one evening, while loading his groceries into plastic bags, he asked her for a dinner date. When she accepted, he was so overjoyed he forgot the sequence of his pin number, making three fumbled attempts before he discovered the right combination.

To walk through New Horizons, carrying a bunch of flowers, was asking for trouble, but Mike had the bearing and looks of a man who could handle trouble. He passed several loitering youths but was unaccosted. He felt no threat, never gave it a thought, his only thoughts were for Karen, his new found lady love. He decided not to rush things. He would court her in the old fashioned way. When he arrived on the landing he heard raised voices. He recognised the anxiety in Karen's voice. She trusted him so much she had given him a key to the flat and he hastily let himself in. Ben held Matt by the neck and was pushing his face down among the pages of his homework, shouting, yelling abuse at Matt. ' Jus keep you fuckin nose out of my business, mummy's boy,' he threatened.

Karen was crying, clawing at Ben in desperation. 'Please Ben, please, please stop it,' she screamed.

Katrina, seething with anger, was punching digits on the telephone.

Mike calmly walked over to Ben. 'Now cool it Ben,' he said, taking each of Ben's arms in a grip of iron. 'What seems to be the matter?' He walked Ben back to the settee pushing him as easily as one might push a pram and forced him into a sitting position.

'Ben's making life hell for all of us,' Katrina answered, 'And he's stolen my mobile, I don't know why he hates us all so.'

'Yes *and* he's taken Kat's wages,' Matt added, 'He's turning mum into a nervous wreck.'

'He's completely out of control, he's beyond me, and now he's getting into drugs, running around with a gang of hoodies,' Karen said, wiping away her tears, 'I just can't handle him, get him to see sense.'

'I suppose you're going to beat me up?' Ben winced, feeling a loss of circulation in his lower arms. 'Teach me a lesson. Back to college and all that crap.'

'I'm not into beating up anyone and I'm certainly not going to start with you, I've too much respect for your family. Now listen to me Ben, just listen to me for a moment. I want you to do something for me.'

'Oh yeah, like what for instance?'

'Well it's for your mum really, I want you to make something for her.'

'Make something! You're sleeping with her. You make something.'

Mike released his grip. 'Actually Ben, since you seem so concerned about it, I'm not sleeping with your mum, but we do love each other and I hope your family will come to terms with that. Your mum told me that after your father left, you were a good son and a useful handyman. She said she couldn't have managed without you. Is that true?'

'Well yeah, sort of, but that was different. She hadn't started seeing other blokes.'

'Well, How would you like a full apprenticeship, working with me and my son Josh? Use that good brain of yours, learn a real skill with your hands, make things in wood, make something really brilliant for your mum. In my workshop?'

'Oh how wonderful,' Karen said throwing her arms around Mike's neck, kissing him on the cheek.

Ben leapt to his feet, 'Who the hell want's to be a boring DIY merchant? Get yourself a life Mike, stuff your fuckin job!'

Chapter 2
Meg's Place

The city had reinvented itself. A few noble structures, classical buildings in natural stone, solid, dependable and conservative stood like sentinals over an industrial age of prosperity and civic pride. Now a new city, a new age, had already dawned. Truly incredible structures, private appartments, shopping malls, office blocks, their windows twinkling with computors, elbowed for space in the very heart of re-development. Huge surpluses from energy rich countries and excessive profits made by far eastern industrialists, had found a safe haven for investments, incredibly, in Anglo Saxon property and money markets. The city's glittering facade was only a pretence of wealth, for in the outlying areas nothing much had changed. In an early attempt to rid the city of it's slums, utility estates like New Horizons Park had been misconceived, leaving run down terraces with their failed corner shops ready for occupation by Asians, who by unstinted effort, were determined to rise above the abject poverty of the third world. Away from the pulsating hub of foreign investment, with preference for it's sprawling mantle, the Asbos, Ben Mackay's gang of hoodies, marked out their territory.

Through the back streets the Asbos swarmed in the manner of howling, prowling animals. They revelled in gang warfare and their own special form of anti- social behaviour. Some of them came from broken homes where the pursuit of pleasure by parents unable to make sacrifices, had cast them adrift. Others had single parents, encouraged to stay on subsistance benefits by complicated, self defeating bureaucracy. Little interest had been shown during their early development and they followed primitive male instincts, testing their audacity, their courage and daring.

Ben however, was different. Ben was not easily identifiable with these perceptions. His mother, although emotionally drained, loved him, made sacrifices, had experimented with the loss of benefits while pursuing occasional maintainance from her ex husband, filled out endless forms and contested the numerous claims for benefit overpayment. For little reward, burdened with a labyrinth of discouraging procedures, she had continued to work, setting her children an example of courage and dignity. And yet Ben, intelligent and rescourceful remained angry. True, he had been denied a father figure with whom he could relate, but his attitude reflected resentment and cynicism beyond his years. He read the newspapers, discussed family circumstances with his brother and thought deeply about things.

Ben reckoned the whole scheme of things throughout history, had been driven by anti-social behaviour. Even religion, which invariably preached peace and goodwill, was guilty of persecution in it's most horrifying form. Warfare too was a salient feature in the development of Mankind, or in his words, 'If collateral damage in Iraq, like blowing kid's legs off was necessary, what's wrong with a little anti- social protest back home?' He had asked himself, ' Why did the government think all this big time anti-social behaviour was necessary?' Was it to ensure the stability of oil markets? Was it the threat of imminent invasion or increased terrorism? Had we been seduced by America? Was it ambition, the delusion of political and historical greatness?' No one knew for sure, but one thing was certain. In the face of no real achievment and serious military reservations, the death toll continued to rise.

Ben considered other forms of anti- social behaviour. 'Wasn't making obscene profits from cheap labour, child labour, slave labour, a form of anti-social behaviour?' The import of food, textiles, technology, diamonds, everything produced by impoverished workers in countries whose needs were so dire, they became easy targets for money institutions, was nothing short of anti-social behaviour. Ben thought there had always been empire building of one sort or another, it was just a case of being in control, making the rules, then you could do as much anti-social stuff as you wanted. Give it plenty of spin and it would go unnoticed. Well, Ben instinctively knew, anti social behaviour was necessary, necessary for him.

He recognised the level of hypocrisy in our society but this served only as an excuse for his behaviour. The first flush of testosterone, emotional shock, the frustrations of his family's predicament and the sense of having a raw deal left him feeling reckless, not caring about himself or the rest of humanity. Fired by unrelenting TV images of luxury and wealth, disillusioned with the childhood idealisation of his father, overwhelmed by the unfairness of it all, he decided to declare war. After all, what price an ASBO? 'If you soldiered for the state, had courage in war, they gave you medals didn't they? Just a different kind of Asbo.' Here on the streets life could be cruel but for Ben and his mates there was a sense of freedom. They could make their own rules, seek out their own enemies, make war on rival gangs and vandalise the trappings of ordered society. They would fight their own wars, win their own battles, earn respect among their own and prove their untried valour.

To night's sortie Ben decided, was to be a 'Crystal Night.' He loved the sound of breaking glass, a big sound, sort of making music, everything falling apart, the end of the world. The Asbos would break as many windows as they could before targeting Rajurs's general store and off licence. Armed with tools stolen from building sites and a couple of petrol bombs, they careered through the back streets, smashing car windscreens or the window panes of an occasional home. A newly opened public toilet for the disabled attracted similar treatment and for good measure, a petrol bomb was tossed through the shattered opening. The most expensive cars received extra damage and one was torched.

Ashraf Rajur, for the convenience of late night shoppers, worked long hours. He had suffered numerous acts of vandalism in the past, but with stubborn pride refused to capitulate. No effective measures had been taken by the police and insurance companies refused any sort of cover at an affordable premium. Therefore, at considerable expense, he installed a first line of defence. The counter was entirely enclosed behind steel bars in the manner of a bank and in the event of an attack on his person or family he had devised an escape route leading to a secure, windowless room at the rear. The corner shop however, remained vulnerable during hours of trading and the steel shutters were only lowered when trading had finished for the day. The plate glass frontage had been fragmented on three previous occasions.

Ashraf sat behind the counter, business today had been very good. Weekly wage packets had reduced the need to give credit and many outstanding grocery bills had been settled. It was late evening, almost ten o'clock and he decided to close the shutters. Suddenly a dark, menacing shadow appeared at the window. Paralysed with terror, Ashraf felt trapped by demon forces, demons with pointed hoods, faces unseen, howling with racial abuse. Wielding a pick axe, one of the gang made short work of the toughened glass as others, stormed through the door. After the initial shock, Ashraf, middle aged and unfit, with despairing bravery, left the sanctuary of his enclosure to remonstrate with the intruders. The Asbos knocked him to the ground, and having grabbed a few plastic bags, began filling them with canned lager, crisps, cigarettes and money from the till. Ashraf, anxious to limit injury to himself, removed his glasses and adopted a foetal position, covering his face with his hands. For some unaccountable reason, this attitude of submission infuriated Pitbull Patterson, a vicious tearaway with a mindless reputation for violence. Hampered by a plastic bag of lager in one hand and a fist full of notes in the other, he began kicking the figure on the ground. One kick fractured an eye socket leaving Ashraf partially blinded. Ashraf's wife came screaming to his assistance and the Asbos disappeared into the night as quickly as they had arrived.

The hoodies had no planned agenda, no record of membership or form of initiation. Their activities were spontaneous, preying on the unguarded, gathering pace, alarming and unpredictable and wherever Ben Mackay, Pitbull Patterson and Skeet Cooney went, the Asbos followed. These characters were the big three, the natural leaders. Skeet was the court jester, unable to take anything seriously other than his Jamaican roots. He believed in black superiority and imagined himself to be vaguely Rastafarian, carefully grooming his deadlocks to prove the point. He wore an ear ring and laughed hysterically as they retraced their steps towards New Horizons Park. Here, the Asbos split up deciding to make themselves scarce, going to ground in their favourite haunts, where, in an orgy of binge drinking, they could boast personal impressions of the evening's adventure. Ben, Pitbull and Skeet felt superior, above this sort of thing. They weren't kids anymore, they were street dealers, they could enjoy the company of people who were really cool, who knew a thing or two, and so they headed for Meg's place where they could drink their lagers, smoke cannabis and relax in the company of like minded adults.

Margaret Kinnear, with her drug dealing partner, occupied a top floor flat on new Horizons. Everyone called her Meg. At the age of fifteen, to escape the abuse of a violent father, she had left the squalor of a Glaswegian home for life on the streets. She had drifted, unloved, uncared for, from one wretched situation to another until inevitably, she found herself pregnant. Against all the odds, she decided to keep the child and in order to enjoy a few comforts for herself and her illegitimate daughter, she had prostituted her undoubted charms as a call girl. Now in her mid thirties, her figure remained that of a teenager. Regular beauty routines enhanced her glamourous appeal, carefully disguising the hard lines of her mouth and with her hair, brassy as a child's Teddy bear, she was still able to turn heads. To maintain her drug habit, she traded in a whole range of narcotics, receiving quotas from dealers higher up the supply chain. She had developed a sad, yet coarse sense of humour but the unforgiving rules of survival in the criminal underworld had taught her to strike quickly. Meg was hard and she was mentally tough. She supported her daughter Kelly at university and ran her drug dealing business with ruthless enterprise and anyone who broke the rules, lived to regret it. Her only visible sign of possible wealth was the gold jewellery she wore, which gave her self assurance. Lost, almost among the clouds over New Horizons, she was able keep a low profile, draw benefits and act the part of a struggling, semi-illiterate, single mum. The authorities had no idea that she owned an expensive villa in the bay of Naples with a fast, luxury power boat on the marina.

Ben, Pitbull and Skeet were new recruits and she was in the process of grooming them for an increase in turnover. Her very first encounter with Ben Mackay however, had stirred emotions which for years lay hidden away in the darkest recess of her teenage memories. She often found herself unconsciously making a fuss over him and was afraid her feelings might interfere with business. She had taken a bath and was relaxing in front of the television, her slender body carressed within the folds of a silk dressing gown, a glass of champagne fondly toying with her lips, when there was a familiar knock on the door.

'Oh, hello Ben, it's you. Ah thought Ah'd spelt it oot, Ah dinna mind you calling on me anytime, but nae the other lads.'

' Aw, come on Meg, we got nowhere else to go. See,' he continued, offering her a plastic bag, 'I got you loads of fags and stuff, the posh ones you're always smokin. We only want a few joints, we got our own lagers.'

'Has anywan followed you?'

' No way' said Ben. ' Look, here's money for some more eee's. We already sold the last lot.' He waited for her to soften up. 'Promise we'll be no trouble.'

Meg studied the handsome, young face. 'Och! ok then, you can sit in the back room, all of you, there's a new telly in there. But Ah want no mess on the carpet, use the ashtrays and keep the windees open.'She paused for a moment. 'And use glasses from the kitchen, put your cans in bags and take them with you when you go.'

The lads showing great respect for Meg and her well appointed flat, removed their trainers, before settling down to enjoy the comforts of her little den, in private. The sweet, cloying smell of 'skunk' cannabis filled the room and the lads began to chill out. Pitbull remarked, 'Cor, that Meg, in't she a cracker.'

'Yeah, she's jus like mah Sasha, know what ah mean?' said Skeet, his eyes rolling in all directions.

'Ere he goes agen, There in't no Sasha, she's all in yer ed,' sneered Pitbull.

'She's real man, beautiful, she's jus beautiful,' murmured Skeet in reply.

'Where is she then? Go on, where is she?' Pitbull taunted.

'She's a new age traveller man, know what ah mean? She's down in Cornwall. I'm meetin her there.'

'Yer're nuts Skeet, a real nutter. Ere Skeet, are we goin ter school termorrer or shall we give it a miss?'

'I'm goin ter Cornwall termorrer, man, I gotter see Sasha.'

'Seen your gran lately?' Ben intervened wishing to change the subject.

'Ere, I gotter better idea. Let's go ter school and have some fun with ole Frankie. E's got us fer maths first thing Monday innee? Well, I appen ter know he's a boozer. I've seen im at it.' Pitbull continued.

'Really,' Ben said, expressing surprise 'It was Frankie who got me expelled.'

'Yeah, e's tryin ter get me kicked out. Me, I couldn't care less, but my ole man's threatened im. Anyway I know e keeps nippin out of class fer a quick swig. E's got a sort of flat bottle e carries round with im, it's special, all silver. I'm thinkin, on Monday mornin we could nick it. Yer know, when he puts his jacket on the back of is chair. Ere Ben, you could come. Wooden alf give im a shock.'

Ben took a long draw on what was left of his joint. 'Sounds like an interestin idea.' Could be fun seein old Frankie grovel.'

The door opened and Meg came into the room. Conversation came to abrupt halt as the boys gave her their full attention. 'Ben, You can come and sit wi me in the lounge, I'm wanting tae have a wee chat with you.'

Ben snuffed his smoke in the ashtray, collected his glass and dutifully followed Meg into the lounge. He felt quite privileged, and when she invited him to sit right next to her, he felt a tremour of exitement. The dressing gown now hung loosely revealing a tantalising glimpse of her shapely legs. Ben thought he recognised an open invitation and wanted to kiss her, but found his desire dampened with shy caution.

'Ben, those ciggies you gave me, you stole them, didn't you?'

'Well, yeah, we done over Rajur's shop. We've been smashin windows.'

'Ah thought so, you're still running wi that gang o hoodies?'

'Well yeah, Rajur's in our territory, it's where we rule, where the Asbos take what they want. We do what we like.'

'Ben, all that's kid's stuff. If you wantae work for me you'll have to gi it up. Ah'm no wantin the cops round here makin trouble over a few ciggies. Do you follow mah meanin

Ben? There's real money out there. A lot more than just pushin ecstasy pills at a quid each'

'Meg, you don't have to worry about cops. There's never any cops about. They're too busy sortin out CCTV cameras and we've wrecked most of those. Any case, they can't see our faces, everythin's blurred and nobody will shop us, their too scared.'

' You're not listenin Ben. If you're gonna run wi those hoodies, you're out of here, all of you. Ah dinna want tae see you're face again.' A veiled threat chilled the apparent warmth between them and Ben felt as though he had opened the lid of a giant freezer.

'I am listenin Meg, but I'm not sure what you're meanin.' Ben offered in a tone of conciliation.

'This place is not mah home Ben. It's the control centre of mah drugs operation, it's just a front. Ah mostly live abroad. Ah've got all the right connections and mah partner organises the muscle.'

'But why let me come here then, visitin, dealin in eees and stuff?' Ben asked, a little confused.

'Because Ah like you Ben.'

'I like you too Meg, I like you a lot.'

'We could have a lot o fun together Ben, an you could make yoursel a lot o pennies if you want on board, but A'll no have anythin tae do wi wee hoodies.'

'You mean I can't come here any more for eees?'

'Not unless you change you're mind aboot runnin around wi a bunch o wild kids. Think aboot it Ben, then you can come an see me, but nae the others. Now you'd better be going, all of you, an take you're rubbish wi you.'

The three Asbos slunk out. 'Ere what's up with Meg?' Pitbull enquired, annoyed that in the middle of a carousal, when he was beginning to feel he owned the place, he'd suddenly been shown the exit.

'She doesn't trust us, thinks we might give her trouble with our anti social stuff, thinks we're a bunch of kids runnin out of control. She warned me that if any of us shopped her we'd end up crippled for life. She means it too,' Ben answered in a quiet voice.

'Well I hope you got some more eees?' said Pitbull anxiously.

'No. She's give me an ultimatum.'

'Never eard of it. What is it, some kind of drug? Don't matter, if that's what the kids want. Praps it's the latest thing,' said Pitbull with renewed enthusiasm.

'You know Pitbull, you're so fuckin stupid. It's a choice. If we want to deal in drugs, we've gotta give up the Asbos. Hey Skeet, what the hell are you doing, climbing on the barrier, get down off that parapet, think you can fly or somethin?'

Ben and Pitbull waited for the lift. Pitbull took out a black felt tip and scrawled across the wall 'Asbos Rule OK', then he added as an after thought, 'Meg luvs Ben.'

The lift arrived and the two lads went in, but Skeet held back. 'I ain't getting in no lift man.'

'Don't be so daft Skeet, It'll take ages down the stairs,' Ben said looking worried.

'I ain't getting in no lift. It's crawlin with spiders.' Skeet's eyes began their rolling motion.

'Yer're nuts Skeet. A real fuckin nutter,' said Pitbull with some impatience.

'Seriously Skeet, you scared of spiders? There's no spiders in a lift, honest, come and look for yourself,' Ben invited.

'The lift's crawlin with em man, jus crawlin. I can see em, same as in my bedroom.' Skeet, screwed up with terror, his lips trembling, his limbs twitching in horror.

'Ok, ok, calm down Skeet, it's ok , we'll use the stairs.' said Ben.

'Skeet, yer mus be fuckin stupid. I in't comin, I'm usin the lift,'

'Ok Pitbull, you use the lift. Skeet's gone all schizo on me and I'm worried about him. Hard to say what he'll do if he's left on his own, I'm takin him to his gran's. See you at school tomorrow.'

'Yer both nuts.' Pitbull scowled, stabbing the lift button, and as the door closed, a bag of empty lager cans jettisoned through the opening.

Constance Cooney, a Caribbean African, was too tired, too scared to sleep. She worked all day as a cleaner and lay restlessly trying to find the best position for her tennis elbow. Five years ago her husband had fallen to his death on a construction site leaving her to struggle on alone. Well meaning authorities, for ease of access, had moved her into a ground floor flat on New Horizons, a position which also made her an easy target for vandals. Attacks were frequent, making her life an absolute misery.

Married in Jamaica, she and her husband had immigrated to Britain with Tina their young daughter. They worked hard, had two more children, a boy and a girl, and after a difficult start, began making some headway. At sixteen, Tina gave birth to a grandson, Marvin. Although Tina refused to name the father, she was a good girl, opting to raise the child at home while helping to run the household. But Tina was young, she was pretty, she yearned for something more out of life and one day, she rang her mother asking her to collect Marvin from primary school. A few days later she rang again to say she wasn't coming home. She had met a white boy with stacks of money and they were going back to Jamaica. She hardly kept in touch and the family never saw her again. Constance was now fifty years of age, still young for a grandmother, but stress was taking it's toll. Since the loss of her husband, she had lost all control over Marvin and she fretted endlessly about his dangerous lifestyle and his well being.

With her mind in turmoil, she continued to shift her weight around the broken springs of a worn out mattress. Her heart almost stopped beating when a loud knocking echoed through the flat. She staggered out of bed, hastily threw on a dressing gown, grabbed her mobile and crept into the hall. She peered warily through the spy hole. Thank heavens! It was Marvin himself, there standing on her doorstep.

She unhooked the security chain and opened the door. 'Marvin, thank god you're arl right' she said with a sigh of relief. 'Where you bin hidin, I bin worried sick. Come in, come in both of you, Marvin you look jes dreadful.'

'I've been cruisin Gran, jus cruisin. I've been lookin for Sasha, lookin all over, but man she's run off with a new age traveller, went to Cornwall an I jus know she's there, waitin for me.'

Ben hesitated. 'I won't come in Mrs Cooney, promised I wouldn't be late home. I brought Skeet back cos he's not well, keeps acting out of his mind. He'll feel better after a good night's sleep, but in the mornin I think he should see a doctor or somethin,'

'What's your name boy? Ah can't thank you enough.'

'I'm Ben, Skeet's mate'

'Well thankyou, thankyou, thankyou Ben, you're a real gentleman. Ah'll take care of him, Ah've cleaned his room jes so everythin's arl lovely for him with fresh clean sheets an new curtains an arl. Come on Marvin, let's get you to bed an in the mornin Ah'll cook you up your favourite breakfast, before you go to school.'

Skeet behaved like someone in a trance and climbed dutifully into bed. Mrs Cooney quietly closed the door and decided perhaps now, she too could get some much needed rest. She lay there, hoping her body would naturally succumb to the weariness in her bones and that sleep might intervene. Precious, soothing sleep however, offered no respite and instead she found herself listening, listening for a disturbance, any sound that threatened to set her nerves jangling. An hour passed in waves of apprehension, until for extra peace of mind, she dragged herself once more out of bed, and satisfied that he was asleep, turned the key in Marvin's door.

Skeet lay there, befuddled, lethargic, his mind unable to break free from a cycle of disturbing thoughts. The image of Sasha floated in and out of an alien landscape. He heard the key turn in the lock and for a moment felt safe from the horrors he knew were gathering before him. Then a little after midnight, Sasha paid him a visit. She materialised like the virtual particles of quantum physics, from nothing, from the energy vacuum in empty space. She was not the red haired warrior queen of his imagination, a Celtic heroine of ancient mythology, nor was she the tall, sultry, dark eyed beauty from Somalia. She came to him as a giant stick insect. he heard the rasping, clicking noise as she stood in the hall and then her long spidery legs wormed their way through the margins around the bedroom door.

Frantically he tore the pages from the books and magazines at his bedside, stuffing them into every crevice, every crack around the door and window. But Sasha lead an army of creepy crawlies and they were out to get him, to possess him, to absorb him. In desperation he took the mattress from his bed and together with the frame, made a barrier across the corner of the room. He crouched behind the makeshift defences, drenched in cold perspiration, his body a paroxysm of terror, knowing there can be no escape, no sanctuary, when the mind is possessed by things of the night.

Chapter 3
Cumber Community College.

Franklin Page Johnson, mercifully, was nearing retirement. He would be leaving the classroom after what seemed a lifetime of teaching Maths. Physically and mentally he felt spent and could hardly wait for the release, which for him was more of a reprieve. In truth he was simply hanging on, but hanging on for what? Well, his pension of course, and yet for some reason it was not that important, not any more. Years of conforming to a national curriculum which changed with the political seasons, together with the undermining of school discipline, had crimped his personality and stifled his performance.

In the early days he had been popular with his students, using unconventional methods to exercise his natural talent for making Maths a fascinating subject. He had often encouraged discussion on new scientific discoveries or posed humourous conundrums, which stimulated interest and lateral thinking while offering light relief.

These gifts had been set aside and the disruptive elements in our modern classrooms had sensed a man, no longer streetwise, unsure, uncool, unable to move with the times, a soft touch, and had conspired to make his life a misery. He could no longer maintain discipline in the classroom, his voice held no authority and chosing not to listen was a favourite option for the unruly. Pitbull Patterson in particular, admired by fellow delinquents for his belligerence, was making his life hell.

His double barrelled name, a legacy of English social climbing, labelled him a snob but his interlect had shaped a career beyond the shallow lives of his wealthy parents. Franklin was a deep thinker and the last few years had been a time for reflection, for examination. Sadly he concluded his journey through life had led nowhere. Where were those rich memories, the satisfaction of giving one's best and seeing a job well done? New priorities, new standards, the worship of different gods, had conspired against him and now he thought he saw the awful truth, his aspirations, his hopes, his dreams, meant nothing, for the cause had been hopeless, useless from the beginning. There had been two passions in his life, two loves. The undying love he held for the glamourous wife he had lost and the love he once held for the teaching profession. Gloria had rejected the boredom of his academic career, refused to give him the children he longed for and finally walked out on him. And now Pitbull, this moron, this thug, this mindless bully, had exposed some underlying weakness in his character over which he tore himself apart in order to discover it's significance. In mathamatical terms the sum total of his endeavours amounted to impotence, failure, zero.

Increasing despondency threatened a nervous breakdown and in order to retain a hold on sanity he cast gloom and doom over the whole world. Mankind, he was convinced, like those animals who had evolved across the geographical time scale faced extinction. In any event, the passing of a thousand million years would see dramatic changes in the sun. It's cooling sequence would make life untenable and eventually destroy the earth. But this vast period of time, giving man a chance to redress the balance of his folly and escape to another planet, Franklin had no doubt, would be denied. Such comic book deliberations were merely wishful thinking.

Franklin believed the end was near, perhaps even in his own lifetime. Not because of faith in biblical prophesies, but more through the weight of scientific observation and his natural leaning towards pessimism. Such thoughts perversely, were his only source of comfort along with the consumption of more and more alcohol.

Franklin, an ex public school boy, once confident, self assured and good looking was now a shadow of his former self. He appeared faded, thin, his lanky frame slightly stooped, a man under siege and given to eccentricity. He had never craved the privileged life of inherited wealth or his wife's manic pursuit of good times and the obscene waste of rich living. She had deserted him years ago for the playboy charms of an aristocratic friend who had pressured him to go into politics. He had seriously considered the promise of a short cut to the treasury but the friend had turned out to be nothing more than a philanderer with designs on his wife. Their marriage collapsed when Gloria eventually left him for the playboy and a Jetset lifestyle, partying around the world, flying high on recreational drugs.

Franklin had been devastated, his mind unable to function, swirling in unknown territory, stranded, beyond his emotional comfort zone. She had been the sort of girl once described as a society flapper, a coquettish creature, preoccupied with finery, and Fran as she called him, would have died for her. When Gloria left, although he despised all those things she felt important, he missed her vivacious gaiety and with her desertion went his joie de vivre. Now he had become a lonely man, living the ordered life of a confirmed bachelor.

It was Monday morning again. How could he face another day at Cumber Community College? Pitbull Patterson and his cronies from New Horizons Park would be ranged against him for their morning's entertainment. Before setting a bowl of cereals on the breakfast table, he poured himself a very stiff brandy. He heard the paper boy rattle the letter box and leaving the brandy, wandered into the hall to collect his copy of the Independent. He slumped at the table and read the headlines. Global Warming was now official, a scientific fact he had instinctively known for years. Governments all agreed that something must be done to save the planet, but of course Franklin knew that nothing effective could possibly be done. In an endeavour to meet the demands of developing nations and a rising world population, the number of vehicles burning fossil fuels, speeding along the highways and byeways of our planet would increase, together with shipping, air travel and animal husbandry. Globalisation would tip the balance, resulting in disaster.

Franklin read the statistics. America, Franklin hated American politics, responsible for twenty percent of CO_2 emissions in our atmosphere was preaching caution to India, a nation responsible for only one percent of emissions. The Greens were busy trying to discourage the African dream, preaching mud huts, no electricity or industrialisation. This kind of double talk Franklin knew, would fall on deaf ears. The developing world would continue to burn coal as well as oil and the level of greenhouse gases would continue to rise over the next twenty five years at least. Of course the end was inevitable, and with down beat fatalism, he forecast a forlorn and very bleak outcome. Only an all out war, a co-ordinated world coup perhaps, by right minded people, could remove those administrations motivated by the influence of oil, gas and greedy money institutions, to salvage something from the wreckage.

Franklin scanned the paper, looking for more bad news. He read the article on anti-social behaviour, the scourge of our towns and cities, and how the government and the police played it down. Smashing windows, torching stolen cars, terrorising whole neighbourhoods, carrying weapons including guns, vandalising property, dealing in drugs and directing verbal abuse, apparently, were not crimes. Government spin called it anti- social behaviour. The police said citizens must be more responsible for their own localities, their own safety. They were not in favour of vigilante groups and there was no need for older people to be afraid of teenagers or place themselves under curfew.

God! Thought Franklin, Wasn't life simply hell? But then, all life forms he reasoned, simply exploited nutrients, jostled, fought, killed off weaker life forms and evolved in order to survive. All life forms, including the lower varieties at Cumber College, were subject to the ruthless forces of nature and the unforgiving physical laws of the universe. Man's ignorance, arrogance and greed, had pushed resources to their limits. The end of it all was inescapable. In his lifetime, he could achieve nothing durable, leave nothing that would survive the inevitable. There was no hope, no continuity. Therein lay an excuse for his failures. At the final reckoning, the world's aspirations would be reduced to less than a whimper, the history of mankind had been one stupendous joke.

Franklin had suffered betrayal. His private life had collapsed when his wife chose another, his professional life had been enfeebled by meddling bureaurcracy, but a tough public school education had achieved it's objectives and Franklin could see no fault in himself. He had lost faith in humanity, gave no credence for his own spirituallity, and yet he remained confident that the world was out of step, marching blindly in the wrong direction while he remained steadfast and true. He poured himself another brandy and shuffled in the drawer for the initialed, silver hip flask, a symbol of treachery and a present from a his former wife's lover. Once he had treasured it, now it represented payment for services rendered and filled him with loathing, but it had it's uses. He recharged the flask with Armagnac, his favourite tipple, tucking it away in the lining of his jacket. Now he felt ready to face the classroom, another day's encounter with the enemy. Before leaving, to use an expression he was particularly fond of, there followed a casual 'defining moment.' He glanced at the financial columns and without realising, triggered a series of events which in his first lesson of the day, would lead to catastrophe.

Cumber Community College, like the surrounding neighbourhood which it served, had a weary, last line of defence look about it and in order to address the social deprivation and emotional needs of it's inner city pupils, much attention had been given to the fabric of the building, resulting in areas of bright paint and jolly murals. These served only to encourage unsightly modifications and further maintenance. The office for standards in education, Ofsted, ignoring allowances for the area which it covered and the enormous stress suffered by it's teachers, had labeled it a failing school.

Franklin never felt guilty about this state of affairs, and fortified by alcohol, swept into the classroom, making a grand entrance. The Armagnac had settled his nerves and in a maverick frame of mind, he decided how the lesson would proceed. Today he would deliver the unexpected, make them sit up, use their brains if they had any. He carefully placed his jacket on the back of the chair and turned to clear the blackboard. He needed as much space as possible for the graphs and diagrams he would draw to illustrate a subject which had nothing to do with the curriculum. So focused was he on his intended instruction, that he failed to notice Pitbull sitting quietly in the front row or Ben Mackay and Skeet, heads well down, at the very rear. The moment offered a perfect opportunity for Pitbull, who with cool deliberation rifled through the lining of the jacket, removed the flask and returned to his desk. The rest of the class were stunned, mesmerised by the shear nerve and audacity of the theft. They sat back open mouthed, with great anticipation, waiting for the outcome.

Franklin, however suspected nothing. He had already noted an unusual calm settling over the classroom and felt confident that a fresh approach might finally achieve something, proving that his instincts and opinions had been right all along.

'This morning we are going to consider the importance of our farming and manufacturing industries. Now, can anyone tell me what they know about our present trade gap?' he enquired, his voice rising to the occasion. 'What is the trade gap?'

' It's to do with imports and exports Sir,' came the reply from a diminutive figure, waving an arm for attention, and very keen to pass on the knowledge his father, a trades union official, had impressed upon him.

'Yes, that's very good Foskett. It's the difference between our income from goods sold to other countries and the cost of the goods we purchase from abroad. Now can anyone tell me how the trade gap stands at present? Is in surplus or is it in deficit?' there was absolute silence. The class knew that Pitbull was out to cause disruption and waited for him to make a move.

'Well, at the end of 2006 there was an all time record deficit for trading in goods of £84.3bn. Now there's a figure we should all worry about. Can anyone tell me how many noughts there are in a billion?' Again there was absolute silence. Thoughts were preoccupied with the mysterious bottle. Why had Frankie brought the bottle to school? What could be in the bottle?

At this point Franklin realised with dismay that Pitbull was sitting in the front row. He decided that attack was the best form of defence. 'Patterson, your school work like your attendance, in terms of value, is close to zero, perhaps you could enlighten us.'

'I dunno do I? A billion I spose.'

Satisfied that Pitbull had been humiliated and his ignorance exposed, Franklin waited for Dina Rajur to answer. She was his favourite pupil, the Asian from the general stores, and in truth he had directed the initial question at her. Dina, who sat quietly in front of him, generally found difficulty in communicating, but understood figures in their most literal terms. She said in a matter of fact tone, 'Sir, there are nine zeros in one billion which may be expressed more simply as ten to the power of nine.'

'Brilliant, well done Dina, you're beginning to think like a mathematician,' Franklin enthused, gloating over the manisfestation of his teaching ability. He had failed to appreciate however, that her uncanny grasp of arithmetic was due to autism, and for most of the time, the pretty little Asian found the classroom environment most stressful. Franklin wrote on the board £84,300,000,000. 'It looks like a great deal of money doesn't it.? And believe me it most certainly is. The bad news is that it is continuing to balloon upwards! But what does this figure tell us? Anyone, Foskett?'

Again there was a baffled silence. Perhaps Pitbull had simply stolen the bottle. After all it looked like real silver and everyone knew that Pitbull was a crook. Perhaps there would be no diversion, no Pitbull side show, and they would have to listen to Frankie's boring rubbish. No way, not for much longer.

'It means that we, as a nation are not making things anymore,'continued Franklin. 'We're relying on the city to bail us out. That £84.3bn is offset to some extent by the so called service industries which made a record £28.5bn surplus. Foreign investments also account for billions of pounds worth of assets. But what happens if those investors lose confidence, withdraw their money?

Thus far, Franklin had immobilised the thought processes of the entire class. He looked at the sea of blank faces. Not one was capable of making a contribution. Without doubt, this was the most boring lesson the class had ever encountered. When oh when, would Pitbull make his move!

Predictably, Franklin gained encouragement from his comatosed audience, believing that each and everyone was riveted to the subject matter. Now, imagining himself to be equal to the task of Chancellor of the Exchequer, he became more passionate. 'If we want to buy a car, we have to go to the French, the Italians, the Germans, the Japanese, the Americans, the far east, or wherever, because in this country, we don't make cars anymore. We don't manufacture ships, tractors, earth moving equipment, televisions, computors, washing machines, the list is endless. We have forsaken our industrial heritage for the soft option of wheeler dealing in finance. What values do such practices inpart? What kind of citizens are we becoming? Is that building a healthy future for our country? Your futures.'

That morning to please his grandmother, Skeet had eaten a king sized breakfast. Remarkably, he felt quite normal but desperately tired. Gradually his head sank, resting on the desk and he began snoring. A titter went round the classroom and Ben decided it was time to put an end to Frankie's claptrap. 'Hey Frankie, shouldn't we be doing geometry? The properties of right angle triangles and stuff?'

'Yeah,' said Pitbull, 'The square on the hippotamus innit?' More laughter.

Franklin froze on the spot. The shock of such a rude interruption by the expelled Ben Mackay hit him squarely in the stomach and his brain felt as though it had been pole axed. The awful reality of the situation suddenly dawned on him. His lesson had been nothing short of inspirational and yet incredibly, no one had been listening. He needed a good shot of Armagnac. 'The square of the *hypotenuse* Patterson, the Theorem of Pythagoras. In a right angled triangle, the square of the hypotenuse is equal in area to the sum of the squares on the other two sides. Turn to page 34 in your geometry books and study the diagram,' he instructed, struggling to regain some composure. Effecting a measured calm, he took his jacket from the chair and put it on. 'Now will you excuse me for a moment, when I return we will endeavour, using only our knowlege of geometry, to prove the theorem.'

With Franklin's deparure, most of the class gathered round Pitbull as he triumphantly produced the bottle, waving it above his head. 'Ere,' he yelled above the racket, 'Frankie's a boozer, anyone wan a swig? Not you Dina, you little smart arse, or you 'Eccles cake' you creep.'

Ben snatched the flask, took a sniff and gulped at the contents, 'It's pretty good stuff,' he said, between swallows, 'Must'ave cost him a bomb.'

Franklin hurried down the corridor, making for the secretary's office, determined to bring the full weight of the law down on Ben Mackay's head. Without knocking he burst into the room. 'Miss Kwidzinski, will you please inform the headmaster as a matter of priority, that Ben Mackay has turned up this morning for a maths lesson. He's been expelled from this school and has no right to be here. His only motive is to cause disruption in class. I feel intimidated by his presence. He's also in breach of his Asbo and the police must be notified as a matter of urgency.'

'Why certainly Mr Page Johnson, I'll speak to the headmaster at once, he's checking on the new health and safety laws. I'll deliver it to him personally.' For added security, before Franklin left the room, she rang the local police station.

Franklin scurried off towards the staff toilets, his fingers already probing for the much needed Armagnac. Horror of horrors! The flask was missing! Of course! Why had the obvious not occurred to him? All that attention in the classroom, the impression of hanging on to his every word, when all the time they were simply waiting for an opportunity to make a fool of him. On no previous occasion had Patterson been anywhere near the front row. Patterson had engineered the plot and Patterson had stolen the flask from his jacket. Signals of alarm peppered his addled brain. His mouth went dry, cold sweat, palpitations, nausea. He crashed through the toilet doors and began pacing in front of the urinals. All his life it seemed, had been a battle against misfortune and now at the last fence, he had fallen flat on his face. But this was serious, his job could be on the line, his pension, his integrity, everything. He locked himself in one of the cubicles and was sick in the pan. He flushed away the remains of his breakfast and was sick again. He lowered the seat and sat with his head in his hands searching for a solution. There was only one thing for it. He would have to retrieve the flask. He would have to lie. He bathed his face in the wash basin, took a few deep breaths and reluctantly made his way back to the classroom.

The class returned to their seats like theatre goers after an interval, refreshed, ready for the second act and there were murmurings of excitement. Pitbull lounged back, his feet stuck out from the desk, knowing he had centre stage. There was an unholy grin on his face. 'Ere, Frankie. You lost summat? You don't look well at all. Need a drink?'

The class waited in absolute silence for the answer. Even the gentle snivelling of Foskett failed to cause any distraction. 'Ere Frankie, we all know you're a piss artist! Ere, exhibit number one.' Pitbull sniggered, holding the flask aloft.

'Foskett, why are you crying?' Franklin responded, diverting his attention, a deep frown creasing his forehead.

'It's nothing Sir.' Foskett whimpered, catching his breath.

Franklin stiffened, his jaw line hardened. 'Come now, I want to know. What seems to be the trouble?'

'I, I fell over that's all'

Please Sir,'Eccles cake did not fall over,' Dina Rajur said in her usual monotones. 'Pitbull punched him in the stomach. He is hitting him many times. Always he is hitting people. All the time he is hitting Eccles cake.'

The incident that followed was quite extraordinary. It would dump Franklin on the scrap heap, destroy his reputation as a scholar, bringing shame, humiliation and rejection. His pension would be made invalid, his career terminated. Paradoxically, it achieved the one thing he most desired, the respect of his pupils. Memories of the Monday morning maths lesson at Cumber Community College would live with them for the rest of their lives.

The whole spectacle was witnessed by the Headmaster, the sports teacher and two policemen who stood in the corridor behind the glass screen. Impressed by good behaviour in the classroom but unable to hear the conversation, their attention was focused on Ben Mackay who showed no signs of causing disruption.

'Patterson, stand up.' Franklin ordered. 'No, by the side of your desk.'

Pitbull obliged, offering Franklin the flask.'Ere Frankie wanna a swig?' he leered, pouring what was left of the contents on the floor.

Franklin slowly took off his jacket and with great calm began rolling up his shirt sleeves in the most precise fashion. 'Patterson, it is time someone taught you a lesson your pea sized brain can understand, you bullying swine, you contemptable ignoramus.' Franklin then launched himself at Pitbull swinging left and right hooks to the body. The surprise and ferocity of the attack took Pitbull completely off guard and he staggered backwards. Sensing he had gained the advantage, Franklin shifted his attack to the head splitting Pitbulls nose which cascaded blood in every direction. Pitbull took another step backwards but before he could recover his wits, an unseen ally delivered the coup de grace. A foot sneaked out, tripping him over, and he fell cracking his head on the floor with a delicious thud. Pitbull was out cold.

It was time for the law to intervene, a perfect senario for an act of public relations. Education was high on the list of governmental priorities and the law must be seen to act swiftly in matters of crime and security where our school children are concerned. The crazy old school teacher had flipped and offered feeble opposition for the two burly policemeent. Our hero Franklin had succeeded in bringing down the full weight of the law, not on Ben Mackay as he had intended, but on himself, and unfortunately in it's most literal form. His legs were pulled from under him and he fell face down in the pool of Almagnac swilling on the floor. A well nourished police officer, sixteen stones of bone and muscle, ground a bony knee into the small of his back and before the exhausted Franklin could give vent to the agony he felt, his hands were secured behind his back.

'Mr Page Johnson! Your behaviour is incomprehensible, disgraceful! How dare you conduct yourself in this manner! In my classroom, in this school!' The Headmaster screamed, his voice reaching falsetto, then swallowing his incredulity, he addressed the police officers, 'Please take Mr Page Johnson to my study. Before you make a formal arrest, I simply must have an explanation from him.'

'Please Sir,' Ben Mackay intervened, rising casually to his feet, 'Mr Page Johnson was drunk. He's always drinkin during school and we all think he's alcoholic cos he's always slipping out of class for a quick nip. He keeps brandy in that silver flask, that's it, on the floor next to Patterson. All Patterson did was to suggest he got treatment, cos it's not fair on us students. He wasn't teaching maths anyway, he kept going on about politics.'

The sports teacher, cradling Pitbull's head, shouted for someone to call an ambulance. He reached for the silver container holding it to his nose. 'Yes it's brandy alright and it's inscribed,' He carefully read the message, 'To Fran. If you don't get the better of brandy, it'll get the better of you.' A titter went round the class.

The headmaster seemed relieved by the information. 'In spite of your record Mackay, it seems we owe you and Patterson a debt of gratitude. In bringing this matter to our attention, you've shown courage and a sense of duty and I hope your appearance at school today means you are turning over a new leaf. I always felt you were an intelligent lad, capable of better things. We will discuss the possibilities later.'

Franklin, suffering an acute spasm of cramp and close to fainting was frogmarched into the Headmaster's office.

'I think we are all now fully aware of the circumstances surrounding this ghastly exhibition, your complete loss of self control and the betrayal of myself and the school. Quite clearly you were drunk, under the influence of whatever beverage it is you carry around in this bottle.' The Headmaster firmly planted the evidence on his desk.

'I'm sorry, but I definitely, was not under the influence of drink,' Franklin replied.

'Come now man! You positively reek of the stuff.'

'Patterson emptied most of the contents on the floor and this police officer took much pleasure in pinning me down among the spillage. I only drink on occasions to steady my nerves.'

' Franklin, we are not fools. We witnessed the whole sorry debacle. You attacked, entirely without provocation, an innocent member of your class, who merely expressed his concern about your addiction. Furthermore, I understand that you had deviated from the curriculum, trying to indoctrinate the class with your own political pursuasion.'

'Patterson is hardly an innocent member of the fifth grade, as you well know. He's a vicious bully, a thug who smokes cannabis in the toilets. He's no wish to learn and because he's afraid of appearing stupid, deliberately sets out to disrupt the class. I thought it was time someone took a stand.'

'Smokes cannabis! In the toilets! I suppose you're going to tell me you saw him while you were in there drinking. Franklin, your argument is no excuse for your behaviour. You have demonstrated beyond doubt that you are unfit to conduct a maths lesson. You have broken all the rules and I must suspend you from all further duties. I shall make a full report on the matter recommending your instant dismissal. Your career I would imagine, is now in ruins.'

'I know you've never liked me and I can see that you're determined to bring me down. Rest assured, I also intend to make a report which I shall make very, very public.'

The Headmaster, astonished by this counter threat, looked to the policemen for support. 'Under the circumstances, I'm surprised by your manner. You show no signs of guilt, no shame.'

Franklin continued, 'You as Headmaster, have failed to improve our low performance rating. Too many children leave this establishment unable to read or write properly. Bullying, drug abuse and truancy are rife and there have been two rape allegations. There's no real form of discipline and most of the teachers are utterly demoralised by the lack of support from you or the authorities. You are a man immersed in educational bureaucracy and enjoying it for it's own sake. It suits your style, unapproachable by parents and teachers alike, you hide behind your secretary, preoccupied with the rules and regulations, making sure the right ticks are in the right boxes. You could try talking to parents and students for a change, you might learn something about your school and the catchment area we serve. You could start with Dina Rajur and Michael Fosket. Then read and inwardly digest the 2007 UNICEF report.'

The Headmaster, perfectly adept at using the right jargon, found his repertoire scrambled by Franklin's string of accusations. Mentally he groped for the right turn of phrase. The big policeman, thoroughly bored with schoolroom dramas, decided it was time he made an arrest. 'Mr Page Johnson, I am arresting you for causing grievous bodily harm to a minor, while under the influence of alcohol. You have the right to remain silent...................'

Chapter 4
Luv is Magick.

Few men took it upon themselves to mess around with Mike, but
many thought him soft where women were concerned, a man with
notions of romance. Those who knew him well, recognised the
more gentle side of Mike's personality, for Mike had been blessed
as a young man with the precious gift of love, a love which had
grown stronger with the passing years. Sheila had introduced him
to the world of music, art and literature and he in turn was the
rock on which they built their life. Their union brought forth
beautiful children, endless discoveries, it never waned, until
malignant fate tore them appart in a cruel vanishing act, leaving
Mike to live their love alone.

Against injustice, especially in it's most violent form,
Mike was capable of raw aggression, but his exploits on the rugby
field had shown physical strength tempered by a sense of
discipline, marshalled by a cool head. He thought he would never
love again, never find a woman like Sheila, with her grace,
intelligence and wit and yet after eight lonely years, something
wonderful had happened. With his new love, he could make no
comparisons. As a child, Sheila had enjoyed the priviledged
background of professional parents and had gained a master's
degree in biology before going on to teach the subject at a
grammar school. Karen on the other hand, was a struggling,
single mum with no money and no qualifications. Even so, there
was an irrepressible vitality about Karen. She had courage,
stamina, and purity of heart. Her beauty shone through the dross
which threatened to bury her and Mike recognised in her, a
kindred spirit. He still nursed an abiding passion for Sheila his
lost love, and his feelings for Karen were stifled by a sense of
betrayal, but the living, breathing love of Karen would not be
denied and Mike desired her, wanted to be near her, feel her slim
body against his, hold her closer and closer, safely in his arms.
Sheila, ever present in his dreams, in his memories, and in his
waking hours, repressed the emotionional intrusion of the
beautiful Karen and he allowed himself only a tender look, a
gentle caress, a lingering kiss, but never pursued his desire for a

more intimate relationship. Now he decided, this must change. He had to be more honest about himself, about his feelings for Karen and his intentions. He would make it a special occasion, inviting her to share a weekend based at his flat overlooking the Bridgewater canal. He wouldn't tell her exactly where, that could be a surprise.

After eighteen years of stability and matrimonial happiness, the loss of Sheila had left him wandering in a featureless desert with little sense of direction. The responsibilty of an eighteen year old daughter and a sixteen year old son weighed heavily upon him but dealing with those responsibilities in a most determined way became an unction for the pain. Among the domestic chores he took upon himself, he discovered the creative art of cooking and gained much pleasure from experimenting with various dishes. On several occasions he had taken Karen to good restaurants, a new experience for her, introducing culinary delights from around the world and he knew she loved Italian food. In one of the many deep cellars located in the hills surrounding Rome, a local wine merchant had discovered a spectacular Frascati and Mike purchased a couple of bottles. It's golden fragrance would accompany the candlelit meal he would cook for them and he planned to make an extra effort with timing and presentation. There would be stuffed mushrooms for starters, lasagne with anchovies and finally something simple but exotic, wild strawberries in lemon juice and clotted cream. A reawakening of all those things he and Sheila had experienced together began to surface, with promise of renewed pleasures. Mike used the appartment at weekends and had turned it into something of a shrine. Secured on the moorings in Castlefield basin was a beautiful narrowboat, in which the family had explored the waterways of Manchester and Cheshire. It had always been lovingly maintained but without Sheila, never left the mooring. The Morgan sports car, in which they had explored the delights of northern Britain, the hood down, Sheila's hair streaming in the wind, sat in the garage, jacked up on concrete blocks, immaculate in racing green, but immobile. These former ventures, Mike now wanted to share with Karen.

Sarah and Josh were both happily married with children and Karen knew that for convenience, Mike lived in a small terrace house near the industrial estate where his joinery shop operated from a modern works unit. He had bought the property as a starter home for Sarah but she had quickly gained her independence. It had also helped Josh his son on the property ladder, and he decided to keep the old house as an investment. She was also familiar with his M registered Volvo estate and it's a giant roof rack and when he arrived at New Horizons to collect her she expected nothing grand. Matt and Katrina had been forewarned. It was possible that she might be away for a couple of nights but certainly no more and they were pleased to see her so happy and thought she looked very attractive, her eyes sparkled, her hair shone, the cares of a working week lifted from her brow, and they shared her excitement.

She walked to the Volvo with natural economy of movement, a flowing gentle grace, and Mike could   hardly believe his good fortune. Karen soon realised that Mike was taking an unusual route through the city and queried 'I thought we were going to your house Mike, you were cooking a meal, showing me your domestic skills?'

'I am love. I know I've never mentioned it, but I also own a flat, overlooking the canal. I stay there weekends.'

'Gosh Mike you're a dark horse. Flats on the canal cost a fortune don't they?'

'Well this one was a bit steep. It was our family home, we lived there when the kids left primary school. Sheila fell in love with it, and because it was close to their new schools and the grammar school where Sheila worked, we bought it. I'd been a top Rugby league player and then with the business doing well and Sheila having such a good job, we could afford it. We weren't short of brass.'

'Yes I can see that, makes sense now you say. Show's how ignorant I am. You know Mike, I've never made a connection with your past. I mean, to think you might be well off. I know you're generous, but you just never struck me as someone with loads of money.'

'Well I suppose I've been lucky,' Mike paused for a moment, 'well in some ways.' he added as an afterthought. 'I was lucky meeting you Karen.' Karen reached across and squeezed his thigh.

Mike's reserved approach to courtship had been a new experience for Karen and over the weeks she found herself increasingly in love with him. She wanted their evening to be something made in heaven and had been ready to give herself to him, but these latest revelations left her confused. Mike was not the man she thought he was. He was more complex, a sporting hero who now ran a successful business and owned property. His former life, married to a woman from an entirely different background to herself, had given him much more than she had imagined. In the middle of her romantic reveries, it had all suddenly surfaced. What could he see in a single, working class mum, living with her disfunctional family, from hand to mouth on New Horizons Park?

It was not until they entered the appartment and Mike had switched on the lights that she was able to shift her thoughts from worrying doubts to her actual surroundings. Her immediate impression was a sense of space, of luxury, of feminine influence and good taste. Furniture, enriched with Celtic design, glowed in the rich, honey colour of English oak, complementing the burnt sienna of a stylish leather suite. A expansive carpet, deep piled, the colour of barley cream, seemed to stretch forever. An original Lowry and other works by lesser known artists and sculptors gave the room a flourish of human expression and in the dining area a china display cabinet, bathed in subdued light, gave hint of further treasures. On the dining table, large, pewter coloured plates were set as table mats and cutlery of the finest Sheffield steel was arranged on a cobalt blue table cloth. A spiral of white candles formed the centrepiece. 'Ooh! Mike what a wonderful place! I don't know what to say, it's all so beautiful, so lovely, just heavenly. Is this all really yours? And to think you've never once said anything about it. I can hardly take it in.'

'It's a bit different to New Horizons I know, but you can rest assured, I haven't rented it to make a big impression. Sarah's the only other woman to come here since I lost Sheila and the place needs to come alive again. That's why I want to share it with you Karen, treat you like the princess you are.'

Karen moved across to the glass doors looking out over the canal. She felt strangely uncomfortable. 'It's very sweet of you Mike to call me a princess, but I can't imagine royalty living in New Horizons. I'm not sure I want to be a princess anyway, living in an ivory tower.'

Mike followed her across the room and stood behind her. He put his arms around her waist and brushing the fragrance of her lovely hair, whispered in her ear, 'You're a princess to me Karen. I know you're stuck with New Horizons but you haven't given way to the welfare state, the culture of 'It's my right.' You haven't fallen into the trap of selfish dishonesty and allowed welfare bureaucracy to run your life. That to me takes moral courage. That's what makes you a princess.'

'Did you make all this wonderful furniture?' Karen asked, changing the subject and faintly blushing.

'Yes, It's some of my early work. Solid oak, keeps me busy, people seem to like it.'

'I love the carved patterns. What a clever man you are.'

'They're Celtic designs, they were Sheila's idea.'

'She must have been very clever too.' Karen hesitated, her thoughts going off in yet another direction. 'Were you serious Mike about giving Ben an apprenticeship? I'm so worried about him. Do you think you could make me proud of him?'

'Of course I was serious, but please Karen, tonight, let's just talk about us. Tonight we're eating Italian with an aphrodisiac for starters,' Mike grinned, letting her go.

He went into the kitchen, opened a bottle of wine from the fridge and returned with two generous glasses. 'Here's to us' he said offering her a glass.

'Oohm! Delicious' Karen gave him an inviting smile over the rim of the glass.

Mike lit the candles, 'Now sit yourself down and be prepared for a gastronomical masterclass,' he joked.

Occasionally, life has a nasty habit of spoiling things and the meal did not go according to plan. The stuffed mushrooms were tasty but too oily. Conversation seemed to centre on how wonderful Sheila had been as opposed to the the disaster of Karen's first marriage. As a result, Mike misjudged the fan oven and the upper layers of lasagne were inclined to be leathery. She made no remarks but Karen wasn't very keen on anchovies either and she left them curled up on the edge of the plate. She began to fidget becoming more and more uncomfortable with her luxurious surroundings. Mike opened the second bottle of Frascati and was now having doubts about the strawberries. The conversation shifted to their children, with Karen's concern over Ben's behaviour effectively blotting out any thoughts of romance. Mike had been unable to get wild strawberries and had settled for a Spanish variety. They looked very red, plump, glossy and succulent, but the first spoonful was pithy and tasteless.

'Let me help you with the washing up,' offered Karen.

Mike groaned inwardly. This was the last thing he had wanted. His princess standing over the kitchen sink. 'No need, everything's going in the dishwasher. You relax in the lounge while I make the coffee. I'll turn the fire on, makes it feel more cosy with the flame effect.'

Karen couldn't settle, she felt restless and while Mike busied himself in the kitchen, she wandered over to the display cabinet. There in pride of place was a photograph portrait of Sheila in her cap and gown. Other momentoes were arranged around the centrepiece with an unusual valentine card in the background. Karen without thinking opened the cabinet and reached for the card. She opened it and there pressed between its covers was a posy of tiny flowers. Beneath the flowers was a poem in Mike's handwriting.

How can I perceive
The mischeivous alchemy of love?
I only know that I loved you.
How can I embrace
The enfolding mystery of love?
I only know that I held you.
And when alone I huddle
Through winter nights and days,
I feel your warmth, my eyes reflect

The comfort of your gaze.
And when I heard
The overtures if spring,
I sang a rhyme for you,
And walked where once we walked
Down Blosson lane,
To catch the scent of wild flowers.
And from their beauty fashioned
A posy in the morning dew
In memory of your unknown grave,
I picked them just for you.

Mike returned with the percolated coffee. The coffee tasted good and for a few moments they sipped gratefully, each wondering how best to resume the conversation. Karen felt withdrawal symptons and Mike felt the evening drifting away from him. 'It's a lovely cup of coffee Mike, but I think you had better take me home.'

Mike felt utterly rejected, 'Please Karen, don't go. I know my efforts in the kitchen have been a bit of a disaster, but so many things seem to get in the way and I lost my concentration. I promise I'll make it up to you.'

'It's nothing to do with your cooking Mike. I hope you'll forgive me but I've been snooping in your cabinet. When I saw the valentine card, curiosity got the better of me and I read your beautiful poem. Can you forgive me, I know it came from your heart and it made me realise how much you loved Sheila. Sheila's everywhere in this flat, it's her home and I feel like an intruder. You still love her Mike. She was an amazing woman and I could never step into her shoes.'

Karen had been frank, she had spoken the truth and Mike now had to face up to his emotional turmoil. An awkward stillness settled over them and Mike was unable to find words which might rescue the situation. At last he spoke, 'It's true Karen.' he stammered, 'Sheila is still very much part of my life. You see, I can't accept that I've lost her. It was the way she went. It was like hitting the pause button on a video and not being able to resume play. She mean't so much to me.'

'I can understand that.' Karen whispered.

And then something quite extraordinary happened. Mike, the big tough guy with the stength of a bull, wept. He buried his head in his hands. 'I'm sorry to break down like this in front of you Karen, you must feel embarrassed and God knows what you must think of me.' Mike swallowed hard, 'I feel like a right twit. I know I've blown it, but I've held down my emotions for too long. It's your honesty Karen, you're so completely honest. That's one of the things I love about you, I do love you you know.' Mike took a deep breath, 'I can love again can't I?' He croaked.

Karen knelt in front of him. She gently took his hands from his face and kissed his tears. 'Of course you can love again, you great big lovely hunk of a man. You must realise how much I love you and tonight you can love me, me Karen, the single mum from New Horizons Park, the girl on the checkout, the one you decided was worth checking out. Let's go to your terraced house and in the morning I'll cook breakfast, a fry up I promise, will rank as a gastronomical masterclass.'

That night Sheila softly stole away from Mike. It was as though she approved of Karen. Softly, softly her presence faded, slipping away from the here and now, leaving only the fragmented memories of their former life.

———————————————

'LUV IS MAGICK.' Skeet blazed forth his message in letters of blue and gold on a star spangled background, adding another layer to the graffiti which covered every accessible space on the walls of New Horizons Park. Skeet was in love, but his love was beyond reason or understanding. Skeet was obsessed with the idea of love, and Sasha, the subject of his intense affections, in reality did not exist. Her person, her creation, was the projection of a disturbed mind, a vision conjured by cannabis abuse which he had smoked from the age of twelve. Classified as soft a drug, it's use had irretrievably damaged the brain, resulting in reality distortion and the onset of psychotic behaviour. At times he chased fantasies of exquisite beauty only to end up fleeing from demons. Sasha was a vision of exquisite beauty, his 'Lucy in the sky with diamonds' and yet try as he may, he was unable to capture her

45

actual features. It was the face of Meg, the drug dealer, the ice queen of New Horizons, who like a siren, lured him on, chasing illusions. She projected feminine guile, the sensual power some women exercise over men and young men in particular. Thoughts of her triggered a desperate need to find Sasha, the private goddess of his dreams.

By a process of irrational thinking, Skeet reasoned that Cornwall was a land inhabited by those who could work magic. Convinced that Sasha was living in the county with a group of new age travellers, he decided to make a break with the Asbos and walk away from the sordid existence of those fools who settled for a life in New horizons. He would track down the mystical tribe in Cornwall where he could be blissfully united with his love.

Before leaving, he had to think of priorities, his essentials for the journey. He needed to contact Ben, his mentor, for a week's supply of cannabis and decided to mug an easy target for the theft of a mobile phone. Without Ben's help and leadership in crime, he had no resources and again he chose an easy target. He waited for his grandmother to draw her pension before stealing every penny he could find in her handbag, causing her anxiety, hardship and stress. Had he asked, she would have offered him money and never chased him for repayment, but in Skeet's mind, in order to save pride, it was easier to steal. The money would fund his drug requirements, pay the train fare and buy food. He gave no thought for the misery he caused. His brain circuits made no connection with the suffering of others and he concerned himself only with immediate needs.

It was late in the afternoon towards the end of April when Skeet finally arrived at Penzance railway station. He wore only a light T shirt and a black leather jacket. his jeans were split at the knees and grubby trainers protruded from the frayed edges of his trouser bottoms. Summer temperatures had fooled Skeet into thinking that warm clothing was unnecessary. His possessions amounted to a mobile phone, half a bar of cannabis, a lighter and a ten pounds note. On leaving the train he suffered a reality attack and for a moment wondered what he was doing in such unfamiliar surroundings. This soon passed as the need to find Sasha intensified. He wandered down to the harbour half expecting to find her gazing out to sea and had to remind himself that she was a new age traveller. To be re-united with his lady love, he had to discover their encampment. He approached a group of teenagers enquiring if they knew the whereabouts of any new age travellers. They thought he looked scary and not wanting him to hang around, suggested he should visit the fair which had arrived in neighbouring Camborne for the Trevithick Day celebrations. They lied saying that new age travellers were camping on the outskirts of the town only a couple of miles away and would be sure to visit the fair. They made no mention that Camborne was twenty kilometres to the east of Penzance. He set off with renewed hope and vigour to hitch hike his way to Camborne, certain that it was the end of a rainbow.

For three miles he maintained a good pace before realising how hungry he was and how easily exhaustion can weaken one's resolve. Trainers are not designed for long distance walking and his heels were badly blistered. The real world sped by in a steady stream of traffic wanting no part of the coloured vagrant trying to thumb a lift on the main road. Gradually darkness closed in and Skeet felt utterly alone in the world. Headlights cast spooky shadows along the hedgerows eventually outlining a stack of hay in the corner of a field. Skeet staggered through the field gate hoping to find a gap in the giant rolls and crawled gratefully between them, already half asleep.

He shivered in his sleep, chilled by the night air, tired of demons, of spiders, of everything and only dreams of Sasha warmed him from within.

He woke early to a dawn chorus and was soon on his way. He reached Hayle just as the shops were opening, and leaving the bypass headed for the town in search of food. Drawn by the smell of fresh baking, he found a small shop selling Cornish pasties and went inside. 'Can I have two pasties please' he said before reaching the counter.

The baker was a little shaken by his first customer of the day, a coloured lad looking half starved, smelling like new mown hay with strands hanging from his Rastafarian dreadlocks, looking more like a scarecrow. The baker was a broadminded

47

individual, a London barrowboy who had moved from the city for a quieter life in the country.'You can ave as many as you like mate. Ain't seen you rahnd ere before.'

'No man. I'm lookin for some new age travellers, know what I mean?'

'Why yeah, ain't no gypos rahnd ere though, Newquay's more likely.'

'I'm lookin for a girl called Sasha, she's livin wiv em somewhere.'

The baker put two hot pasties in a carrier bag, 'You got woman trouble son? Take my advice, move on, leave er aht of it.'

'How much are the pasties man?' Skeet asked, anxious to get back on the road'

'That's ok son, you look as though you need em, they're on the ahse.'

Skeet was thrown by the baker's warmth and generosity. 'Well thanks man, that's really somethin, I mean that's really somethin.'

The baker followed him to the door and as Skeet left the premises he gave him a can of coke. 'Good luck son, but don't think of coming back, cos I ain't giving away no more freebies.'

Skeet made short work of the Cornish pasties, but the coke was nowhere near enough to quench his thirst. Since leaving Penzance it had been his only liquid intake and he now realised that fluids were necessary for sustained physical effort. It would be all hiking and no hitches on the open road and he would have to walk a marathon before reaching Camborne. He began thinking ahead, a highly uncommon practice for Skeet, and instead of discarding the plastic bag, he used it to carry bottles of water. Skeet headed out towards Camborne, stopping occasionally for a breather and a much needed joint. He walked all day arriving once again in a state of exhaustion. Wearily he trudged through the town to join the celebrations, hoping to meet up with Sasha.

The main attraction on Trevithic Day was of course the steam rally. People came from miles around to see this fabulous exhibition in honour of Richard Trevithic, the early pioneer of steam. There is, in most boys, an abiding fascination for steam engines, but Skeet showed no interest whatsoever and headed for the clamour of the fun fair. An ornate caravan caught his eye. A notice board propped against the wheel read, 'Mother Tregenna. Cornish Mystic and Clairvoyant. Crystal, Tarot and Palmistry Readings. £3.' This seemed an answer to his prayers, for surely, Mother Tregenna would know where to find Sasha. He knocked and a young girl appeared in the doorway. 'You want to see Grandma?' she smiled, 'For a reading.'

'Well yeah man, she can do magic, can't she?'

'Grandma's brill, she can see into the past and look into the future,' the girl explained with pride and admiration, 'Come on in, I'll tell her she's got a client.'

Skeet, having been raised by his grandmother, had fixed ideas about how grandmothers should look. Mother Tregenna was nothing like his preconception. Pure white hair fell carelessly across the striking features of her unlined face. She looked kindly and had an ageless quality about her. She had a petite figure and wore a lot of jewellery. Skeet was fixated, he admired jewellery.

'Why, Lord's a mercy! You look like yume on yer last legs biy. Daisy bring him a big slice o' carrot cake and make a cup o' tea, there's a darlin. Why, yume obblin something terrible biy, come a long way ave ee. Where yume to?'

Skeet had some difficulty with the dialect. 'I got blisters walkin. I'm down here lookin for my girlfriend and er, cos you do magic, I thought you'd know where I can find her'

'Daisy, bring some plasters, there's a darlin. You eat yer cake first my biy, then we'll talk about yer girlfriend.'

Mother Tregenna fussed over Skeet and gave him the leftovers of a fish pie. she bathed his feet, washed his socks, put his trainers in the fresh air and fixed plasters over his blisters. She knew she was dealing with a troubled soul and could see death in the boy's eyes. Skeet was unused to the kindness of strangers. His own grandmother, Constance, worn down by poverty and grief, had always been there for him but beyond her caring there was precious little love in his life. He became tearful with emotion, unable to form words which might express his gratitude.Then after a while a wonderful calmness settled over him.

'Now tell me biy, what's yer name, what shall we call ee?'

'My mates call me Skeet.'

'No I mean yer real name.'

'Marvin, Marvin Cooney.'

Well Marvin, I'll look into my crystal, I might see yer girlfriend and I might not. I'll tell you what I see, I wont lie to ee.' Mother Tregenna sat behind her table, removed a cloth from the crystal and gazed into it's depths. She saw dark shapes, strange reflections flickering to the surface. ' I can see *you* in my crystal Marvin……. yume smokin wacky baccy, tidn't good for you, you must give it up…… Yume from up north…… Manchester or such like…… Yume still at school, you should be at school now shouldn't you Marvin?'

'Yeah I'm from Manchester, but I never touch drugs missus, never have. What about Sasha, my girlfriend, what's the crystal say about her?'

Mother Tregenna said nothing, and for a moment she seemed transported. Minutes passed before she spoke. Then she said in a quiet voice, 'Your girlfriend idn't got a name. Sasha's just a name you've gived er.'

'No, she's Sasha, she's definitely with some new age travellers. It's doin my head in keep thinkin about her, I got to find her.'

'Your Sasha's a Fairy Queen me dear, she's all in yer eade, nowhere else, just all in yer eade. You can't be lovin a Fairy Queen now can you? A good lookin biy like you can't spend his life chasin fairies. Now you go back home me dear, back home where yume from, why, there's many a lovely maid waiting for you in Manchester.'

'No your magic's all wrong, I love my Sasha, I'll keep lookin till I find her.'

'Yume lookin after fairies, me dear. You can't find em, not ere, not where we'em to now. '

'Well, where can I find her?'

Mother Tregenna lowered her eyes, 'If you keep lookin, you'll search will end at harvest time, when there's a gathering, I can see it in the crystal. It'll finish come harvest time.'

'But I don't understand missus, I'm not sure what's your meanin.'

'It's time you were on yer way Marvin, I can't say no more. You be going back home, back to school me dear, give up this silliness and stop smokin the wacky baccy.'

'It all seems daft to me, know what I mean, all so stupid. You're just like the rest of em, telling me what I've got to do. Now I suppose you want your three quid.'

'I don't want yer money me dear, but take this lucky charm.' She gave him a tiny piece of jade in the form of a pendant shaped like a heart.'Wear it round yer neck Marvin me dear an when yume in trouble, think of me and t'will keep you safe from harm.'

Skeet sat on the caravan steps, his nervous fingers fumbling with the laces of his trainers. He was confused, unsettled by the session with Mother Tregenna. How could she possibly question the passion he felt for the girl of his dreams? He knew she was out there, waiting for him, yearning for him, a vision so compelling that he must continue his search, and yet he knew she had given him no love, only torment, torment to the point of madness. He thrust his hands deep in his pockets, clutching the pendant in his fist as though he had been offered a lifeline, a link with reality, something to stabilize the crazy workings of his mind.

Skeet wandered around the fair, losing all sense of direction while trying to clear his head and unscramble his brain. He was distracted by a group of young people, each male an Adonis, each woman an Amazonian beauty. They were carefree, laughing and teasing each other. They managed their lives living out of an old Ford Transit while drawing benefits and scrounging, their existence devoted to the worship of surf. Skeet joined in with them, his black skin, hardly noticable against their deep tans, his dreadlocks in keeping with their pony tails and tousled hair styles, his tattered clothing perfectly acceptable among dedicated surfers. He soon found himself bouncing along in the back of the 'Tranny' heading for Newquay and Fistral beach, the English Mecca for those seeking an ultimate ride.

The alliance was short lived. Skeet was unfit, scared of water, had never been near a surf board, and when the surfers discovered him smoking skunk, they refused to have anything more to do with him. They thought he was a surfer on hard times, he had shared their food, slept in their van but now, after their rejection, he was destitute and alone. He made his way into town, even more determined to find Sasha. For a seaside resort, Newquay has more than it's share of club life and Skeet's hopes were raised by the late night revelling. He asked which club was most popular with the younger generation, determined to somehow gain access, certain that Sasha would have the same venue in mind. Finding some difficulty in following directions, he took the wrong turning into a back street and found himself surrounded by hoodies. They were white, half illiterate, racist, and fuelled by alcohol. In a frenzy of violence they knocked him to the ground, kicking and punching him until he lost consciousness. They left him sprawled among the dustbins and binliners at the rear of the club he had been looking for.

He came to in the early hours, pain seering through his body. He thought the rats were giant spiders. He thought the seagulls ripping open the binliners were vultures tearing at his flesh. He decided to ring Ben, the only friend he had in the world, but the mobile phone had gone. As a last resort he thought of Mother Tregenna. His bruised fingers frantically groped each pocket for the pendant. Shock and horror! The pendant was missing.

Chapter 5
Evening Classes

The Pattersons were natural saboteurs. Operating behind enemy lines in times of war, their talents might have earned a military citation and hastened victory. In peacetime however, their unwavering aptitude for creating mayhem was turned on society in general and their own neighbourhood in particular. Practised in every kind of social abuse and able to manipulate the welfare system with Oscar winning performances, they lived a violent lifestyle with theft, vandalism and anti social behaviour high on the agenda. The motivation for causing so much hurt was their need to earn respect, the sort of respect one might show a rattlesnake, and this they achieved in some measure. At the hands of Franklin Page Johnson, Pitbull had suffered humiliation and had lost that respect. A deep hatred for 'Mr.Frankie, fucking Page, fucking Johnson,' provoked his malevolent pride and gnawed at his twisted self esteem. Easily driven to a loss of self control, he decided to settle the score once and for all.

There were few hiding places in the New Horizons Flats. Concrete floors and ceilings, with minimal cupboard space provided little scope for stashing, but Pitbull's father, out of prison after serving five years for armed robbery, had discovered an ideal cavity behind the bath. Pitbull, having an aversion for tools or anything that might suggest work, struggled to remove the hardboard bath panel, fumbling with the screwdriver and chrome, domeheaded screws. He managed to remove the panel, working his head and shoulders into what little space there was at the rear end of the bath, he reached up, feeling for the batten wedged between the bath and the wall. Lodged on the batten, wrapped in an oily cloth was a Browning 9mm, semi-automatic pistol and a box of ammunion.

Given no option, Franklin left his bicycle in the cycle shed knowing that after school it would be vandalised. In a show of great urgency and alarm, he was transported in style, noiselessly sliding past the school gates in a police BMW, heading out for the nearest police station. On arrival, he was dumped unceremoniously on a wooden bench in the corridor and still handcuffed, left to ponder over his folly. For over an hour he sat there awaiting his fate, until at last a police constable approached with a forlorn look on his face. He was a man who had long given up hopes of promotion and whose duties never extended beyond four walls. There was an apology for the delay, he would have to wait a little longer while his cell was being cleaned. 'I'm afraid we've only one cell available at the moment sir and that's being used for storage.'

Franklin responded with weak sarcasm.'Really! Just how many suspects have you got in custody? Aren't you taking a big risk leaving a gangster like me unattended?'

The police officer smiled his resigned smile, but showing some sympathy, removed the handcuffs, ' I think in your case sir, putting you behind bars is not one of our major concerns. We've had an intake of criminals who've recently been convicted and we're not yet ready for 'em. The prisons are full to capacity, too much overcrowding, and we're having to deal with the overflow.'

Franklin was confused. 'But we've been told, by government and police authorities, that there's a significant reduction in crime. I mean every day one reads about light sentencing and early parole. It's simple arithmetic, our prisons should be half empty, shouldn't they?'

'Well I don't know about that sir, but when school teachers with posh accents give us trouble, we've got no chance.'

The policeman wandered off in no hurry while Franklin, now stiff and utterly weary, craved desperately for sleep. The thought of somewhere to lie down made the spare cell infinitely desirable and at that moment he wanted nothing more than the luxury of police accomodation. However, no efforts were made to clear the cell and a second detainee was parked on the bench, a jibbering male wearing a fancy shirt, covered in someone else's blood. The man tipped forward, falling off the bench to lay outstretched on the floor in a drunken stupor, coming to now and again to direct abuse at the petrified Franklin. A teenager, brought in for questioning, steaming with alcohol lurched against him, puking half digested lager into his lap. The three of them looked a sorry sight, unwashed, unloved, smelling like a blocked drain.

After a very long day and a sleepless night, Franklin was finally taken for an interview. It was eight in the morning when detectives, sergeant Bill Erskine and constable Joe Meade decided he was ready for a grilling and would soon, 'spill the beans.' They knew it was an open and shut case. The whole incident had been witnessed by a number of people including the arresting officers and there could be no doubt that a charge of causing grievous bodily harm was safe. However, an assault case requires up to one hundred and fifty bits if paper and is handled by as many as sixty people before procedures allow it to come before the court. With so much administration in mind, the detectives often lost sight of their objectives, in fact they were so tied down by political correctness, government targets, mountains of red tape, trade union officialdom and meetings, neither felt free to proceed in a straightforward manner.

Franklin began the interview.'There's no wash basin in the toilet. D'you think I could clean myself up before we make a start?' He asked in a perfectly reasonable manner, yawning and rubbing his eyes.

The constable detective, ignoring his request, gave him a verbal caution, writing furiously as he droned through the preliminary questions and answers. He addressed Franklin as though rehearsing a script. 'The allegations are that on Monday, June 10th 2007, you took it upon yourself to conduct a maths lesson for the fifth formers of Cumber Community College while under the influence of drink. Patterson, one of your pupils, exposed your irresponsible behaviour before the whole class and in a drunken rage you chose to assault this defenceless boy splitting his nose and causing other injuries which resulted in an ambulance call out for a case of suspected concussion. These are the facts aren't they?'

True to character, Franklin decided attack was the best form of defence.'I resent your tone. You've had me on a wooden bench with couple of drunks for almost twenty hours, no offer of a drink, nowhere to sleep and no one keeping a check on me.

Softening me up no doubt for an interrogation. In any case I need a pee.'

'Your trouble Mr Johnson, is lack of self control, now can we get on with your statement?'

'I've no intention of making a full statement without legal advice. I may not have many rights, but I know interviews should be conducted according to certain rules and procedures. I think in my case you've broken those rules and I want that put on record. Now, if you've no objections, the toilet, I need to go I'm afraid.'

The sergeant, realising that Franklin was not the alcoholic fool he had assumed and was not easily intimidated, decided to change tactics. 'Ok, I'm sorry about the bench and the delay, but we're so overstretched we're almost afraid to bring anyone in. We've had to accommodate people already sentenced, you know, with this latest government move,' he explained, looking for sympathy. 'I think we'll leave it there for a moment while you clean yourself up and I'll see what I can do about organising something in the canteen.'

An hour later the interview continued with Franklin getting the upper hand. he no longer felt censured and humiliated, but intellectually superior. 'What you have charged me with is only true in part. Patterson is not a defenceless boy. He's a powerfully built teenager who is feared by the neighbourhood, school staff and students alike. He's a vicious bully, permanently in breach of an Asbo, and is running the streets completely out of control.'

The sergeant cut in, turning towards the constable. 'Patterson hasn't got an Asbo has he?'

'Not that I'm aware of. I'll check it out.' The constable hurried out to check the records. Franklin continued, 'Initially I felt threatened by the appearance in class of Ben Mackay, who's a similar character and has been expelled from school. He's another one who's in breach of an Asbo, a drug dealing public menace. It strikes me these Asbos are a waste of time. They're never policed or followed up. I read recently that as many as sixty percent of Asbo offenders are in breach of the order.'

The sergeant unwittingly went on the defensive. 'Asbos are very complicated, with the police, local authorities, youth offending teams, registered social landlords, prosecutors, the judiciary and God knows how many other agencies getting in on the act. Government crime reduction guidelines run into pages and pages and the goal posts are continually being shifted. We're not in the business of competing for business, we've enough *real* crime on our plate already.'

'But doesn't it strike you that something's terribly wrong? I'm here, pilloried by the law, my career, my reputation, my retirement pension all on the line, because, through your neglect of duty, I was driven to make a stand against a mindless thug while young criminals like Mackay, Patterson and Cooney are still at large. Isn't it a fact that half your time is spent in the station and only one in every fifty or so police officers is on the beat at any given time? There is absolutely no deterrent out there. Only a small percentage of your enormous resources is operational in the front line. You're like an army in reserve.'

The constable came into the room. 'Er Bill, I've checked out Patterson and Mr Johnson's right. He received an Asbo when he was fourteen, following a school complaint about abusive language and graffitti on school property. He's not been in trouble since, but his dad's got serious form.'

Franklin exploded. 'Not been in trouble since! I can't believe I'm hearing this! Not been in trouble since! What a joke, a wicked sick joke, but of course what you're really saying is, 'he's not been spotted on CCTV.' Why he's nothing but trouble and you'll never catch him on CCTV, he makes sure of that, he runs with a gang of hoodies and it's impossible to recognise any of them, as you well know.' Franklin let that sink in. 'Whatever happened to your promise of zero tolerance?'

The constable turned to his partner for support. 'Mr Johnson, we take every crime very seriously, don't we Bill?'

'I can't help noticing you never address each other by rank, the police were more disciplined when I was a youngster, and by the way, my name is Mr *Page* Johnson.' Franklin was beginning to enjoy himself, filled with righteous indignation, he thought he had the detectives squirming.

The sergeant decided it was time to put an end to the interview which was rapidly becoming an embarrassment. 'I think we've heard enough of your whinging Mr Johnson, you're being very unfair on the force. Our job is far more difficult than you can possibly imagine. Police officers get shot you know, carrying out their duties.'

'I appreciate that and it's an awful tragedy, but lots of people are being shot, teenagers *and* school teachers, not to mention the mistaken identities who end up in y*our* line of fire which brings me to another important matter. Patterson's father is out of jail after being convicted of armed robbery. He's already threatened me and I want police protection.'

The sergeant was ready to crush this bumptious, know all little prig. 'Ken Patterson is out on parole and is already under police surveillance. It strikes me Mr Johnson, it's our children who need protection, protection from *you*. With insufficient evidence on the second charge, I'm recommending police bail while we carry out further investigations and I suggest you contact your solicitor immediately.' He looked down at his notes. 'You're going to need him.'

'Well thank you. I'm glad you're able to see sense. I'll make an appointment the moment I get home. But I don't quite understand. A second charge?'

'I'm afraid you can't go home. Your home is sealed off and is being treated as a crime scene.'

'What on earth are you talking about?'

The police sergeant savoured the moment. He was about to bring Mr Page Johnson crashing down. 'We've received a complaint from Mrs Patterson, the boy's mother. She says you took the boy home after school, on the pretence of giving him extra maths tuition, and sexually assaulted him.'

Franklin left the police station, bewildered, shocked, the most reviled creature on earth. What little had been left of his private world had finally collapsed amid ghastly allegations. He had been unprepared for such pernicious lies. Although totally innocent, his name would be dragged through the courts leaving him marked for ever by this dreadful stain. All he ever wanted was the love of Gloria and the need to share his enthusiasm for maths with those willing to learn. He loved children, at heart he was a family man, all he ever wanted was children of his own and a quiet family life. How could the world treat him so? How could those dreams of happiness, those unselfish aspirations, end in such ignominy? He was nothing more than a shadow, a hollow carcass, a joker in the pack, physically and mentally exhausted. There was nothing left worth fighting for, life had nothing to offer, he was ready to give up, die, sink into oblivion.

In the car park, a small intense looking man was standing by a laundry van. He came over to Franklin and introduced himself. ' Mr Page Johnson?'

'Why yes, er, I er, I'm afraid I can't talk to anyone, not at the moment.'

'Well, I'm Jack Foskett and I want to thank you personally for what you did for my son.' He took Franklin's hand and shook it firmly. 'I'd like you to know I intend to give you my full support in this. I'm making a voluntary statement for the police and I'm going to tell them exactly what went on in that classroom and I shan't rest until something is done about that Patterson boy. My son is also prepared to make a statement.'

The words reached Franklin like distant echoes and he failed to appreciate their significance. 'That's very decent of you,' he muttered.

A VW beetle drew up alongside in ladybird livery, looking like an inflated version of the insect itself and ready for take off. A head leaned out of the window and Franklin recognised the limp hair, cartwheel glasses and retrousse nose of the English teacher at Cumber College. He had rarely spoken to her during school hours, hardly noticed her in fact. 'Why Miss Tonkins what are you doing here?'

'Hello Frank, I see your house has been sealed off by the police and your bike, well, what's left of it, is still in the cycle shed. Now just look at you, here you are with no transport, no home to go to and probably no money on you. Now get in the car and don't argue.'

In a complete daze, Franklin climbed into the car. 'It's very good of you Miss Tonkin, but I don't understand, I can't believe that anyone from school would want to associate with me after what's happened, I'm in such an awful mess, I've reached the pits I'm afraid.'

Miss Tonkin, crunching the gears, headed out of the park to join the stream of traffic. 'Well, for what it's worth Frank, I think you're bloody marvellous. And I'm not the only one.'

Tricia Tonkin could have been the original plain Jane and to describe her as a woman with the fuller figure would have been kindness itself. Unlike Franklin, who had received the best education money could buy and had been groomed for higher things, Tricia, from her childhood, had to fight every step of the way. She was able to cope with the pressure and stress at Cumber Community College chiefly because, as a student, she had attended a similar school. She understood her students, their background, their mistrust of authority, their prejudice and the dire shortage of money which made them hostage to a welfare state. She had that rare gift among academics, the common touch. Though disadvantaged by lack of funds and a broken home, she showed intelligence and stamina, working her way through university to win a degree and independence. Men had been unkind to her, faking love in order to take advantage of that independence, smooth talking layabouts, trying to control her, having their feet under her table while she paid the bills and the mortgage. Now, aged twenty eight and twenty years younger than Franklin, she was mentally tough and nobody's fool.

Franklin always behaved like any gentleman of his generation, with good manners and courtesy, especially towards women, and although for some women, this old fashioned behaviour spelt chauvinism, Tricia found it preferable to the lack of respect she had experienced from younger men. Franklin had also shown courage against the odds, courage against Pitbull, when everyone else was scared stiff of him. Tricia knew Franklin lived alone and decided he needed mothering.

'Frank, I'm taking you back to my home, you can stay with me for a few days while the police do whatever it is they are doing at your house. I've got a spare bedroom.'

'Miss Tonkin, I'm quite overwhelmed,' Franklin swallowed hard, 'your kindness and generosity,' he tried to regain some composure, 'I feel humbled, close to breaking down, right here in front of you.' The lump in his throat hardened as he struggled to reason with her. 'I mean we've never even had a conversation before and I'm ashamed to say I can't remember your first name. I simply cannot allow you to jeopardise you own career in this way. I'll stay in bed and breakfast or something.' He tried to relax his throat muscles, but more emotion surfaced. ' I mean whatever would people say?'

'My first name's Tricia, Frank. I know you've not paid much attention to me in the past, no one ever does, that is until they get to know me, and as far as worrying about what people say, well, I don't care what people say. I'm mad, mad at the way you've been treated, it's outrageous. Pitbull had it coming, no one's ever stood up to him like you did, he treated us all with contempt, everyone was terrified of him and anyone who knows you, realises these charges are not worth the paper they're written on. Anyway, I'm getting up a petition and I've already got most of the teachers on board. And that's not all, Mr Rajur from the corner shop is also getting up a petition from the Asian community. A couple of weeks ago he was robbed and beaten up by a gang of hoodies, calling themselves the Asbos, and he's sure he recognised Pibull's trainers.' Tricia gave Franklin a sideways glance. She caught him wiping a tear from his cheek.

'I think I need a drink,' he managed to say.

'I'll make you a nice cup of coffee the moment we step inside, but from here on in, alcohol is out. I mean it Frank, I'm going to sort you out whether you like it or not. I've decided you're worth salvaging. Think of it as evening classes,' she said with a laugh.

And so began a beautiful friendship. The police searched Franklin's house, downloaded his computor and found nothing. Statements were made by the Fosketts, petitions were received from the teachers of Cumber Community College and a separate statement came from Ashraf Rajur, together with a petition from the Asian community who applauded his teaching abilities and his communication skills. Pitbull was taken in for questioning and the charge for grievous bodily harm was reduced to common assault for which Franklin received a caution. No further action was taken.

A network of yellow tape, snaked around the Franklin address, serving more of a PR exercise than a security measure. It was finally removed, but not before newsreel photographers and the press had taken shots from every angle. Franklin once more took up residence and began to take stock of the situation. He decided to sell the place and might have moved out of the area but for one thing, his 'Evening classes.' The evenings with Tricia had steadied his nerve and he began to smarten up, taking more care with his appearance. He gave up drinking Armagnac, he threw off his despondency, his cynicism, his bitterness, and began to feel young again. Tricia looked forward to the visits which became longer and longer. She denied herself chocolate snacks and late night nibbles, she lost weight, she wore make up, she made an appointment with the hairdresser and changed her glasses for a more stylish pair. The changes were subtle and came gradually and as they drew closer, neither was really aware of any outward improvement. Imperceptibly they were falling in love. Tricia was no Gloria, but Franklin was old enough and wise enough to see the woman she was, faithful, strong and dependable. He put his house on the market and moved in with Tricia and there was so much trust between them, they decided to get married.

A local drama group had chosen a production of J B Priestly's comedy, 'When we're Married.' It is not too challenging for amateurs and the old fashioned humour is easily understood. It seemed appropriate for the couple and they booked seats for an evening's light entertainment. In order to park the ladybird and be sure of a good seat, they decided to leave early and as Franklin stood at the end of the drive giving Tricia the all clear before reversing into the road, he thought he saw a movement behind the Mahonia. It's spiky fragrance suddenly filled the garden as though it had been disturbed. He heard the shots, muffled, spitting hate, death and destruction, the antithesis of everything kind and creative. Those shots were the last impressions Franklin had of this world. One bullet smashed into his lower jaw, another severed an artery in the neck before entering his spinal column and a third went straight through his lung. He spun round and collapsed. Tricia leapt out of the car and dashed to his aid, 'Oh no, Oh for God's sake no.' she screamed, but there was nothing she could do and he died in her arms.

The Patterson's flat now became a crime scene. Armed with a search warrant for the possession of drugs, the police arrived in numbers, a rare occurance on New Horizons Park. And here, Pitbull's reign of terror came to an end, toppled by a sweet natured Springer Spaniel. The young bitch sniffed her way around the flat and with her tail wagging furiously, pawed at the bath panel. The panel was removed to reveal a store of drugs, stacked between the plumbing. Machine oil stained the concrete screed and a sharp eyed detective investigating further discovered the Browning semi automatic. Pitbull's fingerprints were all over it and marks on the bullets, retrieved from Franklin's body, matched the rifling in the barrel. Pitbull was charged with murder.

Franklin received more recognition in death than he received in a whole lifetime. The church was packed. The community, the whole nation, were shocked and dismayed that such a crime could be committed on the streets of Britain in broad daylight. Franklin had given far more than he understood, a clear blueprint for all those students who had ever listened to his teachings. They were ordinary folk, engineers, teachers, craftsmen, shopkeepers, people who never forgot the mathematical groundwork he had given them. A memorial prize for maths was instituted at Cumber Community College and Dina Rajur was it's first recipient. And the fight in the classroom? That would always be a talking point and almost became a legend.

Tricia grieved, her sorrow seemed inconsolable. Even so, there were blessings. Franklin had his faults, had found it difficult to move with the times, had known failure, but for all that he was a man. Tricia had loved that man and together they had discovered a wonderful relationship. Franklin had made a will, leaving everything he owned to her, but that was of little importance, she held a gift more precious to her than any legacy. She was carrying his child.

Chapter 6. The Messenger from God.

The village church, built with great quoins and irregular courses of uncompromising granite, gave little scope for the stonemason's art, its lack of features resulting in a veritable rock of ages. The belfry tower, buttressed at each corner, peered above the rich foliage of a copper beech and the sweeping arms of an ancient yew. Other trees sprinkled sunlight over the gravestones, breaking them into fragments of granite scree leading up to the tower. Near the wicket gate, a mullberry tree, it's sprawling limbs supported on iron crutches, scattered luscious fruit, feeding the birds, staining the footpath. Unlike the meadow grass of larger cemeteries, where mowing with powerful machines is more akin to haymaking, and where gravestones are obliterated and flowers choked to death, this churchyard was beautifully maintained with finely cut grass to match the lawns of the adjacent vicarage. Only the lively twittering of small birds and the gentle cooing of pigeons as they flew back and forth from the louvres of the tower, disturbed the peace and tranquility of a perfect Cornish retreat.

The reverend Robin Reid presided over this idyllic sanctuary and was agonising in his study over the forthcoming Sunday sermon. Agonising is not too strong a word for the task which lay before him. In order to appreciate his dilemma, we need to understand the circumstances which led to a relatively young clergyman losing his faith. Robin Reid was the only child of a military family and had been desperately lonely as a young boy. His father, a high ranking officer and a war hero, had spent much of his time away from home and there had never been a close bond between them. His father, a strict disciplinarian, had given his life to the regiment and his devotion to service and duty was an exemplary model for others to follow. A spartan lifestyle, rigidly imposed in preparation for operational theatres, had finally eliminated the emotional need for women, leaving him with confused sexual orientations. More and more he embraced the idea of combat and began to love the concept of war and the young bodies of his soldiers who might be slaughtered like sacrificial lambs. However, with tremendous self control, he would not allow these dreadful awakenings to surface.

His mother hated war and loathed violence in any form, for whatever reason. Suffering the cold comfort of a loveless marriage and for the sake of respectability, she played the dutiful soldier's wife but secretly became obsessed with a padre, whom she loved from afar. She was earnestly convinced the chaplain shared mutual pangs of desire and could be none other than her soul mate and was so emotionally wrapped up with the personification of her wildest dreams, she typed an unsigned letter, assuring him that one day they would be united, if not on Earth, then surely in heaven. These tortured emotional undercurrents created an unheathy family atmosphere and Robin escaped into an imaginary world where he could play with his chums, a whole cast of invented characters. He gave them different nationalities, different backgrounds and curious dialects which he uttered in lowered tones. His mother doted on him and was unbearably possessive, exercising too much influence over his decisions. Persuading him to take holy orders in the Church of Engand became an all consuming ambition for her son. It somehow compensated for the huge disappointments in her life. Convinced that he owed so much to his mother, Robin felt obliged to take her advice and having left school with good A levels, joined the C of E with the prospect of becoming ordained. At first he showed great promise and might easily have risen through the ecclesiastical ranks to become a young bishop, but having been let loose on the Christian community, he became too controversial and was hurriedly marginalised, banished to the rural obscurity of a Cornish diocese. He married Harriet, a girl so like his mother, she was often mistaken for his sister. To their sorrow they remained childless, but Harriet's faith in the almighty could never be shaken and she instinctively felt the love of God and of his son Jesus Christ.

The usual round of coffee mornings, garden fetes, mother's meetings and other ex curricular activities were not well attended and the Sunday congregation, reflecting the general decline in the number of young people in the village, dwindled into a grey haired gathering of pensioners waiting for the grave. While Robin became increasingly despondent, Harriet who played the organ, remained upbeat. Her love of music had given the church an interesting diversion, a face saving dimension. She set up her piano in the nave directly before the screen which separated it from the chancel and formed a choral society. This attracted several non church goers including a few long redundant tin miners who were still in good voice. She was planning her first recital and there had been some enthusiastic rehearsals. However for Robin, the easy pace and quiet solitude promoted a period of meditation and soul searching and he began to examine his own relationship with God. The truth was, he had never felt the love of God, certainly not in the sublime way Harriet professed. An admission even more painful was the fact that he had never really loved God. I mean, how can you love someone you can't see, someone who never talks back, never embraces you, never fights your quarter or is positively there for you? I mean, who is God, what does he look like, where does he live, where can he be found, is there any proof of his existence? Robin decided, in a Darwinian world of scientific knowledge, sub atomic discoveries and miraculous technology, the C of E needed to address these questions, difficult questions which people preferred to ignore in order to get on with their lives.

More than anything he missed the challenge of working with anti social behaviour problems among youths. He had been an influential worker with a youth offending service but here in the village there was hardly any juvenile crime and he was beginning to feel wasted. The only real impact he could make was to begin a programme of re-education, to speak out against the entrenched ritual and mythological regimen the church stubbornly offered to those seeking comfort and refuge. There were a few souls among his congregation who might listen, who might spread the word. He decided to approach the subject head on, no platitudes, no ancient jargon, no religious dogma, no allegorical references, just plain speaking.

He looked out, beyond the leaded lights and stone mullions of his study, beyond the copper beech, out, out into the colourwash of a pale blue sky, beyond the cottonwool clouds, out, out into infinite, unfathomable space, hoping for inspiration, and he realised he could no longer ignore the nagging doubts of his ministerial career. Perhaps he should leave the church, make an appointment to see the bishop and denounce his vows. Perhaps he should do the brave thing, try to change things from within, in which case he had to be sure of what his ministry actually stood for, even if it was in conflict with his employer. Perhaps this way he would re-awaken his own faith, find his own salvation. He ran his fingers through his hair. Particles of dandruff fell across the pages of his note paper, glinting in the sunlight. He swept them aside in disgust and began tapping out his thoughts on the laptop. After the introduction, he would make notes from which he could elaborate further.

'It is the freeing of our conscience, imprisoned within the fortress of our ego which allows us to distinguish between right and wrong, good and evil. Thoughts arise which check our appetite for self indulgence. We recognise our sins and have more concern for others. There is some guilt, and we have thoughts of forgiveness, of redemption, of salvation and of God. Such thoughts often relate to a crisis in our lives, a terminal illness, something from which there is no escape, when all our powers are exhausted. As a last resort we may utter a prayer to God. For those of us, who by good fortune blunder through life into old age, there are memories, regrets, sadness and hope that there is life hereafter. We are taught from childhood that there is more to life and that God will provide. In the name of God our wars are fought. In the name of God our kings and queens are crowned. In the name of God our politicians are blessed. In the name of God we elect church leaders. In the name of God we are married. In the name of God we consecrate our dead. And yet, for most of us God remains an enigma. Many claim that God is enshrined within their hearts, they know him, trust him, a father figure whom they love and worship, but for most of us, life is a learning process, a quest of discovery, an unfolding of time and evolution with enormous growing pains. Increasingly, superstition and fear are giving way to enlightenment and the church's effort to promote blind faith is not enough. We need to understand ourselves and the nature of the world. If we have souls, we need to be aware of them, to be aware of God.

The church proclaims that the word of God may be found in the Holy Bible and it is true that the Torah or Pentateuch, the first five books of the Old Testament, traditionally ascribed to Moses, form the basis of Christianity, Judaism and the Koran. These works incredibly, have influenced our religious views of morality to this day, even though Mosaic laws make horrific reading. The stories abound with God's reminders of the miracles he has performed, entirely for the benefit of the Israelites, his threats, his punishments and his frightful curses. The Israelites are a race chosen by God and they are instructed to occupy the lands of other other nations requiring a great deal of smiting, killing and destruction. There are laws and ordinances given by Moses and underwritten by God. They are archaic, quaint, punitive, tedious and irrevelent to the struggles of humanity. There is a demand for continual burnt offerings and the sacrifice of animals, details concerning the selling of servants, stoning for adultery, execution of witches and all manner of barbaric practices which civilised nations have long since outlawed. Deuteronomy, the fifth book of Moses, chapter 25, verses 11 and 12, demonstrate in the most awful manner, the controlling mentality of Hebrew priests and their attitude towards women. I quote:

Verse 11
When men strive together one with another, and the wife
of the one draweth near for to deliver her huband out of
the hand that smiteth him, and putteth forth her hand and
taketh him by the secrets:

Verse 12
Then thou shall cut off her hand, thine eye shall not pity her.

The whole work portrays God as a terrifying despot whose prime interest is his chosen race. A man is executed for gathering sticks on the Sabbath and numerous other outrages are committed in the name of Jehovah. Clearly this is not a God we can love or relate to. The stories in this section of the Old Testament, God's creation of heaven and Earth, Adam and Eve, Noah's Ark, and the Exodus from Egypt are dynamic, partisan, curiously exhalted, but hopelessly absurd.'

Robin took a print out of what he had written thus far. Yes, he was satified. He would read it word for word, slowly, carefully, deliberately, before speaking from his written notes. He sat up straight, his desk was too low and his back was aching. He levered his narrow shouldered, six foot frame from the swivel chair and reached for the rusting cockspur fastener to open the window. He thought he heard a piano and realised it must be Harriet composing some tune or other in the church. He looked at his watch, hoping she hadn't forgotten it was nearly coffee time. He stretched, yawned, sat down, leaned forward and continued with the opening address.

'The explosion of a supernova, an astronomical event of such apocalyptic proportions, it defies our powers of description, followed by the aggregation of dust and gas molecules by gravitational forces, gave birth to a disc shaped, rotating nebula with the proto-sun at it's centre. Increased density and friction raised the temperature until nuclear processes gave birth to a star, giving forth intense radiation, heat and light. Other bodies formed in the solar nebula, plantisimals, but lacking the mass and density to generate a nuclear reaction, they evolved into the planets we now observe in the solar system. Our Earth is one of those planets, one of the four inner rocky planets. It is a beautiful, pristine, spinning gem, shining out within the vast reaches of an immense galaxy, the Catherine wheel of stars we call the Milky Way and it's deep blue seas have always, from their very beginning, received light and heat from the sun.

It requires the rejection of logical thought if one is to ignore the frontiers of scientific knowledge, the ever changing evolution of species, the fossil evidence of animals who appeared on the scene and became extinct and the theory of evolution. Only ignorance or closed minds can fail to appreciate all that has been discovered by experiment, the insights of great minds, all that has been astronomically observed, the magnitude of the universe, the distribution of galaxies, and the forces which create the birth and death of stars and the formation of planets.

The Church has an appalling record of supressing scientific discovery and the freedom of speech while feeding ignorance with superstition. In terms of religious import, it is time for the Church to openly reject the mythology which forms much of the Old Testament. It contributes nothing to our understanding of Christian doctrine, it empties our churches and it's contradictions merely serve to confuse. Its place is in the library along with other works of literature, and not in the church. It has no bearing on modern Christianity and it's gross invention of history together with it's baleful narrative is not helpful in our search for God.'

The more Robin wrote on the subject the more he enthused. He picked up a biro, a freebie from cancer research, and had furiously started making notes when Harriet came in with the morning coffee. 'Coffee dear' she said with a warm smile.

'How's the sermon coming along?'

'Fine, like to read it so far?' Robin replied, clicking the print button.

Harriet began reading. Robin, sipping his coffee, studied her face, hoping to see some reaction, dismay, surprise, or even better, outright disapproval. But Harriet read, shaking her head like a schoolmistress who cannot get through to a backward pupil.

'You know Robin dear, you're going completely in the wrong direction with this. You're sitting on the fence. An agnostic who can't make up his mind and has lost all sense of direction. No serious Christian takes the Old Testament literally. It represents early man's concept of a single deity, a vision way beyond those represented by other religions in pre history. A God who has no recognisable form, a God beyond our powers of understanding, but nevertheless a God who is part of our inner being, our soul. That Robin dear, is the wonder of it. There is nothing to be gained by trying to visualise God, an endeavour beyond our faculties. The essence of God is to be found in the teachings of Jesus. If we pursue love, truth and those virtues which enrich our lives we shall draw closer to him. I agree that the Church of England is in need of reform. It's too pro establishment and should give up its ceremonial preoccupation with the monarchy, it's grandiose, memorial pride of place for the aristocracy and the glorification of our wars. Its values should be rooted in Christ, not in Henry VIII. The church should be the true guardian of democracy with powers to scrutinise legislation and veto parliarmentary decisions.' Robin felt repremanded, astonished by her forthright criticism and radical opinions. His brow wrinkled, his eyes blinked as though trying to clear his blind stupidity. 'Wow' he muttered, and then, with the direction of his thoughts rudely diverted, he realised something odd, piano notes were still filtering through the open casement. 'Harriet there's someone playing the piano, in the church, I first heard it when I opened the window and thought it must be you. Is it something you've organised?'

'No, I haven't played it since last choir practice and after that I put the cover back on. We'd better investigate.'

They left the study and hurried over to the church. Unmistakably there was someone playing the piano, a repetitive, aggressive rendering, interrupted by curious chanting. The unearthly sound suggested caution and they quietly opened the door, sneaking in with heads down to occupy the nearest pew at the very rear of the nave. From here they witnessed a performance for which there was no rational explanation, a crazy, mind blowing apparition, a desecration. They sat mesmerised, wits scrambled, trying to make sense of it all.

A black youth, wearing a filthy shirt and trousers, his tangled dreadlocks, spiky, charged with electricity, sat hammering at the piano. He was improvising a form of street music, loud, raw, demanding attention. He used the whole keyboard and nothing he played seemed out of tune. A can of coke and a half eaten pasty teetered on top of the piano. His legs pumped, beating out the time, until suddenly he slewed off the stool, leaping to his feet, gyrating, hips swaying, projecting rhythm into the space around him. With head thrusting and finger snapping he began rapping out his thoughts.

'Ain't workin twenty four seven, no I ain't workin twenty four seven,
Ain't never gonner find no heaven, you'll never get to heaven
In New Horizons Park, New Horizons, New Horizons, New Horizons, New Horizons, in New Horizons Park.
Ain't havin no more schoolin, no I ain't havin no more schoolin,
I'd rather be jus foolin, cos all the kids like foolin

In New Horizons Park, New Horizons, New Horizons, New Horizons, New Horizons, in New Horizons Park.
I jus can't see no point, no I jus can't see no point,
I'd rather smoke a joint, cos there's magic in a joint
In New Horizons Park, New Horizons, New Horizons, New Horizons, New Horizons, in New Horizons Park.'

He went back to the piano, playing with more confidence, changing chords, finding more expression, then darting away, stomping back and forth as though scattering the music among a captive audience, then back to the piano, then more rap.
'My Sasha, she's some bird, she really is some bird
An she's never ever heard, no she's never ever heard
Of New Horizons Park, New Horizons, New Horizons, New Horizons
New Horizons, New Horizons Park.
Ain't sure if she's left me, no I ain't sure if she's left me,
But I was feelin kinda empty, I was really feeling empty,
In New Horizons Park, New Horizons, New Horizons, New Horizons,
New Horizons, in New Horizons Park.
But now she's comin back, I know she's comin back
And we can hit the track, we'll both get on the track
To New Horizons Park, New Horizons, New Horizons, New Horizons.
New Horizons, to New Horizons Park.

He sashayed, still snapping fingers back to the piano, grabbed the coke, stuffed the pasty in his mouth and slumped in the front pew.
'I think you'd better phone the police.' Robin whispered, 'I'll keep an eye on him.'
There was no reponse, Harriet sat transfixed.'Harriet, quickly, get the police!' Robin hissed.
' I don't think so Robin. There is something quite amazing going on here. Can't you see? This boy's no threat to us, he's bearing a message, a message for you. I believe he's been sent, he's a messenger,...... a messenger from God.'

'What are you saying Harriet. That young man's clearly a threat, a vagrant, high as a kite. It's hard to say what he's up to.'

Harriet took Robin's hand, 'Come on we'll go and speak to him.'

In truth, Skeet hoped that he would be discovered and was almost relieved to see the couple who now confronted him. He was more than ready to pour out his troubles to anyone who would listen. At close quarters Harriet thought how good looking he was, and alarmed by the cuts and bruises on his face, opened up the conversation. 'Good morning young man, I must say this is a surprise, we get so few visitors here, we only see those living in the parish and you're a complete stranger. You seem to have taken an interest in my piano, how long have you been playing, you must be in a Pop group or something?'

'Nah, I've never played a pianner, but when I heard the notes I jus knew how to play it. It's really cool, man. Wish I had one.'

'I can hardly credit it, you have such a natural talent and a good ear for music, but surely you've practiced before?' Harriet replied in disbelief.

'Nah, I got nothin to do, so I jus bin tryin it. I found some paper and pencils and bin makin up rap, thought I'd try it with music.'

'It's amazing, I think you'd make a good musician. Where are you from?'

'I see you've broken into our famine relief box.' Robin cut in with growing indignation, taking note of the damaged charity box lying on the floor. 'That money was for people who are starving in the Sudan.'

'Yeah, I see that, its for starvin blacks innit? That's jus why I took it. I'm a starvin black in I? Know wha I mean. Any case, this is a church innit and you're a preacher bloke, always prayin and stuff, an you should know, God don't need money. can't you ask him to help em?'

'You don't understand. We bring these misfortunes on ourselves, we have a choice.' Robin said, determined to gain the initiative.

'Those kids in Africa never had no choice. I never had no choice. We was jus born in a crap situashun.' Skeet continued, with emphatic use of the double negative.

'You're nothing more than a juvenile dilinquent. How dare you behave like this in the house of God. I can tell you're on drugs. You deserve an Asbo, need to be brought into line. I have very good connections with youth offending organisations.'

'God's got houses all over, nobody lives in any of em. Any case he's got no bedrooms, I bin sleepin among the pigeons an they're crappin all over me. Any case, you don't know nothin about Asbos. Man, they're jus stupid, know wha I mean. Any case I already got one.'

For the second time that morning Harriet sensed her husband was arguing himself into a corner. 'Young man, you seem to have been in the wars and I think we need to understand your problems. Now, first of all what is your name and where do you come from?'

I'm Marvin from Manchester. Everybody calls me Skeet cos they think I'm mental.'

Alarm bells rang in Robins head. He was dealing here with a lunatic. 'From Manchester! Then what are you doing in Cornwall and what are you doing in this church?' he demanded.

'Well I'm lookin for Sasha, my girlfriend, She's down here with some new age travellers and man, I got to find her, get her back.'

'Ok, but why come here? There aren't any new age travellers in this village or anywhere near here and you have no right to use this church as a squat.'

'I thought you said it was God's house? An now you're sayin he don't want me here. Even though I'm lost, I'm cold an starvin and ain't got no money.'

'My husband doesn't mean that Marvin, he's just wondering why you came into this church, I mean you're not a church goer are you, not raised Cof E?'

'Nah, this is the first church I ever bin in, but I see on the gate, you're havin a harvest festival.'

'Yes, but what's that got to do with it?' Harriet said, becoming quite entrigued.

'Well, this is where I'm meetin Sasha.'

'What here in this church?'

'Yeah, Ma Tregenna, she told me in Terrific, know wha I mean, that place where they have the steam engines.'

'He means Trevithic, sounds like he's been to the steam rally,' Robin explained. 'I've heard of Mother Tregenna, she claims she's a white witch.'

'Yeah that's it, Ma Tregenna said Sasha would be here at harvest time, when you have your gatherin. Ma Tregenna was really cool, jus magic.'

'But our harvest festival is three weeks away and if you think you can hang around here waiting for your dolly bird to appear, you're very much mistaken. I must ask you to leave immediately and take your rubbish with you.'

'I ain't goin nowhere, this is God's house innit not yours, an he ses I can stay.'

'In that case I shall call the police and have you forcibly removed.'

'Calm down Robin dear, you're over reacting,' Harriet intervened, taking charge of the conversation. Robin turned to her, confused, knowing full well by the tone of her voice that she had already made up her mind, and knew exactly what they were going to do. She sounded like his mother and although fired up for a confrontation, he was not going to argue with her. 'First of all Marvin we want to welcome you to our church and offer you our hospitality. We will make enquiries as to the whereabouts of Sasha and in the meantime you can stay with Robin and myself in the vicarage. All we ask is that you treat us with respect. You can sit with us at mealtimes, help Robin in the garden with his fruit and vegetables for the harvest festival and I can give you piano lessons, teach you to read music. You have a good singing voice and I'd like you to join our choir. But most of all, I want you to help me make the church beautiful, not only for God, but for Sasha when she arrives and together you can both enjoy the service. Will you do that?'

Robin was visibly shaken. 'This is going to get the whole village talking, word is bound to reach the bishop.'

'That is precisely what you want, isn't it, to change things from within? Well here's you're chance. God given, a chance in a lifetime.'

'Cor! Missus, that's really cool. I mean you'd really teach me to play the pianner, let me live in your big house and everthin?'

'Most certainly Marvin, and you can begin by having a hot bath and taking lunch with us.'

Robin scratched his head, dismayed, resigned, unsure about playing the part of a good Samaritan in such bizarre circumstances. Harriet was behaving like his mother, quite sure of herself while he dithered, acting the child again, compelled to follow. Why couldn't he grow up? Where was all this nonsense leading?

Chapter 7 Worcester sauce and Woodshavings.

Ben strutted through New Horizons Park with the brash arrogance of youth, an inexhaustable reservoir of health and vigour, giving him confidence, dispelling all doubts, allaying all fears. He thought he understood the ways of the world, had a good foothold on life and no one, he was sure, could stand in his way. However, certain issues managed to probe his slumbering conscience. He read about the Frankie murder case and wondered whether he had influenced or encouraged Pitbull in any way. The Asbo trail of mayhem had stalled in the aftermath of the schoolmaster's death and everyone understood the facts, Frankie had done nothing to provoke murder. Frankie hadn't been such a bad guy after all, and Ben had come to respect him, an old guy like that, standing up to Pitbull. For the first time in his life Ben felt shame. He deeply regretted his friendship with Pitbull and wished to distance himself from the tragedy. He decided to end his leadership of the Asbos and surprisingly felt a a sense of relief. Meg had given him good advice and he was ready to move on, but he still felt anger towards his mother and failed to understand how she could find so much happiness with the new man in her life.

A fragmented generation of children raised by single parents inevitably leaves a few casualties, and from an early age Ben's family had been deprived of male guidance, constructive influence and fatherly protection. He naturally took on the role, shouldering responsibilities, giving support to his family, caring for them, and as a daughter innocently flirts with her father, so Ben formed a special relationship with his mother, playing the part of grown man, acting like her champion. He wanted her love and admiration, to hear her sing his praises, wanted her to be proud of him, proud of the way he faced up to life. An understanding that his mother needed more than a dutiful son was beyond his comprehension and now this beat up footballer, this DIY freak had muscled in on their life, injuring his male pride, leaving him with a sense of rejection. OK, they had no need of him and he had no need of them. He had already found some one who truly loved him, someone with whom he could make real money, have some real excitement, afford a few luxuries and help himself to the good things in life. The idea of working for a living had no place in Ben's plans for the future, these things had to come easily and quickly with Ben in the driving seat. Street life had taught him a simple truth, the strong take what they want and the weak have no choice but to give it to them.

It was a cheerless Saturday morning. Blankets of grey cloud promised another miserable weekend as persistant rain sluiced litter down the choked gullies. For Ben, New Horizons represented everything he wished to leave behind. He loathed the whole complex and despised most of the people who were obliged to live among the horrors, weak hopeless cases who never complained, never protested. If he'd had a say about it's future, he'd flatten the whole stinking pile. He took the stairs three steps at a time arriving at his mother's appartment without appearing to draw breath. He knocked impatiently and Karen opened the door. 'Ben darling, thank God you're here. You've not been envolved in that police enquiry? We've been so worried, devastated by what happened to that poor school teacher. Please Ben, promise me you had nothing to do with it. Mike's here with some wonderful news about a job offer.'

The words tumbled out as Karen welcomed her prodigal son. 'Matt's gone for fish and chips and a few lagers.'

Ben brushed past her, dumping his weatherproof jacket on the nearest chair, dripping water over the carpet. Karen, stifling a rebuke, tided it away. 'What's this all about, I can't stay long, I've got better things to do. If it's about Pitbull and the Asbos, don't worry, I've packed all that stuff in.'

'Oh Ben! Promise me you had nothing to do with that dreadfull shooting, I can't believe you were involved in any way. Oh Ben, promise me darling, you knew nothing about it. The police haven't been holding you have they, you haven't been charged with anything?'

'Nah. I've done nothin. All I did was go to Cumber, meanin to give Frankie a hard time, that was all. It was Pitbull's idea, I had nothin to do with it, wish I hadn't gone now, listenin to that prat Pitbull. I thought Frankie was really cool, the way he went for Pitbull, an old guy like him, laying him out cold. I'd never have gone if I'd thought it would turn out like this. Frankie was a good guy.'

'A lot of people think you put Pitbull up to it and it wouldn't surprise me one little bit,' Katrina interrupted.

'Kat! How could you say such a thing, accusing your own brother of helping to commit murder. Ben's wild but he wouldn't harm a fly,' Karen defended, raising her voice, alarmed to hear from her daughter the opinions of others. 'Anyway when he hears what Mike has to say, I'm sure he'll see things our way.'

'I don't think Ben had anthing to do with Mr Page Johnson's murder, he's not the sort to bear a grudge, he wouldn't do anything so daft.' Mike reassured, determined to prevent a slanging match. 'I think Ben's a good lad at heart and given a chance could be a credit to all of you.'

Karen, unable to contain her enthusiasm, continued, 'Mike's offering you the chance of a career in his business, he's arranged a full apprenticeship with day release for technical college leading to qualifications. It's a marvellous opportunity for you Ben and even in the first year of training, you'd be earning well above the minimum wage.'

Ben registered disgust,. 'I'm not interested in D.I.Y. it's too boring.

Mike found Ben's depreciation of craft and practical skills somewhat irritating and decided now was a good time to begin his education. 'Ben, cabinet making and high class joinery has nothing to do with D.I.Y. D.I.Y. is to do with house maintenance, mostly decorating or putting up ready made shelves. Even for this work some care and skill is required and carrying out home repairs and improvements is to be encouraged, but our skills go way beyond D.I.Y. We'd teach you skills very much in demand, skills that will always earn you a living.'

'What skills? Using electric drills like on the T.V. ads?' Ben sneered.

'No, our work is a craft. First of all we'd teach you to master the use of hand tools when working with wood, how to keep them sharp, how to form a whole range of precision joints, used in making our furniture. You'd learn about furniture design, how to set out bench work, how to do wood carving, engraving and finishing. You'd learn how to select sutable timber, the use of woodworking machinery and much more.'

'Ok., so it's not D.I.Y., but all you're doin is using up precious rain forest, hardwood trees what take hundreds of years to grow, jus for makin luxury stuff we can do without.' Ben argued.

Karen wasn't listening to her son. 'I've seen Mike's furniture and it's absolutley beautiful. It would bring lasting pleasure to anyone's home.'

Surprised by Ben's remarks, Mike considered how to reply, he hadn't expected accusations from this direction. 'Actually, although our furniture operation is very low key, I've been thinking of shifting away from hardwoods. Josh thinks we should move into shopfitting and general joinery, but that would mean a huge investment in machinery, using sheet materials and softwood, more of a manufacturing set up. Softwoods are renewable, so we wouldn't be guilty of destroying rain forest or desiduous plantations. You might be interested in being part of our expansion Ben, coming in on the ground floor of a new business.'

'Then you'd be talkin more trees, more water, more fossil fuel burnin for electricity and transport, more CO2 emissions. It's all hastle and for what? Makin money for banks, investors and wheeler dealers? No thanks.'

Karen was losing patience. 'For goodness sake Ben what on earth is all this nonsense? Here you are, being offered the chance of a lifetime and all you can do is preach doom and gloom. Whatever's got into you? Kat see if you can make him see sense.'

'I hate to admit it but Ben has got a point,' Katrina said grudgingly.

'Yes, he's got a point,' Mike conceded, 'I can see Ben's no fool, he's been reading all this new info on global warming, it seems to be the main topic of conversation these days and industrial development isn't helping any, I can see that, and to be honest the idea of churning out fixtures and fittings for banks, supermarkets and the like has no real appeal for me, that's why I prefer bench work. Craft and the pursuit of excellence give me more satifaction than mass production and deadlines, but that's an older generation speaking. Bench work's ok for me but not for Josh, not for younger men and their families. I know we have to move with the times, we can't go back to living in caves, but I can't think globally like you Ben, to me it's more like swarm intelligence. I can only think seriously about those I love, making their life better, making them happy and I know that's all Josh wants, and if he thinks a bigger operation is required to make it happen, that's fine by me. One day Ben you'll meet a girl you can love, marry, have children of your own, and I know you'll want to do the same for them. It's about earning love as well as respect, having self esteem, being constructive, seeing a job well done, feeling ok about youself. Do you feel ok about youself Ben? You would you know, if you came to work with us.'

There was a familiar knock on the door. The fish and chips had arrived. Ben felt ravenous and his attention was easily diverted by the unmistakable smell and the two carrier bags Matt was carrying. He swooped across the room, relieving Matt of the one holding the fish and chips. He groped inside for what felt like the heaviest of four wrappings and with a first come, first served attitude, dumped the remainder on the dining table. Karen leapt to her feet snatching the packet from him. 'Can't you, just for once, show some manners? We're sitting round the table to eat these fish and chips and we'll be eating them off dinner plates with knives and forks. Kat darling, can you make a pot of tea while I lay up. Mat put the lagers in the fridge, I've warmed the plates and there's slices of bread and butter, french bread and farmhouse butter from the deli. We'll have ourselves a real treat, all together like a family, even if it is only fish and chips.' Everyone took their places, certain that the Karen might throw the meal in the bin if they messed her around.

'I spose you want me to say grace in keepin with such high standards,' Ben sniggered. He put his hands together and with exaggerated reverence, raising his eyes to the ceiling, offered up a thanksgiving, 'Thanks God for chosin to put food on our table when half the world is starvin, I spose our needs are greater and we must be real special.'

'I hate sarcasm Ben, blasphemy against the almighty when he's not here to defend himself, it's ugly. Anyway God didn't put this food on the table, Mike did,' Karen reprimanded, carefully setting out the condiments, obscure brands of brown sauce and tomato ketchup with Worcester sauce taking pride of place.

'Gosh mum, what's with the Worcester sauce, we've never had that before, bit expensive isn't it? Matt observed, impressed but unable to hide his surprise.

'I bought it for Mike, he happens to like Worcester sauce on his fish and chips and it's our way of saying thankyou.' Ben thought this downright favouritism and responded by reaching for the bottle, peppering his meal with the newly discovered relish.

Much to Karen's relief and pleasure, the family get together went according to her heart's desire and the fish and chips were enjoyed on a different level to your average takeaway. Generous portions, essential for a relaxed atmosphere, promoted good humour and a feeling that having a share in the feast meant all was well with the world. The family warmed to Mike as he discussed Matt's future ambitions in forensic science, chatting easily about teenage fears, the competition they had to face in the big bad world and the disappointments they were certain to experience. He showed a genuine interest in Katrina's hopes for the future and her forthcoming A levels. He gave encouragement, making light of the world's problems, offering them help and support, and in an unguarded moment, Ben agreed to call in at Mike's workshop on Monday morning, 'Jus to give the place a once over.' This was more than Karen had hoped, and for a woman who had never had time for the luxury of religious convictions, it seemed like a miracle, the work of a benevolent spirit who decided her efforts were worthy of a blessing and for all Ben knew, or anyone for that matter, God may well have had a hand in it.

After a few lagers Ben left the party in good spirits, heading for his pre-arranged meeting with Meg. She opened the door for her young lover, standing before him in a see through dressing gown. The lines on her face had softened, invisible in the subdued light and her delicious curves immediately set his pulse racing, his blood pumping. He slipped his hand inside the loose neckline, cupping her breast, kissing her wildly as they half stumbled along the hall, feverishly seeking the intimate fragrance of her bedroom. Ben was infatuated, flattered by the intimacy and the thought that a beautiful, mature woman considered him man enough for her needs. After a fury of love making, they showered, caressing each other with soap and shower gel, cavorting, embracing in a deluge of pressurised water before settling in the lounge with a bottle of Meg's favoutite tipple, ice cool, Moet Chandon. Ben was intoxicated, not with lager or champagne but with a sense of enjoying the best things that life can offer. He felt he had somehow graduated, succeeded where his mates had failed. Things which bring pleasure can be habit forming and Ben decided he wanted more of the same, the highs, the freedom, the paroxysms of ecstasy with the woman he thought he loved.

Wishing to further stimulate a sense of euphoria, Meg introduced cocaine. He'd never before tried snorting cocaine, not because he preferred cannabis, but for economic reasons. Street cocaine, usually a fifty/fifty mixture of pure cocaine and some other innocuous powder like glucose, would cost as much as fifty or sixty pounds a gram on the streets and in the clubs, whereas in Ben's opinion, skunk cannabis at twenty pounds an ounce gave better value. He was intrigued by Meg's ritualised cocaine equipment, items she had collected from antique fairs, a silver framed mirror, a cobalt blue sat cellar encased in silver filligree with a small silver spoon, a masonic jewel, custom made in the form of a silver trowel and a silver cup containing a selection of coloured straws. Using the spoon, she carefully measured one twentieth of a gram from the salt cellar, placing it on the mirror in the form of a pyramid. This she divided it into two equal lines with the masonic trowel and chosing a rainbow coloured straw, with a delicate gesture, inhaled one of the lines through her sweet little nose. She offered a straw to Ben inviting him to do the same. Ben, keen to experiment, snorted his line like a vacuum cleaner, holding his breath, waiting for the rush. First a numbing sensation in the nose and on the tip of the tongue, his temperature rose, blood pressure increased, nerve ends gave the rush of mood elevation and Ben felt in tune with the Gods and supremely confident.

'Cor Meg, coke's really somethin else, makes you feel ready for anythin! Spect there's a downside though, I know it's a lotta money and I don't wanna get hooked, not hooked so I can't do without it, actin like a junkie,' Ben ran his fingers through her hair, moved closer, letting her body lotion wash over him, whispering in her ear, 'Not like I'm hooked on you,'

You canna get hooked on lady, it's nay addictive, not like chinaman, it's jus for havin fun. Some folk canna dae wi'oot though, it helps em deal wi stress.'

'What about overdosing?' Ben continued, wanting to know more, always concerned about his own well being.

'Nay, it's easier to overdose on paracetamol, Ah'm tellin you, it's jus for havin fun. Skunk's more dangerous, hell of a lot more, it can dae your heed in. Too much lady might damage the cartilage in your nose, but even that'll heal if you lay off it for a wee while, you jus have tae be sensible wi it.'

Why lady, not coke or charlie?'

'Cos it makes women randy. When you've had a snort it's better between the sheets, Ah ken it turns me on.'

They sat, sipping champagne, caressing, kissing, floating in a private world enhanced by drug induced make believe. Ben hung on to the illusion, a New Horizon's pent house, lording it over the low life unfortunates trapped within it's substructure until rational thought finally percolated through the haze. 'Meg, there is somethin worryin me. Yer partner, I don't even know his name, never see him around an I know he lives here. What the hell's he gonna do to me when he finds out? Supposin we got caught together, me with his woman?'

'Jimmy's mah minder, he's been wi me since the bad old days. He's a real hard case and clever wi it, but he's jus a business partner. He's got his own room here an sometimes he sleeps over but the flat's in mah name. He's more likely tae have a fancy for you than have any feelins for me. He's gay, like a lot of old warriors, bit like some generals, fancies young lads, but if you really love me Ben, he'll no worry you.'

'Havin a girl like you Meg's a bit scary. Can't say I'm lookin forward to meetin him.'

'Dae you love me Ben? Love me enough tae do anythin for me?

'Pends, I'd do most things I reckon.'

Ben, you've gi'in up the hoodies for me an that's a good start. You trust me enough tae let me look after your money an there's fifty pounds in mah safe an your drivin licence, though God knows how you managed tae keep it, but that's all you've got. Ben if you come in with me, I can make you rich an show you the good times.'

'I'm listenin Meg.'

'You used to love joy ridin, boy racin and vandalism an you've gi'in it all up for me.'

'I'm listenin Meg.'

'How would you like tae have your own sports car an enough money tae keep it on the road, nae stolen, all above board?'

'Well course I would Meg, who wouldn't, it'd be a dream come true, but where would I get the readies?'

'If you come in with mah drugs operation, you'll be rich beyond your wildest dreams. Now listen, Ah'm givin away nae details, nae names, but your first job would be makin a pick up of pure snow, ten kilos of cocaine, smuggled through Liverpool. After we've stepped on it, addin another ten kilos, it'll be worth more than a million on the street. You'll nae be handlin money, all syndicate transactions are laundered.'

'Phew! Sounds like really big business.' Ben said, feeling unsure of himself, 'Sounds very risky. What exactly have I got to do?'

'There's nae serious risk Ben. All you have tae do is join a student party, have a good time. Ah'll gi you the set up, well as much as Ah can. Tomorrow mornin, you'll collect an Express delivery van from a garage in the city. It'll be painted in trade livery and full o car spares for genuine trade deliveries in and around Liverpool. In the showroom you can take a peek at a two year old Audi Quattro, immaculate, wi only fifteen thousand on the clock, taxed and insured. The car's yours if you make a good pick up. D'you follow me so far Ben? Think you can follow instructions?'

Cor! An Audi Quattro! Jus try me.'

'After the first Liverpool drop, you'll heed for a country manor hoose in the Forest of Bowland. It's owned by a Russian multi millionaire, a gang master organising cheap immigrant labour for factories and the food processing industry, but that's jus a front tae help him launder his drug money through Russian and Swiss banks. His real business is cocaine, dealin directly with Colombian drug cartels. The supply chain runs from Colombia to the west coast of Africa, endin up in Liverpool docks. His son goes to Liverpool uni, and he's throwin a party at the manor for all his pals and you're getting an invite.'

'Ok, but who will I be dealin with, the bossman himself?' Ben interrupted anxious to know more about the adventure.

'Nae, he doesnae spend much time there hissell, he's got a manager who runs the place wi some security, but his son gets there a lot. There'll be nae introductions, you won't get to know who you're speakin to, not on this trip, except for the students o course. Don't ask questions, jus mingle an have a good time.'

'Ok, but how do I make the pickup?'

'Now this is important.' Meg carefully placed her champage glass on the coffee table, moving away from Ben she turned to face him, her eyes narrowed, her mouth hardened. 'You'll nae be havin any drugs or booze, you must stay sober and behave wi responsibility. Your invite is to let them give you the once over, they want to check you out as a security risk, you'll be watched, on test, even bugged maybe, so don't breathe a word aboot you're reason for bein there, make up some story, use your imagination. Fall down on this an that's the end of the operation an you'll be in trouble, big time. D'you understan all that Ben?'

'Why yeah, don't worry Meg, I can handle it no problem.'

'Leave the hoose party anytime after midnight and drive round tae the barn at the back. The barn doors will be locked an you'll find a key in the van's glove compartment. Drive intae the barn and you'll see ten new tins o base cellulose paint for car sprayin stacked at the far end ready for your collection. Load em up, lock the barn doors an drive to Birkenhead for the second spares delivery. You'll be on the payroll of the Express delivery firm an you'll have all the delivery notes an paperwork for the goods you're carryin. You'll drive like a responsible employee, dinnae go over the speed limit, dinnae break any traffic regulations, jus behave normally. The van's not long been on the road but if you do break doon, phone the Manchester garage for recovery. Are you absolutely sure you're up for this Ben, rememberin you'll nae get much sleep?'

'For an Audi Quattro! Yeah, I'm up for it Meg.'

'An remember Ben, nae drink, nae drugs.'

The next morning Ben left early, dragging himself away from the cuddling warmth of Meg's embrace. After all the champagne, passion and excitement, he had slept as only the young can sleep and Meg had the good sense not to disturb him. Armed with road maps, delivery addresses and a packed lunch he kissed Meg in the doorway. She said she loved him, wished him luck and as he made his way to the lift, she called after him, 'Dinnae forget to lock the barn doors and put the key back in the glove compartment.'

His mother would have been surprised and pleased with his appearance. Meg had changed his hoodie image, the 'knees out' combat breeches, the filthy trainers, the hooded jacket, for something more presentable and a new look Ben bussed his way to the garage wearing a blue casual jacket, a clean crew sweater, comfort jeans and smart leisure shoes. The garage, Vera Motors Ltd., was impressive with a wide expanse of forecourt, fronted by a row of flags advertising its Fiat dealership. Ben confidently strode into the main office, sure of his credentials, introducing himself to the girl behind the counter. She gave him a welcoming smile saying that Mr Vera wished the job interview to be held privately in his office on the first floor. She led the way and he followed her shapely legs as they skipped up a broad flight of stairs, sending him aggreeable signals, promoting a feel good factor.

The office was uncluttered, a mink carpet, deep piled suggesting a luxury showpiece rather than a nerve centre, and modern, Italian furniture gave it unmistakable style, softened by a spectacular sub tropical plant which stood in the corner adding a touch of serenity. Seated behind the half moon desk was Tonino Vera, a smiling, overweight Italian, the son of a wealthy Neapolitan family, who had married an impoverished English aristocrat. He lacked the swarthy good looks of southern Italians and behind the gold rimmed spectacles, there was a subtle shiftiness.

'So you are Ben, Meg's protégé. She seems to think you're ok and I hope you measure up to her expectations.' Tonino motioned for Ben to take a chair. 'From now on you must change your lifestyle, no more anti social behaviour, capiche? We hold a franchise for the supply of European car parts and accessories and you will be ligitimately employed by this branch of our business, paying tax and insurance in the normal way and you must fall into line like any other responsible employee. Our business with Fiat and the spare parts oufit has nothing whatsoever to do with my drug dealing enterprise and both concerns have no idea that we use their facilities for drug distribution. From here on there is no turning back for you. Meg tells me that you're ok and if I'm satisfied that you're entirely trustworthy, you could go places, but you have to convince me. You speak to no one, the staff, friends, family, no one, about this operation of which you are now a part. Capiche? Only me and Meg will communicate with you concerning shipments of cocaine. What you already know is dangerous and if you fail to honour your position of trust, you will mysteriously disappear. Capiche?

Ben paled, these people were ruthless, Tonino's cold smile, the threats, the point of no return. 'When do I get my Audi Quattro?' he replied weakly.

'It's sitting in the show room Ben, follow me and we'll take a look.'

Ben sat behind the wheel of the Audi 3.2, TT Roadster Quattro, a dolphin grey predator among the gleaming colours of friendly looking, Pandas, Puntos and Bravos. Seduced by the styling and automobile technology, Ben's fearful misgivings were at first compensated by the 'must have' greed of a feral teenager. 'Cor, what a beauty! And she's mine if I make a good pick up?'

'We'll talk about that back in my office. I want you to be quite sure about your commitment.'

They returned to the privacy of Tonino's industrial den. He closed the door as though shutting a safe and remained standing, shorter than Ben, with hunched shoulders and an impenetrable smile. He commanded the whole space. 'The Audi will be yours to use at your leisure, next year, twelve months from today,' he said.

Ben felt crushed by this casual remark, betrayed by his love for Meg, used, exploited. Clearly, the car had been offered as bait. 'But Meg said the car would be mine,'he stuttered.

'Meg doesn't call the shots, I do. She's only one of many outlets and even though we go back a long ways and she's special for me, she has to stay in line. Capiche? Meg says you've got brains, well use them. You're known to the police, you have a record, you've got an Asbo. There's nothing on you, but you're envolved in a murder enquiry and your chances of finding employment are zero. How's it going to look if you're seen driving round in an Audi Quattro? No way! You must stay in our employment for a year at least, come clean with the authorities, get your Asbo lifted, convince everybody you've turned over a new leaf. Do that and I'll re-employ you as car salesman and you'll get the use of the car, all expenses paid, including tax and insurance, which for you would mean an horrendous premium. The vehicle will remain the property of Vera Motors and will be garaged on these premises. You'll get a decent wage as a delivery van driver and regular cash payments for running drugs which Meg will hold over for you until we've got you established as a successful car salesman. I'll be arranging speech tuition for you, expect you to smarten up, change your image and move away from New Horizons. If you play your cards right, in a couple of years you could end up as a sales director and then you can buy your own sports car.'

Ben hung on to every word, dismayed, scared, but curiously excited. 'Cor it's given me somethin to think about, I jus dunno.'

Ben, it's not a question of you having a choice. You've been playing around with drugs from the age of twelve. You're eighteen, soon be nineteen and you came into this with you're eyes wide open. Like I said, you know too much. Ever see a 'Godfather' movie? Well I'm making you an offer that you can't refuse.'

After the Frankie shooting Ben knew the meaning of shame, now he understood the meaning of fear, fear on the edge of terror. 'I spose I'll have to go along with it,' he mumbled.

'Yeah, I *spose* you will. Now here's the keys to a Scudo parked round the back next to our stores depot, it's loaded ready to go. Collect the delivery invoices from the storeman and remember he knows nothing about the pickup. Meg's given you the rest of the details and when you return, another driver will take over on the forecourt. He'll take the consignment to our processing plant. After that you can take a week off while we sort out your employment details and assess your performance, but report back here on Monday week.' Tonino reached inside the breast pocket of a soft leather jacket, recently purchased in Rome and drew out a matching leather wallet. 'Here's fifty pounds expenses,' his smile broadened, 'Now get going and have a nice time.'

The two inside lanes of the M6O2-M62 out of Manchester were choked, the reserve of heavy goods vehicles, jugganauts maintaining speed and engine revolutions by truckers who never took their foot off the gas. In order to break free of these two lanes, lighter vehicles accelerated to speeds well over the limit, a practice accepted as a sensible way of freeing up traffic by making good use of the fast lane. Ben had little motorway experience, but joy riding had given him spacial awareness, sharp reactions and rapid response. He was a natural driver, using the vehicle as an extension of himself, eager to test the limits of a machine, loving all things fast and furious, but now he held himself in check, content to stay tucked away between the freight. At the M6 intersection, the traffic eased and as he continued towards Liverpool for his first delivery he wondered what he was getting into. He loved Meg with a dangerous passion, thought about her every waking hour, longed for her, longed to hold her very close, close enough to fuse, fuse in a paroxysm of sheer ecstasy, and yet, she had lied to him, led him to believe she was running a huge drugs operation when she was just another dealer, keeping shop for pushers and teenage hoodlums.

Mr Vera was the 'Man' and Ben suspected Meg would receive only a small share of the Russian consignment. And what about Signore Vera? What was Meg to him? His mistress maybe! Meg said he'd get a sports car, made it sound as though he'd cracked it, but all he'd done was get a job as a van driver with a death threat hanging over him if he didn't do exactly what Mr Vera wanted. He was angry with Meg, he loved her, had trusted her, but she had fooled him, set a honey trap and robbed him of the freedom he had always enjoyed. He felt scared and sick in the stomach.

The first delivery was made at a car body repair works on a Liverpool industrial estate and the foreman was very chatty, treating him to a tasty snack and a cup of coffee from the mobile café. Ben left the premises on first name terms with most of the staff and in a better frame of mind, he had never worked with other people and their camaraderie left him with a sense of belonging. He back tracked along the M62 before filtering on to the M6 heading towards Preston. His nerves settled, perhaps he had taken Mr Vera's threats too seriously. Fear had shaken his self belief, taken the strut out of his swagger, gnawed at his guts, making him tremble when he needed to stay calm. He refused to recognise the symptons, or accept that the operation was a test of criminal daring which might expose his cool as mere bravado. He loved driving and here he was in possession of a new van with the freedom of the open road stretching before him. Why had Mr Vera been so abrupt, acting as though he was of no account, treating him as an undesirable, an anti social law breaker? He found it hard to believe that anyone would take it for granted that he was nothing more than a yob, a thug, a no hope criminal when he was simply at war, rebelling against authority and New Horizons Park. Surely he deserved more for the risk he was taking, for keeping his mouth shut. Twelve months working for Mr Vera, in Ben'a eyes amounted to a lifetime. He'd not pressed the subject of cash payments or when he could spend it. It seemed Mr Vera and Meg had stitched him up and that he had no say in the matter.

When motorway traffic moves freely, motorway miles soon slip by and there is time for reflection. Ben cruised comfortably, heading north on a six lane arterial highway, intent on running drugs for a syndicate he knew little about, having no control over decision making. It was another part of his journey through life, but a journey rushing headlong in the wrong direction. An underlying lack of confidence, the root cause of his social problems, threatened to surface. Whatever the history, however much Ben stood up for his father, in his heart he knew the truth. His father had been a drunk, a waster, a loser, failing to support his family, leaving them without structure, without example and without money. Ben, the eldest child, had born the emotional brunt of their fragmented family life and traumatised by his father's violent outbursts, found it difficult to function at primary school level, leaving him ill equipped for a secondry education. He might easily have sunk into despair and despondency, dropping out of life to squander his youth on drugs and alcohol, but he had been genetically blessed with his mother's fighting spirit and a robust selection of grey matter which offered some resistance to a downward spiral. In terms of worldly pleasures, good times and a loaded wallet, he wanted his share, without having to graft, without lining the pockets of money institutions, without exploitation in all it's duplicious forms and he felt these ambitions were there for the taking, until that is, his interview with Tonino Vera.

The landscaped ribbon of motorway reeled by, a fast forward tape, mostly unseen by the driver. Meg's route, the shortest, suggested leaving the motorway at junction 33, but tired of motorway, Ben opted for junction 31, taking the A59 towards Clitheroe. The urgency of highway traffic frittered away, freeing his senses, allowing the rich green pastures of Lancashire countryside to add a more pleasing dimension to the journey. He left the A59 running north into a wild region, the forest of

Bowland, a former royal hunting forest but now a country of high fells, open moorland, tree lined rivers, rocky streams and the haunt of the stooping merlin. The B road through Bashal Eaves and Cow Ark eventually follows the river Hodden, a tributary of the Ribble, which meanders from Ribblesdale through Preston before carving a wide estuary between Lytham St Anne and Southport. The natural beauty of the area shared it's calm with the city boy, transforming his backstreet appraisal of all things to one of wonder.

With evening approaching, beyond Dunsop Bridge in the trough of Bowland, cradled between Sykes Fell and Whins Brow he finally arrived at his destination, Hareden Hall, a Victorian manor set well back from the road. Japanese Ivy, neglected, untrained, reached under the eaves, covering the sofits, barge boards and facias encouraging wet rot, already well established. The leaves were turning crimson, covering the walls in a mantle of variegated colour, disguising the perished brickwork. Newly erected scaffolding stood around the gable end where repairs and renovations were being carried out.

A car load of students had arrived ahead of him and were being checked at the gate by two muscular Slavs who were struggling to make themselves understood. They signalled for Ben to drive past, acting as though he was expected and a regular visitor, tapping the window only to suggest that he should park away from the other vehicles at the rear of the house next to a Landrover. Several cars, mostly past their sell by date, and a couple of stripped down scooters were clustered on the newly laid gravel drive. The overgrown gardens were being landscaped and bright yellow earth moving machinery together with an articulated dump truck shared the space. Ben made for an already opened field gate which allowed access to the rear and he motored through to park next to the Landrover. He locked the van and remembering to close the field gate, became consciously aware that his casual attitude to life had been superimposed by Mr Vera's demands. He felt like a stooge, duped unwittingly into playing for a higher league, way over his head.

With some trepidation, he made his way to the front entrance, admiring the carriage lamps each side of the neoclassical porch, which illuminated a heavy, pannelled door, opened to reveal the chequered, quarry floor of a large vestibule with a stained glass inner screen. The screen door also stood open, inviting easy access, but here the welcome lost it's charm. The well lit hall had been stripped bare, the walls showing much evidence of plaster patching and extensive preparation work, the staircase cordoned off, covered in dust sheets. Packing cases were stacked at the far end along with step ladders and other builder's equipment. A fortune was being spent on the place. The local authorities were taking control of all restoration work on the listed property, grateful for the opportunity, energising their expertise, enforcing the most expensive options in order to preserve this valuable piece of English heritage, the wealthy indulgence of a Victorian industrialist. The Russian multi millionaire was only too happy to oblige and no one questioned the source of his wealth, after all, the house would be part of Britain's real estate not Russia's.

Ben, drawn by music and laughter, opened the door to a Victorian drawing room, transformed from an area of woodworm and decay to a creation of it's former splendour, the original marble fireplace remaining the focus of attention. An ornate, plaster cornice separated the ceiling from a sculptored frieze. Skirtings, archtraves and dado rails were generously moulded, carefully mitred and scribed, reflecting superb craftsmanship available even in this day and age. A well worn Indian carpet somewhat out of character, covered the centre area of a newly laid boarded floor, knot free, secretly nailed, stained and varnished around the margins. Brocade window dressings, rich green walls and subdued lighting gave the room an ambience of history and romance and Ben felt himself slipping into a time warp.

At one end the university students stood around a large table which doubled as a bar, replenished from a cellar, well stocked as a matter of priority. The students had each made their contribution, a bottle of wine or spirit, the contents of which were poured into a huge goldfish bowl forming a cocktail full of surprises. The conversation was bubbling, animated, the outpourings of bright young things charged with the excitment of coming together in such unusual surroundings. The students wore their house party clothes, coloured stockings, jeans, T shirts, flipflops or trainers, well suited for a relaxed atmosphere and a marathon of alcohol consumption. On an even bigger table, a generous buffet of mouth watering delicacies, occupied every available space and Ben's gastric juices surged into overdrive. Viktor Ivanovich, their Russian host, had specifically demanded of his son Georgi, that no drugs were to be allowed on the premises, their usage morally offensive to Russian orthodox churchgoers, but for some students, no house party could deliver without a few joints or a snort of cocaine and so Georgi obliged with an assortment of hash cakes, traditional Madiera baking with marijuana as an added ingredient. Indie music, an Arctic Monkeys album, 'i bet you look good on the dance floor,' followed by 'fake tales of san francisco,' throbbed easy dance music, but the lyrics could hardly be deciphered against the chatter and with the volume turned down, no one was dancing.

Two girls sat in the bay window checking on the arrivals. They wore their skirts just above the knee and when they moved, their bare legs flashed prettily in the light from the carriage lamps. Their curiosity had been aroused by the arrival of Ben's van and they studied him as he walked up to the house. They liked what they saw.

Ben was used to throwing his weight around, could be intimidating among his own, but in the present company he instinctively knew his swaggering would appear grotesque and in an atmosphere charged with A level adrenaline, his self assurance built on other's fear of anti social behaviour, disintegrated. His discomfort increased, when one of the girls in the bay widow smiled at him across the room, not a 'come hither' invitation but a warm, confident smile, confident that Ben was a fellow student who could be approached without formalities or caution. Ben had many failings, but a faint heart was never one of them and plucking up courage, he walked over, trying to give the impression of a relaxed, more mature person who had left his wild student days behind. 'Hiyah girls, can I get you more drinks?'

'Please. We're drinking Jack Daniels,' the blonde responded, still smiling. Ben sauntered over to the bar, waited his turn, then ordered two Jack Daniels and an alcohol free lager. The man behind the bar was a Chechen gangster, high cheekbones, cold eyed, thin lips curling down, wearing a dark suit, cut away collar and smart tie.

'There is no lager is alcohol free. For you is straight tonic or water. Is best for you Ben, ok. Say is vodka, is best ok.' An extended arm served the drinks and Ben noticed the curious tattoos, marks of criminal status, reaching down to the wrist.

Ben nodded, unable to challenge the eyes, eyes as hard as gun metal, feeling the pressure while thinking on his feet. What line could he shoot about himself? Lying came easily, he could be a smooth talker, especially where the police or Asbo authorities were involved, it was part of his natural defence mechanism and as he collected the drinks an inspirational pack of lies was already taking shape, a story giving him credibility. He had to convince the blue eyed blonde, the one with the right curves and the shapely legs, had to make her believe he was worth chatting up. He would say that he had his own joinery business, owned an Audi Quattro and was going places. He had recently bought the van from a business friend and in due course, it would be sprayed bearing his own company logo. He was making a tour, meeting clients, visiting a trade fair, and was here to measure up for the new staircase, a specialised job which his firm was able to manufacture. He was running late and had gate crashed the party. 'Two Jack Daniels,' he announced joining the girls on the window seat.

The blonde turned, carefully studying Ben's face. She wore no makeup, her complexion fresh as spring blossom, her eyes violet blue, clear, intelligent, profound, fixed with disturbing honesty. 'We've not seen you around. I take it you're from Liverpool uni? What are you reading?' She asked.

'I'm not at uni, I screwed up on my education, matter of fact, I got expelled. All I ever got was an Asbo.' Ben heard himself saying things that were all wrong, he hadn't meant to knock himself in this way.

'Just as I thought, I can see you've been a naughty boy. So what are you doing here, I mean have you got a job or anything?'

'Yeah, not much of a job though, I'm a delivery van driver, workin for Vera Motors in Manchester.'

'Manchester! The Asbo capital of Britain,' the second girl remarked, having decided that competition for Ben's attention wasn't worth the effort.

'I'm deliverin spares in the area includin somethin for the earth movin machinery. I'm runnin late and gate crashed the party. Meetin you, I'm glad I did. What are you studyin?'

'You're talking to a rare bird, I'm hoping to be a civil engineer with grand designs in mind. You know, building roads and bridges, something that only boys supposed to be interested in. Why don't you re-train for something better, now you've seen the error of your ways?

The conversation was not going according to plan and Ben couldn't understand why he suddenly felt lying so difficult. It seemed he had known this lovely girl all his life and he was surprised how relaxed he felt in her company.

'Well actually I've been offered a start in a joinery works, they design their own furniture. Still manual though, I mean real graft innit?'

'Why that's a wonderful opportunity, I do so admire anything creative. You'd find it very rewarding you know, making things that others can enjoy. You could end up running your own firm, become rich even. You must take it, I can't think what's holding you back?'

'Well my mum's a single parent and it's her boyfriend who's offerin me the job. He's quite a guy really, but I want to make the grade on my own. I don't want favours, specially from him.'

'I was raised by my mother and I've no idea who my father was. Mum's had one hell of a hard time, but she's made big sacrifices for me and everything I've achieved up to now, I owe to her and there's no way I'm going to let her down. You shouldn't be ashamed of help, let pride get in the way, we all need help somewhere along the line and we should be grateful for it and show our love and appreciation.'

Ben had fallen for the girl in the bay window. Chemistry was there of course, and yet her influence went way beyond the 'boy meets girl' encounter. He wanted her respect in a way that met her aspirations and not his. 'I'm Ben by the way, what's your name?'

Before she was able to answer, the Chechen tapped him on the shoulder, 'Ben, you come plice, is message for you.'

Venom lurked behind those snake eyes and Ben didn't argue. 'I'll be back in a tick,' he said to the girl.

The barman took him aside. 'Ben, the boss wants you leave now. These students not for you, you have too much good time. Is not for you. Cellulose is here already, is in landrover. You go now ok.'

'You sure? Meg said it would be in the barn, and what about the drop in Birkenhead? I'll be there hours before they open.'

'Who is this Meg? Some dealer? You go now ok, paint is in landrover. At Birkenhead, you sleep in van, ok Ben. You better get going, eh?'

'Ok,' Ben said, trying to hide his anger and frustration. 'I'll jus say cheerio to the girls or they'll think it's weird.' The girls were watching him and the blonde smiled sweetly when he returned. ' I'm afraid I've got to go, but I must see you again, you never told me you're name. Please, can I have your address or a phone number?'

'Can't we have just one dance, before you go? What's all the rush when we've only just got to know each other?'

'Fraid not, but I'll definitely be in touch, if that's ok. I've never met a girl like you, a girl with class.'

She produced a used envelope from a shoulder bag lying on the table, 'Here's my mobile number and my address at Liverpool uni.' Ben read the the envelope addressed to Miss K. Kinnear. 'My name's Kelly by the way, Kelly Kinnear. I've enjoyed meeting you Ben and for what it's worth I think you should take that joinery job. Meg, my mum, lives in Manchester on New Horizons Park, second block, flat 25. Its on the top floor. You can always contact me through her. Now what's your phone number, where can I write to you?'

A galaxy of fibre optics twinkled from the instrument panel giving the driver, safely cocooned within the van's cockpit, a sense of security, remote from the rest of the world.

Aw fuck! Ben cursed, Kelly was Meg's daughter! To think of it! To be suddenly presented with a tantalising glimpse into Kelly's world. A world of honest endeavour, a world of self discipline, those virtues which encourage happiness and fullfillment. A girl like that, so fresh, so intelligent, so beautiful and so young. How could she possibly know that her career had been funded by drugs and the earnings of a call girl?

Headlights illuminated the rising mists of Bowland, now featureless, smothering the van in a shroud of cotton wool. The vehicle slowed to a crawl.

What had possessed him? Why had he become so infatuated with Meg, a woman old enough to be his mother? How was it that such an attractive woman had no partner, wasn't married? How many lovers had she enjoyed before Ben? She was using him, she had lied to him, taken him for a young fool. What the hell was he thinking about?

The petrol gauge read three quarters full, there were no warning lights, the wipers beat out their steady rhythm, clearing the build up of condensation. The van continued north, approaching the river Wyre and the mist developed slowly into a fog.

Now he held Kelly in his arms, now he looked into her eyes and now his conscience, eroded by anger and self gratification, re- awakened. What was he doing with his life? The way he lived would inevitably lead to disaster. He could see that now. There were honest ways of affording an Audi Quattro, ways which in a sense added to its value. The prize he was seeking meant nothing more than ill gotten gains at the expense of other people's misery.

The van was now running west and as the mist thinned, it accelerated towards the motorway, nose to the road as if guided by remote control. It crossed the motorway to join the A6 instinctively turning North again, probing for junction 33.

He had to see Kelly again, had to explore an option which he had never before considered and had refused to recognise.

Meeting Kelly had torn his world apart, posing new challenges, pointing him in new directions. She had connected with the real Ben Mackay, a man in hiding, and for her, he wanted to be that man. Ben Mackay, a man who might learn to accept social responsibilities, a man who might recognise that progress for humanity requires a contribution from each of us and the world does not exist merely to gratify the needs of an individual. A man who might learn how to be a good citizen. For a girl like Kelly, he was sure he could change his ways.

The van slid into the junction, sweeping down the incline, running south, filtering into the motorway, it's indicator flashing a message of intent. The speedometer steadied at a cruising speed of seventy, chasing the never ending flight path of glimmering cat's eyes.

'For what it's worth, I think you should take that joinery job,' 'For what it's worth, I think you should take that joinery job.' For what it's worth. For what it's worth. For what it's WORTH!!!

The wipers were now at rest, the headlights dipping now and then. Mirrors flared, reflecting the lights of fellow travellers, the fan heater purred, the tyres drummed gently against the tarmac. Huge road signs reared up through the gloom, thrusting information like dummy boards. The van maintained it's speed until linking with the M56 turning west towards Chester.

Those Russians! That barman! Tonino Vera! Those threats! Having dealings with such people was scary. Ben wanted out, but he couldn't just walk away. What should he do? What could be his next move? How could he escape? How could he win back his freedom? Then he realised an awful truth, he had given up his freedom long before meeting Meg or Tonino Vera. Real freedom, the opportunity to make choices, to make honest appraisals, had slipped through his fingers when he started using drugs, when he began stealing, when he resorted to savagery, when he lied, when he broke his mother's heart. He thought about Ashraf Rajur, of Franklin Page Johnson, of Pitbull Patterson. He thought about the offer from Mike Edwards. He thought about his mother's unconditional love. He worried about Skeet Cooney until trying to deal with all these issues became impossible and his mind went numb. He began to feel desperately weary.

Three miles from the M53 intersection which runs north again to Birkenhead, the van pulled into a service station to park in the area for commercial vehicles, an overnight dormitory of sleeping truck drivers. Ben crawled into the rear of the van to get some much needed rest. He curled up between an assortmemt of spare parts and door panels giving no thought to the cocaine, a fortune sealed in tins of cellulose, secured in racks above his head. The engine cooled and as the temperature dropped Ben found difficulty in sleeping. Tired beyond caring, he eventually shivered himself to sleep and dreamed a curious dream.

He was driving a coach load of tourists, among them were his family, Mike, Meg and the Asbos, on a tour of southern Italy. Kelly was acting as guide and courier sitting in the front of the coach talking into a microphone. The driver's position was in the centre of the coach among the passengers and the restricted vision made driving very difficult and extremely hazardous. The roads were simple tracks and the coach finally became stuck near to a remote farmhouse. The farmer, Tonino Vera, offered the tourists a meal and they all trooped off to enjoy his hospitality. Ben stayed in the coach with Kelly and they began kissing. Their embraces became more intimate and Ben's excitement rose to fever pitch. Then someone grabbed him by the hair, jerking his head back. He twisted round in order to discover the identity of his assailent. Transfixed by the eyes of a snake, he vomited with fear. The Chechen barman was holding a gun to his head.

Ben woke to the gutteral throb of diesel engines, the truckers were moving out. He had no clear memory of the journey from Hareden Hall and at first he felt disorientated, unsure of his whereabouts or by what route he had arrived. Gradually he became more consciously aware of what he was doing, and as the purpose of his mission came more into focus, he knew what he had to do.

He made the delivery in Birkenhead without a hitch and returned to Vera Motors in Manchester, making good time. He had only just switched off the engine when another driver took over. He went into the main office, checked the yellow pages for

Mike's business address and asked for a lift to the industrial estate. No one offered, but the receptionist allowed him to phone for a taxi. He paid the fare with his expense money and went looking for Mike Edward's joinery works. A number of units were grouped around a central car park and in one of these he could hear machinery operating behind a closed steel shutter and he decided to enter the workshop through a small door set in it's frame.

Now he stood on the threshold of an industry working with wood, an age old industry, an industry as natural to man as working the soil. It felt good, wholesome and reassuring. He stood there among the woodshavings, breathing in the fragrance, sweet with resin.

Chapter 8 Sasha's in the World.

The Tin Miner's Arms boasted a regular and enthusiastic attendance, more so than Saint Michael & All Angels C of E, it's neighbouring church. A cheerful log fire crackled in the smokey recess of a chimney breast built of random granite rubble and remnants of Delabole slate. Oak beams, iron hard, salvaged from shipwrecks, formed a natural framework for the walls and ceiling and an assortment of high backed benches, some ancient, some with cushions, were arranged around the heavy oak tables. Flagstones, worn smooth by generations of miner's working boots, seemed warmer than a Persian carpet. The Tin Miner's Arms, long time marinated in Cornish beer, French wines and departed spirits, it's plaster impregnated with smuggled tobacco and miner's sweat, promised respite from labour and an escape from the harsh realities of everyday existence.

Members of the church choral society called in after rehearsals. Two redundant miners and a retired mining engineer, those with treasured memories of a once thriving industry, were already seated near the fire. One of the miners, affectionally nicknamed Badger, now worked as a market gardener, renting land from a struggling dairy farmer. He had reinvested his redundancy money in second hand machinery and natural fertilisers to grow organic vegetables for outlets in the neighbouring towns. He drank from his own pewter mug, which received the landlord's special attention, making sure it was kept spotlessly clean in readiness for it's thirsty owner. Badger drank deeply, savouring the fresh, biting flavour.

'What d'you make of Marvin, the young coloured lad?' He asked, carefully placing his mug over the beer mat.

'Anyone can see he's a natural talent, they say he's in one of them bands from Newquay, must be. I tell you though, I reckon he's on the wacky backy.You seen his eyes rollin? All over the place' his pal remarked.

'Harriet loves him to bits, it gets embarrassing at times and I don't think the reverend's too happy about it either, if you ask me he's heading for a nervous breakdown, he so twitchy these days,' the engineer added.

'Funny you should say that,' Badger continued. 'To be quite honest, I think the reverend's a bit jelly. Harriet wanted Marvin workin in the vicarage garden, you know helpin the reverend keep it tidy and that, but Marvin just don't want to know and to be truthful, I think it's me what's upset the applecart.'

'How come?' said the engineer.

'Well, I wanted to make a chicken coop see, keep a few chickens and sell a few free range eggs, bit of an experiment really. Anyway, I could do with a bit o help and for weeks I been puttin out feelers for a good man/biy. Then I thought o Marvin, an asked if he'd like to come an work for me. I said I'd pay him o course.'

The second miner gave the engineer a knowing look. 'What you payin him with Badger? Shirtbuttons!'

'Well not a lot obviously, can't afford it, but I thought he might be interested that's all.'

'And was he?' The engineer was intrigued.

'Well yes, he surprised me. He comes over afternoons and works like a black.'

'That sort of talk'll get you in trouble. What exactly have you got him doing?

'Well, He loves chickens, he's always fussin round em and I'm thinkin of getting some ducks by the stream. We've been makin a dam with some old corrugated sheets and now we've got a sizable duckpool. Marvin's been a great help and I couldn't keep him away even if I wanted to. To be truthful, I think a lot of the biy and I wouldn't like to lose him. He's already drivin the tractor and I've got plans for a small vineyard.' Badger was feeling generous, 'I think I might teach him to drive the old pickup, pay for drivin lessons.'

'Ok, but what about the harvest festival? That's all he seems to talk about. Keeps on about his girl friend Sasha and how she's coming to the service. I don't know what to make of it all? Whatever brought him to the village in the first place? He's got a northern accent, he's definitely not local.' The engineer thought Badger had the answers.

'Yeah, he does keep on about Sasha and Harriet is set on makin the church all special, bit like a return of the prodigal daughter.' Badger agreed.

The second miner drained his glass. 'Anyone can see she's obsessed by it all, givin him piano lessons, treating him like her own son, and now she's says he's doin a solo in the recital. She's spending more time with him than the rest of us, practicin every morning. Think he could be fostered or somethin? They say in the village the reverend can't have kids. Same again all round?'

Other members of the choir were arriving, settling to their favourite tipple and conversations swung back and forth about Marvin and the effect he was having on their choral society, how he had revitalised their approach to the forthcoming recital and the mystery surrounding Sasha, a guardian angel who would appear at the harvest festival.

The reverend Robin Reid was once again engaged in his weekly struggle to write a meaningful Sunday sermon. His pathetic congregation had more than trebled. The whole choir now attended, together with many from the village who had never before entered a place of worship. Robin knew they were not coming to hear a dynamic sermon, or to learn about the meaning of life, or in the hope of salvation and life after death, or for religious instruction. They were coming because they were curious about Sasha and there had been talk of a religious experience, a visitation, a miracle perhaps, at the harvest festival. He leaned over the laptop, willing the computer's electronic wizardry to open the window of inspiration which might get him started. He began tapping out a message for the Sunday evening service.

'We live now in a world of computor technology, a world which indirectly or directly controls every aspect of our lives. It is a technology on which we are becoming increasingly dependent although most of us have absolutely no idea how it works. It has improved communications beyond belief but in a more important sense it has driven us apart, allowing us to mentally escape from ourselves and each other. No other man made machine has so ordered our imagination, so exploited our sub conscious, so dismantled our faculties for loving and caring and so duped us into thinking we have powers we can never possess and that we can reach out and grasp that which is unattainable.'

The reverend's fingers froze on the key board. What on earth was he talking about? He had no intention of preaching about the effects computers may be having on our lives. What did he know about computers? There had been tremedous strides in medicine, engineering, navigation and in all walks of life. More lives had been saved by the use of modern technology, computers and mobile phones than by just love and caring alone. He erased the script.

Harriet came into the study. 'Coffee darling. How's the sermon coming along?'

'Not all that well really, I seem to have lost my convictions, can't speak from the heart any more, every word I write seems to mock me, raising doubts. I think you could help me darling, perhaps we could have one of our little discussions over coffee, it often gives me ideas, gets my thoughts flowing.'

'I'd love to, but Marvin's waiting for me in the church. He's doing so well on the piano, he's quite gifted you know. He only has to hear a tune once and he plays it back by ear with amazing improvisations.'

'All I ever hear about is Marvin this and Marvin that. You're becoming quite obsessed with the boy.'

'I do happen to think Marvin's special. I'm not sure what it is but I'm convinced there's something spiritual about him.'

'What absolute nonesense, he has appalling manners, wolfs down his food with elbows spread all over the table, never says please or thank you, leaves the bathroom in a disgusting mess and shows no respect for me whatsoever.'

'The boy's never had a chance in life, never knew his mother and has no knowledge of his father. All he needs is a little TLC.'

'I think he's on drugs. You're preoccupation with him, treating him like our son is very dangerous. And what's all this

106

nonsense about Sasha, the mysterious girlfriend? You're treating the harvest festival more like a home coming.'

'I've spoken to Marvin about Sasha and I'm absolutely convinced that she's a new age traveller. They met in Manchester and were very much in love when something happened which tore them apart. I think they made a lover's tryst and I believe Marvin when he says she will arrive here for our harvest festival. The boy is entirely honest, having a depth of sincerity which is easily recognisable and I can't believe that he's lying, I mean why would he?'

'Alright, alright, I'm being too cynical, but how on earth did they decide on our Church for their reunion, a place of worship so remote from Manchester? You realise of course that there are people in the village who think we may be dabbling in the occult? Some older folk think that the arrival of Sasha for an harvest festival may be an omen of some sort. The very idea of a new age traveller, a free spirit, all tattoos, bangles and beads, threatens a pagan intrusion on all that we hold sacred. The whole thing is quite preposterous, sheer madness.'

'Robin darling, don't you see, this is a test of faith. You are being confronted with your innermost doubts and fears. You have a choice. You must either accept Marvin as a herald, an angel if you like, who has blessed you with his spiritual intervention and embrace the fact, or turn aside like the Pharisee who passed by on the other side. The older generation of Cornish folk are still very superstitious and you should know better than taking their gossip on board. The very fact that only a small percentage of our population as a whole attend services, reflects the nation's innermost yearning, which in this day and age the church is unable to address, leaving us spiritually starved and morally adrift. The arrival of Marvin and Sasha will help you regenerate Christian values in a way which people will take seriously. Be brave Robin darling, break with convention, minister to those who fall among thieves. '

'Harriet, I feel crushed by my own impotency, you should be in the pulpit, not me and I'm truly sorry, sorry that I can't get off the fence, not without your help. I've no wish to disappoint you, but Marvin just doesn't relate to me. I've tried chatting with him, tried to get him interested in the garden, shown him books in the library, tried to gain his confidence, but everytime I try, he simply shies away. He's more interested in working down on Badger's small holding, for which of course he's getting paid.'

'Why don't you leave your sermon for a moment and join Marvin and myself for a music lesson. I think you'll be impressed. I've decided to do something quite exciting at the recital, I'm letting him do a solo, a song more along the lines of a negro spiritual. He wants to play his own version and I've not interfered. I've heard it a couple of times and I think it's brilliant, quite remarkable.'

'Negro spiritual? Surely Marvin's not able to perform that kind of music, it's so completely at odds with rap and all that rubbish. I mean, you say he can't even read music! As a matter of interest, what have you chosen for him?'

'Sometimes I feel like a motherless child.' After all he is a motherless child isn't he?'

'Not any more, if you have anything to do with it.'

The pair left the study and wandered over to the church with Robin taking up a position in the front pew. Skeet was busy composing rap and before Harriet could take up her position beside him, he leapt from the piano stool and ignoring Robin, gave her an involuntary kiss on the cheek. 'Mornin Harrie, you're lookin real cute man, know wha ah mean,' he said, addressing Robin as though he was a stranger. Robin was furious with such blatant familiarity.

'Marvin dear, I want you the play 'Motherless child' just as you've been practising, Robin would like to hear it.'

'I'm doin somethin different wiv the tune, I fink it's real cool man. I done it special for you Harrie.'

Skeet composed himself, his hands resting lightly on the keys, his head lowered, turning slightly as if about to peer over his shoulder. He remained in this position for over two minutes. Robin, convinced that he was about to witness an embarrassing attack of stage fright and a fumbling display of incompetence, noisily cleared his throat. Harriet gave him a repremanding look. Skeet slowly raised his head and began to play. The words poured forth from the very depths of his being, a haunting sound, echoing with rich, weeping overtones. The music was compelling, strange, with a 'Pied Piper of Hamelin' quality, beckoning the listener to follow each note, carried aloft on a sly wind, swirling among the church rafters, always beyond reach, a soulful message, ranging through infinite space on an endless journey in hope of finding the gates of heaven.

'Some *times,* some *times,* some *times,* some *times,*
Some *times* I feel, some *times* I feel,
Like a motherless child.
A *long* ways, A *long, long* ways,
A *long, long, long ways* from *home.* '

Skeet continued his improvisation, ending in a more disciplined cadence, he spun round on the stool, grinning. 'Well Harrie, what yer fink, why you cryin?'

Harriet deeply moved by the performance, whispered, 'Marvin, that was beautiful, absolutely divine and I feel privileged in helping you discover your natural ability. It made me realise, I can't teach you music, you're already a better musician than I'll ever be.'

'Nah, I can't play like you Harrie, read all that music and stuff, you're really cool man.'

'Marvin you'll soon learn to read music, but you have something I never had, you have music within you. You know Marvin, I think your music is more suited to the guitar and I'm sure you'll find natural expression with this instrument. I know a very accomplished player who plays the acoustic guitar and I'll arrange for you to meet him.'

The reverend Robin Reid, rendered speechless by Skeet's ability, at last found words offering his support, ' Marvin, if you decide to play the guitar, we'll buy you one to practice on. I had no idea, I never for one moment, not for a moment realised.......'

'You saying reverend, you'd buy me a guitar, I mean to have my own guitar, jus to play when I want?'

'Yes Marvin, to play whenever you want.'

'Well man, that's really cool. I'll play it jus for Sasha at the harvest festival, I'll play her a love song, tell her how much I love her.'

The recital proved to be the most inspiring event the village had ever heard or witnessed. The repertoire included songs from the ever popular musicals, Oklahoma, West Side Story and the Robbie Williams' score 'Angels'. It lifted the community out of the doldrums, made them more aware of their own ability, made them more receptive and helped enlighten the introvert nature of their countrified existence. Everyone had enormous respect for Harriet and responded with great enthusiasm to her humorous cajoling and determination. Skeet's performance was the highlight of the evening, elevating his status to that of a potential celebrity and people were mystified by the appearance of a provincial star in their humble, and some thought dreary, little church. Harriet had insisted that members of the choral society wear suitable uniforms, there had to be high standards both in performance and presentation, especially if they were to go on tour, an ambition which, with Skeet in the ensemble, she felt well worth while. Dressed in a green blazer, white shirt, cutaway collar and tie, Skeet was the darling of them all. The chiselled good looks, the cascade of Rastafarian hair, the handsome profile, highlighted with a glittering earring and flashing white teeth, sent a warm glow of West Indian sunshine into the hearts of all those in the audience. Members of The Women's Institute, the gardening club, the cricket club and the girls from the riding stables all wanted to know Skeet. He revelled in his new found popularity and had time on his hands for everyone, smiling or laughing with them and always ready to listen. Harriet loved Skeet, he was her protégé, a gift from God, a son who could take away the pain and fill the emptiness left by nature's cruel denial of motherhood.

It became common knowledge that Marvin and Sasha were to be married in church and the wavering reverend Robin Reid would conduct a special service, conjoined with the harvest festival, which would constitute a fundamental break with tradition. Marvin the wandering minstrel from up north had no family connections in the area and Sasha, the wandering new age traveller, had never been seen in the parish. They had not been confirmed and were not members of the church of England. No Banns had been read in church. Certainly, the reverend was planning a service which for high church, was liberal in the extreme. The whole event would be nothing short of a sensation and no doubt the bishop would have some say in the matter. The reverend of course had no such plans and was entirely ignorant of the part he was expected to play in the rumours circulating around the village.

As time went on, Skeet became more and more involved with Badger and his ambitions for the organic market garden. Badger exploited the situation to the full and gave no thought to the damage such heavy work might do to a musician's hands, but Skeet was nobody's servant and with money in his pocket was liable to do anything, other than conform. One day, with harvest festival approaching, Badger took a scheduled trip to Newquay and Skeet went along with him. The Toyota pickup, dangerously overloaded with produce, it's catalyst converter no longer functioning, set off in a cloud of exhaust fumes. Badger had several deliveries for restaurants and green grocers, including the collection of empty crates for the return journey. He was thankful for Skeet's able assistance, whose strength and agility speeded up the whole enterprise. After the day's transactions he sat in the cab counting the money and was more than pleased with the total earnings. He was feeling generous and decided it was time Marvin received some wages. He had worked every afternoon for three weeks and when there was no choir practice, most evenings. The occasion was worthy of a little speech and before handing over five, ten pound notes, he reminded Skeet of his good fortune in finding employment and how lucky he was to benefit from the generous nature of his employer, a weakness which all his life, he had carried like a cross. Skeet was overjoyed, 'Cor, thanks Badger, that's really cool. First wages I ever had, I'm not coming back wiv you though, I've got a letter to post an I want to look over a few guitars. I'll make my own way back on the bus. Tell Harrie not to worry, I'll be back tomorrer, I'll stay over wiv some friends, some surfers I know.'

'You sure biy, now don't go spendin all that cash.'

Skeet climbed out of the vehicle, 'I'll be ok Badger, you bin really cool man, see you termorrer.' Without more ado, Skeet wandered off, he had a letter to post before tracking down a night club dealer for a much needed supply of skunk cannabis.

Skeet's grandmother Constance, was getting worried. She was used to Marvin's comings and goings but had neither seen or heard of him for weeks. She thought she might inform the police, but previous complaints about intimidation and anti social behaviour had received little response and shown a general lack of concern. In addition Marvin already had an Asbo and this fact alone, was enough to discourage any envolement with the police. The increasing stress, inflamed her arthritic knee, brought on severe headaches and gave her sleepless nights. She was making herself ill with worry and was close to giving up her cleaning job, when one morning relief came in the form of a letter. She recognised the handwriting. It was from Marvin:

Dear Gran

I'm ok an livin at the vicarage wiv harrie and the vucar an I'm Lernin the pianner and stuff an It's reelly cool an I'm lernin the Gitar as well an harrie ses I'm reelly good. My sasha is comin to the harvest festival which is on october 10 an its on in the mornin an evenin as well in the church an I'm in a quire playin the pianner an singin an I want you an Ben to come. Ma tregenna ses Sasha is defintly comin. Here's the adress

The vicarage
St michaels and all angels
Penhethlyn

Cornwall.

Constance read the letter several times, trying to make sense of it, her relief giving way to serious concern. The Sasha episiode was developing into something quite bizzare. Constance was blissfully unaware of Marvin's heavy devotion to cannabis, but knew the awful truth behind his terrifying nightmares and his mobid obsession with Sasha, the fixation which had taken control of his life. She realised she had to contact Ben without delay, praying that he would bring Marvin safely home to New Horizons.

She made a few enquiries and soon discovered Ben's home address. She rang the number and Karen answered the phone. ' Mornin Mrs.Mackay, Ah'm Constance Cooney, Ah live two blocks away, on the ground floor, an Ah'm ringin about mah granson, Marvin. Ain't seen nothin of him far weeks then arl of a sudden Ah jes got a letter from him. He's done drivin me crazy with his goings on, him bein in Cornwall an arl, he needs a doctor real bad. Your son's his best mate and Ah jes done got to see him, do some talkin with him, Ah've bin worried sick.'

'You mean my son Ben? I've heard him mention Skeet. Is he your grandson?'

'Yeah, he's mah granson an Ah'm worried sick. Ah jes don't know what he might do, an Ben's the only one Ah know who could help him. Where can Ah find Ben Mrs Mackay? Is he livin with you?'

' Well, not exactly, but he's often mentioned Skeet. Isn't he running with that gang of hoodies? They're up to no good, playing around with drugs and making our lives a misery. Ben's given all that up now, much better behaved, settled down with a regular job. He's a delivery van driver, works for Vera Motors in the city. He comes and goes as he pleases and I don't want him mixing with that crowd again. I suggest you ring the police.'

'Mrs. Mackay, Ah've done rung the police till Ah'm blue in the face. Arl I want is far Ben to bring him home to me, that's arl. Your Ben's a lovely boy, he's good an kind an he's bin jes wonderful with Marvin. He understands his problem an knows how to handle him, Marvin'll listen to him. Ah'm pleadin with you Mrs Mackay, Ah jes need to talk with Ben, that's arl.'

No one had ever before spoken of Ben in such glowing terms and Karen allowed herself a moment of pride. It seemed that at last her eldest son was getting his life together. 'Ok Mrs Cooney I'll give you his mobile.'

Ben fumbled for his mobile. These days, living in two worlds, he never knew what to expect. Was it from the world of those who faced their responsibilities, his working mother, Matt or Katrina, the world of Mike and his son Josh, who made beautiful furniture or hopefully Kelly, the beautiful university student whom he wanted as a girl friend? Or was it a call from Meg and a world poisoned with narcotics, or perhaps one of Tonino's gangsters, a world of violence and extortion?

Ben had enjoyed his week at Edward's joinery, his introduction to making carefull measurements, calculating increments with acurate precision, the mastery of woodworking tools, finding an element of discipline and control within himself, and even more, discovering a true friend in Josh. He decided that Kelly was right, this was what he wanted to do, this was what he wanted to achieve. He was no fool and he'd tried to do the sensible thing. Following the week's break, he'd confronted Tonino, informing him that he wanted out, assuring him that information concerning undercover dealings in cocaine were safe with him, he knew how to button his lip.

But having proved himself on a drugs run, Tonino was disappointed with Ben, 'I warned you Ben. You think this is some kid's game we're playing? You work for me, you understand, for me, no one else, not ever, capiche? You go messing with some other outfit and your dead meat. I know you gotta beautiful sister, a beautiful mamma, capiche.' Tonino smiled, his tone changed, 'Look Ben, I'm sure you're a smart kid, you gotta be the way you handled that pickup. Just relax, take it easy, don't make such a big deal out of it, do as I say and you'll be fine, no problems. Anyways, you got a couple of weeks holiday coming up. Meg's taking you to Napoli!'

From that meeting onwards, Ben realised he was living a lie, lying to his mother, lying to his familly, lying to Mike and

Josh, lying even to Kelly, lying to the whole world. 'Who is this?' He said, trembling into the mobile? He listened, as Constance poured forth her anxieties, begging him to call and see her that same evening and without hesitation Ben agreed. He was genuinely concerned about Skeet.

Ben read the letter from Skeet, 'I know every now and then he goes mental, must be cannabis, it's damaged his brain cells, he's been really into it as long as I can remember, but I don't understand this stuff about Sasha. I never met her Mrs Cooney, have you?'

'Sasha's arl in his head. When he was twelve, he done got envolved in a gang rape. She was only fourteen, a pretty little redhead, older than her years, Natasha she was called. Marvin done nothing but he saw what happened an it turned his head.'

'Cor! I never knew he was mixed up with that, it was a big scandal at school, but there was no proof, we all said we knew nothin about it an it all got covered up. There were loads of interviews, social workers, police women and stuff but no charges were ever brought, but we all knew who it was, it was Pitbull and some of the Asbos. I should have said somethin, I knew it was wrong, I respect women, I got a sister an I knew it was wrong, but I didn't say nothin. I spose Skeet was traumatised, jus like Natasha, she's never got over it, she's so quiet and scared.'

'Ah think Marvin's done gone insane an Ah'm beggin you, Ah'm prayin Ben, you'll do this far me, an please Ben, let me pay you, Ah've got savings. Ah jes want him back home, get him to a doctor before he finds real trouble.'

'You don't have to pay me anythin Mrs Cooney. Skeets my mate an I'll bring him back, I promise. The harvest festival's on Sunday an I'll travel down Saturday night, I'm workin all day Saturday.'

'God bless you Ben,' Constance threw her arms about him, unable to hold back the tears, 'Ah jes can't thank you enough, You bin so good to him, there's not many in this God forsaken world like you, you're such a good boy, I spoke to you're mum on the phone, she mus be so proud an arl.'

Ben left the flat wandering how he was going to keep his promise. He was afraid to use the Vera Motor's van and there seemed only one thing for it, he would have to ask Josh, ask him if he could borrow his car. He knew this would be asking a great deal. And now that he had turned down Mike's offer of a good job with lame excuses and more lies, he was uncertain how things stood between them. He expected Josh to say no, in which case he would have to take the van and risk the consequences. But to his surprise, Josh said ok and even went further, he offered to travel down with Ben incase there was any trouble.

Robin and Harriet were worried about Marvin's excursion into Newquay and were greatly relieved when he returned to the vicarage. Badger had given them the details and they were expecting to see him the following morning, but tensions increased throughout the day and later that evening, having made a decision to report him missing, hopes and expectations were restored when Marvin rang the door bell. He stood at the front door with a carrier bag, looking nervous and tired. Harriet gave him a welcoming hug, 'Marvin! We were getting so worried, especially when you missed choir practice, it wasn't the same without you.'

'I'm ok Harrie, I've seen a guitar I like.' Then offering her a pink envelope, 'Here I bought you a present.'

Harriet, feeling very emotional, opened the envelope and took out an inexpensive necklace, a silvered chain with an amber coloured, heart shaped pendant.

'Why Marvin, how lovely, I shall always treasure it, how sweet, how thoughtful of you to think of me.'

'I want you to wear it Harrie, it'll keep you safe from harm an you'll always be thinkin of me.'

'Marvin, how could I ever forget you? You'll never know what a difference you've made in our lives. But darling, let me get you some supper.'

'It's ok Harrie thanks, I got some pasties in my bag, an I'm so tired with all that walkin man, all I want is some kip.'

'Let me get a plate, I'll heat the pasties and you can have them in your room.

Robin's fixed up a telly in there for you, so you don't have to watch our programmes all the time. Get a good night's rest and in the morning you can take a nice hot bath. Would you like ketchup with your pasties? I'll bring a knife and fork with a napkin.'

Harriet and Robin slept soundly assured that things were back to normal and all was well with the world. In the morning at around ten o clock, Harriet knocked on Marvin's bedroom door. There was no reponse. She decided he needed more sleep and left him undisturbed. Two hours later she tried again but there was still no reponse. She decided to quietly check on him. The bedroom door had no lock but some obstruction lay behind and try as she may, it refused to budge. She called Robin and he began hammering the door shouting 'Are you alright Marvin? Please open the door, are you alright? Harriet's cooked breakfast, please Marvin open up!' Then, using his shoulder, he put his full weight against the door and after some considerable effort managed to force open a gap wide enough to squeeze through. Drawers, removed from the tallboy were heaped against the door with some of their contents wedged under the threshold. Inside, they were met with a disturbing scene.

The room stank of cannabis, stale lager and vomit. Chunks of uneaten pasty, smothered in tomato ketchup, were spread all over the carpet, trodden into the pile. The up ended bed frame, matress and bedding, together with other items of furniture had been used to build a hide in the far corner and shreds of newspapers, magazines and library books were stuffed into every crevice. There were burns on the TV set and Marvin, squatting in the middle of it all, shook violently, with sweat pouring into his eyes.

Robin found himself unable to move, 'Oh my God,' was all he could manage.

Harriet, reacting on impulse with motherly love and compassion, knelt beside him, gathering him to her, as if he was a child, stroking his hair, rocking to and fro.

'There, there,' she hushed, 'You're safe now, you're quite safe.'

In morbid silence, with distressing attention to detail, they cleared up the mess. This was not vandalism, not wanton destruction, this was the work of a demon. The incident shook them to the core and Robin wished to distance himself as far as possible from Marvin and his drug abuse. Such behaviour confirmed Robin's first impression, Marvin was on drugs, a psychotic whose welfare was beyond their knowledge or capacity. He must be admitted to hospital at once, where he could no longer exercise a dangerous influence over Harriet. Robin thought Marvin ought to be sectioned under the mental health act and made confidential enquiries, explaining the circumstances without giving specific details, only to discover that a compulsory admission was out of the question. A patient had to be assessed as abnormally aggressive or seriously irresponsible, whatever that meant, before he or she could be held against their will. No one could be detained for drug dependancy or harmless schizophrenia. Admission had to be on a voluntary basis. On hearing this information, an element of fear crept into their nightly slumbers and Robin had nightmares about being murdered in his sleep.

A day later, Harriet went into complete denial over the experience, recognising only the attractive side of Marvin's personality, his warmth, his generous nature, his musical talent, his striking good looks and most of all the satifaction of knowing that she had a special relationship with him. She could only follow her maternal instincts and had absolute faith in her ability to save him from further torment. She easily pursuaded Robin that his proposals were harsh, lacking Christian charity, showing weakness in the face of adversity, turning his back on someone in their hour of need, and as usual Robin succumbed to her arguments, blaming his personal lack of conviction, his dithering, and his infuriating dependance on her strength and support. Niggled by the uncomfortable truth in her accusations, Robin failed to recognise that Harriet might have ulterior motives. His worries were further exasperated when he received a telephone call from the Western Times. 'Had he opened a soup kitchen at the vicarage, offering shelter and rehabilitation for drug users and vagrants? Was he making a stand against Cof E accepted practice, planning to marry non believers, new age travellers Marvin and Sasha during a harvest festival service? When could they arrange an interview?' Robin, slamming the phone down, refused any further communication.

Things were settling down, getting back to normal when Friday morning came, only two days before the harvest festival. Robin, Harriet and Marvin sat at the breakfast table. Badger had sent them a dozen free range eggs with his compliments, and half of them, now boiled, nestled in a blue rimmed basin, waiting for their hallmarked silver egg cups and teaspoons. Other delicacies were on offer, farm butter, home made marmalade and several slices of toast, precariously overloaded in a toast rack designed for more delicate appetites. The aroma of percolated coffee settled their nerves but conversation steered painfully clear of those things which were uppermost in their minds. Robin and Harriet watched in clinking silence as Marvin crammed slice after slice of delicious toast and marmalade.

The Western Time's latest edition arrived with the post and Robin, excusing himself from the table, retired to the conservatory. With trembling hands, he examined the newspaper and there on the front page was a picture of Marvin and Badger. The article explained how Marvin, a busking, new age traveller had received a message from St Agnes, the patron saint of virgins, calling on him to attend the harvest festival at Penhethlyn where he would be reunited with Sasha, the love of his life. A group of travellers, located on Bodmin moor had said it was a clear example of how their simple lifestyle could change a world corrupted by greed and materialism and how it would eventually break down religious dogma. They would convoy down for this very special wedding, their women decked in wild flowers, their menfolk playing flutes and drums and they looked forward to meeting a clergyman who was not afraid of radical thinking.

Feeling close to a nervous breakdown, he called Harriet and showed her the article. She read it carefully, then burst out laughing. 'What hilarious nonsense. Isn't this just typical of newspapers, never get their facts right, latch on to anything which might cause a sensation?'

'Harriet I'm astounded you find it all so amusing, I see absolutely nothing to laugh about. Marvin's gate crashed our life, turning it upside down and now we're threatened with something quite dreadful and I had no way of foreseeing this, this, this latest *obscenity*. I could end up being excommunicated, ridiculed, become a national laughing stock.The whole thing is preposterous. I'm going to phone the police at once, put a stop to it.'

'Robin darling, here you go again, over reacting. You're taking the whole thing too seriously. If you phone the police you'll simply make matters worse. Stay true to you're convictions. Preach a sermon worthy of the occasion. There's nothing to fear, nothing from anyone. All this talk of a marriage is ridiculous and you know it is. Marvin's never once mentioned a marriage or said he wanted to marry Sasha.'

'But don't you see Harriet, Marvin's a threat to us. We have no idea what he might do when under the influence of drugs. He may have weapons as well as drugs hidden away, we could easily be murdered in our beds!'

'You really are afraid aren't you? Harriet replied with puzzled surprise. 'Now you're being paranoid. Why, Marvin has a most gentle personality, there's not an aggressive bone in his body, he's a sensitive boy, gifted, warm and thoughtful of others. He's suffered a great deal and needs our love and understanding and I intend to help him all I can,' she hesitated, letting her remarks sink in. 'With or without you.'

Robin was shocked speechless by what amounted to an ultimatum, a parting of the ways, a possible breakdown of their relationship, a rejection of all they had meant to each other, after years of happy marriage. So this was how she really felt, she'd never been happy, never fulfilled, their marriage had been a sham. Harriet wished she hadn't said those last words. If only she could take them back, she'd never mean't to wound him so deeply. 'Robin dear, I'm sorry, I didn't really mean that, it just slipped out. Now why don't you go to your study, finish that great sermon and I'll bring you some fresh coffee.'

Robin went to his study, his shouders drooped, his thoughts a kaleidoscope of failure, fear and broken dreams, his eyes vacant, seeing only a reflection of himself, the lonely little boy with his make believe pals.

Saturday came, the day before the harvest festival, offering no choice, no escape from the study, the leaded lights, the stone mullions, the copper beech and the lap top waiting for inspiration. For weeks Robin had thought about how his contribution might grace the occasion only to find his ideas thwarted by frightening developments. The article in the Western Times had promised an invasion of non believers. In what form could he present his sermon, in what direction should he lead his congregation? Harriet had lost patience with him and the more he thought about it, the more he realised he was unable to cope. Here was an opportunity to cross the line, to preach those things he believed, just as Harriet had encouraged, but in the face of mounting pressure, he buckled.

He decided to regurgitate a traditional harvest festival message, the kind of misguided worship, in an age enlightenment, he felt had no relevance. How could he praise God for a bountiful harvest when hardly anything was grown locally? People bought their produce from supermarkets, where the vast majority of food came from abroad. The wonderful exhibition of fruit and vegetables, arranged with such care and attention in the church were mainly the result of Badger's brave attempts to find a market among the wealthy and more discerning. Flowers and other contributions came from private gardens and their tiny green houses. But what sickened him most was the fact, that on this planet, twenty five thousand people a day were dying of starvation, most of them children under five. And yet, in the face of these appalling figures, more and more acreage was being used for the production of opium, hemp, coca, corn and sugar cane for ethenol, palm oil and soya beans for biodiesal. Of course this was not God's fault, although he was not sure he believed in God, it was simply the process of natural selection, survival of the fittest. There could never be a harvest that would satisfy the hunger of an exploding world population. We were simply lucky to be the ones having the lion's share, for the moment. How could we thank God, simply because we had loaded the dice in our favour? What was more important was to build a new culture based on ethical thinking, following the words of Jesus Christ in thought and deed. The church, unable to grasp the import of science and discovery, simply bored people and had no influence over the world's affairs. In schools, Christianity had been relegated to a dispassionate study along with other religions and only a small diminishing number of the population regularly attended church.

Robin's train of thought was interupted by a knock on the door. He thought it must be Harriet with the coffee but the door remained unopened. ' Come in,' he said unable to hide his disappointment. It was Tom, the verger.

'Sorry to disturb you vicar, but there's strange goings on in the belfry and I think you should know about it. Look what I found up there.'

'Strange goings on? Well, what have you found?'

'I found this stuff in a plastic packet and a sheet of paper with weird scribble all over it.' He handed over the items looking very agitated and concerned.

Robin quickly placed the herbal cannabis in a draw and opened the sheet of paper. 'Well thank you Tom, If you don't mind, I'd better examine this alone.'

Harrie is my mum
Ben and Badger best mates
the reverend is a twat

Marvin needs Sasha
x x x x x x x x x x x x x x x x

Sasha did my head in

Marvin

Black
Spider
rules

Black Spider evolved
with Sasha in him

Tribe   leader

Sasha
don't
know how
much Marvin
loves you

Badger is one
of us

Shadow black
is in one and
one is in him

Harrie is one
of us

Black Spider
says Sash can't
come to the
harvest festival

The reverend
is a
TWAT

Ben is my best
MATE

Black Spider stole
my Sasha

123

Robin tried to grasp the meaning of it all, the revelations of a disordered mind, the incoherent ravings of a private hell. He looked up 'twat' in the Oxford English Dictionary. A stupid, unpleasant person it said, along with other equally unattractive definitions. Something had to be done. After some frantic searching, he discovered a website dealing with cannabis psychosis, www.priory.com/psych/cannabis.htm and logged on. He printed pages of information on the subject, noting that in chronic cases the symptons known as Amotivational Syndrome were usually permanent and with continual usage, became acute. There was nothing else he could do. He rang the police. He explained in some detail how they had unwittingly given refuge to a wandering psychotic, a Marvin Cooney from Manchester whom he knew for a fact was in breach of an Asbo and probably had a criminal record and whose behaviour was becoming quite threatening. Marvin was in possession of an illegal substance, a package of which he had confiscated for their analysis. Even more alarmingly, Marvin had attracted an army of new age travellers who were descending upon the church for tomorrow's harvest festival. He feared a demonstration of some sort. The police said they would check up on Marvin and promised a police presence in the vicinity of the church. However, they could not restrain new age travellers from worship, but if there was to be a violent or disruptive demo, reserves would be called upon to break it up and restore order.

Feeling more relaxed, Robin locked the evidence in a draw and returned to his notes for the harvest festival sermon, a subject which in his mind, seemed to have disassociated itself from church services. A welcome reprieve from negative thoughts arrived when Harriet came in with the coffee. 'Coffee darling. Any inspiration? Decided how you're going to make tomorrow's service special, special for Marvin. Its going to be such a big day for him isn't it? I do hope Sasha arrives early, he'll be so disappointed if she's not here for the morning service.'

'Well actually darling, I'm having real problems. I find the whole concept of a church sevice, celebrating the excesses of the Western World, quite nauseating.' He took a sip of coffee, peering over the rim, making sure he had Harriet's undivided attention. 'The hymns, the prayers, congratulating ourselves on getting more than our fair share of God's bounty, how we've earned it and how deserving we are.'

'I'm not sure I follow.'

'Harriet darling, consider the facts. In order to survive, in order to supply our brains with the enormous amount of energy they require, we have to consume food, in one form or another, it's a fundermental requirement of all living things. You agree?'

'Well of course it is and that's what our Thanksgiving's all about, the fact that the earth can supply our needs.'

'Today food production is achieved by machines, the intensive farming of animals and the exploitation of cheap labour, quite often near slave labour, the latter having always been the case. Our slaughter houses, like the Israelites' Tabernackle, run with the blood of slaughtered animals, going flat out to keep up with the demand for meat, a commodity which only half the world can afford.'

'What a dreadful thought.' Harriet wrinkled her brow. 'You've decided on going vegetarian? D'you know, I've been thinking along the same lines.'

'No Harriet, I'm being unduly sentimental, I'm not going vegetarian but one has to admit, if the millions of turkeys bred for our consumption over the Christmas period, had any influence over their fate, they would most assuredly vote to stay alive. I know such thoughts are ridiculous, hypothetical and darkly humourous, but I'm trying to illustrate what the world distribution of food means in humanitarian terms.

'Oh really! Robin, whatever is this leading up to? What *do* Chrismas turkeys illustrate in humanitarian terms?

'Forget about turkeys, I'm talking about the world distribution of food. It's a picture of greed, of ruthless financing, of market control by companies hoarding food, supplying genetic seeds and agricultural chemicals, supermarkets intensifying competition by their monopolies, the devastation of our rain forests, the exploitation of labour having to work for a living below the poverty line and shameless waste. It's not a wholesome picture is it? In any event millions are left starving and desperately undernourished. What value a C of E harvest festival?

Isn't it time the church spoke out about these things, did something at a political level instead of playing around with token charity and pouring forth endless platitudes?'

'Robin darling, I think you're off in the wrong direction again. Religions can never, should never, become directly involved with the secular world. Religions can have no control over the misery caused by earthquakes, floods, hurricanes, drought and other natural disasters, no more than they can minister to all the worlds material needs. All religions are there to help us rise above these things, to restore our faith in the life hereafter, to show us how to love one another. Faith is a private affair, a matter for each individual conscience, a matter for the soul. People attend church because for centuries they've recognised that faith can lift us above the physical laws of the universe. Your thoughts are too heavy, too preoccupied with politics. Tomorrow must be a simple message of faith, of hope and the joy of sharing. The offerings in the church do not represent our gloating satisfaction, they are given with humility and love.'

Robin decided now was the time to produce the evidence. 'Harriet, I think there's something you should be made aware of, it may help you to see things in a different light.'

'I've no wish to see or hear anything against Marvin. I know he has problems but so have you. All of us, including Marvin, have been working to make your church beautiful and you've never once given encouragement, never really got involved or shown your appreciation. You've never taken the trouble to get to know the people in the village or understand the lives of your own flock, let alone Marvin. You just bury yourself in books. How can *you* understand the needs of humanity?' Harriet, more than ever aware of the increasing rift between them, quietly excused herself.

As she left the room, Robin noticed how much greyer she seemed. He slumped into his chair. She was right of course.

Sunday came, October the tenth, the day of the harvest festival and with it an invasion of new age travellers. They came in the early hours, waking the neighbourhood, a noisy procession of clapped out diesels housed within clapped out buses, Ford

126

Trannies and ancient motor homes. After driving back and forth through the village, they broke the lock on a field gate giving access to the village green where they parked in random disorder, encroaching on the hallowed cricket pitch to form a scrapyard encampment. An hour before the service, they set off for the church, looking like refugees in the aftermath of a nuclear war. They paraded an assortment of clothes, Asian, Oxfam and just plain rags. The women, wearing garlands of wild flowers, singing and dancing with their children, waved banners and evergreen branches, accompanied by their menfolk who made music on whistles, flutes and home made drums.

Following their departure, a second invasion arrived in the form of a police detachment. They sported bright yellow jackets and appeared well organised as road tax discs, illegal tyres, dodgy numberplates and vehicle road worthiness were methodically checked. They had a search warrant and when the travellers returned to their vehicles, a thorough drugs bust was intended before moving them on. Police security vans were lined up for the arrests and a police helicopter hovered above. They soon had an audience, as villagers on their way to church, gathered in amazement to witness the fun. Police in such numbers had only been seen on television and there had never been a policeman in the village since the much admired and respected PC James Harris used to slog sixes all round the village green back in the seventies. Many of the younger onlookers had never seen a policeman in their entire lives. The officer in charge sent two constables, a man and a woman, to attend the church sevice. They were to report to the reverend Robin Reid and radio back if there was a disturbance of any sort.

The new age travellers arrived at St Michael and all Angels in good time, determined to occupy the front pews where they could be near the action. A few regulars were already seated, but having found themselves engulfed by the acrid smell of wood smoke, the great unwashed and the unnerving familiarity of unruly children, decided a strategic retreat might be more conducive to silent prayer. A steady stream of the curious and the converted filled the church. Robin watched from the study window and his composure gradually disintegrated, giving way to knee trembles and a facial tic. He repeatedly removed his glasses giving them a vigourous polish as though trying to erase the scene.

There was a knock on the door, the police had arrived. Robin opened it and almost embraced them. 'Thank God you've arrived,' he gasped. 'The young man you are looking for is in the vestry, he's unmistakable, he's black with Rastafarian locks.'

'I don't understand sir,' replied the policeman. 'What man?'

'The young man who is terrorising us, the one on drugs, the one who is dangerously psychotic, the one in breech of an Asbo, A Marvin Cooney from Manchester!'

'We don't know anything about a Marvin Cooney sir, we're here to drug bust these new age travellers and prevent a demo. They're illegally parked on the village green and causing obstruction.'

'But I specifically asked for Marvin's removal as a matter of priority, I gave details and you promised to check up on him.'

'I'm afraid we've no instructions on Mr Cooney sir, I think we've enough on our plate dealing with these new age travellers. We've no information on Mr Cooney and as far as we are aware there has been no complaint against him. We can escort you into church if that'll make you feel happier?'

'No, that would look ridiculous and most unseemly for a church service. I'd rather you keep a low profile, take up positions at the rear. The whole thing's getting completely out of hand, I've no idea what to expect, other than a complete farce.'

'Very well sir, just calm youself, we'll keep an eye on things, if there's any trouble we have plenty of reserves in the village.'

Harriet took her usual position at the organ. She played softly at first but in order to drown out the rising din from new age travellers, involuntarily found herself competing with a determined crescendo. The choir, bravely advanced down the aisle looking sombre in their long black cassocks and less than white surplices. Skeet's demeanour impressed the congregation, making them feel good about themselves, he was living proof that Saint Michaels had no colour prejudice and that the Christian message extended to all races. The reverend Robin Reid, with faltering steps, mounted the pulpit. This was the biggest congregation he had ever faced and he felt intimidated by such a huge gathering of new faces, a sea of vacant expressions, the unimpressed countenance of non believers. The new age travellers were not in the least interested in what he had to say and clearly had no respect for the sanctity of the church. Their children were already munching on apples, crunching through carrots and generally helping themselves to the offerings arranged with such artistry before the chancel.

In a croaking voice he addressed the congregation. 'Today we are gathered together in gratitude and thanksgiving for God's wonderful bounty. We who live on this "sceptred isle" have been shown the promised land, a land flowing with milk and honey, and in all humility we thank God for our merciful deliverance from want. Let us pray.' As if to enter into the spirit of things, two young mothers in the front row bared their ample bosoms and began breast feeding their babies. The reverend's eyes blinked morse code. He cleared his throat. 'Let us pray,' he repeated.

'WE WANT SASHA! WE WANT SASHA! WE WANT SASHA!' The new age travellers chanted. Hovering behind the baptismal font, the police officers called for reserves, then descended upon the rabble in order to organise an eviction. The sight of policemen bearing down the aisle sent Skeet into a panic and he broke ranks, making for the small door which led to the bell tower, his favourite hiding place. The new age travellers in no hurry, dispersed, leaving behind heaps of detritus. They reassembled in the churchyard. 'WE WANT SASHA! WE WANT SASHA!' They persisted. Most of the congregation left with them, gathering outside, where a confrontation between the police and the new age travellers looked promising, offering real entertainment. One of the more responsible citizens ran back inside the church. 'Marvin's up on the roof of the tower,' he yelled. 'He's waving his arms about and shouting something.'

Before taking after Skeet, the policeman had a few words with the vicar, 'I'll try and bring him down, don't let anyone else into the tower, the situation could be delicate. I'm afraid sir I shall have to ask you to clear the church. The morning service will have to be cancelled.' He turned to the policewoman. ' Don't take any risks with the crowd outside, wait for reinforcements.' He then climbed the narrow stairs, exercising caution, and on reaching the roof of the tower, found Marvin dodging from one castellation to another shouting at the crowd below. 'SASHA'S IN THE WORLD, SASHA'S IN THE WORLD, SASHA'S IN THE WORLD.'

Police constable Bruce Davidson kept his distance and in measured tones spoke like an understanding father on a family day's outing. 'Just calm down, just calm down. Now listen to me son, there's no problem here, no one is going to harm you, I'm here to help, understand? There is absolutely no problem here, I'm here to help. You have a problem? You can talk to me, I'm here to listen. Whatever it is we can sort it out. Together.'

'Skeet seemed less agitated but more emotional, a tear ran down his cheek, 'Sasha's in the world,' he said.

'Yes I know Sasha's in the world and the world is one hell of a tough place to be in, but we all got to do the best we can. Now I take it you're Marvin?'

'Yeah I'm Marvin, Marvin from Manchester, I live in New Horizons, and it's cool man, so cool. Sasha she's left me, she ain't comin back, I jus know she ain't comin back.'

Now listen Marvin, I was your age once, I got my heart broken, just like you, and you know what I did?'

'What did you do man?'

'Well Marvin, at first, I felt like crying but then I thought hell, I got to get on with my life, so I worked harder, tried to do something useful and d'you know, that pain went away. You're young Marvin, a fine looking lad, I'd be proud to have you for my son and you got to move on, keep working, get on with your life and I promise the hurt will go. I'm here to help you do that, you can trust me Marvin, I only want to help.' The constable edged nearer. 'There's no way I'm going to arrest you Marvin. Let's go down together, like mates, where we can quietly sort this out.'

In order to watch the drama unfold, groups of onlookers took up strategic positions in the churchyard. A murmur went round and even the new age travellers appeared subdued. All eyes were focused on a black youth as he pranced back and forth on the roof of the tower, a messenger on high, arms waving against the white clouds. Robin and Harriet stood together near the base of the tower. 'Please Marvin, please come down, there's nothing to fear, we all love you,' Harriet implored at the top of her voice. For a moment Skeet disappeared from view and everyone breathed a sigh of relief, confident that the lad had responded to Harriet's plea and that the police officer had pursuaded the youth to come down or perhaps made an arrest. Then suddenly he was standing on the very edge, his arms outstretched, 'SASHA'S IN THE WORLD,' he shouted at the sky. Then he was falling, his surplice candled like a failed parachute, falling, falling, falling for ever. His body slammed into the grave stones and in that moment the demons left him, left him never to return.

'Oh my God,' Harriet screamed and instinctively took a step forward to where his body lay.

Robin restrained her, 'There's nothing you can do, he's beyond our help, let the police deal with it, God rest his soul.'

'Take you hands off me *Judas*! Don't ever touch me again.' Harriet broke free, but hesitated as a young man ran through the crowd reaching Marvin ahead of her.

'Skeet, Skeet it's Ben, what have you done? It's Ben, come to take you home.' Ben knelt beside Skeet's lifeless form, gathering him into his arms, 'Oh Skeet,' he sobbed, 'You crazy fool, you crazy bloody fool.'

'Harriet!' Robin caught her arm, 'Marvin was mentally sick, he was beyond our help, surely you can see that now. There is no Sasha. Sasha was all in his head. Surely you can see that, she never would have materialised, I mean how could she?'

Harriet seemed in a trance, the harrowing tension left her face and a faint smile played around her lips, her voice whispering, distant, 'Ah but she has....... I see them together........ Marvin and Sasha........ She's very beautiful, just as Marvin described........ She has red hair with a white ribbon and she's dressed in green...... they're walking hand in hand along the footpath...... Now they're leaving....... through the wicket gate.'

Chapter 9 Where the Heart Is.

Marvin's grin, a flash of Caribbean sunshine, had gone forever. It had lightened her day, restored hope and healed the wounds of family breakdown. With the loss of her only grandson, the chance of finding happiness drifted away from Constance Cooney and her world no longer held a promise. Only the memories persisted, making no sense, having no purpose other than torment. Each day she lived again those early years, when as brave immigrants, she and her husband had faced the cultural shock of colour predudice, racism, and disillusion. Each day his death on a construction site remained chiselled in her mind, like an epitaph on a tombstone, a stark entry in the accident book, a requirement under the Health and Safety Acts, giving the date, the time and the circumstances, along with a list of crushed fingers and broken limbs. Each day she thought how Marvin, as a child, had been left in her care. Her daughter, faced with the option of leaving her son with her mother or losing her boyfriend, had chosen the former, relinquishing her responsibilities and any love she might have for her family in favour of a new life in Jamaica with her white boy friend, spending his huge inheritance. Constance also had a son who'd shown early promise as a musician, but due to heroin addiction, had wasted his talents in a third rate band, playing gigs at beer festivals and obscure village halls. The memories, the unremitting toil, the futility of trying to maintain standards, gradually fossilised until they became nothing more than a distant dream, a disfigured mural on a crumbling wall. The hours, the days came and went and Constance went through the motions, but she had given up on living, the struggle had been too much, the misfortune, the final tragedy, overwhelming.

For the residents of New Horizons, life became even more intolerable. After losing Ben, their undisputed leader, the Asbos regrouped and a breakaway unit formed, staking out fresh territory within defined boundaries, gathering each evening around a collection of giant recycling bins sited in a deserted pay and display car park, a no go area for motorists, even though a permanently wrecked pay machine promised free parking. Pitbull had become something of an Asbo hero, I mean he'd taken out a

132

school master, he'd used a firearm. No one, but no one, messed with Pitbull. A pistol! What a prize! What a possession! That was so cool, really wicked. Now, showing off a firearm, carrying a gun, meant no fooling. This was how it was on the street, this was no playstation and the more reckless gang members earned status by carrying a pistol of some sort, ideal for the face saving, territorial wars which had to be fought, ideal for enforcing payments on drug deals, ideal for getting respect. That was central to gang culture, getting respect, doing what the hell you liked, binge drinking, marijuana, crack, whatever, violence, violence against authority, violence against the old and the vulnerable, punishing those who showed no respect. Law abiding citizens said the gangs were out of control, evil scum, sick minds intoxicated by the thrills of juvenile terrorism, but gang members felt very much in control, were self governing, making their own laws, their own rules of engagement.

The breakaway Asbos sensed that Constance was vulnerable and began a programme of intimidation. There was no set pattern, no timetable for their frequent attention. They considered it low key activity, just good fun, shouting racial abuse, smashing eggs against the window, stuffing filth through the letter box, piling beer cans and takeaway litter against her front door. Constance gave up praying and became a nervous wreck, close to losing her sanity, unhinged, caught in a quagmire of dispair and bereavement and quite beyond the reach of recovery. Mercifully, from an unexpected quarter, deliverance was at hand.

Mike Edwards was planning to offer Karen an old fashioned proposal of marriage. For him this was a big step, and uncertain of her response, he felt the time and the place had to be just right. He hated the less committed approach where each party steered clear of the inevitable challenges, giving their individual needs priority, preferring the illusion of continual courtship, an arrangement he thought lacked strength in adversity. He had already made plans and was looking forward to sharing them with her. It was lunchtime and he sat in the office enjoying corned beef sandwiches, improved beyond belief by the addition of onion rings and tomato ketchup.

At heart Mike was a family man. Josh and his wife Melanie, Sarah and her husband Darren, his grandchildren, Sean and Celia Edwards and Bonnie Brown made his life whole, nurtured his paternal instincts and gave him pride in their achievments. He wished he could see more of them but they lived such busy lives, there were so many pressures, so much going on. The traditional role of grandparents had changed with more and more of them acting as unpaid babysitters, helping to ease financial budgets while their parents worked. Mike's generosity had been a great help but lack of daily contact made him feel somewhat dated. Children now lived in a world so remote from his own upbringing that his conceptions, his standards, his criteria were hardly relevant. His grandchildren perferred a one to one with computor games and there were times when in their company, he felt obselete.

His love for Karen dispelled any significance this might have and he felt young again, refreshed, hungry for a new life. The more he thought about Karen, the more he treasured every waking moment, his love readily embracing all that was beautiful in the world and all that was good and kind. What a wonderful thing is love Mike thought, so easily expressed in the joy of giving, giving freely with no strings, no conditions, no ulterior motives, no lost leaders. This was the kind of giving he had in mind for Karen, all that he given Sheila, all that he had given his family.

Loving Karen though, had made his life complicated. It now carried unwanted baggage. Karen already had a young family who had experienced violence at home, a family without a father, a family which included Ben, a young man with an Asbo who was always in trouble with the police, who ran with street gangs, messed around with drugs, had been involved with a shooting and had witnessed a tragic suicide. Mike had offered help, Josh had offered friendship and yet Ben inexplicably, had rejected these lifelines and Mike suspected that he had been drawn into organised crime. He had discussed the problems of criminal behaviour among children with his daughter Sarah who was studying politics at the Open University. She was very much envolved with a charity scheme dealing with youngsters in the city who were struggling with life and in particular those already in custody. She had political ambitions and had chosen to write a dissertation on the structure of society in Britain today. Mike knew she had her mother's intellect, he valued her opinions and was very proud of the way she had matured. In answer to his queries she had given him the introduction to her essay and he had been carrying it around in his brief case for a couple of days. Now he decided was a good time to read it.

He read it through carefully and her words struck a chord, making him crucially aware of the inherent problems of New Horizons Park, the Mackay family and his emotional involvement. Of course, he grumbled about things, health and safety regulations, red tape, government interference, taxes and the weather but had never taken politics very seriously, he'd always been too busy getting on with life. Sarah's research and observations into anti social behaviour prompted a shift in his perspective, adding a new dimension to his outlook on life and the discovery of a political conscience. He read the introduction again.

'Throughout history, anti social behaviour, the emergence of dark forces, has reflected in its most primeval form, the immoralities of the ruling classes. When man made laws shackle the poor, remove the hope of privilege and prosperity, depreciate the achievments of those without influence, remain deaf to cries for help while favouring those with wealth and power, civilisation is fouled by a mounting residue of dissidence which in turn spawns rebellion, undermining it's foundations and is the inevitable forerunner of collapse. The decline may be controlled with harsh punitive measures and even in this age of enlightenment, many still advocate the return of flogging and the death penalty. In Europe, the weight of liberal thinking and the sensitive issue of human rights, have outlawed the notion of an 'eye for an eye,' meeting abuse with abuse, violence with violence. However, civilisations continue to suffer the excesses of those who gain control, the corruption of power, the casualties of ruthless competition, the inbalance caused by greed and the ransom imposed by oil and gas monopolies. In western democracies these ills are now cleverly disguised and are not so easily defined or recognised, nothing is what it seems and new words are used for deceit.

In Britain, lose hard earned income on a short fall pension scheme and it has been missold. Inadvertantly lose out on a buy one get one free offer and it has been misrepresented. Lies from politicians are merely spin. Extortion, as practiced by banks, credit card companies, local authorities, and other self regulating professions, is disguised in small print and legal jargon, designed to lure the unwary, resulting in a soaring, trillion pound record of personal debt. The internet, that miracle of communication and learning, is also a highway for sleaze, electronic scams, deviant voyeurism, the seduction of children and a means of escape from the realities of life. Moreover, the fabric of our lives entirely depends on our exploitation of the third world, profiteering from cheap labour in eastern Europe, cheap goods from new industrial economies such as China and countries around the Pacific rim. We now depend on the import of foreign skills, both professional and manual and in our efforts to maintain control while avoiding real work, find ourselves buried in an avalanche of benefits at one end of the social scale and a crushing overburden of bureaucracy at the other. Our resolve is weakened by a labyrinth of superfluous laws, our common sense is devalued by disproportional risk assessment and elaborate health and safety regulations, our personal responsibility eroded by injury lawyers capitalising on claims for compensation.

Young people can no longer afford a home and few jobs offer security while immigrants deservedly earn as much money from the economy as the tax payer distributes in benefits for the unemployed. Bureaucracy has become a parasite, sucking the life blood from those who do meaningful work, destroying initiative, making redundant those tools with which we are able to compete, anaesthetizing our sense of adventure and ingenuity while squandering the rewards for creative vitality.

The strength of a nation is assured when opportunities and mentors for the young are made available at all levels of society.

A strong foundation in agriculture, manufacturing and all forms of engineering provides a healthy structure for the employment of school leavers, where the results of their endeavours are essential to our every day life and are easily recognisable, where demands on physical and mental ability stretch beyond the government's preoccupation with paperwork, the retail industry, money institutions and get rich quick middle men. Sadly, our foundations are crumbling. We were once infamously described as nothing more than a nation of shopkeepers and we are closer now to that description than ever before. Is it any wonder that so many young people are frustrated and their anger paraded in the open, publicly, before our eyes, an ugly spectacle of increasing disorder and drug abuse in every town and city?'

'Phew!' This was strong stuff. Could his daughter's observations be true? Were things really as bad as that? Wasn't it all a bit over the top? Were there such deep cracks in our society? Was our great country steadily going into decline? Were our politicians institutionalised, out of touch? Mike knew Sarah had political ambitions but this was all a bit doom and gloom. Was she preaching communism, socialism, or some other 'ism, was she a Tory or a Liberal? Mike had no idea but there was no mistaking the evidence of decline. In his lifetime he had witnessed the dismantling of British industry, coal, steel, textiles, shipbuilding, cars, motorcycles, trucks, heavy plant, electrical goods, computors, televisions, radios and many more. All gone. Even the proposed new aircraft carriers, the future pride of the British fleet, might have to be built abroad, or built piecemeal in small yards.

Mike had always voted Conservative, he believed it was better for business, for free enterprise. That was what he believed until Maggie Thatcher came to power. Corrupt unions, demarkation and strikes had brought industry to it's knees and the 'Iron Lady' had tamed them, but she was no visionary and with shopkeeping mentality had forsaken British industry, leaving the patient to die in order to stock our shelves with foreign goods and foreign investments. Mike thought she gained pleasure in punishing the unions, the 'moaning minnies,' and from then on he lost faith in politicians no matter what party. He empathised with the general direction of Sarah's work and certainly, New Horizons was a perfect illustration of how problems among the young had been allowed to fester. He wondered if he could do something about it, make a useful contribution, come up with new ideas for the kids on the streets of Manchester. He'd keep it on the back burner, play around with the idea. First though, love beckoned, he'd made plans for the future and that future included Karen and a proposal of marriage. He wanted to mark the occasion with something worthy of a sweet memory, a place, a time that would remain precious to them for the rest of their lives, a new experience for each of them, a new beginning, free from the intrusions of past happiness. He had studied the brochures and finally settled for a weekend together at an exclusive hotel in the lake district, a blissful escape from the disfunctional pressures of New Horizons Park. There, nestled against a backdrop of dreaming lakes and cosseting hills he would make his proposal of marriage and explain his plans for their future. After the lunch break he worked with a light heart, knowing that in the evening he would be with his new love, confident that his idea of a weekend away together would make her happy. He would make no mention of his intended marriage proposal, all he had to do was arrange a suitable date.

As usual the evening began with flowers and sweet talk before moving on to more serious business, 'Karen, I've been doing a lot of thinking, I mean about us, about you and your family, stuck here in New Horizons Park.'

'Have you love. Me too, I've spent a lot of time thinking about us, thinking about you, how impossible it all is.'

'Impossible? Nothing's impossible love, not for us.' Mike replied, looking a little crestfallen, 'Is it?'

'Mike, I can't understand what you see in me with all my family's goings on, it's asking too much. First there was Ben's involvement with that Patterson boy and that shocking murder, and now the tragic death of his pal Skeet, Marvin Cooney, the coloured lad. You know Mike, he's terribly upset about it and I'm beginning to feel I can't cope with much more. I can't get Skeet's suicide out of my mind, it's so awful, such a waste of a young life. I mean what is Ben getting into, it's his attitude, his behaviour, he doesn't seem to care anymore, about anything, even himself. After he turned down your job offer, I've had my suspicions, I'm sure he's up to no good, I just know there's something underhanded going on, something to do with drugs.'

'Karen love, you ask me what I see in you. Well, for starters I see a beautiful woman, then I see a woman with principals and what's more, a woman with guts who does her best to live by them. I see the girl on the checkout, a woman who deserves to be loved and I'm the lucky guy who loves her.'

'Oh Mike, you're impossibly romantic.'

'I know Ben's a worry Karen, I can't understand him either, he was getting on so well with Josh and was obviously enjoying his new job when he suddenly decided to throw it in, for no real reason, I couldn't make it out, but I still believe he's a good lad at heart, just give him time, he'll come round.'

'I'm sorry Mike, I know you must think I always put my children first and it's not that I don't love you, I do, I've come to love you more than any man I've ever known, but I can't relax knowing that something awful may happen to Ben.'

'Karen love, I understand your worry as a mother, your love for your children, I feel the same about my kids and I'd think a lot less of you if you were any different, but you musn't sacrifice your own happiness for a wayward son, he'll not think any the better of you. I love you Karen and if you'll let me, I want to make your life easier share your problems, so we can face them together.'

'I do appreciate your support Mike, more than you'll ever realise but it's not fair on you, expecting you to shoulder the mess I've made of things. It's all got out of hand, it's gone too far, it's all too much. You once asked me if *you* could love again, now I'm the one with doubts. I'm not sure if *I* can love again, knowing that Ben's always going to cause trouble.'

Mike put his arms round Karen who now seemed close to tears,' Don't take on so Karen love, I know how upset you are. Can't we just go to our favourite pub, have a quiet drink, talk this through. I've a holiday suggestion to make, a surprise, something I hope will cheer you up.'

'I'm sorry Mike for getting so emotional, I can't help it, I feel like weeping buckets, feel myself going to pieces, but I mustn't crack up, I can't afford to. Sorry darling, yes alright, ok, we'll go somewhere where just the two of us can talk, but first I promised Mrs Cooney I'd call round, give her what little comfort I can, she seems in such a dreadful state, I think she may need help of some sort.'

'I take it that she's Skeet's mum, she must be devastated.'

'No she's Skeet's grandmother. Apparently his mum abandoned him when he was quite young and his grandmother's brought him up. I don't know her that well but she phoned begging me to ask Ben to bring Skeet back from Cornwall and that was when your son Josh offered to drive Ben down. It would have been a big problem for Ben and I was very surprised when Josh came forward the way he did. He must get on with Ben or he wouldn't have offered. The Edwards and the Mackays do seem to get on well together don't they?' Karen smiled weakly,

'You're so right Karen, you and me, we're made for one another and I've got a good feeling about Ben, he's not really such a bad lad. Josh is a good judge of character and if I hadn't thought Ben worth an investment, I'd never have offered him a job in the first place. I honestly believe someone has a hold over him, but like you I've no idea who it could be. Changing the subject, where does Mrs Cooney live?'

'Oh she lives on New Horizons, two blocks away on the ground floor.'

'Come on then, we'll both go, see if we can be of any help. And then I thought we might try that new place on the canal, it was an old warehouse and they say it's got loads of atmosphere, bit more up market with no teenage binge drinkers.'

'Sounds lovely.'

In fading daylight they left the building and with approaching darkness an unmistakable yet familiar menace closed in on them. Karen took Mike's arm and held on grimly. She had intended to visit Constance in broad daylight knowing full well that few residents ventured out in New Horizons after dark. Even in Mike's company she felt intimidated, each shadow posed a threat, each brooding alley harboured evil intent. They could so easily decide against visiting Constance, risking the long walk through a no go area and instead take the shorter route where Mike always parked his car, the more quickly to enjoy a relaxed evening in pleasant surroundings.

' Mike I'm worried we might run into a street gang, they're always on the prowl and it's getting late, I think we'll give Constance a miss, I'll give her a ring, make other arrangements, trouble is I'm working tomorrow.'

'No need to be scared love, you'll be alright with me, I'm not letting a bunch of unruly kids dictate what we can do or where we can go. Skeet's gran is calling for help and it seems we're the only ones listening. We'll go and see her just as you promised.'

'Well if you think we'll be ok, but even with you I feel scared Mike. You read about it every day, there's so many of them and they carry weapons you know.'

'I think the whole situation is scandalous. People afraid to leave their homes after dark, creeping around like scared rabbits, it's time something for real was done. It's no good just keep changing the rules, all these cock eyed ideas on paper.'

They were almost there, only another fifty metres, when a gang of hoodies emerged from nowhere. Fuelled by a cocktail of amphetamines and lager beer, they began throwing eggs at the Cooney front door. They were white boys whose behaviour seemed governed by the reptilian complex of their brains, usage of the neocortex having been long abandoned, a sort of reversal in evolutionary terms. One of the gang, after shouting abuse, urinated through the letter box. Another began spraying graffiti over the brickwork while a third heaved a bottle at the window, which shattered, sending shards of glass flying into the room. Constance ran into the kitchen, where she fumbled desperately with her mobile phone.

With no hesitation Mike charged down on the mob and grabbing the bottle thrower by the scruff of the neck, whipped off his hood, debagged him and held him, his ankles pinned in track suit bottoms. 'You don't look so tough now do you son. What the hell do you think you're playing at? I'm making a citizen's arrest.....ugh.'

A heavy blow behind the ear brought Mike to his knees and a Catherine wheel of stars, exploded inside his skull. Mike's head began to clear and he staggered to his feet but a second blow, a knife wound in the back, drove into his ribs, puncturing the lung. Mike collapsed on the pavement coughing up blood, gasping for breath. Then followed a vicious kicking free for all led by the bottle thrower who, incensed by the humiliation of losing his trousers, went beserk, aiming kicks to the head, intent on doing as much damage as possible.

Karen froze, paralysed with fear. It was like watching a Stephen King horror film, evil spirits, jackals gathering for the kill in a desolate landscape. She could feel the wickedness, invasive, crushing her will, sapping her strength and yet her love for Mike overcame that fear, her limbs began to move, dumbly she went forward to face a violent end. She tried to drag away the nearest assailant, but was thrown violently into the gutter. She managed to get on her knees and crawling between threshing legs and flying boots threw herself over Mike's huddled body. 'Stop, stop, oh my God, you'll kill him, stop it,' she screamed. The hoodies tried to drag her off but she hung on screaming at the night, begging for mercy. Mike, still conscious felt her warmth, her body next to his, 'Please Karen, just get out of here, phone the police, you can't reason with these scum,' he winced through gritted teeth.

'I'm not leaving you Mike,' Karen sobbed.

'Ere, that's Ben Mackay's ma innit.'

'Yeah, better leave her alone, that stupid bastard must be her new bloke. E 'int givin us no more trouble, I think we've beat enough shit out of im.'

The hoodies disappeared as quickly as they had arrived, leaving the pair stunned and disorientated with Mike in considerable pain. It had all happened so quickly, it made no sense, it defied all rational thought. The attack had been frenzied, mindless, insane.

Mike struggled to his knees and they knelt facing each other, holding on for dear life. With his shirt covered in blood, his face already swelling beyond recognition, Mike's response to the beating was typical, 'Karen, I know one thing for sure, *you* are some woman. You can't imagine just how much I love you?'

'Mike you've been stabbed, we must get you to hospital, get an ambulance, must get a dressing on that wound. The mobile, it's in my handbag, I can't see it, they must have taken it. I'll see if I can get Constance.' She was still crying.

Having managed to dial 999, Constance huddled in the kitchen like someone caught in an air raid, terrified by the explosion of broken glass and the unearthly noise of a mob on the rampage. When she heard a woman screaming it triggered a small miracle. Constance lived a simple enough life, a natural carer, working for white folks, trying to stay on top of things. She usually only made friends among her own people but Marvin had crossed the cultural barriers of a multi racial society and his close friendship with Ben, a white boy, broke new ground for Constance. She'd been looking forward all day to meeting Ben's Mother and instinctively knew those screams were her cry for help. She'd been the one who needed help and Karen had responded without hesitation. Now the tables were reversed and Constance discovered she also had courage. She was outraged, ashamed of her own fears. She decided to face the enemy. She marched through the hallway in a defiant mood, no longer cowed into submission, quivering, under siege in her own home. She threw off the security chain, opened the front door with force enough to tear it off it's hinges and began screaming a verbal broadside at anyone who might be in range. She stopped suddenly. The hoodies were nowhere to be seen.

'Oh Mrs Cooney, Constance, thank God you're here. Please we must phone for an ambulance, it's very urgent, Mike's been stabbed in the back and he's bleeding horribly.'

'Oh my God, we mus get him inside, get some compression on dat wound, stop awl dat bleedin, I'll done phone right away.'

That night only five people were available to deal with the emergency, the three victims, Mike, Karen and Constance who deserved awards for bravery and the two ambulance paramedics who often faced physical abuse while carrying out their duties. The police response was late, which often was the case with incidents on New Horizons, although they did appear on the same day. They grilled Constance in the manner of dealing with a prime suspect but she was unable to name any of her attackers. In due course they would examine CCTV footage and make a futile appeal for witnesses. All other resources might just as well never existed. Similar acts of gang culture violence, fuelled by drugs and alcohol were regular occurances all over the country. This latest New Horizons assault had almost resulted in a murder and yet lack of information would mean that no charges would be brought against the perpetrators. Nothing it seemed could arrest this growing menace, a truly frightening aspect of our modern society.

Acting the many parts in a comedy of make believe resources, comfortably parked within our numerous community organisations, were legions of hands off operators who masquaraded as workers in the fight against anti social behaviour, their skills in the art of non doing were highly developed, their ability to confine all activities to a production line of computor print outs, shredders and paper recycling depots, without parallel. They could be found among the sweet talking politicians who promised everything and delivered nothing, the piles of inert deadwood in our council departments, government quangos, the busy bodying, office bound social workers and control freaks in the health and saftey executive, to name but a few. Meetings were their excuse to get away from the computor, preferrably during the middle of the morning, when new guidelines could be invented. They were no help when it came to dealing with anti social behaviour or anything else for that matter.

Constance had only ever worked as a cleaner and much of her time had been spent cleaning hospitals. In her work, she always gave more than was required and had aspired to becoming a nurse. Finding herself in the front line, with the injuries of others to think about, fears for her own well being dissolved and her caring manner naturally took charge, giving her the presence of mind to deal with the emergency. She made sure an ambulance was on the way, stressing the need for urgency. She effectively stopped the bleeding and thoroughly cleaned Mike's wounds using a mild anti septic. She wrapped him in a blanket and finally made a pot of tea. Mike and Karen were impressed. In the middle of a life threatening situation they had been saved by a good Samaritan, the very lady who initially was the one who needed help. In these circumstances it was difficult to express sympathies or offer condolences over Marvin's death, but Karen couldn't thank Constance enough for the way she had calmed their nerves and the way she had ministered first aid treatment. In return she offered friendship and support and Mike promised to get something done about the hoodies. He had friends in the police force, friends in high places. They chatted about the everyday problems of living on the high rise estate until twenty minutes later, Mike, labouring for breath, was stretchered into the ambulance, followed by Karen, who still visibly shaken, was trembling with anxiety.

'Mike is going to be all right isn't he?' She asked the paramedic in attendance.

'Yes he's going to be ok.'

'But why is he having so much difficulty breathing?'

'His lung appears to have collapsed. His blood pressure's ok and he's not in shock. He's probably bleeding into the lung cavity, but I don't think he's lost too much blood. When we get him to hospital, they'll drain the cavity, give his lung time to heal. The rest of the damage looks worse than it is, it's mainly superficial. It obviously means a great deal to him, having you near, but try not to let him talk.'

Mike lay there, more bewildered than shocked. He'd been a fool, tackling that gang of hoodie teenagers. He'd underestimated the opposition, their strength in numbers. He'd exposed Karen to danger. How stupid! How irresponsible was that. He wasn't being macho, wasn't being brave, he just hated bullying, all those kids ganging up on Constance, a defenceless woman. What was happening in our society, what failures had given rise to the violence, drug and alcohol abuse among the youth of today. Squinting through bruised eyes, cheeks puffed, face grotesque, Mike looked up at Karen. In the subdued lighting of what seemed like a mobile operating theatre, she shone like a guardian angel. Karen had shown real courage, his precious love, this woman holding his hand, this woman whose beauty ran deep, this woman who had risked everything to save him further punishment, now made his love for her unbearable. A tear ran from the corner of his eye. 'Karen,' he whispered. 'This isn't quite how I'd planned things but..........'

'Please don't talk darling. Not till we've got you to hospital.'

'Karen, I know I'm not exactly the kind of beau you'd find in a woman's magazine but.........'

'No you're not exactly, but you *are* my kind of beau. Now please darling don't have so much to say.'

'Karen, will you marry me?'

'Darling, Are you sure you're ok, I mean your head is quite clear? You've taken an awful beating you know. '

'I've never been more clear about anything in my life.'

'But this would mean spending the rest of our lives together?'

'Well yes, I suppose it would.'

'What a lovely idea.' Karen kissed him tenderly on the forehead. 'Why of course I'd love to marry you Mike, now lets have some hush.'

Chapter 10. The Lady and the Liver Bird.

Tonino Vera enjoyed enormous wealth. Wealth inherited from a Neapolitan family and their dealings with Cosa Nostra, that deeply ingrained criminal sub culture, the Sicilian Mafia. His family had demonstrated enterprise and business acumen in property, especially in the construction of cheap flats for letting in Sicily and around the bay of Naples. They had exercised control over these developments at all levels, the purchase of land, the planning procedures and the actual building operations and were of course the landlords who collected the rents. The business, although relying on corrupt officials, had given the impression of being wholly legitimate and along with many other companies, provided a useful source of money laundering for the Mafia whose initial wealth came from narcotics.

The Mafia is an organisation with one set of rules and one power structure which is clearly understood by its members and whose criminal activities present worrying and significant distortions in the global ecomomy. Things however, in Naples had changed. Organised crime had broken with Sicilian tradition and a Mafia within a Mafia had spread through the city, it's beauty and tourist appeal now blighted by a descent into evil. Naples was perhaps the worst possible example of a European society riddled with violent gang culture. The Neapolitan Camorra, or system as it is known, is an underworld of vicious hoodlums, continually at war with each other, undermining the city's integrity, edging it ever nearer towards the abyss of a dark age. Their business is illegal dealing in weapons, narcotics, toxic waste, fake branded fashions and construction. Reprisal killings and murder are high on the agenda and a Camorrista, or senior gang leader, is lucky to live beyond forty years.

The old Mafia was no longer interested in Naples and Tonino had attended many family meetings whose bosses were looking for new enterprise in Europe. Britain, they had decided was that part of Europe where they were most likely to gain a serious foothold. Italy had born the brunt of English speaking, economic migrants, fleeing from poverty and perscution in Africa to find jobs and a new life in the UK. Smuggling routes across the

Sahara through Libya and the Italian island of Lampedusa were dangerous but well established and many eventually found their way to Britain, a country unable to seal it's borders, with no record of illegal immigrants or control over those who exploited the labyrinth of it's welfare system. Illegal workers also came from India, China and Malaysia and national insurance numbers were ten a penny. The Mafia recognised that immigration out of control created social pressures and an ideal climate for crime and the recruitment of drug dealers. In support of their plans, Britain had further obliged by reducing it's navy, it's coast guard observation services and it's customs and excise officers and the Mafia bosses were especially interested in Britain's new gambling act, which preyed on the vulnerable while encouraging what they considered to be Britain's work shy, get rich quick, criminal underbelly. In order to increase government revenue, the floodgates had been opened for more betting shops, touch screen roulette machines and super casinos. The idea of super casinos had enormous appeal for the investment of Mafia money and visions of recreating a pre-Castro Cuba seemed a distinct possibility.

At his most recent Mafia meeting in Syracuse, Tonino had reported that Britain's prisons were filled to capacity and that in his opinion the judiciary was steadily losing its grip on law and order and that emphasis in Britain had shifted from building a great nation to the pursuit of personal wealth and the price of shares. Moreover he confirmed, the country was awash with alcohol and illegal drugs. The Turks were shipping heroin into Britain through the container port of Felixtowe which on average handled one container a minute. The Russian and Spanish Mafia were smuggling cocaine through Liverpool docks which in a year handled thirty million tons of freight. It was impossible to check even a small percentage of such a huge volume of merchandise and Tonino calculated a very low risk factor and affordable detection. He further revealed secret Home Office figures which quoted an £8 bn a year rake off from drugs dealing by as many as three thousand wholesalers and seventy thousand street dealers and it was decided that the Mafia must have a lion's share of the action. Tonino had a good business brain, he was married to an

English aristocrat, he spoke very good English and was their ideal choice for heading a pilot scheme in Britain, making contacts, exploring the potential of setting up a multi million pound drugs operation, fronted by legitimate business.

Tonino never rushed into anything. He believed in a policy of groundwork and research in order to achieve long term results. Vera Motors had been an established legitimate business for all of five years before he felt ready to make a cocaine deal with the Russians. It had taken that long to employ trusted henchmen and make the right contacts. The operation had worked well, the Mafia bosses were pleased and he was now in a position to expand in other directions. Success depended on his ability to build a good team and within his organisation he had carefully established a criminal hierarchy whose allegiance, although well rewarded, was based on fear. Tonino had no children and that family bond, central to Mafia activities was missing. He now required a right hand man, someone he could trust implicitly, someone young and strong, someone with intelligence and daring, someone close to his heart, someone like a son. Therein lay Tonino's weakness, an Achilles heel for which his formidable suit of armour offered no protection. He had the Italian, innate love of family with its overiding passion for a son who would be an extension of himself, a reflection of his own machismo. Tonino's marriage had been expedient and had opened many doors but his wife had suffered one miscarriage after another and was unable to fullfill his dream.

Tonino had shown Ben Mackay the harsh, uncompromising side of a high ranking Mafiosa, although during their first encounter, underlying, paternal instincts had stirred, promoting thoughts of family and what pride and pleasure a son might have given him. He had taken to the lad and decided to groom him for a life of organised crime, secretly hopeful that Ben would recognise in him a father figure and eventually be his second in command.

Recent events left Ben in turmoil. Each day he thought about Kelly, bombarding her with text messages, unsure of the best way to win her undying love. The death of Marvin had shaken him to the core and he could see that like Marvin, his life thus far had been wasted, an ugly profile which in no way matched his true character. Love and grief now tore at his heart. Equally upsetting was the news that his mother had agreed to marry Mike, a father figure whom he half respected and who now lay in hospital recovering from a stab wound inflicted by youngsters whose names he could name. Should he betray his former gang members? What the hell could he do to redress the balance? Tonino Vera his employer, a man always unavailable, unapproachable, a man who lived in shadows, had summoned him to a private meeting and against his will he felt obliged to keep the appointment. He guessed it was something serious. He was scared. Had he done something wrong? Nervously he presented himself at the reception. Once more the girl with the shapely legs led the way to Tonino's office, but this time there was no feel good factor.

'Ah Ben, come in come in.' Tonino said, placing an arm around Ben's shoulders, then offering a chair facing the desk. His face broke into a wide grin as though relieved and glad to see him. 'You ok Ben?'

'Yeah, I spose so.' Ben bravely decided to speak his mind, 'Look Mr Vera, I've bin thinkin.'

'You been thinking Ben? What have you been thinking?'

'Well I bin thinkin, I don't really want to deal in drugs anymore.'

'You don't want to deal in drugs! What d'you mean you don't want to deal in drugs. You've been street dealing in drugs since you were out of diapers.'

'I know, but I just bin to my mate's funeral, Marvin. Drugs sent him crazy. He threw himself off a church tower an I know it was drugs what killed him.'

There was a long silence. Tonino leaned back in his chair and lit a cigar. He carefully studied Ben's face. He blew smoke at the ceiling, he opened a drawer in his desk and drew out a package, his manner changed, his voice softened, 'Here's five hundred in cash and I've put another two grand in Meg's account for you. That's for doing such a good job on your last pick up. Ben, I'm impressed.'

'Cor! Mr Vera, two grand, I wasn't expectin that sort of money, I don't know what to say.'

'Listen Ben, you need to get you're head straight. Taking drugs is a recreational pastime, no different to smoking, gambling and drinking. Over do it and you'll screw yourself. Tobacco and booze cause more disease and death than cannabis or cocaine ever could. Costs the NHS a fortune and yet the government is happy to allow double standards. You can see it every night on telly, one minute there's a NHS health warning on the dangers of smoking and a help line for those who want to give it up, next you'll get a couple of dramas where everyone is smoking like there's no tomorrow. Dramas put out the stronger message wouldn't you say? We all know the government makes millions out of gambling, tobacco and alcohol, it helps pay their salaries and expenses, jobs for the boys, it's just good business sense and there's no way they'll be giving up this great little earner, whatever the casualties. It's just trade Ben, giving folks what they want, helping em relax, letting em have some fun.'

'The way Marvin died wasn't fun, he was livin in hell.'

'Dying with lung cancer ain't fun, being alcoholic ain't fun, its just people being weak and irresponsible. That's the way life is, it ain't fun, its dog eat dog, but that doesn't mean you can't make a few extra bucks. That's what it's about for all God's children, making a few extra bucks, getting some sort of life. Ever read history books Ben?'

'No I was expelled from school, they could do nothin with me cos I never listened, but I'm listenin now Mr Vera, listenin to every word.'

'Its no different now to when Britain traded opium for goods made in China, back in the 1800's. The Brits drove up China's addiction until it reached dangerous levels and with their superior forces, nicked Hong Kong and made sure the trade continued. Of course now, Britain's hasn't got the military clout but it's pretty damn good when it comes to financial wheeler dealing. I wouldn't lose any sleep over it Ben if I was you. That two grand's only the beginning, stick by me and there'll be more, lots more, more than you can imagine.'

'I can see what you're sayin, it makes sense, but sposin I get caught?'

'You won't get caught Ben, not if you follow my instructions to the letter, and even if you did, you'd only get a short sentence and don't worry, I'd make sure the returns were well worth some time out in jail. I don't want to have to threaten you Ben, not like when we first met. I want us to get on well together, I want you to trust me, trust me like I was your own father.'

Five hundred pounds in ten pound notes was more cash than Ben had ever had in his immediate possession. He fingered the thickness of the brown envelope. It felt very good, very promising. Swayed by Tonino's confidence, his manner and style amid an ambience of wealth and good taste, he visibly relaxed, shifting his weight from the edge of the chair. Excited by the prospect of spending money, he thought of the two grand Meg held in trust with the promise of more to follow. He was special, he was valued and he belonged. 'When's the next run?' he asked.

'Next week, same place, Hareden Hall. I'll let you know the exact time. This one's a much bigger consignment, one hundred kilos of pure cocaine, and you'll drive a Ducato, one with secret compartments in the rear, behind the fitted shelves. The shelves are stocked with small parts and fixings but the whole thing dismantles quite cleverly, giving access to the space behind. The coke this time is in one kilo packs, not in tins, so be very careful how you drive. On your first trip the weight of cocaine was close enough to the weight of celulose to give you extra cover, but this time, if you end up on a weigh bridge, even if you're within your axle load, an inspector might be bright enough to realise there's unexplained additional weight which might prompt a search. For this reason you'll be given a safer route for the return journey. There's nothing to worry about, spot checks on goods vehicles are few and far between, it's just an extra precaution. I'm pleased to say Ben, considering your record, your driving is immaculate. This consignment will be worth twelve million on the street, so keep it that way, capiche? Same instuctions as before, with an extra three panel deliveries in Liverpool. Now Ben, something more. After work tomorrow, I think you're ready for some elocution lessons, change that lazy street talk, stop dropping your G's and T's and try pronouncing a few vowels.'

'Ok, Mr Vera, if you say, but I can't see nothin wrong with how I'm talkin.'

'And you can drop the Mr Vera stuff, call me Tony. If your going to be a car salesman in my showroom, I don't want you sounding like some uneducated, smart arse kid off the street. You've got to give people confidence, handle deals, work out hire purchase details, make a good impression. Being a main dealer's a bit different to selling bangers on a car lot. You see Ben, I believe in a bit of class as well as a bit of savvy.'

'Cor! Tony, you mean you're givin me a job in the showroom?'

'Yes, when you're ready Ben. You're an intelligent, sensitive kid, not too reckless, bit nervous, but cool with plenty of guts, bit like your mama, and you've shown me a few leadership qualities. I happen to know you've got a good mama Ben, a bad father maybe, but a good mama. Believe me, family means everything, having parents who are always there for you. Anyway whatever, so far, I like what I see and I might have plans for you Ben, big plans. Please don't disappoint me.'

'Me, workin in the showroom, sellin new cars, cor! That would be absolutely brill, I can't wait. Give me a chance like that and there's no way I'll let you down Tony, you'll see.'

'Ok, now here's my home address, get yourself there tomorrow evening, round about seven. I won't be there but my wife Letitia will be and she'll help you with your speech. My wife has class, her diction is perfect, she's an English aristocrat, a Lady, she was Lady Hamelton before I married her. Call there tomorrow evening and introduce yourself, see how you get on, she'll be expecting you. Oh, and don't discuss any business with her. I never discuss business with my wife, ever, capiche.'

'Ok Mr Vera, er Tony, I'll be there.'

'Ok Ben, now report back to the spares department there's a delivery waiting for you. Oh and Ben, you can take the Quattro for elocution, but after seeing Letitia I want it back on the forecourt, I don't want you swanking around with you're mates having it end up on New Horizons, take a taxi home, capiche?

This last minute invitation from Tonino was a clever and most powerful seduction. For most young men, sports cars represent all the positive things in life, beautiful girls, beautiful bodies, beautiful wealth, beautiful energy, beautiful freedom, beautiful everything. Driving out of the city, mesmerised by performance, luxuriating in pristine comfort and intoxicated by the smell of soft leather, Ben had a glimpse of what life might have to offer. He decided this was what he wanted, all those things which on New Horizons Park, seemed unattainable. Here was a chance to make it. Confident that at last he was on the right track, he resolved to keep going, unable to see that he was heading down a one way street, a street leading only to disaster.

Tonino's English residence was a large modern house of individual design set in a quiet cul de sac with four other properties in half acre plots not far from Manchester airport. They were occupied by the families of international businessmen who commuted abroad, mostly high performing sales executives, dedicated company men whose application to work no one doubted. This fast lane, middle management profile suited Tonino Vera's needs and within the community he was considered to be a valuable tax paying asset.

Ben drove quietly past the heavy, wrought iron gates, left permanently open, giving an impression of welcome and transparency. After a light fall of rain, the brindled paviors of a large parking area glistened in the headlights and he parked sensibly, keeping clear of the double garage door. Ben had dressed well for the occasion and had invested in a pair of leather shoes which were rather uncomfortable. Even so he felt out of place, sneaking almost, trespassing on hallowed ground where in due course he would be called upon to explain his presence. With some reluctance, he walked slowly to the porch and rang the bell. A Philipino maid answered the door, and without asking for details, invited him to step inside.'If you will follow me please, Mrs Vera will see you in the sitting room.'

154

Mrs Vera stood before him, composed, haughty and unsmiling. She appeared to be looking down her nose. She had the grooming, the high forehead, the fine features and carriage of noble birth, that special bearing of someone whose demeanour is unchanged whatever their circumstances. Tax and the mismanagement of land had impoverished the Hamelton's family estate and Letitia had fallen upon hard times. Before the final reckoning, in order to prolong the illusion of well being and maintain the status quo, she had taken advantage of a holiday with friends in Naples, where the charms of a handsome Italian offered a convenient solution to her problems. Tonino had rescued her from poverty, could afford the lavish lifestyle to which she had been accustomed and restore the trappings of wealth and privilege which she had always known was her God given right. Outwardly she bore all things with equanimity, but inwardly she knew she had betrayed the principles of those who feel they are born to rule. 'I presume you are Mr Benjamin Mackay. Mr Vera seems to think your natural abilities are worthy of some refinement and I must say, unlike some candidates, your outward appearance at least is tolerable. Mr Vera is convinced that one only has to associate with good breeding and the mystique of upper class will rub off. Poor deluded man. However, we will endeavour to disguise the fact that your present standards were aquired from parents who live in the gutter and I do so hope the learning experience is not too painful for youh. Please sit down, I want you to read something for me. I take it you're able read?''

Ben had never understood the importance of education. Science, History, Languages, Literature, all those subjects which meant preoccupation with books, periods of confinement and the imposition of discipline. To him it represented the frittering away of uninhibited youth and he was convinced that learning of this sort made no difference to survival on the street. The prospect of being schooled by a lady of noble birth, someone who appeared to have arrived from a different planet, an aristocrat showing no trace of humility, who would always talk down to him, unable even to recognised him as a fellow human being, filled him with dismay. The lady in question now stood before him, dressed in a tailored jacket, an ankle length jersey skirt and a bright chiffon scarf, all beautifully assembled with impeccable taste. She spoke with arrogance, pronouncing vowels in a way that made Ben feel distinctly inferior, leaving him lost for words. After an embarrassing pause Ben finally engaged in conversation. 'I wasn't bred in the gutter missus. My mum is an amazin woman, super cool and brave with it. She's worked all her life as a single mum to raise three kids, an her standards are far higher than yours. Matter of fact she's a better woman than you could ever be. Your just a stuck up snob. You might speak posh, like you've got a mouth full of plums but I int fooled one little bit. You've never had to work for a living, you just ponce around posin. An by the way my name int Benjamin, it's Ben. 'Ben could hardly believe what he was saying and regretted it instantly. He wondered whether he had gone too far. She had made him angry and he had over reacted. Perhaps he should make an apology.

Letitia, unruffled, looked directly into Ben's eyes. This handsome looking boy was another of Tonino's proteges which meant he was nothing more than a small time crook, streetwise, perceptive, but possibly mean and vicious and yet he was defending his mother, saying she had high standards. She sensed a breakdown of Ben's relationship with his mother. 'I am impressed Ben. I like the way you stand up for your mother. You must love and respect her deeply. She is very lucky to have such a champion for a son and I'm sure she is very proud of youh.'

Ben lowered his eyes. 'Mum loves me I spose, but she int proud of me. She's proud of Matt and Katrina, my brother an sister, but she says I broke her heart. I was expelled from school an I've bin runnin with gangs and stuff. Only thing I got is an Asbo. Look missus, I'm really sorry about what I said, shootin my mouth off, I mean I don't really know what you're like do I? I mean all that la di la stuff you hide behind.'

Letitia gracefully lowered herself into an arm chair, 'Please sit down Ben, you're rather tall and I can't have *you* looking down at *me* can I? It seems neither of us like being looked down on. Ben I accept your apology, although I suspect it was forthcoming because you're afraid of what Tonino will do when I explain to him how you came here for help and chose to insult me.' Letitia understood the meaning of fear and for a fleeting second it betrayed Ben's composure, alarm weakened those bright eyes, the vigour of youth visibly sagged.

'I int afraid of Tonino.' Ben stammered.

'Ben, are you fool enough to be so brave? I don't think so. Have no fear, your outburst can be our little secret. It is true that you don't really know me and you can never appreciate what I have suffered at the hands of my dear husband, but as you so rightly observed, I behaved like a stuck up snob, I forgot my manners and it was I who first insulted you. Your reposte made me realise there is something about you more worthy of consideration. I want you to listen carefully, I want you to understand how easily one's life can lead to damnation. In a curious way I found your brutal response honest and refreshing, you treated me as an equal and compared with your mother, a lesser individual. You see, I recognise that I have wasted my life. When I was young, it never occured to me that I should make my own way in the world, I suppose it was my upbringing, and unwittingly I married an Italian mobster in order to continue living the sweet life. I have lived in fear ever since. I have suffered physical abuse, death threats and male chauvenism in its most obscene form and I am hopelessly trapped in a criminal underworld with no means of escape. My reward for staying silent and living a lie is occasional pampering, red roses, pink champagne, living in luxury. You said I act posh, la di la, well, it is true and it is all I have, all I have to offer, an ugly posturing charade, a performance of denial sustained by heroin addiction. You Ben, recognise me for what I am and have found the courage to offer me a mirror in which I clearly see my own reflection.'

'I honestly didn't mean to upset you, I spose I really jus feel guilty about my mum and took it out on you. No, I was wrong about you, you are a Lady, still got class, whatever you say about yourself, you're a real, genuine Lady an I want you to learn me proper English if you can find the time.'

'I am ashamed Ben to use my title, I am no longer a Lady and you may call me Letitia. I shall be happy to *teach* you English Ben, not learn you English. You are the one who will be learning.'

'Well I think you're a Lady, Lady Letitia, a titled Lady, you're too honest about yourself to be a snob. Ok *teach* me.

Please! Tonino said I sound like some smart arse kid off the street an I don't want to sound like that anymore. I want to go places.'

'You do realise Ben that you are heading in precisely the same direction as myself, lured on by thoughts of easy money, money made at the expense of other people's misery, criminal money?'

'Tonino said it was givin people what they want, gamblin, drugs and stuff.'

'Ben, if you continue in this direction, you will destroy yourself and it is no exaggeration to say that you are on the road to hell.'

'It's not jus the money, I like the risk, the adventure, the buzz.'

'All that will soon lose it's appeal. You cannot live your life with total disregard for the rest of humanity. In the criminal underworld, there is more ugliness than beauty, more greed than generosity, more hate than love. You must first live your life in pursuit of that which is spiritually beautiful. It is not the pursuit of money which brings happiness. Have you ever fallen in love Ben?'

'Well er, yes. I'm totally in love, in love with a girl at Liverpool uni but I'm not sure she loves me. If I can earn loads of money, she might take more notice of me an I could impress her, show her some good times.'

'Ben, you are being drawn into a life of violence, murder, drug traffiking, extortion and prostitution, the causes of so much human suffering, a life consumed by greed, a life given to lying and deceit. This is not the way to win your love.'

'Surely it int that bad is it?

'No it's not that bad, it's much, much worse. Ben, please listen to what I am saying, I have a proposition for you. I shall be more than pleased to help raise your social standards, but you must promise me something.'

'Promise something?'

'You must promise me that you will give up your association with Tonino as soon as possible. I don't know how envolved you are, but you must get out before it is too late.'

'It's not goin to be that easy, I'm in quite deep and he *has* threatened me. I'm not sure if he was really serious but when I first met him he more or less said I would disappear if I crossed im. He was ok the last time we met. He arranged for me to see you and let me drive the Quattro, matter of fact he treated me more like his son.'

'Oh! he was serious, believe me, he was really serious. This is worse than I thought. When his paternal instincts are aroused the situation becomes even more volatile. I was unable to give him children and he so much wanted a son.' Letitia bit her lip, 'this is going to be difficult but I am determined that you shall be rescued from his clutches. I need time. I must give the situation a great deal of thought,'

'Please don't take any risks over me. Honest, I can look after myself.'

'Ben, you may visit me each week on this same day at the same time and I look forward to helping you improve your speech. In addition, we can explore the world of literature and I'll make arrangements for us to enjoy a late supper. I've decided to begin our reading sessions with a great classical work and I've chosen a book by the Russian author Fyodor Dostoevsky, Crime and Punishment. We'll read it chapter by chapter, discussing it's merits as we go. It is a long book and will give us plenty of time in which to make our plans.'

Euro Express Car Parts and Vera Bodyworks were housed in two adjacent factory units located on the same industrial site as Mike Edwards Joinery. Each Vera enterprise had a good reputation for quality workmanship and excellent service. The parts and accessories franchise ran two Fiat Ducato vans which were permanently based and serviced on the premises. The units were divided by mezzanine floors which provided extra storage space. The upper floor of the bodywork shop had been partitioned to form a narrow corridor, one and a half metres in width, across the entire rear end of the main building and it was in this well ventilated area that covert drug processing, packaging and the manufacture of ectasy pills took place. This shortening of the upper floor, in a building of considerable length, where passages between the system shelving made it appear even longer, presented an optical illusion. The space at the rear had no windows or doors and was accessed through a removable panel in the ceiling of the ground floor. The two businesses were managed by Tonino's nephew, Roberto Vera and his imported Russian bride Nadya, introduced as a matter of convenience by the accommodating Viktor Ivanovich of Hareden Hall. Nadya was a comfortable, well rounded woman, a voluptuous little package, whose wide hips, ample bosom and slim waistline, projected an hour glass figure. Roberto was not a tall man and the fact that she hardly reached his shoulder in high heels was altogether to his liking.

They enjoyed each others company and were always laughing and Roberto called her his Russian dumpling. Nadya could speak only a smattering of English and Italian, but Viktor had chosen Roberto's bride with care. She could count. In fact she could count very well indeed. She understood balance sheets, profit and loss accounts and for the legitimate side of the business, her book keeping was immaculate. Her real talent however, was the way she recorded the complicated transactions and money cleaning activities of the drug dealing side of the business. She was used to exchange rates in pounds sterling, euros, Colombian pesos, Russian roubles and Swiss francs. No transaction escaped her scrutiny and the Italian Mafia relied on her records for accurate information relating to their deals in Britain.

Ben made his way to the familiar industrial estate and reported to Roberto for details concerning his next collection. He was introduced to Nadya and the rest of the staff but nowhere in the entire building was there any sign of drug handling or any clue as to where the packaging and processing took place and he was given no information about the secret room above the bodywork shop. He was impressed by the whole set up. It was hard to believe that behind this legitimate, well equiped, well maintained, thoroughly professional organisation, there lay a huge drugs operation. He collected the Ducato along with items for delivery and the necessary paper work and left early, hoping to avoid the heavy traffic on the M62. Driving the Ducato was a dream, the cab section, elevated much higher than a car, gave him a feeling of being in command, of looking down on lesser mortals. He was riding high, riding on a cloud of glowing expectation as thoughts centred on his arranged meeting with Kelly in Liverpool. Text messages had ricocheted back and forth, their seductions multiplied in a stream of abreviations, breathless promises, mounting passions and undying love, further intensified by their separation and the heat of their first encounter. On the strength of this electronic romance and the virtual mind games it projected, Ben had spent most of his money on a piece of jewelry and a bouquet of flowers. The idealisation of love had awakened the need for giving rather than taking and the flowers were carefully wrapped in a reservoir of damp cloth and the necklace, chosen after much searching and deliberation, would add emotional drama, cementing their relationship, when the time came for him to leave.

Ben made his deliveries like a bird on the wing, arriving in Liverpool with time enough in which to express his ardour and renew his courtship, before continuing on to Hareden Hall for the main purpose of his mission. He had arranged to meet Kelly outside the university art gallery in Oxford Street and when she appeared his heart summersaulted for sheer joy. He ran to meet her, embracing her, kissing her before offering the flowers with boyish enthusiasm. 'Kelly! You're lookin cool, jus beauiful, like a model or somethin. Meetin you here is like we're film stars on a Hollywood set. You're some babe Kelly, I can't stop thinkin about you, I've bin thinkin about you ever since we first met. Hope you like the flowers.' Ben was disappointed, there had been a lack of reponse to his first greeting, it's spontaneous embrace, the hungry kiss.

Kelly appeared flustered and embarrassed. 'Yes the flowers are lovely but I can't go carrying them around all morning. We'd better go to my lodgings in Toxteth, get them in water, I've got a room in a house there along with some other students, but we've got to talk Ben, I need some answers, answers to some serious questions.'

Kelly climbed into the van and following her directions, Ben headed out for the Toxteth area. She lived in a run down terrace house, owned by an unscrupulous landlord who owned similar properties in the area, letting them exclusively to students who accepted the living conditions and were too preoccupied with studying in the close proximity of boy meets girl interactions to complain about the disrepair and grotty furniture. He never carried out any serious maintenance and made a rich living from student grants. Ben was quite shocked by the state of the place which seemed to be occupied by animals rather than some of the nation's highest school achievers. Kelly found a suitable container in the kitchen for the flowers and much to Ben's disapproval, placed them on a table in the communal area for all the students to enjoy. They made their way up the stairs where Kelly shared cramped quarters with another girl in the loft conversion. There were no chairs and they sat on the bed. 'Ben,' Kelly began, 'How well do you know my mother?'

Ben, stunned by a question that set alarm bells ringing, chose to waffle,

'Your mum? Er, I'm not sure what you mean, I mean how can I know her, I've never even met her.'

' You're lying to me Ben. When we met at Hareden Hall, you gave me you're phone number, not your home address and you've never made contact through my mother as I suggested. It so happens I rang her a couple of days ago and I mentioned your name. I said you were my new boy friend and how much I liked you. She was shocked. She said you lived on New Horizons Park and she knew you all too well. She didn't paint a very pretty picture and begged me to have nothing more to do with you.'

There was an awkward silence between them. Ben groaned inwardly, 'Ok. I'm really sorry I lied, but I only knew you're mum in passing. It's true, I used to have a bad reputation but honestly, I've changed, I've given up runnin with gangs and stuff. Now I want to make somethin of myself.'

'Mother said you were dangerous, a drug dealer, and I know you're lying.'

'Now hang on a minute Kelly. How well do *you* know you're mum? You made out she was hard working, made big sacrifices.' Ben hesitated, he had no wish to hurt Kelly's feelings with some awful revelation, 'I mean what was she like, when you were a kid, when you were growin up?'

'Kelly shook her pretty head, the blonde curls fell across her face, 'I'm not prepared to say,' she answered, looking vulnerable. Ben yearned for her, longed to take her in his arms, comfort her, carress her.

'I love you Kelly, I love you so much, I'd do anything for you, anything to make you love me.'

'Would you Ben, would you really? My mother was a prostitute, a call girl, then one day she slept with an Italian crook and became his mistress. I never met this Italian guy and have no idea who he is but I know she's trapped by her association with him. I know there's violence in her life and I know she's mixed up in a drug dealing racket but she's always tried to protect me from the darker side of her life, giving me the benefit of the risks she's taken, making sure I don't go down the same path. She's been a good mother, she could so easily have rejected me at birth but she chose to raise me in the most awful circumstances, against all the odds, and she's given me nothing but love and although her lifestyle disgusts me, I love her dearly. I'm only telling you the facts because you already know them. She says she's having an affair with you, enjoying your young body. You spend most your spare time at her flat and you're just one of her many street dealers.'

Faced with such exposure, stripped bare of pretence, Ben trembled like a lost soul on the day of judgement. Hopes and dreams lay in ruins, his world had collapsed. 'I love only you Kelly,' he whispered.

'No, you don't love me Ben, you love yourself. Our text messages held only the promise of love. We were considering our own needs, seeing what we wanted to see, hearing what we wanted to hear, we weren't searching for each other, listening to each other's hearts. You scare me Ben, living a life without scruples for the sake of money. You build only stumbling blocks for others. When you first asked me what I wanted to do with my life, I said I wanted to build bridges and I wanted to build a highway into your heart, but I see you now for what you are.

Sending me text messages of love while you were sleeping with my own mother made them worthless. You're one of life's scavengers, taking what you want wherever you can, whatever is on offer, with only thoughts of satisfying your own appetite. I could never love a man who is unable to give of himself, has nothing to offer mankind, someone who steals from life and gives nothing back. Now please, I want you to leave, go back to you're lover and never, ever communicate with me again.' Kelly led the way down stairs, showing Ben the front door, closing it in an act of dismissal as though getting rid of garbage. She ran up the stairs, back to her room, where she threw herself on the bed, burying her head in the pillows, trying to smother the sobs.

Ben walked to the van in a state of shock. Numbly he drove instinctively, feeling unbelievably wretched, unable to register what was going on around him, wanting to scream obscenities at the world. Soon his anger gave way to deep sorrow and tears, unsolicited, ran down his cheeks.

Chapter 11 The Ways of the World

The wisdom that comes with maturity helps us deal with rejection in a philosophical manner and it may be personally instructive, but for youngsters it is more deeply felt and can be devastating or even destructive, especially in young relationships when overtures of love are so easily cast aside. A cruel dismissal will shatter the fragile self confidence of youth, the naive belief that the world is waiting for what young people have to offer, the fresh bloom, the rapturous sex appeal. Rejection inevitably leads to self reappraisal and Ben, suffering inwardly, his mind still reeling from Kelly's dreadful insight and her ruthless character assassination, consciously replayed their last moments together, his brain rewinding a mental tape recorder, again and again, listening, analysing the replay, hoping to discover a new angle, a different interpretation, which might offer a reprieve and an excuse for an argument in his defence.

All day his mind had been preoccupied with self searching. Tonino's praises for a job done so professionally meant nothing to him and when evening came, he found himself in the familiar territory of New Horizons making for his mother's flat. He was a child again, he was ready to confide in her, seeking his mother's comfort, her understanding, her reassurances and her love. The warnings from Letitia, a woman who had suffered first hand from the evils of organised crime and the repugnance Kelly had shown for his lifestyle had given him a glimpse of how the world perceived his ambitions. He now considered how he might escape from the life he had chosen and the awful consequences which threatened if he dared betray Tonino's trust. Bravado had given way to deep seated fear and he was ready now for an outpouring of all those things which he knew would destroy him. His mother would listen to him, share in his misgivings, offer consolation for his emotional turmoil, teach him how to win back his love and set him on the right path. He had lost his key to the flat and knocked sheepishly on the door.

Katrina opened the door, somewhat shocked by Ben's appearance, his out of character grooming and dress sense, the high necked shirt collar, the figure hugging cardigan, neatly tucked into stylish jeans, it's horizontal stripes setting off Ben's broad shoulders, and the heavy buckle of an Italian leather belt. She immediately sensed a shared tension between them, 'Oh it's you,' she said, without enthusiasm, searching the tired but familiar, handsome face, 'mum, Ben's here,'she called through to the kitchen.

Showing some impatience and ignoring Katrina, Ben brushed past her, certain that he would receive his mother's undivided attention. Once inside the flat he realised that he was interrupting something and should have rung first. His mother, Matt and Katrina were busying themselves getting ready to leave. It seemed to him they were setting out on a very important mission. 'Hiya mum, wonder if we might have a little chat, I mean just the two of us, there's somethin important I want to say, about what's been going on.'

'Ben darling, I'm so glad you're here, we're just off to see Mike in hospital and now we can all go together as a family. He'll be so pleased to see you, he's always asking about you and we've all been wondering what exactly is going on and why you left your job at Mike's joinery. It was such a marvellous opportunity and Mike said how much promise you showed and how well you got on with Josh, we're all baffled why you left so suddenly. Anyway we can talk about these things in hospital, we'll go in my car, it'll be a bit of a squash but I'm sure we'll manage.'

'Oh, er, you're off to visit Mike, in hospital. How is he?' Ben felt obliged to acknowledge the fact that he understood the circumstances.

'He's doing very well, we're hoping he'll be home for the weekend. Ben darling, we haven't time now for a chat and think I know what it is you want to talk about, you want to give me the names of those hoodlums who were making life hell for Constance, who attacked us and knifed Mike in the back. Well, I'm determined to see them arrested and you can give me their details later. I'm proud of you Ben for offering to come forward, I know how difficult it must have been.'

' Sorry, I seem to have come at the wrong time, caught you when you were all goin out, when you've obviously got more important things to do than waste time with me. I can't see Mike

166

right now cos I got more important things to do as well. Anyway, I didn't come here to give you the names of those kids. I wanted to talk about something else, something that affects me, there was lots I wanted to say, but it don't matter, not now.'

'But surely you can find time to visit Mike in hospital. I know it will mean a lot to him. He so wants us to be part of his family and I want it too, now that we're getting married. Please Ben, come with us, please come, if not for Mike, but for my sake. I can't understand why you see Mike as such a threat. You know very well, I love you as much as any mother loves her son, and you must know I'll do anything for you, I'll always be there for you Ben, whenever, and for whatever reason. Please don't come between Mike and myself, please let me have some happiness. I'm sure one day you'll find love and then maybe you'll understand.' Karen paused, struggling to maintain her composure, 'Mike has offered you nothing but friendship and a wonderful opportunity, surely at least you can show him you care.'

Karen's undivided concern for Mike's welfare gave the impression that other family troubles were of secondry importance and that treatment for Ben's wounds would have to wait. Ben had been ready to reach out to his mother, make amends for the damage he had done to their relationship, thereby winning her approval and esteem. Now, crushed emotions gave way to rising anger. 'Well that's just it, I don't care see. What you and your boy friend decide to do is nothing to do with me, leave me out of it. I've got my own plans.' Ben, suffering further rejection, abruptly turned his back on her and before slamming the front door, shouted back, 'And another thing, I int shopping my mates for Mike, you or anyone else.'

He ran down the stairs at an alarming rate, choking back unwanted tears, cursing himself for every word he had said. Why had he reacted with so much anger against his mother, why couldn't he show her the respect she deserved, when all the time he loved her so much? Why had he said he didn't care when in reality he had discovered that loving someone meant caring, caring more than pride would allow him to admit?

167

Ben had only one other bolt hole, a warm, titillating retreat with it's little luxuries and it's sensual boudoir, an hedonistic sanctuary in the jungle of New horizons and a den of iniquity, Meg's place. But here there would be serious issues. Meg knew about his professed love for her daughter and the outcome of their meeting in Liverpool. How was she going to react? On what terms would she now receive him? His driving license was in her safe keeping together with a substantial sum of money held in trust. Ben wondered whether he could re-kindle his former passion and hoped that recent events would not lead inevitably to further rejection.

Nervously, and a little breathless after using the stairs, he reached the highest level of the block and presented himself outside the flat, hoping that she would be there and the whole complicated love triangle could be sorted out as quickly as possible with no change in their feelings for each other and no recriminations. Meg answered the door. Meg had the figure of a woman who could wear anything, however cheap, however unpretentious and still look very good. She wore a short skirt with a simple blouse and her legs were shapely even though her tiny feet were clad in slippers. She looked alluring as ever. She smiled sweetly at Ben, and leaving the door wide open, without saying a word, led him into the lounge.

'Ben ye look all stressed oot. Ah cannae remember ever seein you in such a state. Would you like a beer or somthin?'

'Thanks Meg, I really jus wanted to talk, sort things out between us.'

'Ben, dinnae feelin sorry for yersel, just cos mah lassie turned you down. You were never really in love wi her, it was all jus textin, jus infatuation. She's not your type, she's more interested in lads wi a profession in mind.'

'No way is it infatuation Meg, I've fallen for Kelly in a big way. She's the best thing that's ever happened to me and honestly Meg, I would do anything to get her back. I appreciate everythin you've done for me, and I'll always care for you Meg, but with Kelly, I could have made something of myself, instead of jus bein a crook, and let's face it, that's all I am, jus like she said, jus like you told her.'

'Ben, now listen tae me, face up tae facts. Ah had to tell her. Ah didnae do it jus to get you tae masel, I did it for her. Believe me, Ah've had to make much bigger sacrifices for her than risk losing a lover. Ah'm no lettin her get mixed up wi Tonino and his set up and that's where it would lead if she took up wi you.'

'I think we could've made it together, given a chance.'

'Nae Ben, you've already made your choice. You want tae get rich quick, you want tae live like a lord, wi a silver spoon in his mouth wi all the trimmings and nae havin tae graft. You dinnae want hard work, you want it easy, all the way, and now like me, you're in too deep. You think you could change, but you couldnae. To some extent Ah blame mahsel, Ah shouldnae had lead you on.'

'I could change Meg, I could change for your daughter. I never wanted to be a criminal. I know it's not you're fault and you're right, it was the money. When I see how hard my mum's had to work, what a struggle she had jus lookin after us, I thought it was smart dealin in drugs, thought I could show off to my mates, throw my weight around, beat the system.'

You cannae beat the system, no matter which side o the law you're on. You've turned your back on the established system only to join another, a system o organised crime, and they're both driven by greed, money, power and privilege and each system has it's own methods of dealin with anyone who is a threat to it's security, both equally violent and both equally terminal. I dinnae think you realise who you're dealin with and how big this drugs operation is.'

'I beginnin to, I'm certain it's run by the Italian Mafia and I'm tellin you Meg, I feel scared.'

The pinched anxiety, plainly visible on Ben's face, for a brief moment, softened Meg's heart. The smiling, laughing optimism of her young boyfriend had been drowned in a deluge of disappointment and regret. 'Ben, Ah know Ah'm old enough tae be your mother, but for all that, men still find me attractive and If Ah'd wanted a new man in my life, a new relationship, Ah'd have nae problem, but I didnae want that, I've been hurt too much and now, Ah value mah independence far more. Wi you though, it's different, you make me feel ten years younger and Ah fancy you. We're jus made for each other Ben, you and me, and I ken we'd make a good lookin pair if we went oot together. You must still love me Ben or you wouldnae be here.' In his pocket, Ben held the presentation box containing the necklace he had bought for Kelly and his mind began to wander, he looked vacant. 'You do love me Ben?……Just a wee bit?'

'You're beautiful Meg but loving you is scary.'

'Ah realise sooner or later, you'll want a younger woman and maybe a few bairns and Ah won't ever stand in you're way, Ah'm not a jealous or possessive sort. We're good together and Ah think we should hit the good times while we can. Tonino thinks a lot of you and if you study him you'll go places, live the good life, nae graft, wi bags o money, richer than you can imagine, fine houses wi swimmin pools and fast cars.' Meg put her arms around Ben's neck, kissing him dreamily on the cheek, folding the soft, warm contours of her body into his, 'Lets have a wee toot, open a bottle of Moet and plan our holiday together. Next weekend, your goin to Naples, crewin mah powerboat on a drugs run. Dinnae worry, there's nae risk whatsoever, it's all carefully set up wi the authorities. For a couple o weeks we'll have mah flat all to oursels, our own little love nest and while you're fallin in love wi Italy, you'll fall in love wi me, all o'er agen.' She thrust her hips against him, her eyes under long lashes fixing his, fluttering their promise.

Ben was already aroused, intoxicated, unable to deny her siren pleasures, the whispering charms of a woman whose sensuality sent him flying among the clouds which billowed around the heights of New Horizons Park. He lifted her off her feet, and kissing her lips until they were breathless, carried her into the bedroom.

Letitia had chosen Dostoevsky's Crime and Punishment because she hoped the work would not only improve Ben's speech but would give him some insight into human behaviour. In the words of a Russian critic, who tried to explain the feelings

170

inspired by Dostoevsky, 'Fyodor was one of ourselves, a man who had suffered more deeply and we are profoundly impressed by his wisdom, the wisdom of the heart which we seek that we may learn how to live.' However, she soon realised that her version of the translation was unsuitable. Ben lacked the patience required to absorb the faultless grammar and the Russian names, whose pronunciations gave him problems, causing long interruptions in reading the text. Letitia decided that good newspapers were an easier alternative. Ben had warmed to Letitia, showning her respect and when he was with her, he made an effort, dropping his lazy, casual way with words in order to please her. Ben had looked forward to their early meetings as an opportunity to drive the Audi sports car, cruising in style among the press of utility vehicles, but after his disastrous meeting with Kelly, the suppers, the tuition and the friendship which had developed became more important.

A Philipino cook, the house maid's cousin, had prepared a delicious home made soup with a variety of herbs and vegetables, thickened with ripe Stilton cheese, the whole accompanied by crusty rolls. The soup was served in a piping hot tureen with capacity enough for many seconds and Letitia gracefully served each helping with a solid silver ladle bearing a crest on it's flared handle. She chastised Ben about his table manners, made him stop wolfing it down while grunting his obvious appreciation. Ben noticed that Letitia had only one small helping and he remarked on her restraint. 'Letitia, this soup's sensational, I've never had soup like this before, it's so tasty, we always have the cheap tinned stuff at home and that's only when it's on offer, two for the price of one. Why aren't you havin more? Sorry hav…ing more, I feel I'm being greedy, when you keep giving me extras.'

'I'm being treated Ben, for heroin addiction and I'm taking methadone under a doctor's prescription. I find difficulty in facing food, I seem to have lost my appetite, but no matter, its pleasure enough watching you enjoy your soup. Please have your fill, but take your time and remember, no sucking on the spoon.'

Ben was suddenly overwhelmed with an uncommon sense of caring. He was beginning to experience this feeling more often and it was becoming a nuisance, it made life more complicated, thrusting unwanted obligations on his unwilling shoulders. The thought that Letitia, an intelligent, titled lady, a woman with grace and bearing, a real Lady whom he felt priviliged to count among his friends, should be heroin dependent and subject to abusive control, filled him with horror and concern. He almost dropped the spoon in the soup, pushed back his chair, tension crossed his face, worry lines creased his brow, 'I feel a bit sick,' he confessed. 'I've been so busy feeling sorry for myself, thinking I was the only one in the world with problems, I forgot you had problems more serious than mine. Truth is, I've managed to screw things up. The girl I wanted so much has split with me because I'm dealing in drugs. I've lost my mum's respect, because I won't take the offer of good job. She's not a fool, she knows I'm messing with drugs. My best mate killed himself because his brain was shot through by drugs and now you, a lady with real class who has been so patient with me, helping me to sort out my head, tells me she's trying to kick heroin. On top of all this I feel trapped in a life of crime. I've reached a sort of moral cross roads and guess what Letitia, I was ready to unload, talk it all through with you because I knew you'd listen, show me sympathy and give me some help but I see now, I'm only thinking about me. Letitia, I know there's nothing I can do to help, but if there is anything, anything at all, I will, honestly, anything.'

'That's very noble of you Ben. I'm rather flattered by your concern, to think a handsome young knight in shining armour is coming to my rescue. Oh, the irony of it all. When I was your age, nothing would have pursuaded me to consider a boy with your background. How blind, how stupid we are when we're young. You know Ben, I can see in you, the makings of a gentleman.

'Me, a gentleman, that's bit of a joke is'nt it? I can't imagine me ever being a gentleman. A Toff with an Asbo? Some title.'

'It may not be immediately apparent, but when I've finished teaching you how to behave in society and the importance of good manners, you'll be a gentleman right enough, a gentleman through and through. Now Ben, to more serious matters. There is something you can do for me. It will be asking a great deal of you and I shall quite understand if you refuse.'

172

'I'd find it difficult refusing you anything, Letitia, just try me.'

'First of all I need to ask you some questions, soul searching questions which require an honest answer. It is perfectly clear, that at the moment, you are not a happy man. You are beginning to understand those truths which only hard work, heartache and the experience of life can teach us. The deepest joys, the chance of real happiness are to be discovered in simple things, natural things which lie all around us on the very threshold of life. For you happiness lies in restoring a relationship with the girlfriend you are so obviously in love with, winning back your mother's respect and taking on a worthwhile job which builds your self esteem and offers a healthy future. Do you understand Ben, what I'm trying to say? Is this what you really want, in your heart?'

'I understand what you're saying Letitia and to be honest with you, I am beginning to feel like I'm missing out on life. I want all those things you've mentioned but it's too late, I've reached the point of no return, I'm in too deep with Tonino, he's got a hold over me, just like he has over you and I can't get free of him, not without making myself a target for Mafia hit men. Next weekend he's sending me to Naples, on a big drugs run, and there's no way I can back out, no way. All I can do is make the best of it, enjoy Italy and keep taking the money.'

' If you were offered a chance to be completely free of Tonino, the Mafia and the whole drugs scene, a chance that would envolve some risk to yourself and a short spell in prison, would you have courage enough to take that chance?'

Ben pushed his soup further away, his throat went dry, he wasn't sure he was hearing things correctly, 'Hmn, what risks? More risks than I'm already taking? Going to prison? I don't understand what it is you're suggesting. Sounds a bit scary Letitia. Tonino warned me about discussing his business with you. Haven't we said too much already? I mean the place could be bugged.'

'You may speak freely Ben, I've had the place checked over thoroughly for bugs by an expert. Tonino is so confident that his money and my heroin addiction give him complete control, he's never once considered me a security risk. In any event, he never confides in me and that is where you may be useful. My monthly supply of heroin is split into daily doses which are flushed down the toilet and he's not aware that I'm receiving private treatment for my addiction. You may rest assured, our conversation will never be heard beyond these walls. You still haven't answered my question Ben. Do you want to be free of Tonino?' Letitia studied Ben's face. For a moment he seemed to have lost contact, then after the initial shock, surprise and curiosity drew a nervous smile. Letitia knew she was taking risks, enormous risks with this young man. She had made a decision based on her intuition which was by no means foolproof, but she felt confident and no longer cared for her own safety.

At that moment Ben made the most important decision of his life. He sensed a common bond, a connection between himself and the woman who faced him across the table. Here was someone he could believe in, someone like Kelly, someone he could trust and for whom he would make sacrifices, offer his fidelity. He had no problem with the decision, there were no dilemmas, he would shift his allegiance, loyalty imposed by coercion, from Tonino to Lady Letitia. He replied without hesitation, 'Ok, get me out of this mess and I'll go along with anything you say.'

'Are you absolutely sure Ben. Even if it means facing a short term in prison?'

'I'm absolutely sure Letitia.'

'Very well. On your next visit, before the Naples trip, I want you to arrive an hour early. We'll drive to a secret rendezvous where I want you to meet someone. You can be chauffer. Say absolutely nothing about our arrangements to anyone.'

Letitia's charismatic charm had performed a miracle, a metamorphosis, an awakening of desert seed. It had begun with Kelly's revelations, the contempt she had shown for Ben's life style and the rejection of his love. A young love, a courtship

174

pursued by him with assumed arrogance and self assurance which, after early expectations, had failed the first test. Ben's association with Letitia had gone beyond the teaching of grammar, the use of good diction and an introduction to English literature, it had given him a sense of obligation and he had responded by giving Letitia his respect, his affection, his care and compassion. Life on the street had been about a different kind of respect, easily recognisable, rooted in fear, the law of the jungle. Letitia had shown him what respect really means, an appreciation of intellect, the recognition of virtue and those responsibilities with which real love is nurtured.

Ben's love for his family had been burdened with so much baggage, he had been uncertain of his role in the scheme of things. He now felt liberated from these pressures, free to examine his motives and his conscience. It was as though a great weight had been lifted from his shoulders. The world took on a different perspective, there were new priorities, fresh ambitions, a lighter outlook and a feeling of empathy with the rest of mankind. He was ready to make a contribution, ready to share the world's struggle in its effort to distiguish right from wrong.

Ben was used to the single minded flow of traffic on the motorway, but now, in the hospital corridor, he found himself on a different sort of highway. Various contraptions, running smoothly on casters, relied on manpower to whisk patients through the complex. Medical staff with nervous energy hurried back and forth and visitors too, some looking grim, herded together along the hospital's main arteries. Ben, falling in with lane discipline, followed the colour coded lines set into the vinyl floors which led to the various departments and eventually to the appropriate ward. He entered the ward, uncertain of how to handle the visit after having so recently ignored his mother's plea to join the rest of the family on their hospital visit. Ben's imagination stopped short when it came to the need for Hospitals, it had never before been part of his agenda and his pace slowed as he approached the nurses' station.

'Can you tell me please where I can find Mike Edwards?' He asked, appearing uncomfortable and beginning to doubt the wisdom of presenting himself unannounced when he could so easily have joined in with the family's visit.

A nurse came to his assistance. She was a robust, wholesome, no nonsense looking woman with intelligent eyes, clearly in charge, unable to suffer fools. She spoke with an Eastern European accent and although struggling with recently acquired English, spoke with unmistakable authority. 'Pleece have you to use antiseptic? It is dispenser, spirit gel, on wall, just inside entrance doors. I think you to miss.'

'Oh sorry, I didn't see it, never realised.'

'Yes, is important for us. We not to want problem with C-Diff. Now is to have extra care. We are more cleaning.' She smiled sweetly at Ben. 'I think you young rugby player, yes? Many rugby players to visit Mr Edwards. He is in section on right, at far end. He is by window. You to wash hands first pleece.'

Ben dutifully returned to the dispenser, gratefull in way for the few extra moments in which to rehearse his speech. It would be like going for an interview. No, with his family almost certainly crowding the bedspace, it would be more like going to confession. The whole place made him feel uncomfortable, it was too hot, too squeaky clean. The hospital administration had finally woken up to the fact that a high standard of cleaning is just as important as a high standard of nursing. A new cleaning contract had been given to a firm employing Polish workers who took their responsibilities seriously, going that extra mile, cleaning thoroughly every nook and cranny.

Ben suddenly found himself at Mike's bedside. The walls and window cill were festooned with get well cards but there were no other visitors. Mike was peacefully asleep. Ben's expectations of a difficult and sensitive converstion had been thwarted, he had imagined every scenario but this. A welcome sense of relief helped him relax and he tiptoed out to get a chair, determined not to wake Mike under any circumstances. There were three other male patients in the room who, inspite of health problems, enjoyed sharing the company of a sporting hero. One of them, out of curiosity and keen to share the familiarity of family and friends, decided to quiz Ben.

'Mike's just had a load of visitors, I think he's a bit tired. You his son?'

'No' Ben shook his head not wanting to engage in conversation. 'I'm not going to wake him, I'll just sit quietly for a bit. If he doesn't wake, I'll leave him a note.' Ben read the get well cards, sat down, listened to the steady breathing, studied Mike's craggy features, softened, tranquil and unguarded, while in repose. He decided to write a few lines before leaving. He found a pen in the bedside cabinet and chosing his mother's card with its message of love, wrote on the back:

Dear Mike,

Glad you're making a good recovery. There's so much I want to say and I realise now what a right prat I've been and I'm really sorry. Thanks for looking after mum and I'm glad you're marrying her. Hope I can be at the wedding. Thanks too for helping Marvin's gran. It really shook me when Marvin killed himself and I've changed. It somehow disconected me from the life I've been leading and I'll never forget how Josh ran me down to Cornwall. One day perhaps I can do something worth while for him. Here are the names of the four ringleaders, the hoodies who put you in hospital…………..

Cheers Mike, give my love to mum, will be in touch, Ben.
PS Hope you can keep the job open for me.

Air traffic droned overhead as Ben drove on the A34 through the Wilmslow area with Letitia seated beside him. She obviously knew the route well and was very clear and precise when giving Ben directions. Ben never tired of driving, but the Audi had it had lost its spell, its swank. It no longer gave him a sense of privilege, of having arrived, rather it made him feel like the lackey he had become.

'Ben, take the A535 to Holmes Chapel, drive on through to join the M6 at junction 18, heading south, then on down the motorway to the Sandbach services. 'Pull in to the car park area,' Letitia instructed.

'Ok Letitia,' Ben replied, 'Is that where we're having our meeting?'

'Yes, we'll be meeting a high ranking police officer, the man who is heading Manchester drugs squad and an MI5 agent. You'll see a police car in the far corner alongside a white police van. Pull in behind them.'

Ben's faith in Letitia visibly wavered as flutterings of fear ran through his frame, the natural response of a highly tuned, early warning system. The mention of a police officer and an MI5 agent made him acutely aware of his predicament and its dreadful uncertainty. 'This all sounds a bit heavy Letitia, surely I'm not that important.'

'This is a very serious matter Ben, involving several nations in their fight against organised crime and I'm introducing you to people at the very highest level. I don't think you realise what a difference your contribution will make, especially where efforts to stop the infiltration of Mafia controlled drug operations in Britain are concerned. Have faith in me Ben and listen very carefully to what is said.'

Ben decelerated into the services slip road, cautiously following the signs which gave directions for cars only. His sweeping headlights settled on a police patrol vehicle and a large security van. The van looked formidable, very secure, very safe, as though designed to carry the crown jewels. He pulled up behind them, anxiously switching off the headlights, wanting to get the whole thing over with as quickly as possible. Two traffic policemen exploded from the car and Ben was certain he was about to be arrested, but surprisingly, they hurried off in the direction of the service buildings to grab a coffee. Two more men emerged from the rear doors of the car. They were big men, dressed casually, pausing only for a brief conversation, before moving easily through the shadows of the dimly lit car park. One of them appeared to enter a code before opening a narrow door in the back of the van, the other approached the passenger side of the Audi, Letitia lowered the window. 'Good evening Chris, I hope we haven't kept you waiting,' she said in a relaxed tone, as though arriving late for a dinner party.

'Hello Letitia, no, no, not at all, we're in no hurry. It's good to see you again. Last time we met was in Naples I believe?'

'Yes and we visited the Etruscan Tombs where we ate the most gorgeous food and drank the most gorgeous wine. Do you remember? In one of the caves? You were so gallant.'

'How could I ever forget? And this I take it is Ben Mackay, the young man who is going to help us with our enquiries?' He nodded in Ben's direction. 'I'm afraid Letitia, this meeting hardly lends itself to exotic surroundings and Mediterranean sunshine, I can only offer the basics. As you know our conversation will be part of a covert operation and the implications of taking a risk with Ben Mackay, requires a good deal of caution. I mean, on record, he is nothing more than an anti social teenager. If the proposal had come from anyone other than you, I wouldn't have give it a second thought. We'll have our little get together in the back of the police van, you'll find it warm but somewhat short on comfort.'

The van had electrically operated, fold away steps which made rear access much easier but apart from this innovation, no other consideration had been given for the welfare of prisoners for whose transport the vehicle was intended. All four climbed aboard, taking up positions on the padded benches which ran the length of the rear passenger area, Letitia and Ben on one side and the two men on the other. Chris the police officer, wasted no time and immediately addressed Ben. 'First of all Ben, I have to inform you that we are aware of your association with Tonino Vera and the trafficking of cocaine. We have enough information to arrest you here and now, enough at least to take you in for questioning. However, it's extremely difficult to break the Mafia code of silence and even more difficult to unravel the complicated machinery of money laundering. We rely mostly on catching dealers with drugs in hand or actually on the table so to speak and we need more direct evidence against those at the top of the chain. You Ben Mackay, if I'm not taking you immediately into custody, must convince me that you are willing to help by providing that crucial evidence. Are you willing to do this? Even if there is some risk to yourself.'

Ben sat staring at the floor, his mind failing to project the implications, the possible outcome. 'I'm willing to help Letitia,' he replied miserably. 'She's helped me get my head straight and I want to do somethin in return, I'd like to see her dump Tonino, get free of him.' He raised his head, looking directly at the police officer. 'If that's possible,' he added, knowing full well he could never make it happen.

'No, it's not possible, not for you, however noble your intentions. Surely you must realise that by placing her confidence in you, Letitia has made herself even more vulnerable. I've no idea how strong is your allegiance to the Vera family or to what extent Tonino has control over you but if you were to betray her trust, you would be handing her a death sentence. Why on earth she's taking this risk I can't imagine. She says you're an intelligent lad, she says you're kind and you're thinking straight but that's not what it says on your records. Is it? And I warn you, unless you give me, here and now, some real information, specific details of your association with theVera set up, names and places, the whole works, I shall seriously bust your ass, capiche.'

Ben was rattled, annoyed, tired of hearing this sort of speech, the threats, the pressure. He was the one who felt betrayed. 'No way do I want to put Letitia's life at risk, but what about my life?' He complained. 'If Tonino found out I was here shootin my mouth off, make no mistake, I'd be dead meat.'

'We are talking a big operation here. An international drugs bust, centered on major cities including London, Manchester, Amsterdam and Naples. We've been working on it for some time and it's gradually all coming together. It's no skin off our nose Ben, but here's the deal. Work under cover for us on Mafia infiltration and maybe we can swoop within weeks. To protect you from possible reprisals, you'll be arrested along with the other suspects, called as a witness but will refuse to co-operate. You'll get sent down, moved around from one prison to another, making it difficult to track your whereabouts and when we think it's safe, you'll be quietly released. You'll probably only serve a few months. When you come out you'll receive financial support and training in whatever you want to do, with an option to join the police force. You'll be able to start a new life and don't worry, we'll take very good care of Letitia.' The policeman leaned back hoping for a positive reaction.

All eyes turned on Ben. He hadn't expected this from Letitia. Cornered like a rat, he'd been presented with a fait accompli. This had been a clever gamble by her and she tensed, waiting for his response. Ben needed time, time alone, time to think, but there was no time, no avenue of retreat, he had to make a decision. His fingers came together in an attitude of prayer, probing the soft underside of his chin. His first thoughts were of Kelly in Liverpool and Meg in her New Horizons flat. Could he betray Meg, the woman whose charms he was unable to resist, even though she was old enough to be his mother? She had seduced him with vixen cunning, lured him on with the practiced arts of a courtesan, drowned his senses in champage, twisted his mind with cannabis and cocaine. He didn't love her but he had been captivated by her, fallen under her spell, under her control. He realised how much she had used him, lied to him, groomed him, before handing him over to the sharks. He felt no sense of guilt about putting a stop to her, but saw it more as an opportunity to get even with a devil woman, the woman who had set out to poison his soul. Could he do it knowing he would lose her daughter Kelly, for ever? There was no real choice, he had to risk it. He thought of his mother, Matt and Katrina, of Mike and Josh. His mother would approve, would be proud of her son if she knew he'd worked undercover for the police. But of course she could never know and neither could Mike or Josh, or any of them. There would be no James Bond glamour, no accolades for helping a police investigation with undercover work and like most agents he would be pressed into service, pilloried by circumstances which suited the establishment. He would be little more than a copper's nark. And then he thought about Marvin, tragic Marvin, destroyed by cannabis, who took nothing seriously, always fun loving, always laughing and he felt he owed. Ben sighed, and with resignation turned to Letitia, he sounded disappointed, 'I wasn't expectin this Letitia, you puttin me on a real spot, under so much pressure. It seems you've simply handed me over to the police.'

'There was no other way Ben, no other way to rescue you. Can't you see, you were in too deep. I had to be cruel to be kind. But this is a way forward, a move in the right direction, it's tearing up that one way ticket to hell and giving you a fresh start, a new life. You must focus on that. Please Ben, if you have any respect for me, please, please take this opportunity.'

The MI5 agent intervened. 'Ben, you are ideally placed to help us in our fight against drug abuse and organised crime. Co-operate fully and I can assure you we will keep our side of the bargain. Remember that drug abuse is responsible for so much suffering and misery in the world. It destroys lives, young lives. Seven thousand assaults are reported each week in the UK alone, many of them fatal, and most of these are drugs related. Murder, extortion, prostitution, the white slave trade, child abuse and theft are some of the crimes fuelled by drug dependency. Money transactions relating to the sale and manufacture of illegal drugs distort the global economy. I want you to bear all this in mind before making your decision.'

After this reminder there followed a long silence, the atmosphere became more intense, minutes seemed like hours, until suddenly, it all came pouring out.

'When I was at school, I dealt in ecstacy and crack and I smoked a few joints. Meg, Margaret Kinnear was my supplier. She lives in flat 25, second block, New Horizons Park. I don't have dealings with her anymore, cos we both work for Tonino, but I'm livin with her and we're off to Naples next week on a big cocaine run. Anyway, one evenin, this was after I'd been expelled, Meg introduced me to snortin coke and offered me the chance to own a sports car. That's where it all started, with the Audi Quattro....................'

Ben told them everything he knew about Tonino, about Vera Motors, Viktor Ivanovich, Hareden Hall, Roberto Vera, Nadya, Euro Express Car Parts and the hidden processing plant. He told them about Meg and their planned trip to Naples. He held nothing back and as each revelation unfurled, the interview turned into an interrogation, with a stream of probing questions. Details were recorded on tape and Ben was instructed to pass all future information on to Letitia, especially concerning the Naples drug run, the ports of call, the ETA's, the names, the dates, the whole package. Finally they were allowed to leave, and Ben slumped into the Audi driving seat feeling utterly drained yet strangely elated. Letitia, like a mother who is proud of her offspring, leaned across, kissing him with maternal spontaneity. At last she had managed to achieve something, she had brought down a mobster, the insanely jealous, controling meglomaniac, whom she had married. It gave her no sense of revenge, no pleasure but in so doing she had rescued a young man from the brink, given him back his life and that thought filled her with a warm glow.

The policeman and the MI5 agent were left to discuss what had transpired. They were already planning the finishing touches to their painstaking investigation, operation Retiarius, the name given to Roman gladiators who fought with a net and a trident. With this new information they would be able to launch simultaneous raids on targets where huge caches of illegal drugs would provide irrefutable proof. The acquisition of direct evidence against higher levels of the Mafia organisation in Britain had proven extremely difficult and this was considered a breakthrough. Finally the MI5 agent remarked, 'Letitia's been an Interpol agent for two years and up to now she's only fed us crumbs. After we learned about her heroin addiction, we considered her a security risk and seriously thought about taking her out.'

'I hope by that remark, you don't mean what I think you mean,' the police officer ventured.

'It means by dear Detective Inspector, that she was due to meet with an unfortunate accident, but quite against the odds, Lady Letitia Hamelton has turned in a star performance.'

Chapter 12 The Lost Generation.

Mike's unwelcome spell in hospital, more frustrating than painful, gave ample time for reflection.The chance to read a novel, follow the sports columns, analyse the fortunes of his old rugby club or thumb through pages of illustrated magazines, seemed more like an exercise in time wasting. He needed time to think, to think long and hard about armed gang culture, the tooth and claw levels of society which threaten to rip apart the ordered fabric of our towns and cities. He tried to understand the motives behind the attack on Constance and the mindless fury which had led to a knifing, a skirmish which could so easily have ended his life, his future hopes, his dreams and the joy of his forthcoming marriage to Karen. How close had he been to heartbreak and tragedy? Ben had given him the names of the ring leaders and Mike considered passing on the information to the police, but although Mike had many friends in the police force, he no longer believed they gave value for money. In spite of early releases and light sentencing, everyone understood that our prisons were bursting at the seams while increasingly, minor anti social behaviour, which inevitably leads to more serious crimes, was ignored. Only police and government spin, based on the number of self regulated cases dealt with, kept pace with the actual increase in crime. Nobody was fooled. Reports of a reduction in specific crimes simply meant that fewer cases in this category had received police attention. Over a period of twelve months two and a half million violent crimes had been committed in Britain leaving the victims of crime and anti social behaviour without compensation or in some cases, justice in the courts. Propaganda to the contrary could not erase this appalling figure. In consideration of these observations, Mike decided to do his own policing. He would track down his assailant, carry out his own enquiries, explore the motives, risk a charge for kidnapping and make a citizen's arrest.

On leaving hospital Karen wanted Mike to convalesce. She wanted to make a fuss of him, nurse him back to full health, but for Mike the period of inactivity had been long enough and he immediately began making enquiries. He quickly discovered the home addresses of the prime suspects, three lived on New

Horizons Park and one in an area he was unfamiliar with. All four ringleaders were known to carry knives and were members of a gang still calling themselves the Asbos. They continued to terrorrise the area around New Horizons Park and most of the residents felt scared of them. Their newly appointed leader, Winston Macdonald, a sinewy Caribbean Scot known as Macca, was particular fond of brandishing a weapon and Mike decided to tackle him first, certain that he was responsible for the stabbing. Surprisingly, Macca's home address was located on a small, council housing estate adjacent to New Horizons. The residents here had made an effort with their homes and some had purchased houses from the council at preferential rates. They were a hardworking community who were prepared to make sacrifices in order to maintain standards. Gardens were well cared for, modest improvements had been made and the whole represented all that is welcoming and commendable in English society.

Mike discovered that Macca's house had fallen behind the others in this respect and as he walked up to the front door there seemed an air of desperation about the place. The doorbell hung forlornly, dangling on wires ripped through the door jamb and Mike hammered on the spilt panelling with a growing sense of outrage. Lack of response added to his frustration and he turned to more closely examine the front garden where further evidence confirmed his initial reactions, obviously the occupants of this blot on the landscape were a rough lot, lacking in community spirit and having no consideration for others. The garden presented an area of neglect, a dumping ground for items of discarded furniture, broken toys and litter. A dozen empty beer bottles, their contents recently consumed along with vodka night caps, were heaped against the boundary wall. The whole area was choked with deep rooted weeds, predominantly docks and dandylions, spilling their liberal helpings of seed over the neighbour's flower beds.

A large, slobering, over friendly dog answered the door, almost knocking Mike off his feet, smothering him with a warm tongue and a cold nose and Mike was obliged to make friends while trying to hold the dog at arms length. A pretty, coffee coloured girl in her early teens, with dark shadows around even darker eyes, appeared from behind the door. 'Get down Asbo, Asbo get down,' she said, tugging on the dog's collar.

'There's a good boy, there's a good boy,' Mike said, making a fuss of the dog.

'What did you say his name was?'

'Asbo, he's Winston's dog, a timber wolf cross,' she answered with pride.

'Asbo! Interesting name for such a well behaved dog, well, I mean, he seems very good natured. Anyway, good morning to you. I'd really like to have a word with Winston if he's at home.' There was a moment of indecision, 'If not I can call back later.'

'You're not the police are you?'

'No, no, I'm not the police, I'm Mike Edwards, Winston and I met recently in rather unpleasant circumstances and what I have to say to him is very important.'

'Winston's seein to mum at the moment so you'll have to wait on the doorstep. I'm sorry but I'll have to close the door cos of Asbo. No, perhaps it'll be ok, he seems to have accepted you, so you can wait in the living room if you'd rather. I'll tell Winston you're here, he won't be long, I'm makin a coffee for mum, want one?'

Mike followed the girl through the hallway taking note of the stair lift which ran up a straight flight of stairs and a wheelchair parked next to the first riser.' It sounds as though your mum has a mobility problem. I take it Winston's you're brother and he has to be there for her in the mornings?'

'Yeah, she's in a wheel chair, she's had a stroke and Winston has to help her on the toilet and get her washed and do her hair and stuff, while I get breakfast.'

I know it's the weekend, but surely there must be carers to do all these things, especially on school days?'

'Winston's been expelled so it's no problem and I'm always mitchin off. We get school inspectors round all the time but they can't do nothin. I'm Sophie by the way. Did you want a coffee Mr Edwards? You can sit down if you want to, not on the settee though cos the springs have gone. Get down Asbo! I better put him in the kitchen, he's really takin a likin to you.'

'Yes, thanks Sophie, I'd love one.' Sophie dragged Asbo into the kitchen, closing the door behind her as Mike settled into the least shabby of the two arm chairs. The room was dreary, tired of this world. Efforts to maintain cleanliness were confined to the bits that showed and table legs, chair legs, anything made of wood, bore the scars of Asbo's powerful jaws. The curtains were still drawn, dull and lifeless, the carpet threadbare, covered in the dog's greasy hairs which stubbornly resisted the futile efforts of a worn out vacuum cleaner. Nothing in the room offered welcome or comfort and Mike's initial idea of making a citizens arrest seemed hardly relevant in such deprived circumstances. Although hot on the trail, closing in on the quarry and near to exacting some sort of justice for Constance, Karen and himself, he felt thwarted, baffled, his sympathies unwillingly aroused.

Mrs Macdonald came down the stair lift, struggled into the wheelchair which awaited her for ease of access and wheeled herself into the living room. 'Oh! Lucky me, I have a gentleman caller. Sophie!' She yelled, 'I thought I asked you never to answer the door when I'm not up and about?'

Sophie appeared with the coffees. 'Mum, I had to answer the door cos Asbo was tearing it down.'

'Keep Asbo in the kitchen, he's becoming nothing more than a confounded liability.' Mrs Macdonald swung round in the wheelchair, 'I hope you're not another useless social worker, no I'm sorry, I can see that you're not a social worker, you seem quite normal, a man with a mission I'd say. Not a copper I hope. If it's to do with Winston, I really don't want to know. Winston's a good boy and a marvellous son and I couldn't possibly manage without him.'

Mrs Macdonald spoke with studied concentration, occasionally sluring her words and Mike's sympathies were instantly aroused. Her face still had beauty but her hair, brushed so lovingly by Winston, was prematurely grey and her features were half frozen in a stupid grin. A thin stream of saliva dribbled from the corner of her drooping mouth. 'No Mrs Macdonald, I've already explained to Sophie here that I'm not a policeman, but I do want to have a word with Winston.'

'Well. If you're not a social worker and you're not a copper, who are you and what is it you want with my Winston?'

'Well hmn, my name's Mike Edwards and hmn, indirectly, you could say that I'm concerned about his future. I represent the residents of New Horizons Park and you must be aware Winston's running with a gang of hoodies who are causing anti social problems in the area.' Mike paused, unsure of how to approach the subject of the gang's knife attack. 'Surely Mrs Macdonald, Winston shouldn't be helping you with your toiletries when there are professional carers available to provide this service. He should be at school or trying to get a job.'

'I'm afraid it's not as simple as that Mr Edwards, I'm Mary by the way and it's a long story.'

Mike was beginning to lose sight of his objectives. 'Well Mary, if you could explain your circumstances, perhaps I can help in some way. That's why I'm here, I've not come to make your life more difficult than it already is, I want to help improve your situation, if that is at all possible.'

'I must say, I'm warming to you Mr Edwards. There's something about you, I think you're a gentleman, on the outside you seem such a tough character, with your broad shoulders and your broken nose, but you have kind eyes. Yes, I'm able to sense these things. I'm quite sure you're perfectly genuine. It's quite rare these days you know, to meet someone who is genuinely sympathetic to the needs of others. Since having a stroke, I've had to deal with an army of social workers, people so constrained by government initiatives, guidelines and procedures, so preoccupied with covering their own backs, they're incapable of independent thought and unable to do anything constructive.

'But what about Winston?' Mike interrupted, somewhat embarrassed by Mary's perception of his character.

I *am* getting very concerned about Winston. I've no idea what he gets up to outside of these four walls but he acts as though he wants to fight the whole world. It all seems so unfair on him. His father walked out on us five years ago and he's the sort of outdoor lad who needs a father. He was doing well at school, he played junior rugby for a local club and loved sports until something happened which set him back.'

'What happened?'

'He was having a boy's rough and tumble in the playground with two other lads who played rugby. A dinner lady reported him to the form teacher for violent behaviour and this was placed on his school record. He was categorised as a bully who was liable to cause harm to other children. Included in the category were sex offenders and drug dealers. The whole thing was completely over the top. Rugby players know how to take knocks and they're certainly not bullies. Now a teacher stands watch in the playground making sure the children do nothing which might lead to a court action for negligence or damages. After this incident he simply lost faith in the system, he rebelled, he refused to work, then he gave up sports and became disruptive in class and ended up getting expelled.'

'Mary, this is Britain today, stuffed full of government initiatives, rules and regulations, decisions made by busybodies sitting around tables who have no in depth knowledge or experience in any trade or profession, out of touch with the practicalities of life, unable to recognise those things which actually build the long term wealth of a nation, handing out cushy numbers to fat cats who just work the system. Politicians, lining their pockets with expense accounts, banks, hedge fund managers, playing with percentages on borrowed money, lawyers exploiting the divorce laws, encouraging claims for injury, undermining personal responsibility to the point where it has become a cult. Government quangos, milking industry for all their worth. It's all about putting the right ticks in the right boxes.'

'I can see Mr Edwards, sorry, Mike if you prefer, you've given this a lot of serious thought and I entirely agree with you. You know, I think *you* should be a politician, you seem like the sort of man who might help change things.'

'I know I'm sounding off, but I'm beginning to wake up, I mean, what sort of nation requires joiners like myself to wear industrial goggles when using a measuring tape, then sends it's troops into battle without the proper equipment? I don't want to bore you Mary but it makes me mad thinking about it. I've had it up to here and I think we've all had enough, it's time to go to war and it's funny you should mention about me going into politics, but now my business is in good hands, I've been seriously thinking about it.' Mike steadied his train of thought, he hadn't come here to talk politics, he'd come to make a citizen's arrest. 'Mary you're very easy to talk to and I'm sure we could chat all day about putting the world to right, but I still don't understand why you're not receiving the proper care, I don't want to get too personal but are you able to manage a bath or a shower on your own, do your own cooking and that sort of thing?'

'The problem is Mike, I own this property and have some modest savings, which means I have to pay for any services I may require. I'm well educated, I've been a librarian for most of my working life, until I suffered a stroke twelve months ago. My husband had a good job too, as a probation officer, representing the coloured community, with a special interest in race relations. When we married, we had no money and went on the housing list. Soon after Winston was born, we got this house on one of the better Council estates. We liked the location and some of the residents had bought their house from the Council and we both worked hard to buy ours. That was six years ago, before my husband's special interest in race relations went further and he took a special interest in a younger white girl. She did research for him and he left me to live with her. She must have done a very good job because while I was burying my head in books, they carried on an affair right under my nose. It all came as a shock and the stress of going through a messy divorce, the financial worries and Winston getting out of control, brought on a nervous breakdown and then as I say, twelve months ago I suffered a stroke. It's all very, very sad and for no reason at all Winston blames himself. He's a very frustrated and angry young man.'

'But you must have explained all this to the authorities?'

'It's not as simple as that Mike. After six weeks of NHS free care I had to deal with everything on my own. Oh, I've had no end of callers, occupational therapists, key workers, you name them I've had them, filling out their forms, making various assessments, promising this and promising that, but delivering absolutely nothing. The only thing available to me is a disability allowance for which I've had to answer over eighty questions. After that, all I'm left with to face the future, is this house and my savings, which is little enough considering I've worked so hard. Ok, the state owes me nothing, that I can accept, but across the road, the state has housed a man for free in one of the maisonettes. He's reached retirement age and just finished a prison sentence, apparently he's got at least four children by different women and he's been in and out of jail for most of his life. He's given absolutely nothing to society and must have cost the tax payer a fortune. The flat's been redecorated and carpeted and he's been given a choice of colours for the new fitted kitchen. Obviously his case history helps support a network of social workers and I suppose it's a good excuse to create more red tape but the whole thing seems topsy turvy. Doesn't give one much incentive to work does it? Not like the story in the bible where the servant who hid his money and earned nothing had to give it to the one who worked and showed a profit. Sorry Mike if I'm talking like a librarian, '

'No Mary, I understand exactly what you're saying and I remember that parable from school days, but what about your children having to care for you, surely there's help available?'

'Again it's not quite so simple. Because I'm considered to be financially independent, the social services are not concerned about my children having to care for me, unless any stress on the children is brought to their attention. I'm reluctant to do this because there's a very real danger of my children being taken into care. It's all very complicated with different people from different departments, recommending different procedures. There's so much form filling, coming and going, two or three hourly investigations for mother and children with the local authority also getting involved and none of them seem to inter-communicate. We could have what's called a Common Assessment Framework with our case going before a multi agency panel and I *could* get free respite breaks for Winston and Sophie but then I'd have to pay for local authority carers. If I employ a carer privately, even if I'd known them for years, they have to be checked out by the authorities for a criminal record. You just wouldn't believe how many people it takes to achieve so little. I know we've been struggling and how standards have fallen, but I don't want social workers getting the wrong idea.

Winston's not interested anyway, not in those sort of holiday breaks.'

'What about the stair lift, I noticed it when I came in?'

'I paid for the stair lift and for equipment to get in and out of the bath.'

'What you really need is a big shower tray, they're so much easier.'

'I'm afraid I really can't spend any more money, we'll have to manage as we are. Things are gradually improving. I can transfer myself from the wheelchair and actually stand for a few moments and I've started helping in the kitchen. The children have had to do a lot of growing up and they've been brilliant, absolutely brilliant and I don't want to keep nagging them about the cleaning. '

'I can see you're all getting a raw deal Mary, which makes what I want to say, much more difficult.'

'Sophie darling, please draw the curtains and tell Winston there's a man here to see him.'

'Why don't you spend your savings, treat yourself to new carpets and a three piece suite, get the place decorated, pay for carers and enjoy a few extras until you qualify for all the benefits.'

'Well, I suppose its pride, but it's also a matter of principal and fairness. It's a bit like old people having to sell their homes to pay for residential care. Surely decent citizens in a western democracy should have the right to expect proper National Health care and not be means tested, stripped of their hard earned assets to fund a top heavy social services system. I value my independence though, I want to beat this thing if I can and get my life back together. I don't want to be at the mercy of state benefits, having my life taken over by welfare officials, praying for the giro cheques and the handouts.'

Sophie called down from the landing, 'mum, Winston's gone back to bed. He's fast asleep.'

Mary continued, 'sorry about this Mike, but on top of having to care for me, he's staying out late at night. I'm desperately worried for him. He's already been given an Asbo and he's not supposed to be out after ten but he just lets the whole thing go over his head and he won't listen to me. He just keeps flouting authority and nothing seems to be done about it. It was on the news the other night, anti social behaviour costs the country three billion a year and over seventy percent of offenders break their Asbos and continue to commit offences. He's a good lad really and I feel our educational system has let him down. He's one of the lost generation.'

'The lost generation?' Mike interrupted, looking puzzled. Mary was getting into her stride and was determined to give voice to her opinions.

'Yes, I would go as far as to say that, a lost generation. To begin with, at primary school, everything is fine. Children are given a chance to be creative, explore their ability and interact with what is going on around them and teachers give them more individual attention. During their time at primary school, standard assessment tests are introduced in two stages, one at the end of year two and a more formal one at the end of year six. The results of these tests are used to stream children into secondary school and also determine where each school stands in the league tables. The schools therefore tend to focus on cramming for SATS results and many children are over stressed by the pressures placed on them. Not all children respond to this style of education and for many, school is not a happy place to be.'

'I suppose Winston was one of those children?' Mike offered.

'He was, but the problem goes beyond primary level. In theory, parents are given a choice about which secondary school they want their children to attend and because good schools are often over subscribed, schools become more selective. Some parents will move home to be near a good school. The end result is that at one end of the spectrum, good schools remain good because they've more children with good SATS results and at the other, low performance schools remain low performing, because they've more children with poor SATS results. Winston went to a school, struggling in the league tables, a huge school with far too many pupils and too many over stressed teachers. He became nothing more than a statistic.'

'I read somewhere that standards have been dumbed down to improve success figures. I must say I find that hard to believe, but a lot of children seem to have problems with natural communication skills, unable to read or write properly. D'you think there's any truth in it?'

'No, it's not true. GCSEs and A level standards are high, especially in the core subjects of English, Maths and Science but a wider range of less academic subjects are available to students who may find them easier to get passes and look good on paper.'

'So what happened to Winston?'

'Well, classroom overcrowding and the big school environment made things worse. Secondry schools also concentrate on the next level of SATS, key stage three, which is used to decide which GCSE set is most suitable for each child. As I said before, this SATS orientated approach to education doesn't suit every child. Some children get severe withdrawal symptons and some rebel against a system which they find demoralising, either way, far too many children are being let down, and many believe that the subject matter itself is being weakened. Needless to say, Winston became a rebel.'

'Ok, I can see what you're getting at, but what d'you think should be done about it?'

'To begin with, SATS should be scrapped. Most of the subject matter is government fed into computors anyway with teachers and students alike following the curriculum like so many automatons. Students like Winston would benefit enormously from properly organised sport, school teams with their own colours and inter- school fixture lists. Sport at Winston's school was a casual ex curriculum affair, undertaken by teachers who were prepared to give some time to it with no clear commitment. Computor games and text messaging are quick fix substitutes but they don't teach children how to behave in society. Even more important would be the introduction of workshops where rudimentary technical and industrial skills could be taught, linking in with technical colleges, agriculture and industry itself where opportunities for life experience would extend beyond the classroom. This form of education should be considered just as important as purely academic work with equal amounts of resources put into it. Government quangos and social schemes which meddle in this category should also be scrapped and the initiative given back to teachers and industry. I'm sure Winston would have responded if a training programme had been available to him. Too many children are now at risk, their potential lost to drug abuse and gang culture, a lost generation.'

'There's a lot of sense in what you're saying Mary.'

'To some extent I blame myself, I was so busy with my own career, I couldn't see what was going on. It wasn't until Winston received an Asbo that I woke up to the situation. I was determined to make it up to him, he's a bright lad and I felt sure I could help him through it, but then my own life fell apart.'

'Would you say that Winston is capable of serious violence?'

'Oh goodness me no, he's like his father, very physical, very strong, but he can be so gentle. I've heard him using bad language though, which I hate, it sounds so aggressive. There's never been any swearing at home, He must have picked it up from those street gangs he runs around with. Why do you ask?'

'Mary, What I have to say may come as a shock. A few days ago I was discharged from hospital after being admitted for a back stabbing. I could easily have lost my life, fortunately the wound only punctured my lung and I made a good recovery. A gang of youths was terrorising a Mrs Constance Cooney, a widow who lives alone on New Horizons Park. She recently lost a grandson in the most tragic circumstances. It was a bit foolhardy, wading in against so many, but I was outraged by such a cowardly attack on a vulnerable old lady. I think you should know your son Winston is the leader of that gang. They call themselves the Asbos and are behaving worse than animals, completely out of control, vandalising property, warring against other gangs, stealing from cars, smoking skunk and dealing in drugs. Winston's known to carry a knife and I've every reason to believe he's the one who stabbed me in the back and then along with the others, began putting the boot in.'

'Oh my God! I can't deal with this, not any more, I've reached the end of my tether.' With her good hand, Mary covered her eyes, 'For weeks now I've been expecting trouble, but not this, it's simply horrendous, to think he might have been facing a murder charge, it's terrifying. I've no reason to disbelieve you, I've had enough warning signs and I've ignored them, afraid to face facts. If the police had stayed on his back this would never have happened, but there's never a follow up, never any police available to deter gangs from street crime, we never see any police, I sometimes wonder what they do all day. You see Mike, Winston's been so good to me, so caring, I simply closed my eyes to the inevitable, knowing I couldn't take any more knocks. I've been in complete denial about Winston, had to, just to survive.' Mary began to weep, her stricken body heaved with each little sob as Sophie tried to comfort her. 'I'm so dreadfully sorry, I suppose you've informed the police and you've come to tell me he's going to be arrrested?.......... I'm glad you've made a recovery though.......... I feel utterly devastated.......... I don't know what to say to you.........so sorry, so sorry,' Mary wailed.

'I'm sorry too Mary, having to add to your troubles, but Winston must be punished for his crime, he must be taught a lesson, shown the error of his ways before he does end up on a murder charge. Actually I've come to make a citizen's arrest. I want to confront him, as a victim, before I take him down to the police station, by force if necessary. Now I'm going up to his bedroom and I'm dragging him out of bed and he's going to have to face us both with an admission of guilt. '

The sound of Mary's wailing grew even louder but its forlorn appeal did nothing to weaken Mike's resolve as he reached for the door leading to the hall way. The door suddenly burst open and Winston appeared dressed in underpants. 'Oh Jesus, it's you is it, makin mum cry, I'll kill you, you bastard.' With that he launched himself at Mike, his fists flailing before headbutting him on the nose. Mike staggered back surprised at the strength and fury of Winston's attack. However, the early initiative was quickly snuffed out. Winston's youthful sinew was no match for Mike's raw power and he gathered the twisting, wreathing torso of his young adversary into an iron bear hug.

'Let go of me you ugly bastard,' he gasped, choking the words out, 'I can't breath, yer breakin me ribs.'

'Never mind about breaking your ribs, I ought to break your neck.' Mike threw Winston on the settee where he slumped like a rag doll. He gave a half hearted kick at Mike's legs and Mike cuffed him hard around the ear. 'Now listen to me you little squirt. It was you wasn't it who stabbed me in the back?'

'Yeah! Yeah! Yeah!' Winston taunted, 'so what? You asked for it.'

'I recognise the voice. You were the one who said Karen was Ben Mackay's mum. You got scared, scared of Ben, and said to leave off. That was you wasn't it?'

'Yeah! Yeah! Yeah! An I ain't scared of Ben Mackay.'

Asbo began barking while trying to chew his way through the kitchen door and Sophie, whose sympathies lay with her brother, bravely let him out. In one huge bound Asbo leapt at Mike and with his tail wagging furiously began licking his face. He thought everyone was playing a game and was keen to join in the fun. 'Now, all of you, just calm down. Sophie, will you please get this dog off me, he's too friendly for my liking and I'm not looking for a face wash, not at this moment in time.'

The dog's misreading of the episode broke the tension and he went quietly back into the kitchen. Mary stopped wailing and Winston with his ear still buzzing, started deep breathing exercises. Mary, Winston and Sophie turned their attention to Mike, a stranger, an intruder who had come among them to seek justice. Filled with apprehension, they waited nervously, anxious to know the measure of retribution. Mike held the floor. 'Mary, forget about the authorities, I'm going to arrange for a carer to call in for an hour each morning during the school week. She happens to be the daughter of one of my employees and I know the family well. She's a lovely girl whose just finished training as a class room assistant and is finding it difficult to get a job. She's a very caring person and I know she'll be only to pleased to help. She'll get you started for the day, make breakfast, get Sophie off to school and do a bit of shopping. You'll have to pay her cash of course, but I'm sure it'll work out a lot cheaper than paying the Council. Sophie you're a bright little lassie and it's important you don't miss out on school work.'

'That's all very well Mike, and I appreciate you're trying to help, but over the weeks, costs would soon mount up.' Mary pointed out.

'I think it's more important that Sophie attends school and for the time being you're going to have to spend some of your savings, but in the long term, what this family needs is more income and that is where you Winston, can make a big difference.

'Me,' Winston questioned, looking sullen and confused.

Mike continued, 'When I came here I had every intention of hauling you off to the nearest police station and then throwing the book at you. I wanted you punished severely, behind bars at the very least. But having met your mother, I've going to try something different. I know I could end up with egg on my face, but I'm willing to give it a try. Your mother said you enjoyed playing rugby.'

'Yes, he was very good,' Mary reminded. 'He's lots of cups and medals in his bedroom. When he was twelve he won the under thirteen player of the year award. I loved watching him play, I was so disappointed when he gave it up.'

'What position did you play Winston?' Mike asked.

'I played in the centre, sometimes on the wing, I was pretty good, quite fast.'

'Like the game?'

'Yeah, I loved it'

'I'm an ex professional rugby league player, I wasn't a bad player either.'

'Yeah I know, I found out who you are. I've heard your name mentioned, you're Mike Edwards, used to play for the Saints, people say you were a great player in your day.'

'There were better players. Now listen to me carefully Winston, I'll tell you what I'm going to do. I'm going to get you a job. A pal of mine runs a hi-tech metal casting works and you can work there for a few months to see how you get on. You'll be well paid and you'll be able to give mum some financial help. You'll learn a lot about metallurgy and if you work hard you'll be given a full apprenticeship. Now as far as rugby is concerned, years ago, I used to be a defence coach for Bradford Bulls and still have connections with the club. They run a rugby league academy for talented players. It's a new venture between Bradford college and the club and it offers a chance for young people to combine rugby training with academic studies. I'm not promising anything but if you want, I'll take you to Bradford for a trial and if you're good enough, I'll try to get you a place at the college. You'll have to take your GCSEs and work very hard. If you prefer to take this route and have ambitions to play rugby league, I'll help sort out the finances and the accomodation. We may be able to get a student's grant or loan, I'm not sure, but we'll work something out and incidentally, if you do get to join the academy, you can watch the Bull's home matches for free. Now Winston, are you prepared to give it a go or are we going right now to the police station where I can bring charges against you for grievous bodily harm and you can bring charges against me for assault and kidnapping and knowing how things stand at present with the law, I'll probably be the one who ends up being arrested and you'll be allowed to go free. Now What's it to be?'

There was stunned silence. Then Mary wept openly. Asbo whimpered behind the kitchen door. Winston was speechless. Then finally, he gathered himself.

'Mr Edwards, would you let me stand up please?'

'Yes, I'd rather talk to you while you're on your feet.'

'Mr Edwards, can I please shake your hand?' Winston offered his hand. 'I'm really sorry for what I did, I was so high on drugs and booze I didn't know what I was doing. I know it's no exuse, but meeting you, I've never felt so ashamed.' Tears rolled down his cheeks, 'I can't understand why you're doing this for me and mum.' He choked.

'Well to be perfectly honest, neither can I.' Mike answered taking Winston's hand.

Winston shook Mike's hand as though hanging on to a life line, 'I'd love to have a trial for the academy, and if I'm not good enough, I'll take the job anyway. I promise Mr Edwards, either way, I won't let you down.'

'Well young Winston, we shall see.'

Chapter 13 See Naples and Die

The city of Manchester rose to prominence in the late 18th century when steam powered machines launched the early, raw dynamics of a cotton spinning industry. From the proceeds of cotton, fortunes were made and impressive buildings were erected as a lasting monument to the city's industrial wealth. The glory and extravagance of civic spending was achieved by the ruthless exploitation of the impoverished mill workers who suffered the miserable conditions of overcrowded slums. Political reform finally came, championed by the outspoken voice of a local newspaper, the Manchester Guardian, but metamorphosis was painfully slow. Slum clearance and smokeless zones had to wait until the 1950s and by then the textile industries were already in decline. The character and heart of Manchester, a brave new city, remains the same, dour, resilient and as uncompromising as those stiff, horizontal iron wings we see on the Angel of the North.

On the other hand Naples is a city like no other. Italy had been divided among various mercantile city states until unified in the 19th century. Under a succession of various kings, including Murat, Napoleon's brother in law, the kingdom of Naples had dominated the South, maintaining it's independence from the Papal States and the North. Naples lost its pre-eminence when the Italian patriach, General Garibaldi, having fought a victorious campaign in Sicily, marched unchallenged into Naples and King Francis ll was expelled. The annexation of the kingdom of Naples to the rest of Italy soon followed bringing with it severe problems. For centuries Naples had been the capital of a nation, a cultural, social and political hub, now it had nothing to administer, the city had no effective commercial base and was left with a top heavy bureauracy which inevitably led to more corruption. Naples existed in a state of flux, overrun by terrorists, deserters, stragglers and thieves, ridden by corruption, murder and organised crime. Sadly today little has changed and crime in one form or another remains a serious blight on the city.

And yet Naples is a city of incredible beauty. The historic centre of Naples is one of the select World Heritage sites, a place to be preserved at all costs, where renaissance art, sculptures and treasures from cultures dating back to the Romans captivate our souls. It is also a city of music with its songs and great classical works. Naples has it's own unique character, magnificent churches, monuments, piazzas, streets and alleyways, it's feast days, the local colour of it's people, grandeur amid the poverty and slums, love and passion amid the crime and all this cradled in a broad sweep on the spectacular bay of Naples with the dark outline of Versuvius brooding on the skyline, reminding us that we are only mortal.

Manchester and Naples have only two things in common, slum clearance and crime. In Naples, an effort to clear up the city began as early as 1885 displacing thousands of Neapolitans, resulting in mass emigration. These efforts did nothing to reduce organised crime and to this day, the city remains a Pandora's Box of social ills. The old adage, "See Naples and Die," meant that after seeing Naples, nothing else could match its beauty except perhaps the delights of heaven. Now the adage may be taken more literally and those who engage in any level of crime do so at their own peril.

Although Ben had never travelled abroad, the prospect of working in Naples as an undercover agent among some of the world's most dangerous gangsters, held no fears. He considered his Manchester street credentials more than enough to see him through and he was looking forward to the adventure. In fact, he was more concerned about Meg and the demands she would undoubtedly make on him. The date of their departure finally arrived giving Ben his first experience of flying and as they flew over the Swiss Alps, Meg let him sit by the window to enjoy the view. The couple were met at the airport by a Mafioso escort, who summoned up a gleaming limousine in which he chauffeured them in style around one of the most beautiful and picturesque sea fronts in the world, cruising quietly along the Via Nuova della Marina and the Via Caracciolo towards the little harbour of Mergellina.

Meg's 'Italian Place,' turned out to be a spacious appartment with spectacular views over the harbour, the bay of Naples and beyond to the azure blue horizon of the Tyrrhenian Sea, a sea within a sea, that part of the Mediterranean which is encompassed about by the land masses of Corsica, Sardinia and Sicily. Ceramic cool floors, classical décor, elegant Italian furniture and examples of Capodimonte art, reflected in a most intimate way, the centuries of Italian culture which graced the city. Ben gazed out of the window. Naples had cast its spell on the lad from Greater Manchester. In surroundings like these, making love to Meg might not prove so difficult after all.

For two glorious weeks, Meg and Ben lived a life of pleasure, a Roman 'dolce vita' comparable with that suggested by the murals to be found among the ruins of neighbouring Pompeii. The sirens of self indulging love beckoned from the isle of Capri and the luxuriant groves of Sorrento across the bay and in the marina, Meg's super streamlined power boat, Seducente (Seductive) with it's generous sun deck, nudged impatiently at it's fenders, waiting to take them there, skippered by Francesco, the Mafioso chaufeur, a minder always available on the end of a mobile. Their holiday, lubricated with iced buckets of champagne and dosed with regular snorts of mind blowing cocaine, dissembled their senses as they slid more and more into a decadent lifestyle.

Ben however experienced withdrawal symptons, withdrawal, not from the abuse of alcohol or drugs, which he had tried unsuccessfully to moderate, but from other things, the sordid affair with Meg, her cloying pretence, the menace behind the trappings of drug money and the events which had taken over his life. Although hell bent on wasting his life on anti social behaviour and drugs, Ben had recognised the sacrifices which love demands. His mother had shown him the strength of her love and support, Mike had shown him the virtues of hard work, giving value for money, helping others less able. Marvin, Josh and Letitia had shown him the meaning of friendship, and Kelly, his first love in the bloom of youth, had spelt out the selfless realities of true love, its enduring need to give, to provide for a relationship. Yes, he could see now the folly of his ways and where it had led him. He had wanted to talk it all through with Mike in the hospital, but now life seemed beyond his control, his future had been taken over by dark forces and through every waking hour, fear with sinister stealth, gradually possessed him, until it became a demon perched heavily on his shoulder and with acute awareness, he felt very, very afraid.

The days came and went and each morning, Ben lay sprawled on the bed thinking about his commitment to operation Retiarious and the implications of what might lay ahead. As instructed by MI5, every forty eight hours, with furtive use of his mobile, he kept Letitia informed. The ceiling fan purred above him while Meg spent hours in the bathroom, trying to disguise the creeping ravages of age and the damage caused by a history of drug taking. Ben's listened to the shower, which seemed to run for ages, followed by periods of quiet concentration, interrupted by the flushing of a toilet, the sprinkling of a bidet and the tinkling of glass on ceramics and he wondered what on earth was going on. How could anyone spend so much time on self beautification? A tremor of cold, shocking comprehension made him recoil at the thought of her practiced little deceptions, her avoidance of too much physical activity, and her preference for drinking sessions rather than taking in the sights. Meg, the woman he thought he loved, the fantasy of his dreams, had become a walking nightmare. He could no longer face sleeping with her and when Meg realised she had lost her physical hold over him, she resorted to longer drinking sessions and heavier doses of cocaine.

This situation continued into their third week, when an invitation arrived inviting them to an evening party at a villa overlooking the clear waters of Posillipo situated a little further round the bay. Meg was very excited and before leaving for the party, she spent longer than usual on restoration work. Francesco duly arrived in a Ferrari red coupe, whisking them along the Via Posillipo, Ben, tanned, looking every inch a Greek god and Meg beside him, her peroxide hair, wild in the fragrant sea breezes, the chariot born vision of a Celtic Queen. No one could deny, they made a handsome couple.

Ben's idea of a good party was a coming together of young people, a repeat of the one he so vividly remembered at Hareden Hall when Kelly had plucked at his heart strings. What a party that had been! Loud music, oceans of booze, marijuana and girls, girls, girls. If only he could have stayed to the end, some of those promises he dreamed of with Kelly might have happened.

At the Villa Rosa he was looking forward to the Italian alfresco version of a similar event and was disappointed to discover that it was nothing more than a social gathering of families and their relatives. Long tables were set beneath the hanging fruit of orange trees, ripe and ready for picking. Trailing geraniums, mimosa and bougainvillaea daubed their colours across the fading ochre of stuccoed walls and the scent of jasmine, aromatic herbs, basil, oregano and sage, infused the senses with intimate seduction. The tables were heavily laden with the very best of local produce, luscious offerings of wine, fruit and salads from the mineral rich slopes of Mount Vesuvius and other mouth watering delicacies readily available throughout the meal. Provision had also been made for the numerous children who attended, well behaved youngsters of all ages, wearing their stylish clothes, free to mingle, chattering and chirping away to each other in the background.

When all the guests had arrived, people casually sat down around the tables and in a gesture of goodwill to their foreign visitors, Meg and Ben were given pride of place at the head of the table next to the revered grandmother, nonna Vittoria Vera, the mother of Tonino and his three brothers. She plumped into her chair, struggling with obesity, flaunting her gold, flashing her diamonds, enjoying the attention like a true matriach, the maternal vision of a woman who has done her duty. Meg understood the Italian's enthusiasm for good food and wine, how they were able to share earth's bounty among family and friends, savouring each morsel in an act of celebration and she joined in their exuberance, chatting easily in broken Italian across the table. Ben was more attuned to the convenience of gobbled takeaways on the hoof and he struggled to capture the mood. He had always indulged his appetites in a selfish way, allowing himself the excesses of anti social behaviour, but this experience held the promise of a generous invitation, people were making each other happy, it was warm, welcoming and altogether more pleasurable. He turned to Meg,

'I didn't expect anythin like this Meg, these Italians really know how to enjoy a get together, and they think a lot of you. '

'Och aye, the English canna dae feasting, nae like the Scots, the Italians and the French. They're so uptight, worryin aboot table manners an the business o getting through the next course. The Italians enjoy sharin the pleasure o eatin. It's a bit like makin love,' she pinched Ben's thigh, 'takin more time o'er the foreplay.'

Over the next few hours, a succession of small servings followed leisurely one after the other. The jugs of wine and water were never allowed to stand empty. Friendship cast her net, love overflowed. Children were presented as being each family's most precious asset and their unhindered presence eliminated any posturing or pretence, making such behaviour ugly and dishonest. Ben finally entered into the spirit of the party, absorbed by the whole experience, from the casual quartering of ripe water melons to the spicy morsels of aragosta. He reponded easily and naturally to the inquisitive interest shown by the younger children, winning over their parents, making language difficulties less and less of a problem. Wine and water continued to flow, interrupted by cries of ' Salute, Viva Italia, Viva Inghiterra,' and in a more subdued manner, with glasses raised to the heavily seated nonna Vittoria, 'La madre.'

The men eventually drifted to the games room for business discussions and a gambling session. In an act of male bonding, Ben found himself hugged and embraced by influential members of the brotherhood, accepted unconditionally as one of their own. Stronger drinks were now on offer and assuming that being English he would appreciate the gesture, Ben was offered a bottle of Black Label to be consumed on the premises. Francesco, addressed by all as the capitano, could manage enough English conversation to act as interpreter which allowed Ben to join in the discussion. Everyone became pleasantly tipsy and increasingly vocal. After a few hours of serious carousing, Francesco and three other men returned to the patio where they huddled together around a table set apart from the women and children. Ben was invited to join them and Francesco explained that it concerned a briefing for their forthcoming voyage in the the Nuvola Distante. They took their drinks with them, collecting a few tasty morsels on the way. Francesco spread a tattered chart across the table.

The Nuvola Distante was a pretty, ninety odd tons, topsail schooner berthed on the Naples waterfront. Built at St Malo in 1905, she was purchased by a Scottish distillery for the whisky trade across the North Sea and named the Scottish Maid. Vera construction rescued her from the scrap yard, carefully restoring the ship to her former glory, manning her with a professional crew. She was renamed the Nuvola Distante and launched in the guise of a tax relief charity, giving disadvantaged teenagers with behavioural problems, a character building experience under sail. She also sailed on adventure trips for the disabled and was regarded with admiration and affection by the city's dignitaries. Behind this benevolent façade however, she was still operating in trade envolving business transactions worth millions of euros in cocaine and cannabis which she took on board at Lampedusa, landing her cargo at Syracuse and Mergellina by the ton. The Vera family also installed a powerful diesel engine giving the Nuvola Distante twelve knots against adverse winds and better control through the Straits of Messina.

The bottle of Black Label was half empty and Ben found it hard to concentrate. Francesco outlined the details of the voyage, their individual duties, times of departure, times of arrival, natural hazzards, the shipping forecast and the weapons they would carry and he made sure Ben understood all that was being said by repeating everything in English, but there was no mention of cocaine or illegal immigrants. This was to be a whole new experience for Ben. How would he cope with a voyage under sail, days at sea with a gang of ruthless criminals, posing as their shipmate and partner in crime? A wave of nausea made him suddenly weak and afraid. With grim, absolute certainty, he knew he was in the presence something evil.

In the early hours Capitano Francesco, demonstrating an iron resistance to the affects of alcohol, drove Meg and Ben back to their flat. He drove with extra care and was more talkative on the return journey. Ben would join the crew of the Nuvola Distante on the following Monday when Francesco would collect him shortly after midnight. Seated together, Meg studied Ben's profile. He looked so young, so handsome and she cuddled closer to him, the urgency in her body straining against his. Ben gazed through the window, transfixed by the glimmering lights around the bay, unable to respond. They arrived at the flat. There were the usual exchanges, 'Ciao, Ciao, Va bene,' and then finally, after all the excitement, the two of them were left alone.

Meg ached for her young lover, her passions aroused by an evening of bacchanalian delights and the assurance of knowing that her desire for carnal pleasures would be fullfilled in the most delightful manner. They showered together, a habit which usually preceded their consummation between the sheets and first made love on the cool, wet, terrazzo floor of the bathroom before continuing with leisurely foreplay on the king sized bed. As their love making continued, Meg sensed a distancing between them and she became troubled. 'Ben, darlin, you're nae makin love tae me. You're makin love tae someone else. Dae you nae still love me Ben?'

'I still love you Meg an no way do I ever want to hurt you, but I got too much on my mind, I mean what the hell am I doin here anyway? Livin some sort of make believe? I mean you're keepin most of my money leavin me with nothin much an I'm bein pushed deeper and deeper in the shit. It's true innit? Francesco and these guys are really scary and now on this trip they've got me carryin a gun an I've never carried a gun, swore I never would, not after Frankie. Sounds to me like they're expectin big trouble. Honestly Meg, I couldn't do murder, not like Pitbull. I'm scared of what I'm getting into, I mean this sort of life in't getting me nowhere.' Ben checked himself, he shouldn't be going on like this, he was supposed to be a secret agent and should be showing some enthusiasm. What really troubled him was a sense of betrayal, he'd informed the police about Meg's activities. This sneaking act of treachery would be her reward for the love she had shown him. How could he live with himself, knowing what he had done? Somehow he had to rescue her. 'Thing is Meg, I don't want to see you get hurt.'

'You were nae makin love to me were you? You were thinkin of Kelly.'

'Meg, why don't you give up the drugs scene? Surely you've got enough money to get right out of it, live abroad somewhere.'

'You're still wantin mah lassie, Ah've known it all along an Ah'm telling you, she's nae for you. Ah could see it, at the Villa Rosa an Ah realised then you'd make a good family man, Ah watched you, wi those kids, and Ah ken you want a younger woman who can give you bairns, and Ah ken ah canna do that and in time Ah know you'll find a lassie who will, but Ah love you Ben. Ah canna help maesel.'

'Listen to me Meg, you've got to get free of Tonino and the Vera crowd, start a new life.'

'Ben, you ken as well as Ah do, that's just nae possible for either of us, nae if we want to go on livin. It's nae possible for you and it's nae possible for me and Ben darlin, are we nae good together? Dae you nae want to live the sweet life and hold on tae it while it lasts?'

'That's just it Meg, I know it can't last and the longer we go on livin like this, pretendin our life's a ball, the worse it'll get between us.'

This remark, heavy with disillusion, stripped away the veneer of Meg's lifestyle. Meg was not a happy woman. Happiness is in the measure of that which is freely given and Meg's life had been driven by survival and its ulterior motives. For the first time in their relationship, Meg's emotions surfaced. After a lifetime of regrets, of broken promises, of missed opportunities, of shame and heartache, her love for Ben tore apart the mantle she had carefully woven to face the world. For once she let her feelings rule her head. 'Ah'm old enough to ken what love means,' she said, trying to hold back the tears. 'An Ah love you Ben, so much.'

Ben wandered across to the window, then turning, he faced Meg. Her features had softened and she looked younger, more vulnerable, holding nothing back, a woman very much in love. In two strides Ben had gathering her in his arms, kissing away the tears, kissing her neck, her lips, her cheeks. 'Please don't cry Meg. I know how tough you really are an I jus can't bear to hear you cry. I love you too Meg. I spose I always will.'

Everyone has their price. Philipino maids have theirs and it may be described as peanuts but Letitia's maid was different, her earnings not only included the humble wages for which Letitia was responsible but also regular payments into a Swiss bank. Tonino trusted no one, least of all his wife and her relations. More recently he had placed her under private surveillance using the most subtle approach. He had persuaded her to advertise for a home help, who in return for a modest allowance and living accomodation, would attend to her personal needs. Suzi spoke English in a manner which suggested she had only recently got to grips with the pronunciation while in fact her English was perfect. She was a versatile cook, her ability in the kitchen, especially with a wok, was full of eastern promise and her standard of cleanliness maintained at the very highest level but her real talents lay elsewhere. Before her association with Tonino and the promise of big money, she had worked on a Korean assembly line, manufacturing computors. Her manager discovered how clever she was and she trained as an electronic engineer only to suffer further exploitation by her employers. Hopes of aquiring wealth in this way or by marrying a rich husband eluded her and life became a treadmill. Eventually, in a bid to improve her standing in the world, she illegally immigrated to Italy, finishing the last leg of a long and hazzardous journey aboard the Nuvola Distante. On arriving Tonino gave her a job working for the Mafia on surveillance systems. She was attractive and he seduced her before arranging her seemingly innocent employment in the Vera household.

Suzi tried every trick she knew in order to confirm Tonino's suspicions, she checked out the data on Letitia's mobile, bugged her car, her tea tray, changing locations on a day to day basis, until one day she gained access to the writing cabinet and Letitia's sofisticated laptop and was able to hack into a secret file where she discovered months of encoded messages. It was impossible to break the code and although Ben's voice had cropped up several times in bugged conversations there had been no real evidence, nothing which might incriminate Tonino or his partners in their drug dealing operations, no reference to Mafia activities. However, it was enough for Tonino. He called for a meeting of the Mafia bosses in Naples and flew out there with Letitia on the pretence of giving her a well deserved break from January blues and an English winter. A couple of weeks lazing by the pool on the terraced gardens of their sumptuous villa, with a flunkey to answer her every whim, would help dispel the lingering depression of English grey skies. The Mediterranean, Italian skies, Italian sunshine and Italian food like mama used to make, would do wonders for her constitution. His real intention was to have her murdered.

At the meeting of the bosses it was decided that no further risks could be taken. The enterprise in Britian would have to operate under a new guise. Letitia and Ben would have to be wasted, preferably in Italy where hit men could more safely be organised. They had their own terminology for murder. 'Wasted' and 'hit men,' sounded macho and businesslike, unpleasant but inevitable, delivered with chilling indifference and a total disregard for human life. In an atmosphere of conspiracy and guarded friendship, evil intentions simmered below the surface with violence uppermost in mind. The death of Letitia would be assigned to a getaway driver who specialised in mowing people down with a four wheel drive. Ben Mackay would be hit during his forthcoming voyage on the Nuvola Distante. Jimmy, Meg's minder, would join the ship in order to carry out the mission.

Letitia had always loved Naples, the city had cast its spell, securing a place in her heart when she was young and the magic had never been broken. She lay, shaded under one of the trees which landscaped the pool, dappled in the sunlight as it filtered through the leaves. She tried to relax but the demands of operation Retiarius were sapping her will to survive. She had faithfully relayed every message from Ben to her contact in MI5 and the pressures were mounting. She feared for Ben's safety. Had he been caught in the act of making suspicious phone calls? This had been a weak link in the flow of information. She sensed danger, Tonino had been more considerate of late, a shift entirely out of character. Suzi the housemaid, had been far too familiar and seemed to be watching her every move. Had Tonino finally blown her cover? For months now, she had used methadone in the treatment of her heroin addiction. She had struggled on alone, desolate, without friends, without support, without love and her life had spiralled into a dark pit of depression. Dispairing at her own weakness, she resorted once more to heroin. Only heroin, delivered directly into the bloodstream from the point of a delicate needle, rescued her from terror, offering in its place a distortion of reality, a short circuit of self destruct masquerading as relief, a brief spell of comfort in the form of a resigned death wish.

The thought that she may have rescued Ben, her protégé, from Tonino's evil clutches saved her from total oblivion. There were times when her mind was crystal clear, a sanctuary of respite free from corruption where she was able to forgive herself. Ben had aroused maternal instincts, had opened the window of her soul letting in the light. She had ventured to look and what she had seen hadn't been so bad after all, for there she had seen a glimmer of hope, a chance of redemption and in these moments of sanity, the return of self control and dreams of one day returning home leaving this awful business to the due processes of law and order. Home to the dear English countryside where memories of a carefree childhood filled her with nostalgia. She smiled briefly at the thought, perhaps she was getting over anxious, paranoid even. Wasn't Naples a beautiful city? Wasn't this villa the last word in luxury? Wasn't her manservant Carlo a most charming companion, showing genuine concern for her welfare, ministering to her needs with hands on care and attention and the practiced demeanour of a male nurse? These thoughts did nothing to allay her fears as dark clouds continued to gather, just as she knew they would.

Letitia groped for the blanket, trying to hide her agitated body. The tremours were back, the cold sweats, the panic attacks. The awsome task which lay before her reared itself like a monster from the depths. How could she, a woman of noble birth, raised on high principals of morality, schooled in gentility but circumspect rather than brave, have taken on such an evil giant? All her life she had paid dearly for the teenage frolics of luxurious self indulgence, the broad highway of wealth and privilege. Unwittingly she had fallen into the hands of the devil incarnate and now by the grace of God, sought to bring him down.

However, it was not God who walked with her through the shadow of death, it was a young man, his life hanging by a thread, who acted as her agent in the field and the faceless, nameless puppeteers of MI5. During the last few weeks of operation Retiarius, her nerves had failed and as it neared its final conclusion she became increasingly dependent on regular shots of heroin. She needed one now.

Carlo, the manservant, thirty something, handsome in a boyish way, appeared custom made for menial sevice. He doted, he fawned on Letitia, he understood her drug dependence, referring to it as a problem shared, earning her sympathy by explaining his own heroin addiction and the humble circumstances of his birth in the back street slums of Naples and how his poor mother had suffered at the hands of a drunken husband and how she had raised six children in the most appalling conditions. He crossed himself, eyes raised to heaven with a murmered prayer, promising theVirgin Mary that every euro he earned would go towards his mother's welfare. In less than a week his warmth had gained Letitia's trust. Only his eyes were cold. Each day he shopped for their provisions on a battered Vespa with a panier basket strapped to the back, leaving his latest SUV with it's menacing bull bar at home in the garage.

Carlo was behind schedule. Tonino had given him two weeks in which to make a hit and time was running out. He made regular checks on Letitia waiting for an opportunity to strike and today he watched her from the kitchen window. He noted how restless she was and how those beautiful hands, musician's hands, pawed at the air. Tonino's stuck up junkie whore badly needed a fix. He sauntered through the flower beds armed with an hypodermic syringe, fully charged with a massive overdose of heroin. 'Mia bella Lady Letitia, Iya think you notta well. Iya think you wanna a good fix eh? '

Letitia lay back, exhausted, the last vestiges of mental reserve utterly drained. Dear Carlo understood her suffering and like a good son would lovingly deliver the necessary high. Without a word she offered him her arm. He very gently held it, caressing the alabaster skin, tracing the blue veins beneath, following the needle tracks.

The curtain came down on Letitia's world, the last scene a fading vision of the marble statues, Roman heroes, Roman gods, standing guard over the blue lagoon that was her swimming pool. Her body lay in repose, as cold as marble, whiter even than the statues. But unlike the statues, there appeared a smile on her face.

Chapter 14. An Island of Intrigue.

The mobile phone arrangement between Letitia Vera and Ben Mackay had certain advantages. Mobile phones are so popular their usage in public arouses no suspicion, they're very convenient and easy to carry. Ben's phone had never been registered and all messages to and fro concerning MI5 activities were instantly erased. Direct access to the software recordings retained by the mobile phone company was exclusive to MI5 who monitored the information by entering a code number and whenever Ben or Letitia phoned each other, they began their conversation with a secret procedure.

Ben had one more day before joining the crew of the Nuvola Distante and he decided to phone Letitia for any further instructions, bringing her up to date with the latest developments. While Meg was still sleeping, he quietly took himself out on the balcony. He breathed deeply at the rush of morning air, absorbed the panoramic views of the bay and tried to relax his nerves before thumbing the digits of his mobile phone. He could hear the ringing tone and waited for Letitia to answer.

'Hello,' came the reply in that haughty telephone voice Letitia always affected.

'Hi Letitia, Ben here, I've finished reading the book you gave me.' He paused waiting for the pre-arranged reply which should have been, 'Have you done all the exercises?'

'Ok Ben, I'll send you another. Looking forward to your cruise on the Med?' Suzi replied, sounding posh in muffled tones.

Ben hastily closed the conversation. Something had gone terrtibly wrong. His first thoughts were for Letitia, nobody, but nobody had access to Letitia's mobile. Instinctively he knew something dreadful had happened to her, which meant they were on to him. Perhaps he should do a runner, but to chicken out was not in his nature, he felt he had obligations to Letitia, to Meg, to his family, to Skeet, poor Skeet, fatally damaged by drugs, to Mike and Josh even. Delinquency had led to serious crime and he no longer felt the buzz of belonging to a gang who could never play it straight. He'd earned a kind of respect on the streets but in the Mafia he was nothing. Kelly had shown him the challenges of facing one's responsibilities, of honest endeavour and Letitia had helped him face those challenges. There was no going back even though he knew now that his life was in real danger.

Capitano Francesco arrived, taking the steps leading up to the appartment two at a time, his stocky figure deceptively agile for a man approaching fifty years of age. A younger Francesco had sailed in the Merchant Navy as first mate in possession of a master's ticket, but having been held partly responsible for a collision at sea, had ended up on the beach. He wore a peaked cap and a pale blue sweater with Nuvola Distante printed across the back. He rang the door bell and as Ben opened the door he turned to go, as though having no time for pleasantries, 'You ok Ben, let's go.'

The Nuvola Distante strained at her moorings as if yearning to reach the open sea. She was a fine vessel, her masts, spars and rigging, blocks and tackle, halyards, stays, sheets and shrouds, deadeyes and chainplates, immaculate, and all in perfectly good running order with not a sloppy rope fall in sight. She had been refitted by a traditional shipwright using selected hardwoods in the hands of the finest craftsmen. Cargo hatch covers had been replaced with raised coamings, rectangular portlights and a coachroof. Formerly the helmsman had steered the vessel in all weathers abaft the mainmast while standing on the open deck, now a generous self draining cockpit, half covered by a wheelhouse, provided shelter for the helmsman and those keeping watch. It also housed the compass and electronic aids to navigation. The new superstructure shone with marine varnish in fetching contrast to the laid decking which swept in silvered teak towards a thrusting bowsprit. The sails hung in their gaskets, flaked down in readiness for making sail and a rigid inflatable hung in davits, well secured over a raking transom. The schooner seemed alive at her mooring, her white hull breathing in the salt sea air, promising adventure, an unction for the tired souls of disillusioned landlubbers.

Ben was tired, Ben was disillusioned and Ben was certainly a landlubber. He felt metally and physically drained as they drove down to the marina, nervous at the thought of a passage at sea, but as they neared the Nuvola Distante his spirits lifted. The sheer scale of the kind of vessel he had only ever seen in paintings or on picture postcards struck him with awe and wonder and when he set foot on the deck, he was unable to disguise his excitement. The cargo space below had been converted into comfortable living accomodation for disabled persons with a communal sleeping area for the crew, but on these trips the accomodation arrangements were reversed and the crew occupied the cabins. In their usual quarters, canvas bunks extended from rollers secured to the ship's sides and were supported by straps from the deckhead.

For the purpose of smuggling cocaine, the bunks were stowed away providing ample space for a large consignent of drugs. Very occasionally the schooner shipped illegal immigrants into Italy, but these were not refugees escaping from poverty, people who wanted the chance to work for a living, hoping to send money home for their struggling families, or the victims of war and political oppression, or girls caught up in the white slave network, these were invariably characters who were already established criminals with powerful connections in drug trafficking and arms dealing. They paid enormous sums for the opportunity of extending their multi million pound operations throughout Europe.

Ben followed Francesco, stumbling down the companionway in a daze to be shown his berth in one of the cabins. Ben sensed a distancing in their relationship, the avuncular approach had cooled, the lines on Francesco's bearded face were deeper, the creased forehead more pronounced as his weathered good looks took on an expression of command. 'You musta change your clothes, weara your Nuvola Distante sweater and your sailing gear. Isa in this locker, ok, you're wet weather gear isa in this locker, ok. I want you musta listen carefully Ben. At sea, the crew isa for three watches, four hours on, eight hours off, two men on each watch, the rest allaways on call. Isa understood ok? I want you musta stand watch with Bruno, he isa very good seaman, isa my number one, understood, ok? Me, Iya no standing watch, the skipper isa not standing watch, ok, and I wanta you obey my orders, every times, you understand Ben, ok?'

Ben nodded, 'Yeah, ok Francesco, no problem, I'm really

up for this. She's an amazin ship! It's my first time on a sailin ship and I'm definitely up for it. It's really cool an I want to learn all about sailin and stuff, I won't let you down Francesco, fact is I'm lookin forward to it. Honest, I'll give it one hundred percent.'

Bruno, the first mate was also a professional seaman, a fisherman, who like his father before him, had smuggled goods into Italy for years. A short, powerfully built man of indeterminate age who loved back street brawling, womanising and bouts of heavy drinking ashore, but with a heaving deck under his feet, remained sober and steady as a rock. For Giovanni the engineer, crewing on board the Nuvola Distante was something of a hobby. In addition to his links with the Mafia he ran a legitimate business rebuilding scrap diesel engines, especially ancient pumps, which he exported to the third world. His mechanical genius with diesel engines was the perfect cover for a ruthless conman. 'China,' the cook was also an experienced seaman, Chinese of course, straight from Hollywood. His podgy fingers could do wonders in the galley but he was known to be careless with a chopper, and not just in the kitchen. The fifth crew member was a Vera blood relative, a Mafia PR man who kept a close eye on everyone. He had studied both Italian and international law and could be described as an intellectual. Jimmy the psychopathic hit man, no one ever got to know his surname and Ben, the reluctant MI5 spy, made up the full compliment. There were no introductions and Ben, having never been in contact with the 'muscle' element of Meg's partnership, had no idea who Jimmy was. These seven characters made up the crew of the Nuvola Distante, dangerous, shady customers on a voyage for the damned.

The Nuvola Distante cast off her moorings and motored out into the bay. A winter gale, an early reminder of the Mistral, that cold, strong, northwesterly wind which blows down the Rhone valley across southern France, had spent itself against the western shorelines of Corsica and Sardinia leaving a fair breeze for the schooner as she cleared the bay dipping her bow into the Tyrrhenian Sea. With the beautiful Isle of Capri falling astern, Francesco ordered a comfortable spread of canvas and the regular crew, each one a passionate seamen who loved his ship and the escape she offered from their murky dealings on the land, turned to with a will. Only Jimmy stood alone, a sinister figure, cold at heart and unapproachable, secretly afraid of water, hating every moment. Francesco stood at the helm watching Ben's enthusiastic response to orders, admiring his young strength as he hauled on the sheets and halyards and in a moment of weakness felt sorry that Ben's newly discovered brotherhood at sea would be snuffed out by a Mafia hit man, a man incapable of feeling, a man having no empathy with those who go to sea.

The Straits of Messina were directly down wind and Francesco lay off a few degrees bringing the wind across the starboard quarter on a course towards the primitive island of Filikudi, the most westerly of the Aeolian group. The islands were some one hundred and twenty miles away and the Nuvola Distante with her sheets eased was making about nine knots. Francesco wanted an easy passage, taking no unnecessary risks and though it meant navigating the islands and the Straits of Messina in darkness, this suited him, he had no wish to draw uncalled for attention to their exact position. Visibility was good and he knew the sea area like the back of his hands. He set the watches to begin at sixteen hundred hours and turned in for a few hours sleep leaving Bruno in command. He gave instructions to be called if the wind changed or if a problem arose and at the very latest, on their approach to Stromboli, the active volcano which would be sighted off their port bow, puffing small quantities of lava and ash about every twenty minutes, it's glow serving as an aid to navigation. At sixteen hundred hours Bruno would stand down for eight hours rest before rising for his watch, from midnight until four in the morning with Ben, the Inglese, a kid, with no experience, whom he couldn't help liking. Before taking to his bunk, falling in with Bruno's eight hours rest, Ben enjoyed the remaining hours on deck. He plied Bruno with endless questions and Bruno, who could hardly speak a word of English, answered with much use of sign language, laughter and leg pulling. Ben's favourite position was sitting astride the bowsprit, just forward of the stemhead where he could look back along the schooner's rolling deck, or look up to wonder at the swaying, majesty of her sails and rigging, or look down the knife-edge of her clipper bow as the tensioned bobstay sliced glittering swathes across the fathoms of deep blue water.

With Stromboli on the beam, Francesco gybed the schooner, bringing the wind on the port quarter to sail between Stromboli and Lipsari before shaping a course for a passage through the Straits. The wind, now reduced in strength to force four, maintained its direction and Francesco set a square topsail to run before the wind, assisted by a favourable current running south, through the Straits and on down the east coast of Sicily. Bruno had suggested they call in at Syracuse for a spell ashore, he thought the crew would appreciate the gesture, having performed so well and worked so hard under sail. He made no mention of the doctor's wife, a professional lady whom he'd met in a fashionable bar, a woman who liked a bit of rough and was always ready to renew their aquaintance, but Francesco refused, he had more serious matters in mind. The Nuvola Distante ghosted through the Straits of Messina, only the creaking of her timbers and the sighing of the wind in her rigging betrayed her position at sea.

Ben's midnight watch passed like a dream. Using powerful binoculars, he reported the lights carried on all shipping sighted in the vicinity and Bruno explained the recognition of lights and what they meant, and how to work out the course and speed of other vessels in relation to the Nuvola Distante and whether there was a need to avoid a possible collision. In contrast to their earlier banter, little conversation passed between them. The Milky Way arched across the celestial canopy spilling stars in its wake like florescent diamonds on black velvet. A vast, heaving bosom of whispering salt water cradled the schooner, seemingly aloft, floating effortlessly in space and time. The wind strength fell, giving way to a land breeze blowing from the shores of Sicily. Bruno ordered the crew on deck, where, leading from the front, he directed sail changing operations. They took in the square topsail, shook out reefs on both fore and aft mainsails giving Ben a chance for his first experience on the helm. The schooner heeled gently on a close reach and Ben thrilled as she surged ahead, feeling her power through his fingers on the wheel, through every tendon, every muscle, as his body flexed, feeling every subtle motion through the balls of his feet.

Ben's first watch at sea ended. He felt exhilarated but weary, keen for more adventure, but desperately in need of recuperation. He collapsed gratefully into his bunk and lulled by the motion of the ship, gradually drifted into a shallow sleep. He woke with a start, switched on the bulkhead light and checked his wrist watch, it was only five in the morning, he still had seven hours of stand down, long enough to relax, to settle into a deeper sleep, but he was now wide awake, acutely aware of his dangerous predicament and the role he was expected to play, starkly conscious of a lurking, unknown factor, which under the guise of a romantic voyage under sail, might lure him into a trap. With some reluctance he fumbled the zip of his sleeping bag, feeling restless, ready for a breath of fresh air on deck and in bare feet quietly made for the companionway where a steep flight of steps led up to the wheelhouse. He paused on the lower tread. Pietro Vera and Jimmy the odd ball, had taken the midnight watch. They were discussing something in English. The cabin doors were open and Ben took the next step in order to hear more clearly. He took a quick peek just above the threshold. Pietro was at the helm. Jimmy sat, coiled like a spring. Their lower faces were dimly illuminated by a subdued compass light. Jimmy's eyes were dark, menacing, hollowed out of a shaven skull. Both men looked hideous.

'When dae ye want me tae hit the Sassenach? Ah'm thinkin the sooner the better. We can gi him a burial at sea.' Jimmy said, screwing his face into a half smile.

'No, no I don't think so. Only Francesco knows about our little problem. Jimmy, I want you to listen very carefully. First we pay our respects in Lampedusa, where for convenience, we have our own mooring buoys in the outer harbour. Then when conditions are right, we'll drop anchor off one of the beaches and under cover of darkness we'll load our consignment. It's very heavy work and at this point I think Ben may be very useful?' Pietro gave Jimmy a knowing look.

'Och aye, he can dae mah work for sure, Ah'm nae here tae work like a dago, ah'm here tae carry oot mah business. So when am Ah daein the hit?'

'Once the coke's on board, we'll make our way back to

220

the harbour where a private launch will take all the crew ashore for a little serata ricevemento, you know, wine, women and song, beautiful women and beautiful wine, Malvasia from Lipari, I'll bring you back a bottle. You, Jimmy, will take the anchor watch, staying on board with Ben. When we've gone, that's when you strike. But there must be no shooting, Ben's not carrying a gun, he's unarmed and you have nothing to fear. We want a nice clean job, no blood, no mess, ok?'

'Och aye, an thanks for the wine, but Ah never touch alcohol an Ah'm nae interested in the lassies. The hit's nae problem. Ah'll just break his neck.'

Pietro continued in lowered tones, 'bring his body ashore in the ship's tender, I'll let you know where to land. Vera consruction is building a new harbour installation in Lampedusa and we'll make sure Ben has a nice headstone, about fifty cubic metres of concrete.' The rest of the crew will think he's jumped ship. Ok?'

Ben lost all feeling in his legs, he had no grip on the handrail. The Nuvola Distante increased her angle of heel, and for the first time at sea he knew he was going to throw up. He staggered back to the cabin, crashed into the louvred door before doubling up over the wash basin, wrenching at his stomach muscles, his body shaking, his natural defences coming apart. This wasn't a late night horror movie, a three star shocker with all the latest special effects, or some heinous story doing the rounds in a recycled paperback, bedside reading before sleep dismissed the drama for what it was worth, oh not this time, this had been for real, so final, so matter of fact, like standing in the dock, hearing your own death sentence. With shaking hands he locked the cabin door hovering behind its flimsy line of defence, expecting to hear faint echoes, murmerings of this ghastly conspiracy. But there was no sound, only the familiar creaking of a sailing vessel and the rush of water against her hull. He collapsed on the bunk, too weak to get into the sleeeping bag. The chilling description of his murder, rehearsed by two souless killers and the terrifying details of the disposal of his body, obliterated all thinking processes.

An hour passed before Ben calmed down. He became more rational and began to consider his position. What was happening to him? What circumstances during the passage of his young life had led to such a dreadful conclusion? He needed to grasp, to fully understand his motives for making the journey thus far and at first he tried to think defensively, to go back to the beginning, back to the Asbos, back to the environs of New Horizons Park. Why did society treat gang culture as though it had descended upon them like a plague, a phenomenon peculiar to modern life and times, a disease from outer space, alien to human behaviour? Hadn't there always been gangs in one form or another? The only difference was their power and whether they operated within the accepted laws of the establishment or made their own laws. Ben thought their objectives were the same, to gain power, to have control. He reasoned, money institutions were gangs who exploited wealth, oil companies were gangs who exploited energy, political parties were gangs who exploited bureaucratic control, supermarkets were gangs who exploited retail, armed forces were gangs who exploited violence, and the Mafia was a gang who exploited fear. All these gangs, directly or indirectly were in some measure ruthless. Hadn't the Asbos been just a little gang, kicking against a society which had submitted to the control of big gangs, gangs so powerful, they were able to subjugate half the world's population? People who found a comfortable niche in the system played the game according to the rules and had no wish to rock the boat, but the under privileged, those unable to find expression, those whom society swept under the carpet, well, some of these people rebelled. In Ben's mind these arguments were unassailable and yet they no longer held their appeal. His passion for them had been exhausted and although they held an element of truth, he now realised that in no way did they excuse his enthusiam for anti social behaviour. The notoriety, the respect from other gangs, the buzz he'd felt, had been addictive and had meant more to him than making a serious effort at school with it's possible risk of failure and now he realised the course he'd taken, opting for an easy way to beat the system, had ended in a dice with death.

As a child Ben had witnessed the results of alcohol abuse and his father's violence towards his mother. He had been raised on New Horizons Park, where decent folk who wanted work, who longed for independence and self esteem, found themselves buried in a lower strata of society, along with the idle, the unemployable, the under achievers, petty criminals, drug dealers and social misfits, where welfare benefits further emasculated the community, weakening it's resolve, leaving an indelible smear across the records of each and every unfortunate who struggled to break free. With little room to manoeuvre, Ben's maverick approach to life had spiralled out of control descending into violence. It had been a natural regression, instinctive for boys who rebelled against a regime of theory in the classroom, who wanted a more practical influence in their lives. Anti social behaviour was the negative side effect of a nation which had lost touch with it's rank and file, where real work and the development of skills was at a premium, where bureaucracy had filled the gap, taken control, robbing people of their personal responsibility. The Asbos had raided shops, broken into warehouses, stolen cars, anything they were able to sell for cash, vandalised property and public amenities and traded in drugs. They went looking for gang fights, relishing the confrontations in their very own private war for territorial surpremacy, proud of their wounds, showing off their battle scars. Certain victims had been targeted, beaten half to death in order to spread fear, guns had lead to fatal reprisals and against this epidemic of social mayhem the suffering made headlines of indignation, but continued without healing or hindrance, leaving it's trail of anarchy and hatred.

Ben's thinking processes twisted, turned, backtracked, but his body no longer registered these confused ramblings and he lay quite still considering the uncomfortable images of his former behaviour in a more rational state of mind. The way forward now became crystal clear. He wanted no part of a criminal lifestyle and recognised the self delusion in hiding behind the emotive arguments of the dispossessed. Asbo behaviour, falling in with Tonino and his drug dealing no longer seemed the natural and logical thing to do. Idle hands and easy money had never inpressed the people he most admired. Now he was a reformed character, rescued at the point of no return by the influence of Mike Edwards and his son Josh, who by their example addressed social problems from within the sphere of good citizenship, building stepping stones not stumbling blocks. The unrequited love he felt for Kelly made him realise his attitude to life, fostered by male pride and jealous envy, had been a way of getting revenge and had it not been for the flawed but courageous Lady Letitia, for certain, he would have pursued these unhealthy preoccupations to the point of self destruct. She had drawn him back from the brink, setting up the unbelievable transition from the leader of a street gang to an undercover agent for MI5. Now he had a chance to prove his real worth.

However, his daring, his bottle, was still being tested just has it had been when he'd led the Asbos. This was a new challenge, the gaunlet of a warrior culture within a different kind of gang culture which still held dubious attractions for the alpha male. With the unknown fate of Letitia preying on his mind he tried ringing her again. Ominously the phone line was dead. The full import of the risks Letitia had taken on his behalf bore down on him like a dead weight. Now he understood what exactly she had tried to achieve and the price she may have paid. Her actions, prompted by maternal love, had almost certainly resulted in dire consequences and the thought made him feel helpless, worried and concerned, feelings which gave way to desperate anger and the need to get even. His snivelling fear gave way to iron resolve, now he knew what he had to do. He wanted a chance to begin again, to wipe the slate clean, to become a joiner, to work alongside Mike and Josh, to convince Kelly that he was worthy of her love, to make amends to his mother, his brother and sister, but first he must brace himself for the deadly mission which lay ahead. He had to honour his promise to Lady Letitia and do all that was necessary to free her from the clutches of Tonino Vera. In this calculating frame of mind, a course of action slowly took shape.

Knowing in advance what Pietro and Jimmy were planning gave him a God given advantage, the element of surprise, and he knew also that at some point only he and Jimmy were to be left on board. This is when he'd have to make a move, when he'd turn the tables on this bunch of crooks and if it was his life or Jimmy's on the line ok, he'd make certain Ben Mackay would be the last man standing. His first priority was to learn all he could about the running of the Nuvola Distante, how to get her under way, how to cast off moorings or raise anchor, how to operate her diesel engine and how to navigate using the compass, sat. nav. and charts. Mentally drained, sleep came at last, half waking, half dreaming, taking possession of his troubled mind.

Ben dozed through the remainder of the standown in the manner of a wild animal, eyes closed yet somehow visually aware, body at rest yet deceptively alert and he immediately responded when Bruno shook him for the midday watch, 'Ok capitano Inglese mucha beauty sleep eh?' Laughing and already in good humour they joined Francesco, Giovanni and China in the wheelhouse where Ben made a special effort to remain lighthearted. The wind remained steady, backing westerly force three, the visibility excellent. The eastern tip of the Maltese archipelago lay on the starboard beam with Valletta and it's Grand Harbour, one of the finest natural harbours in Europe and a regular port of call for the Nuvola Distante when carrying tourists. A skyline of vanilla walls, forts and ramparts, the dome of Carmelite Church and the ordered spread of it's flat roofs, all drenched in the sunlight, beckoned Francesco. He loved Valletta, for him a city of sweet memories and taking the helm, he sailed towards the harbour entrance as though making a sudden decision to sail around Gozo at the western end, but it was only a distraction, a chance to further satisfy his nostalgia. Those ashore with time on their hands watched the schooner. She was a familiar sight, 'Look,' they said, 'There's the Nuvola Distante, what a beautiful ship! What a sight under sail! She does so much good for the disabled you know, may God bless her, keep her safe.' Other's who wished to show off their superior knowledge said, 'I see she's carrying a civil ensign and flying the Vera sail training pennant. Italy could have no finer ambassador, she's a credit to the nation.'

Sailing close inshore Francesco lay off his approach to Valletta, rounding the eastern tip of the island, close hauled, following the Dingli cliffs along the southern shoreline. A small group of tourists were visiting the Madalena Chapel perched on the highest vantage point and some were scanning a fleet of fishing vessels with shared binoculars. When they caught sight of the Nuvola Distante, she took their breath away. A white, seabourne vision of absolute splendour, a free spirit, a ghost ship, a creation of those ancient mariners whose romantic endeavours had been drowned in the depths. They watched with longing, wanting a share in the historical experience, envying the good fortune of those on board. Mediterranean cruise ships passed the Nuvola Distante and a sighting was considered a surprise bonus in their itinary. Ferries, plying from Porto Empedocle in Sicily to Linosa and Lampedusa, often sailed in company with the schooner and the passengers crowded the decks to watch her progress, waving their arms at the crew of the Nuvola Distante as though greeting a much loved relative. She stirred their hearts with feelings of patriotism, with echoes of former glory, of adventure and heroism, a golden era, when their forefathers had discovered the world in the magnificent age of sail.

Francesco ordered a change of course freeing the wind to sail on a close reach for the island of Lampedusa about ninety miles west of their position inshore of the Maltese coast. On the following morning as they approached Lampedusa he radioed the harbour enquiring whether he could berth alongside rather than pick up his usual moorings. The port authorities confirmed that he could berth on the end of the western pier which formed part of the inner harbour. This pleased Francesco, it made getting ashore so much easier. During the passage from Malta Ben had familiarised himself with the workings of the ship, acting the part of a rookie eager to learn while making a special effort to remain cheerful and friendly towards the rest of the crew. He kept well clear of Jimmy though, and at every opportunity studied his frame, the way he moved, measuring his wiry strength and agility. Physically he decided, Jimmy was not so intimidating, Ben had youth on his side. It was Jimmy's personality that he found unnerving, the way he looked at people, unable to disguise the smouldering, volatile nature of a psychopathic mind.

Before entering the harbour Francesco started the engine, the crew lowered all sail, folding each one neatly in their gaskets before motoring towards the western pier. Fenders were lowered, warps coiled for easy handling and the crew stood by, ready to cast lines ashore. Francesco took the helm and with hands skillfully fingering the engine controls, gently manoevered the vessel alongside the jetty while earnestly bawling commands at the crew. The ship was made fast, rope falls were coiled, hitched to cleats or belaying pins and everything on deck was left clean and shipshape before the crew was allowed off duty. Most of them went to their cabins for a change of clothing and a freshen up. China, who had been taking things easily, returned to the galley. He had been making careful preparations for the evening meal, a sweetener, held in the main saloon for special guests who had been invited to renew their acquaintance with Vera sail training hospitality. The guest list included Mafia links with the Lampedusa drug smuggling racket, agents acting on behalf of illegal immigrants, air traffic control officers and of course the principal harbour official. Thirteen in all were seated around the table and in such circumstances, Ben couldn't help thinking it was an unlucky number.

A hubbub of laughter, following the irrepressable flow of smutty, Italian jokes and loud mouthed ribaldry drifted through the open skylights from late afternoon until the early hours on the following day. China launched his entire repertoire of Italian cuisine, limited in scope, but generous in proportions with enough wine and spirits to stock the bar of a cruise liner. These appeared on the table in quick sucession as empties were cleared away. Throughout the evening Italian was spoken in various dialects making it impossible for Ben to follow the conversation. Francesco placed Ben next to Jimmy, unhappy with the arrangement but knowing that at least they spoke the same language and hopefully wouldn't feel excluded from the rest of the company. Ben was horrified, he would have rather given the party a miss. Jimmy opened the inevitable dialogue. 'Ah'm thinkin ye mus be Meg's toyboy, are you no? Ah'm Jimmy her partner, her minder d'ye ken.' He directed his remarks to the meal in front of him without giving Ben a sideways glance. The words probed, mocked, menaced like poison darts. Ben pretended he hadn't heard and continued eating.

'We've nay had the pleasure but she's telled me all aboot ye an Ah've been watching ye Ben Mackay an Ah can see why she's got the hots for ye, nae doot she thinks you're a bonnie braw laddie.'

'Yeah, I know Meg from New Horizons. She mentioned you once or twice, said you were a hard case, but I never realised you worked for Tony Vera, I thought you were your own man. Funny how I never saw you around though. And another thing, jus for the record, I in't a bonnie braw laddie and I in't Meg's toyboy either, we happen to love each other. Corse, everyone knows you got a liking for *bonnie laddies* and I spose you can't get your head round me lovin Meg, but it true all the same.'

Jimmy wanted confrontation, especially with those on his hit list. For him, putting each contract on a more personal basis turned a cold blooded murder into a private dual. Honour, perversely had to be satisfied and the whole process gave him a tremendous kick. Ben's cheeky reponse was a huge turn on and in addition he felt sexually aroused. Ben wasn't just another victim, he was now an object of desire.

'Ben Ah'm thinkin maybe we could be pals, nay need tae fall oot over Meg. Ah ken ye like her and ah ken she's somethin else between the sheets, but ye need tae mind, all the years Ah've known her, she's never been wi'oot a bloke.' He paused to consider how best to lure Ben away from the present company. 'Och aye, Ah ken Meg's nae mean lassie. Ah got some photees o her back in mah cabin, photees o her posin nude. You'll nae have seen em, they're her private little collection, but if you want tae see em, we'll slip oot an Ah'll show em ye, ye can chose which ones ye want, Ah'll gi ye a couple.' He reached under the table, pinching Ben's thigh in a suggestive way and when Ben drew away he gave the flesh a cruel twist.

'Get your stinkin hands off me you bent perv. Jus keep away.'

Jimmy studied Ben through narrowed eyes savouring the prospect of having been given a free hand in the manner of his death, a deed unhindered by any feelings of empathy, pity or remorse, eyes the mirror of an empty soul, a predator devoid of all thought save the devouring of it's prey. He could hear the click, as Ben's neck gave way in a vice like grip. 'There's somethin aboot me ye havnee reckoned wi mah bonnie laddie. You're talkin tae a wolf, ah think like a wolf, ah act like a wolf an ah see like a wolf, an all ah can see the noo is you're bones wi the flesh all tore away, jus you're bones Ben Mackay, all white, with nae flesh on em. That's what ah see ma bonnie laddie.' All evening he'd been sipping fruit juice but suddenly he stood up and without looking at the label, took a long swig from the bottle in front of him. He turned, clicking his tongue in a strange guttural manner, as though rehearsing the sound for his own benefit. 'Di ye hear that, well, that's the last you'll be hearing from me ye bonnie braw Sassenach.' With this final gesture he left the table. No one took any notice but Ben was visibly shaken.

In the early hours, having drunk themseves sober, one by one the party goers tumbled down the gangway. Mafia lines of communication had been reinforced, deals had been struck and a criminal agenda concerning bribes and corruption had been addressed item by item, in a casual manner, with satifactory results. Arrangements were made, time schedules were sychronised, there would be no hitches. During the hours of darkness the Nuvola Distante would take on board a consignment of pure cocaine, fifteen hundred kilos in all, worth seven hundred million euros on the street and in addition, on the hour of departure, four illegal immigrants would be smuggled aboard.

There was much handshaking, much backslapping, much embracing, as they staggered into the vehicles parked on the quayside. Everyone had been payed handsomely for their services. The harbour master in particular was pleased with the night's business and as he settled himself behind the wheel of a fishmonger's van, craftily borrowed from an accomplice, the keys to a luxury flat on the bay of Naples bunched heavily in his back pocket.

The crew slept through the morning. Only Ben found sleep impossible. Late into the afternoon Francesco roused the crew. A light breeze continued from the north west leaving calm waters in the lee of the island, perfect conditions for an anchorage further down the coast. The Nuvola Distante left her berth and under engine headed out to sea. She rounded the headland nosing into the next bay, where the irregular shoreline was skirted by the Via Cala Francese, a road running along a narrow strip of land between the airport runway and the sea. Francesco made for a deep inlet at the eastern end of the bay and dropped anchor as close inshore as possible, leaving enough sea room to clear the bay without difficulty. The runway ran close to the western shore, its length terminating less than two hundred yards from the Via Cala Francese, offering a convenient link from one side of the bay to the other.

A thin veil of cloud hastened the fading light until the Nuvola Distante gradually melted into a canvas of ultra marine sea and blackened cloud. She carried no riding lights and under cover of darkness launched the rigid inflatable. Bruno took charge of the landing party while Francesco and Jimmy remained on board. Francesco hissed last minute instructions until, with Bruno at the controls, the splutter of an out board engine drowned the urgency in his voice. Bruno hardly opened the throttle but even so, the lightweight tender showed a surprising turn of speed. Pietro, Giovanni, China and Ben arranged themselves around the central control column, heads craned forward, eyes straining into the night.

Ben felt strangely alienated from the whole operation, an unwilling accomplice whose function has been relegated to that of an onlooker. The rubberised fabric of the inflatable and its wooden thwarts were wet with condensation and he could feel the damp seeping through his cotton slacks, through his clammy fingers, threatening to drown his resolve. At the very first opportunity, as soon as they hit the beach, the possibility of making an escape, stepping out of of this gathering nightmare seemed a more favourable option and he shivered at the thought. The boat gently butted its way towards the shore, a menacing wall of darkness, black against black, an impenetrable, featureless barrier closing in on them from all sides.

Ben could only think of tomorrow when he would be forced to face the horror of an attempt on his life, in a manner unknown, by a character whose very demeanour froze him to the marrow. And yet for some perculiar reason he was not afraid. He was surprised and somewhat relieved by the cold calculating frame of mind which had suddenly possessed him allowing him to function, to think clearly. He'd never felt this way before and the total absense of fear disturbed him. He'd shrugged off the old familiar Ben Mackay, metamorphasised somehow, into someone he was unable to recognise, someone dangerous. He tried to reinstate the person he'd left behind, to reassure himself that nothing had really changed and he tried to recall the faces of the women he loved, Kelly, Meg, his mother and his sister. He tried to reach out to those whom he respected, Letitia, Mike and Josh, but his mind's eye failed to give any one of them a face. He could only think of himself and his survival. Perhaps he was becoming like the men who now huddled around him, perhaps he had always been one of them, a hardened criminal, a ruthless mobster, a killer.

Suddenly out of the gloom, deceptively near on the port bow, a light flashed. Ben blinked in disbelief, but unmistakably it flashed again. Bruno throttled back, then altered course towards it. He beached the craft on a narrow spit of sand where three men were waiting for their arrival. Bruno carried a small anchor ashore making it fast higher up the beach. Then, without a word of recognition, all eight men filed up the sandy tracks leading to the road where a small truck had been parked. The three onshore men climbed into the cab and making as little noise as possible, the landing party loaded into the back of the vehicle. The truck drove towards the harbour stopping short of a sharp bend in the road, at a point where it ran very close to the end of the runway. Francesco had given orders not to wear an article of white clothing and before leaving the truck Bruno produced a pot of grease paint, instructing the crew to blacken their faces. Ben followed Bruno as they headed for the runway, his mind now a complete blank, unable to fully appreciate the scale of the operation. The party positioned themselves among the scrub, beyond the glare of runway lighting, and waited.

In less than thirty minutes a propjet, chartered by Euro Express Car Parts to carry freight for Tunisia, circled the airport, interrupting its return flight to make a perfect landing in

Lampedusa. It used only half the runway but continued to taxi the whole length. At the end of the runway it swung through 180 degrees before coming to a halt, its engines still running. A side door opened and seventy five plastic bales, each containing twenty sealed, one kilo packets of pure cocaine, jettisoned onto the tarmac. The door closed and the plane taxied back to the airport terminal. Shouldering one sack at a time, without haste, the smugglers humped the consignment from the airfield to the waiting truck, a back breaking job, undertaken with willing enterprise. During the operation, Pietro kept an eye on the road. The truck drove back to the beach where the load was passed down to the water's edge. Bruno completed the transfer making several trips to the unlit Nuvola Distante, delivering each load on a reciprical compass bearing. Using one of the halyards, the sacks were craned on deck and when the whole crew were back on board, the illicit cargo was safely stowed below. After the night's work, with muscles aching, everyone turned in for a much needed rest.

    Everyone that is except Ben. He locked his cabin door and wedged it fast, painfully aware of his vunerability, and being unarmed, feeling at a serious disadvantage. With this in mind he'd taken a kitchen knife from the galley, placing it under his pillow to lessen the odds. Thus far the schedule outlined by Pietro during his watch with Jimmy had gone according to plan, there had been only one deviation. The Nuvola Distante would most probably return to her berth alongside the pier and not pick up mooring buoys as Pietro had suggested. It was only a minor detail but it was enough to add an element of uncertainty. Ben decided, that in spite of weariness he must remain ever watchful and never let Jimmy out of his sight. He dozed, slipping now and then into a deeper sleep only to reawake at regular intervals with a violent start.

    As predicted, directly after noon on the following day the ship motored back to her berth on the quay. There was no private launch. Instead, the truck which had been used for the previous night's work, arrived with total disregard for secrecy or any fear off legal intervention. The crew piled into the wagon, joking about their V.I.P. treatment and the luxury of their humble conveyance. In a flurry of excitement, high expectation and aftershave lotion they drove off for an evening's celebration and the carnal pleasures of Pietro's night out for the boys. Following Francesco's orders, Ben stayed aboard. He leaned over the rail to see them off, counting each man as they climbed into the vehicle, looking out for Jimmy, anxious to know exactly where he was, but to his dismay Jimmy failed to make an appearance. A deathly silence fell over the ship. Ben considered this latest development. He was on deck, Jimmy was below. Ben decided that he had no option but to stay on deck. He sensed Jimmy laying in wait somewhere in the bowels of the ship, waiting for the unguarded moment, like a snake in the grass for it's blundering prey. The situation was desperate. Should he simply run away, disappear into the night? How could he, knowing he was trapped on an island with little chance of escape, with no food or money, where he would inevitably be hunted down? For the first time in his life he needed more than a willingness to kill, he needed the killer instinct, the ability to kill at close quarters, to look his victim in the eye, to feel the sweat, to taste the fear. Now he was thinking like a cornered rat, now he knew what he had to do. He stationed himself in the wheelhouse, sitting directly opposite the head of the companionway, his kitchen knife at the ready, his back arched ready to spring. Jimmy would eventually come looking for him and when he reached the top of ladder using both hands to steady himself, his body fully exposed in the hatchway, Ben would drive the knife between his ribs.

Ben patiently waited, his resolve, his adrenalin, keeping sleep at bay, his nerves stretched to their limit, his body braced for action. Darkness fell and Ben switched on the main wheelhouse light. As he did so there was a shuffling in the companionway. Jimmy was mounting the ladder. Suddenly Jimmy's upper body was there, right in front of him, just as he'd hoped, his arms reaching out for the handrails, his chest presenting a perfect target. Ben relaxed for a moment, then with brute force, plunged the knife deep into Jimmy's rib cage. Jimmy hung on for a moment, his wound pumping blood. Incredibly he made no sound, then after fixing Ben with an evil eye, he lost his grip, teetering for a moment, before collapsing to land with a heavy thud on the floor below. A surge of relief swept over Ben, his initiative had worked, he had slain the dragon and yet he remained tense, immobilised by shock, unable to grasp that his would be assassin lay dying, almost at his feet. Incoherent mutterings, broken by unearthly groans, were wickedly reassuring, most certainly the death throes of an evil monster, a man who would soon be a rotting corpse.

Ben felt sick, very sick. He had taken someone's life, not in anger, not under the influence of drugs or alcohol, not in a frenzy of self preservation, not while the balance of his mind had been disturbed, but in a cold calculating way, in Jimmy's way, the way of a ruthless killer. The awful revelation of what he was capable of scared him. It had all been so easy, so easy to plan, so easy to kill. He rushed on deck, doubled up over the rails and threw up violently. He recovered for a moment and again his stomach wrenched as if to discharge the bile secreted by such a murderous act. He gripped the rail feeling weak and exhausted when suddenly his animal instincts for survival were aroused by a sense of fear and inpending horror.

The footsteps across the deck were soft, shuffling and slow and before he could turn he felt his neck clamped in the steel sinews of a death lock. The knife had missed Jimmy's heart and with supernatural reserves, driven by rage and revenge, he had withdrawn the blade, discarding the weapon in favour of destroying Ben with his bare hands. Ben almost passed out, but with lightning reflexes, knowing he would be unable to break the grip of what must surely be the devil incarnate, using all his strength, he heaved himself and Jimmy over the rails into the sea.

Ben was a natural swimmer and he took a huge gulp of air before hitting the water sinking fathoms down into the harbour's murky depths. This last ditch reaction saved Ben's life. Jimmy was insensitive to most dangers, but the thought of being drowned, buried alive under a huge weight of water, was for him the one thing that registered blind panic. He immediately released his grip. He couldn't swim. He began a useless, frantic struggle for breath until his mind finally imploded, shrinking down to a capsule of claustrophobic light. The groping sensation of fingers, curiously detached, clawing at gravel on the sea bed, was the last thing of which he was vaguely aware.

Ben, now high on adrenalin, swam towards an iron ladder, bolted for the convenience of small craft, on the vertical face of the quay. He heaved himself up one rung at a time, giving his body a chance to recover from the effects of a do or die effort, then grasping a ruptured shoulder muscle, he staggered back towards the Nuvola Distante. Before going on board he prowled the length of the pier looking and listening for Jimmy, but Jimmy had disappeared into oblivion. It would be several days before his body was recovered, floating among the flotsam and jetsam of the inner harbour.

Having satisfied himself that Jimmy was no longer a threat, Ben returned to his cabin, changed into dry clothes, poured himself a drink and sat for a moment, contemplating the man he had become. He felt incredibly strong, invincible, ice cool. a new Ben Mackay had emerged from the mortal combat which had been thrust upon him, he had graduated from an unschooled tearaway, a social community problem, a civic embarrassment, to a self contained secret agent. He had achieved this status without special training, without a suitable education. As far as the MI5 bosses were concerned Ben was expendable, they had no great expectations of him, he was merely an item, a wild card, a long shot. But now Ben warmed to the idea and felt ready to embrace the role. He'd make them sit up, take notice, make them see he had what it takes. Street crime had been training enough, had toughened him up, had helped subdue feelings of guilt or concern for the welfare of others. Now he could wage war with the law on his side and when circumstances permitted, could exercise power over life and death.

He needed to relax, to think clearly about his next move. He realised that somehow he must escape before the crew discovered he'd not been dispatched and that Jimmy was missing. He had to leave the island. During the voyage Ben had taken great care to understand the ship's engine controls, how to slip moorings, and as many aspects of handling the schooner as possible. He felt brave, in control, ready to turn the tables on these Mafiosa hoodlums. While the crew were ashore celebrating the success of their enterprise and the prospect of huge returns, their bellies bloated with food and wine, Ben would make sure that on their return they'd be in for a shock. The Nuvola Distante and her precious cargo would have already sailed without them.

Ben retrieved the murder weapon intending to throw it overboard when clear of the island. He cleaned up the evidence of blood, already sticky and drying in the companionway and climbed into the wheelhouse, praying that Francesco had left the engine ignition keys. Francesco had seen no reason to remove these and as Ben flicked them over, he noted the fuel gauge registered three quarters full. He pushed the starter button and after the second attempt, the diesel throbbed into life, idling in low revolutions. He studied the charts and with the parallel rulers laid off a course for Malta. He had no understanding of magnetic variation or compass deviation but could see that Malta lay about one hundred miles east of Lampedusa. Having worked out a compass course he went ashore to slip the fore and aft bowlines from their bollards. The ropes lay slack and easy to handle. He took the gang plank in a couple, of strides and set about hauling the lines inboard. The stirrings of a sea breeze pushed the schooner away from the quay held now only by fore and aft springs. Ben hauled in the gang plank and tried to release the forward spring but the rope had stretched taut with the weight of the ship, jamming the turns over a cleat. He went below heading for the engineer's store, took an hacksaw from Giovanni's tool locker and raced back on deck to cut through the remaining lines.

Francesco had moored the vessel facing the end of the pier for an easy departure. Fortune favours the brave and the ship drifted away from the quay. Had the wind been been more northerly she would have held fast against the harbour wall and would have required a great deal more skill to get clear, but everything seemed to be going Ben's way. He took the wheel, eased the engine controls to slow ahead and steered for the harbour entrance and the open sea. He began feeling very much in control, heroic even, confident that he held all the necessary credentials for an undercover agent and he liked the feeling, he liked it a lot. His early resolutions about working with Mike, about trying to impress Kelly, making things right with his family, no longer held their appeal. He'd found a life of adventure, he'd discovered an inner strength, he needed no one. He was alone, a complete novice, with a seventy five feet schooner, registered at over one hundred tons, motoring due east at six knots on a calm sea. He could never in his wildest dreams have imagined such a situation. A thousand miles away, a thousand cares away, over the heat of the Sahara desert, massive air turbulance was building. The Sirocco, a desert wind from North Africa, had a surprise in store.

Chapter 15 Come with me and be my Love.

Mike Edwards had no patience with cunning or mind games, he simply met problems head on and dealt with them accordingly. There had been highs, sporting heroics which had earned fame and long term financial stability. He was influential, a popular figure whose genuine humility and good sense had attracted a wide circle of friends and an adoring family. There had been lows, injuries and the tragic loss of his wife, but he had never been a quitter and in the manner of his performance on the rugby field, he hammered aside the opposition. He'd always felt confident, in control, able to make the right decisions, that is, until he met Karen. His love for Karen had changed all that. Never before had he been caught up in anti social problems and the trials of young people whose lives had been damaged in some way. It seemed to be an upshot of modern living, a social blight which had sufaced against a background of micro technology and western affluence, problems which years ago had been ignored, buried in the avalanche of conscription for war and the exploitation of labour. Mike's barnstorming approach wasn't working and he felt baffled.

It began with the hospital note, the message from Ben, the apologies, the remorse, and the information concerning his attackers. Mike's enquiries had led to a cesspit of organised crime and he could see no immediate solutions. Now he faced sealed lips, veiled threats and sinister implications. Weeks had gone by with no contact from Ben. He'd mysteriously disappeared leaving no details as to his whereabouts and Karen had been so worried, Mike had reported Ben missing to the police. Even so, his friends in the force were no help, they appeared to be stalling for time. He'd tracked Winston down, got himself involved with another family drama and events had now taken a very nasty turn. It seemed Ben had moved on from anti social behaviour and was now involved with an international crime syndicate. Karen became increasingly on edge and Mike, having no wish to add to her concerns, found it difficult to give her all the facts. He kept his fears to himself and continued to comfort and reassure her. The festive season hardly registered and the hoped for family feast with its Christmas crackers and turkey centrepiece had seemed more like a last supper.

The winter was exceptionally mild and the new year began with bright sunshine. In the countryside there were signs of an early spring. Some said it was global warming, others said it had happened before but whatever the reason, the new year held a promise of reduced winter fuel bills and a fine summer. Love had given Mike a new direction, setting him free from the trappings of happiness in years gone by. He kept the canal barge which he had fitted out so beautifully but decided to sell the luxury flat and the Morgan sports car.

During this spell of winter sunshine, thoughts of raw weather were forgotten and the beguiling warmth gave him a crazy idea. He decided he and Karen needed a break, an escape to the country, away from New Horizons Park and the shadow it had cast over their lives. He suggested they should take a week's holiday, living aboard the narrowboat boat exploring the Manchester canals. They could cruise the Cheshire ring, a circuit which includes several canal systems, through the heart of Manchester, then beyond into the rural countryside that spreads across the Cheshire plain. It is an interesting tour of many contrasts, ranging from an heritage of industrial archaeology to the remote beauty of the Macclesfield canal. Mike was used to working the lock systems, blessed with endless reserves of strength, they presented no difficulty. Karen loved the idea, a whole week, just the two of them, a chance to gather their thoughts, to ease the burden of gathering uncertainty, to find in her head a moment of stillness. She knew Mike was deeply troubled. His efforts to minimise her fears were plainly obvious, he was holding back, holding back information concerning Ben's disappearance. She knew he was trying to protect her, but she had to know the worst, not knowing was unbearable. She secretly shared Mike's conclusions, the holiday was an opportunity to get away from New Horizons, to discover the truth, to think more objectively about the future and face whatever problems there were simmering below the surface.

They made their break in February. Temperatures were high for that time of the year but there had been periods of heavy rainfall and an occasional gale. They gave this little consideration, the narrowboat was well provisioned and furnished out with every luxury including an efficient heating system. Undaunted, they set forth on their adventure with all the enthusiasm of teenagers. On the face of it everything seemed to be going Mike's way. His immediate family were secure, he had money in the bank, a successful business, had influential friends in the right places and time on his hands with the woman he loved, but the problems associated with his extended family made life complicated, threatened his happiness and thwarted his ambitions.

The barge gently chugged its way past extremes of modernism and industrial spoilage giving Karen a whole new perspective on the city, and leaving this behind, joined the Peak Forest canal. They passed through Marple Locks and decided to make their first stop. They moored against its charming waterside and set out to explore the area, an excursion which inevitably led to a comfortable pub with a log fire. They mellowed, soaking up the ambience, willing it to absorb their hearts and minds with the promise of a relaxed holiday. They were in no hurry, and at that moment in time, this was where they wanted to be, sharing an intimate space in front of a log fire, nowhere else in the whole world. They hardly noticed the man with close cropped hair sitting quietly in the corner, a thick set man, wearing a black leather jacket. He was reading a newspaper. When they left, he took out a mobile, made a phone call in lowered tones and moved over to the window. He watched them with callous interest as they make their way back to the canal barge.

The Macclesfield canal drew the couple further into the surrounding countryside. On this stretch there were no locks until the flight at Bosely, a few miles beyond Macclesfield and they hoped to enjoy hours of lock free cruising. A cold wind blew from the north east, and sharing the tiller, they huddled closer for warmth. They felt easy together, leaving aside the need for emotional caution, or outward show. During the trip they often made love and there were moments of passion, passion tempered with understanding which left them rejuvenated rather than exhausted. Mike was never demanding, he was gentle with Karen and she always responded, opening to him like the petals of a flower in the morning sunshine. They began to relax, to observe the natural world around them, and the world seemed a safe place for their love. The wind gradually increased threatening a gale and they cuddled together feeling how lucky they were, knowing they had each other, knowing how secure and strong was their love and the thought of it warmed them to the core.

The canal runs for twenty six miles to link up with the Trent and Mersey canal and Mike decided to moor on a quiet stretch where they could prepare a simple meal and crack open a bottle of wine. Karen busied herself in the kitchen opening a can of soup for convenience, serving it piping hot with grated parmesan and garlic bread. They sat at the dining table facing each other. The soup was one of Karen's on offer 'cheapies,' her employer's version of Scotch broth and it tasted surprisingly good.

'Isn't this simply divine, so remote from our lives in Manchester,' Karen remarked.'

'As far as I'm concerned, it's as near as I'll ever get to heaven,' Mike said, helping himself to another slice of garlic bread. 'What I mean is, with just the two of us, it's always like being in heaven..... For me anyway.'

'Oh! Mike, who could have guessed how romantic you are, and you being such a tough guy?'

'I'm not that tough Karen.' If anything I'm too soft.'

'Being soft hearted doesn't make you weak, it makes you strong, makes you more human.'

'I'm not so sure about that. Look what a mess I've got myself into with that Winston boy. Honestly, I was completely out of my depth, shouldn't have interfered.'

'You've never said much about it. Did he get that trial for Bradford Bulls?

'Well yes, but it didn't work out as planned.' Mike slowly finished his soup and placing each hand on the table, leaned back and sighed. 'I've not told you the full story Karen. I can now see I was wrong, I didn't want to cause you more hurt, I thought I could handle it, but my getting involved with that Winston boy has led to a whole new ball game.'

'I've known all along there was something on your mind and I knew you'd tell me in your own good time. It's about Ben isn't it?'

'Yes, it's about Ben.'

'Ever since we left Marple, clear of the built up areas, Ben's been in the back of my mind, I can't stop thinking about him, I mean where is he? We've not heard a whisper from him, not since he left you that note in hospital.'

Mike sighed again. He looked resigned. Couldn't they just for once have some free time, the two of them, together, away from the hostility of New Horizons Park and the on going drama in Karen's family? God, it seemed impossible. 'I had the impression he wanted his job back, but he's not been in touch,' he said wearily.

'Sorry Mike darling, I'm trying not to think about Ben but I can't help it, every now and then a wave of terror comes over me and I'm very afraid. I know it sounds as though I'm fussing, but it's like an empty feeling in the pit of my stomach, knowing he's in serious trouble, I just know it.' Karen was close to tears, 'Mike, his life may be in danger. Sorry darling if I'm getting paranoid but I can't ignore these feelings. I mean, shouldn't I be doing more about it, getting the press involved perhaps.' She made an effort to regain her composure. 'When you informed the police, was there something more I should know about, have they found a lead, come up with any clues?'

'No, nothing, nothing at all. It might seem daft, unbelievable perhaps, but I think there's some sort of conspiracy going on. Matter of fact it was because of all the cloak and dagger stuff and the way they warned me off, that I started making other enquiries.' Mike took her hand in his, trying not to cause further alarm. 'Karen………'

Karen quietly interrupted, 'it's guilt I suppose, knowing I've failed him. I blame myself. I've never mentioned it before, but a couple of months ago, when you were in hospital, he came round to see me. We were on our way to visit you.' Karen paused for a moment trying to recall exactly what had been said, 'I think he wanted to confide in me and looking back I'm sure it was a cry for help. At the time I never realised, he's always been so independent, always rejected any advice I gave him. I remember now, I was fussing around looking for car keys, rushing as usual, I should have listened, heard him out. I asked him to come with us to the hospital but he wasn't interested and went out slamming the door.'

The beauty of the countryside with its hidden treasures along the canal beckoned, but the spell had been broken. Mike hardly knew where to begin. 'That note he left me in hospital was a complete turn around. Ben was genuinely cut up about Marvin and was ready for a change of direction.' Mike gazed through the porthole, willing himself to enjoy the greenery, to savour the moment, but love for Karen and his concern for her peace of mind took over, she deserved to know all the facts. There had been serious developments following his association with Winston Macdonald. His efforts to play the part of a social worker had led to a web of organised crime. 'It must have been difficult for Ben, shopping his mates, giving me the names of those hoodies. It was a bit of crucial evidence, took some guts and without that I'd never have tracked down Winston Macdonald, the lad who actually stabbed me, but a lot's happened since then and the whole thing's got a hell of a lot more complicated. One thing's for certain though, and you must believe me Karen when I tell you, Ben is a reformed character. It's not just our doing, someone else has befriended him and it's been a turning point, he's changed, he's grown up.'

'Has he really Mike? There's more though isn't there. You've told me the good news, now you must tell me the bad news. Some crook's got a hold over him, he's been threatened. Mike, I know you're trying to protect me and I love you for it, love you so much I can read your thoughts and I can sense there's something more, something I should know about, as his mother, isn't there?'

'Well it began with that note, him accepting me as part of the family and being glad we're getting married. He said then he wanted to come to the wedding and hoped I'd keep his job open. You know that's true, you've read the letter.'

Karen tensed, begining to show real anxiety, 'Yes but is he ok?'

It was happening again. Mike felt as though he was competing with Karen's motherly love, an instinctive love, profound, incomprehensible with no strings. He wondered, was her love for Ben stronger than her love for him. Mike's love for Karen had no reservations, he loved with an open heart and could never be jealous of Karen's abiding love for her children but he realised that to win Karen's love completely, he had to share his love with her children. This was going to be difficult where Ben was concerned and somehow he had to break the news gently. 'Yes love, as far as I know, I'm pretty sure Ben's ok.'

Karen, relieved by Mike's assurance, visibly relaxed. In her mind if Mike said Ben was ok, then he must be ok. 'Of course I've read the letter, over and over and that's what I find so worrying. If he felt that way, why hasn't he been in touch? He's been acting strangely for weeks and I always know when he's lying. It's about money isn't it? He owes money to a drug dealer.'

'No, it's not that, but drugs are involved and I think we're dealing with a big crime syndicate here, too big even for the police to handle.'

Shock registered on Karen's face and the worry lines were even more pronounced. 'Have you any idea where he might be?' she said in a quiet voice.

'He's in Italy, Naples I believe.'

'In Italy!'

'Yes, in Italy.' Mike shook his head, hardly able to grasp the fact himself. 'I think love, I'd better tell you exactly what I've managed to find out. It all began with Winston and his trial for the Bradford Bulls. It wasn't easy getting him a trial, with so many waiting for a similar chance, but I managed to arrange it and when the great day arrived I called round to collect him as promised, but he'd cleared off, done a runner. His mum said he'd worked himself up into such a state, he just couldn't face the ordeal. She said he had no self esteem, no confidence, and the day before the trial he simply lost his bottle.'

'Sounds like a familiar story.' Karen nodded, hanging on to every word.

'Remember, I'd mentioned it before, Winston was coloured, English mum, Nigerian father, a boy from a broken home left with an invalid mum. She'd had a stroke following a messy divorce and I felt sorry for the family. Well, apparently his father was a bit of a disciplinarian, expected a lot from him and was always putting him down. Mary said their life was all about her husband and his ambitions. They met at university, he was a probation officer, clever bloke but it sounds as though he had a chip on his shoulder, bit racist, I'm not sure.'

'What happened about the job you found Winston. At the metal works?'

'That didn't go to plan either. Bill lost a big order for metal casting and couldn't take on any more staff, so I gave Winston a job in the joinery, took him under my wing so to speak. The idea was that he could earn money to help pay for his mother's care. He was mitching off school to look after her and I thought a decent job would give him an healthy interest in life, get him away from street gangs. I realise now I went over the top, but more recently he started to trust me and I've got to know the lad. Surprisingly he's coming on well, treats me like his father. He might even make a joiner. Seems crazy when you think he almost killed me.'

'I don't think you went over the top, I think you've been wonderful towards him,' Karen offered.

'Well, Winston gained more confidence and started to confide in me so I asked him about Ben, about street gangs and what they were all up to. He said Ben had been the leader of their gang, a gang calling themselves the Asbos, and then suddenly he left and got a job with Vera motors. They played around with cannabis and some of them dealt in drugs. A woman called Meg was their supplier, apparently Ben was her toy boy. She lives in a top floor flat on New Horizons and spends a lot of time in Italy.'

'But why haven't you told me all this before?' Karen pleaded.

'I honestly don't know. It was a private thing and it all developed so quickly. I didn't want to lead you down a blind alley, add to your worries, give you false hopes. You see Karen, I never intended to meddle with their lives, not like polititians, trying to take control, or turn Winston into a case file on a computor and focus on that like social workers do, I wanted to do something positive. I was testing my own theories I suppose. You know I'm always banging on about the importance of trade and industry, how real work makes for good citizenship and how we've lost our respect for those things which form the cornerstone of our existence? Well here was a chance to put my money where my mouth is and I was afraid of failure.'

'Yes I see that and I happen to believe in you Mike, everything you stand for.'

'Anyway, I checked out Meg's place in New Horizons and drew a blank. The flat was locked up, apparently Meg was on holiday. Her neighbours said she was just a single mum on benefits, trying to keep her daughter at university. She kept herself to herself and hardly ever spoke to anyone but there seemed to be a lot of comings and goings. So, following up what Winston had said about her, I checked with the police but they said she had no record, they knew nothing about her. I know none of this really makes any sense.'

'If she was on benefits, how come she could afford holidays abroad?' Karen marvelled, anxious to know more about the mysterious woman who'd got her claws into Ben.

'Exactly! By now I was beginning to feel like a private detective and was certain I was on to something which might throw light on Ben's whereabouts and the drug scene in New Horizons. So I followed this up with a call on Vera Motors, asking for the Boss, an Italian, a man well known in business circles, called Tonino Vera, you know the type, Freemasons, Rotary, on the board of this, on the board of that, usual drill. Apparently he'd also married into English aristocracy, a real social climber. He was unavailable and you've guessed it, they were on holiday, in Italy.'

'Couldn't you find out where they were staying?'

'It was a big set up, a main dealer in Fiat cars and commercials but everyone there acted dumb and when I enquired after Ben they said he wasn't employed directly by Vera Motors but by one of their subsideries, Euro Express Car Parts. This name rang a bell. They have a depot on the same industrial estate as Edwards Joinery and I drive past it almost every morning. So that was my next port of call, Euro Express Car Parts. I said I wanted to see Ben but they were quite rude, aggressive almost. They asked me if I was his father saying he'd failed to turn up for work and could consider himself sacked. So I got tough with them and hoping they wouldn't ask for ID, I lied, saying this was part of a plain clothes police enqiry concerning Ben's ASBO and demanded to know what address they held for him. They said he was lodging with a Miss M. Kinnear, Block 2, Flat 25, New Horizons Park. Of course I'd already been there, it's Megs place on the top floor.'

Karen looked flabbergasted. 'I'm having difficulty getting my mind round this. Ben never said he was living with this Meg woman. Still it's something of a relief, He's obviously sunning himself in Italy while she's paying the bills.'

'Love, I'm afraid it's not as simple as that. There's more. I didn't like the look of Euro Express. It didn't feel right. The secretary was Eastern European with a strong accent who kept saying she didn't understand me. Her husband was the boss, another Mr.Vera, same family, and was unavailable, in Italy, I suppose. There were a lot of foreigners working there and some of them looked a bit shady. There was a body shop next door which seemed a hive of industry with a few delivery vans parked up. It was obviously a very professional set up and surprisingly the work was a high standard.'

'You should have gone back to the police.'

'That's exactly what I did and I was given a private interview with the head of the Manchester drugs squad, a Detective Inspector Chris Williams. And listen to this, he said I was interfering with a huge undercover operation investigating the Mafia. The Italian police and MI5 were envolved. They were dealing with the trafficking of cocaine here in Britain and abroad on a huge scale, and you're not going to believe this, Ben has got himself involved. He's was safe and well in Italy, living in Naples but for his safety and our own I must keep right out of it and say nothing to anyone. I'm telling you because I think you have a right to know.'

'Thank you for telling me Mike.' Karen managed, unable to appreciate the implications.

Karen cleared the table, nervously clattering the dishes. She was lost for words, silence, dumbing down her thoughts took possession of her and as she leaned over the sink her body shook. Unable to hold back the tears she began to sway back and forth, willing herself to maintain some hold on reality. The wind gusted around the barge and a sprinkling of rain splattered against the galley window. Mike stood behind her and gently taking her shoulders, turned her body to face him, holding her close, restoring her to herself, allowing her to hear the rain, to watch the rivulets tracing their course across the glass.

'Karen darling, everything's going to be ok. Ben's going to be ok. Now listen, we're not far from Macclesfield. We'll head there, find a quiet pub, have a meal, relax, have a couple of drinks and talk this thing through.'

With deliberate calm, they made ready to continue their journey and within a couple of hours the narrowboat arrived in Macclesfield. They moored alongside the quay and determined not to show haste, leisurely changed their clothing before seeking out a suitable watering hole. They collected drinks from the bar and settled in a quiet nook. It was warm and inviting, offering a brief respite from the indifference and indignities of the world outside. Karen was beginning to relax a little when their peace was rudely interrupted. Mike's mobile rang and he reluctantly fumbled for it in the breast pocket of a windcheater which hung on the back of his chair. 'Hello, Mike Edwards speaking.......... Oh! It's you Josh'. For several minutes Mike listened to the message without comment. Karen watched, holding her breath while Mike's face registered disbelief, horror and despair. 'What! Oh my God no' He heard more, then with more tension in his voice, 'we'll make our way back tomorrow............ perhaps you could collect us ....We're moored up in Macclesfield............Ok Josh, ok, see you tomorrow, bye.'

Certain that some awful fate had befallen her son, Karen looked distraught, 'What's happened Mike?' She asked weakly.
Mike looked grim. 'I'm afraid Winston will never make a joiner,' he said. 'He's been shot. His body was found slumped between some re-cycling skips in a run down car park. And Mr Vera's

wife, a former Lady Letitia Hamelton, has died in Italy from a drug overdose. Apparently she was an heroin addict.'

Carrying a leather briefcase, a thick set man with close cropped hair, wearing a light raincoat, walked casually out of the shadows which deepened on the approach to the canal. He climbed aboard one of the barges which ranged along the length of the quay. For ease of access it was roped in hard against its fenders and the new paintwork shone under the steady glow of a streetlight. Mike had chosen the berth for added security. The man wore skin tight gloves and holding a pencil torch between his teeth, with surprising ease, picked the simple two lever lock on the cabin door. He lowered himself into the cabin and opened the panel to the gas cylinder compartment. He took two packs of high explosive from his brief case and carefully lodged them behind the butane gas bottles. He wired the detonators through a timing device from the leisure battery, setting the timer for 24.00 hrs when Mike and Karen would sure to be on board, and would most probably be asleep in their beds. He left everything as it should be and after a final check, prepared to leave.

The sad news of Winston's death weighed heavily on Mike. A sense of bewilderment and failure decended upon the couple and a resigned weariness left them feeling exhausted. They decided on an early night, knowing that sleep would not come easily. Perhaps in the morning they would see things more clearly and be able to make sensible decisions. In troubled silence they made their way back to the boat where in each other's arms they hoped to find some comfort. Dark forces had other plans. At midnight an unholy explosion would reduce the barge to a wreck blasting it's occupants into eternity.

'There's someone on our boat, I can see a light flickering inside.' Karen whispered with alarm as they approached the quay.

'A light? My God you're right love, something's going on here, could be a thief, hang on a minute, let's see what he's up to.' The couple moved back into the shadows.

Karen groped for her mobile, 'I'd better ring the police.'

In a society where we are constantly being pursuaded that we are unable to look after ourselves, Mike was an example of someone who still held a considerable measure of self belief. 'Just hang on a minute while I check it out. You stay back here love, promise I won't do anything daft.' Mike made a small detour, approaching the boat towards the bow, taking cover behind a parked car.

The thin shaft of light was suddenly extinguished and a heavily built man emerged from the narrowboat interior. He was wearing what appeared to be a plastic raincoat and was carrying a briefcase. Mike noted the footwear, black trainers, and how quietly he moved in them, light on his feet, like an athlete. 'Hey you there, you've broken in, you've been aboard my boat. ' Mike challenged in a booming voice as he broke cover to bear down on the intruder.

The man froze for a moment, as though poleaxed. Then recovering his senses, tried to make a gettaway, deciding to run for it. But Mike had already closed in on the suspect and with a bone shattering rugby tackle, drove his shoulder into the man's thigh to bring him fully stretched, crashing to the ground. Mike was quickly on his feet and grabbing the man by the back of the collar, hauled him upright. The man was facing outward, his mind working overtime in defence mode. Then with a vicious, jerking, back head butt, he smashed Mike in the face with such force that it split his nose and for a moment Mike lost his vision. No longer holding the brief case, the man's hand instinctively dived under his raincoat lapel. 'Mike!' Karen screamed, her legs carrying her unwillingly towards the scene, 'Mike for God's sake watch out, he's got a gun!'

Mike responded with superhuman strength. He pinned the man's lower arms to his side in a massive bear hug, lifting him clean off his feet, before lunging towards the street lamp. With heels kicking into Mike's shins and repeated back head butts, the man struggled to free his arm in a desperate attempt to use the gun. In a few strides Mike slammed his adversary into the concete lamp standard, crushing his own hand in the process. The man's head whiplashed against the pillar, several ribs caved in and his body sagged. In considerable pain Mike let go, leaving the unconscious mystery man to collapse in a heap on the ground.

'Karen threw her arms around Mike, 'Oh! Mike, Oh Mike! your poor face!'

'It's all right, I'm ok love,' he gasped, breathing heavily but still managing to smile. 'Better phone the police, I'll get his gun.'

With trembling hands, Karen had some difficulty in convincing the police that it was a serious matter. No, the man wasn't just a thief, he was armed with a gun. No, it was not a private residence, it was a canal barge. Yes, they were on holiday even though it was the middle of winter. What exactly were they reporting? Surely not a theft when nothing appeared to have been stolen. Were they sure it was a real gun and not just a replica? Why had her boyfriend beaten this prankster senseless? It sounded more like a case of grievous bodily harm against the complainer. Most of the on duty officers were dealing with reports of more serious incidents. The ambulance service was also over stretched but an ambulance for the injured party accompanied by a WPC. Would hopefully arrive within the next half hour.

'If the police are taking that long, we'd better tie this guy up before he comes round, there's plenty of rope on board.' Mike decided. 'Then we'll make ourselves a cup of tea.'

Confused yet outraged by the brutal audacity of this hoodlum, they showed little mercy in securing the man's arms and legs. The thin rope cut into his wrists, acting a like tourniquet, effectively reducing blood circulation. A cold drizzle set in, adding to their misery and satisfied with their work, but aware their prisoner might suffer from exposure, they covered him with blankets before returning to the comparitive warmth of the barge where utterly exhausted, they brewed a much needed pot of tea, the English way of dealing with stress.

The man on the quay, motionless under a pile of blankets, still held a threat for Karen. This alien being, whose motives were not understood, had posed some sort of threat and was, Karen believed, an harbinger of evil. Mike, her man, her lover, her hero, had subdued the monster and rendered him harmless, but Karen felt sick and wished to distance herself from his ugly presence.

'Mike darling, your hand's horribly swollen, and your poor face, we must get you some hospital treatment the minute the police arrive, and your poor nose, it's still bleeding horribly and we're running out of tissues.'

Mike was restless. Pain was beginning to take over from adrenalin. He peered through the window, checking up on the prisoner. 'Karen, his briefcase, it's lying there in the middle of the road. Might give us a few clues as to what this is all about.' Mike went out to retrieve the briefcase, worried that he might have killed a man who was little more than a thief. He drew back the covers to examine the face of their armed robber. The eyes were closed and he was breathing with difficulty, but was obviously very much alive. Relieved but concerned about the man's welfare, he rejoined Karen on the barge, determined to give the police a shake up. Mike examined the weapon the man had been carrying, it was not a plastic replica and it was loaded. Together they went through the contents of the briefcase. It contained a few electrician's tools, a pencil torch, a coil of wire, some insulation tape and a sketch of the barge's interior layout. The positions of the leisure battery and the butane gas compartment were ringed in red. The implications were obvious. 'Karen, forget the tea, we've got to get out of here, there's a bomb in the gas compartment!'

The second call to the police produced an entirely different reaction. Within minutes four squad cars arrived, a fire engine and two ambulances. The whole area was cordoned off. A police check on Mike Edwards had revealed that his safety had been a matter of concern. The bomber was placed under immediate arrest and bundled into a security van. Mike gave the pistol and briefcase to the investigating officer and after some discussion it was decided that only an Army bomb disposal unit could deal with the problem. Some nearby properties would have to be evacuated.

Mike climbed into the ambulance, his shirt was soaked in blood, his hand was giving him hell. 'We'll have to stop meeting like this,' he joked. It was almost midnight, time had passed unnoticed in a kaleidoscope of shocking events. Karen put a comforting arm round him and with uncanny perception, glanced at her watch. The whole scene was suddenly illuminated in a blinding flash of white light. A deafening roar shook the quayside as shockwave after shockwave numbed the senses. Everyone instinctively ducked as the barge exploded. Fragments hammered down on the roof of the ambulance and a fountain of canal water, dredging up stinking mud, sprayed the whole area. The ambulance crew quickly gathered their senses and slammed shut the rear doors. Mike took a last look at what was left of the barge. The scene was devestating, apocalyptic. The barge was now burning fiercely. Only the crumpled framework remained.

On the way to hospital, Karen showed signs of delayed shock. 'This is all my fault,' she said in a forlorn voice. 'Dragging you into my family affairs.'

'Don't ever think like that love. Remember the last time we were in an ambulance together? What you did for me that evening showed me the measure of your love. My love for you is the same. I'll do anything to make you happy.'

'But Mike darling, your beautiful boat. I know it's insured but it was so special for you and nothing could ever replace what it meant to you.'

'I doubt whether my insurance will cover an act of terrorism. Anyway, honestly, I'm not worried about it. The boat was never a prized possession, something I had to have for myself, it was more an expression of my love for Sheila. That's all in the past. Your love Karen is more precious to me than a canal barge. I can only thank God we've survived, but I'm shocked, really shocked to think someone wants us out of the way, that someone would go this far.'

'I feel the same about you Mike. I couldn't bear to lose you and I know like Sheila, you've got grand ideas for me, a big wedding and a big house, but darling it isn't really necessary you know, just as long as you'll never stop loving me.'

Mike put his arms around Karen, 'I'll never stop loving you, not while I'm in the land of the living, but I'm worried for us Karen, very, very worried. What the devil have I got us in to?'

Chapter 16. The Loss of the Nuvola Distante.

A few heavy chairs were set around a cheaper looking table, it's laminated top giving an unnatural shine. A couple of filing cabinets and a large chest of drawers made of similar material punctuated the blank walls. There was also a computor table, but no computor, and instead a solitary vase with artificial flowers gave the appearance of having been rescued from a car boot sale. For secret meetings dealing with Security and Intelligence, the huge space available was of comic proportions and the ceiling much too high. A louvred window presented a panoramic view over the metropolis, but today the louvres were half closed and the room was lit with energy saving light bulbs hidden behind expensive lamp shades. A wall to wall carpet, grey, deep piled, muffled the sound of any movement. The Head of MI5, the London Police Commissioner and two senior MI5 officers sat at the table, an assembly of grey heads, grey faces and grey identities. They each had a dossier which they carefully shuffled, re-examining the contents as if to remind themselves of the subject matter. They had the resigned look of those who have spent a lifetime taking orders.

The Head of MI5 chaired the meeting and with an air of conspiracy, began as though addressing partners in crime. 'Operation Retiarious, the fisherman,' she smiled, letting them know she understood the Latin translation. 'First, let me say, what a splendid effort you've all made in this investigation. Co-operation between our services has been excellent and we now have sufficient information to make our next move. It has been through your perserverance that our agents in the field have uncovered details of an extensive drug racket in cocaine, run by the Italian and the Russian Mafias, centred in the north. We're now in possession of names, locations, and enough details to make our next move. As you know, we've been working with Interpol and Italian Intelligence on this and we must now organise a joint meeting with these agencies to ensure we all have the same objectives.'

One of the MI5 agents decided to interrupt. For much of his life he had been employed in dangerous situations and looked tougher than his associate, who after leaving Cambridge with a brilliant degree, had spent most of his time in the back room. Both men were approaching retirement. The tough one still liked to think he was working for the good of mankind in a battle against evil. The Cambridge man had become more and more cynical over the years. The tough guy had a loose frame and looked very fit. He spoke in a quiet voice. 'Let's not get carried away congratulating ourselves. Our success is almost entirely due to the Lady, and the way she groomed a certain Ben Mackay, the young rookie we've thrown to the lions. Even as we speak his survival chances are pretty slim. The Lady acted with tremendous courage in this investigation with little thought for her own safety. We know she was murdered and her death is a tragic loss but I think her achievements should be recognised and placed on record. Furthermore, we shouldn't give up on Ben Mackay, let's get him out of there, offer him some proper training and honour the promises we gave Lady Letitia. I'd be happy to look after him.'

'I know Chris Williams, head of the Manchester drug squad was very upset on hearing about Letitia,' the Police Commissioner added.

'Well he would be wouldn't he. I believe they once had an affair,' the MI5 Chief cut in, anxious to dismiss the part Letitia and her toy boy protégé had played. 'Letitia was a junkie, a security risk and a serious liability to this department.'

The tough guy simmered, 'Cut the crap. The Lady was never a security risk. Hell! We were more of a threat to her than she ever was to us. If the Mafia hadn't murdered her, we probably would have.'

The MI5 chief fixed the tough guy with a penetrating stare, all seeing yet sightless. 'I suggest you keep your opinions to yourself, try using your brain instead of your mouth. That sort of talk could make *you* a security risk.'

The Cambridge man and the tough guy had an understanding. In the murky underworld of espionage, where trust no longer has a meaning, where betrayal, violence and deceit are tools of the trade, an unlikely friendship had developed, a comrade in arms relationship where the two agents watched the other's back. The Cambridge man intervened. 'What the hell does it matter how we managed to nail this outfit? No one's ever going to hear the details anyway. Surely it's more important now to iron out the political details.'

The sightless eyes softened, came back into focus, studying the three other faces in turn. An uncomfortable silence followed. All eyes were now on the chief.

'First let me make it clear. There will be no arrests,' she said emphatically.

The Police Commissioner could hardly believe his ears. For months he had trained a special squad in readiness for this final assault on cocaine, an awesome task which would strike at the very heart of organised crime in Britain. 'I don't quite understand,' he said, beginning to feel divorced from the proceedings.

'In my ignorance I thought we were going to tackle the drugs problem. Ok, we're intercepting the occasional yacht, launching raids on run down terrace houses with a team of heavies and a convoy of police vehicles. Ok, we're smashing down doors, dragging half asleep street dealers from their grubby bed linen. Ok, we're making sure it's all televised in the interests of public relations, but honestly, I'd hoped for something a bit more ambitious, I'd hoped we were going for those who are in control of drug trafficking. Obviously I've got it wrong.'

'The Cabinet does not want to make arrests,' the chief continued. 'It's a question of resources and having to consider the far reaching political implications. Taking on the Italian, Russian and Spanish Mafia and the Colombian drug cartels would be a hopeless endeavour and would require the equivalent intervention of a military campaign. The costs would be enormous and it is doubtful whether America, Russia or Europe would come on board. Such an undertaking is out of the question.'

'Are you saying that we condone the abuse of drugs and the damage it does to young people?' The Commissioner continued, with some resignation in his voice.

'The government's position on all drug abuse is to reduce the demand through the enlightenment and education of our children. This may take a couple of generations, but there is no serious alternative. In the meantime we must try to exercise some measure of control and the best way to achieve this is by having inside information. Operation Retiarious has given us an oportunity to access that information in the most direct way. We can now identify some of the key figures who are behind the main sources of drug distribution in Britain. With heroin it was the Turks, with cocaine it's the Italians and the Russians'. The chief wrote something on her pad. Her solid gold biro flashed as the sun broke through the clouds to throw a beam of light across the table. She had a captive audience. 'We've made a deal with Mr Tonino Vera and more importantly, also with Mr Viktor Ivanovich of Hareden hall.'

'A deal for Christ's sake! I can't believe I'm hearing this. What about the amount of drugs coming into the country? Surely something must be done about that!' The Commissioner's thoughts were now drifting towards his pension. He wanted no part of this.

'You all know very well that checking the millions of tons of freight which pour into the country by road, sea or rail is a practical impossibility. Such a measure would halt the flow of commerce, bringing the country to a standstill.'

'This deal!' The Commissioner now realised that his role would remain unchanged, there would be no challenges, no arrests, no satisfaction of having been part of a genuine war against drug abuse. Now he was simply curious. 'What exactly are the *arrangements* we've made with Tonino Vera?'

'Tonino Vera will scale down his drug operations in Manchester but will retain his business interests in Britain and will continue to be a tax payer. He has offered to finance the running and construction of several luxury casinos in some of our major towns and cities and these businesses will be entirely legitimate, forming a huge source of revenue for the government. His drug trafficking in Britain will constitute a means of controlling the level of street trading and we will receive regular classified information concerning these activities. More arrests will be made at this level and the noose will gradually tighten. All we have to do now is iron out the details.'

'And what about our Russian friend? Same medicine I presume.'

'Viktor Ivanovich is an entirely different proposition and much more important.'

'The Policeman leaned back in his chair, folding his arms in the manner of one who wishes to act merely as a spectator. He liked to think of himself as a man of principles, but these revelations made him feel impotent. It seemed that Britain could not afford principles. 'Much more important! Important for what reason? The mind boggles.'

'Viktor Ivanovich came from humble beginnings. He was born into poverty, his grandparents were professional people who died of malnutrition in a Solviet labour camp and surviving family members are dedicated anti- communists. Viktor was determined to get a better life and sold drugs in order to help his parents and provide for himself while studying at Moscow university. He earned degrees in geology and chemistry and is now head of a huge gas corporation in the Ukraine. He also owns a fleet of liquid gas tankers and it is on these ships that he continues to smuggle cocaine. He sees no harm in it whatsoever and considers the drug less harmful than alcohol. Furthermore it increases the profit on each shipment and enables him to be more competetive with gas prices. He also brings in illegal immigrants which in his opinion, is an act of humanitarianism, helping people, who like himself as a young man, wish for a better life. Our investigations have concluded that this is a non profit organisation which provides much needed manual labour.'

'Surely with this information we can easily intercept these cocaine shipments. I mean, is he aware that we know exactly what he's up to?' The policeman was by now exasperated and beginning to look his age. His private belief that positions of high office in any organisation should not be filled by women, was now being confirmed in the most forthright manner.

'With the help of Tonino Vera we are happy for the time being to simply monitor these illegal practices.'

'Am I dreaming this or have you lost all sense of duty and common decency. If this is the case, please accept my resignation forthwith. The men who serve under me deserve to know that the sacrifices they make in the course of their duty is in the interest of justice and fair play. We are trained to uphold the law, to apprehend all criminals and never turn a blind eye. Such practices are treated as corruption, just in case you've forgotten.'

'Hang on a minute,' the Cambridge man interrupted, 'Just listen to what the chief has to say before you start moralising. We're talking politics here. This is more to do with energy resources and the nation's prosperity than cocaine. Your average copper is really only interested in his salary and his pension scheme. Stop being so bloody holier than thou.'

The chief ignored the Police Commissioner's outburst and continued in a calm voice. 'Viktor Ivanovich has been shipping gas to us from Qatar at some considerable cost to ourselves. His company is now in the process of building a new pipeline from the Ukrainian gas fields to Odessa where natural gas can be shipped directly into Europe making us less dependent on Russia who has control over the present pipeline. He has signed a trading aggreement with Britain which will doubly increase our imports of liquid gas at much reduced prices and has made a significant investment here in Britain for the construction of gas storage facilities which is vital for our economy. In short, Mr Viktor Ivanovitch likes Britain and we in turn, I can assure you gentlemen, like him.'

'I see,' the Commissioner mused with a faraway look in his eyes, 'Well then, it seems that between you, you've taken care of everything. And what about Margaret Kinnear the dolly bird drug dealer? We tracked down her residence thanks to Mike Edwards, the ex rugby star, who's been been making enquiries about the Mackay boy. Apparently she's on holiday in Italy. I suppose she's going to be made a Dame,' he added sarcastically.

In her youth, The Head of MI5 had been a striking young woman, tall, athletic and very clever. What she had lacked in femininity she made up for with willowing grace and dazzling charm and she had attracted certain men with whom she loved to compete. However, there wasn't a submissive bone in her body and her assertive and uncompromising attitude discouraged any possibility of romance. She was well able to cope with the burden of office, but now, her jaw line had stiffened, her eyes had lost their sparkle and she found it difficult to smile with spontaneity or even laugh. Her private world was a world she preferred to escape from, it was lonely, with only unwanted thoughts for company and there was nothing in it to laugh about. 'Margaret Kinnear gave us a problem, she knew too much and arresting her would have opened a can of worms. We had decided that she must be eliminated and asked ToninoVera to do it on our behalf, but the problem was made difficult by the fact that she has a daughter at Liverpool University.'

'Surely that's no problem for MI5, just another accident. Can't let anyone get in the way of our cash flow can we?' The policeman was getting angry.

'Please try to be more objective and less emotional. We are discussing matters which concern our reserves of energy. Energy is our number one priority. If we run short of fuel everthing starts to collapse, the whole fabric of the nation comes apart. And spare us any moralising about casinos. Government revenue from gambling helps to fund hospitals, schools and infrastructure.' The chief gave the Commissioner a look of confounded incredulity as though taken aback by his naivety and lack of savvy, she added thoughtfully, 'and of course police pension schemes,' she paused to let that sink in, then continued, 'The murder of innocents is not part of our agenda and anyway, fortunately for us, Tonino Vera has solved the Kinnear problem in a most convenient way.'

'Oh yes, it's all very convenient. Just how convenient is it for Christ's sake? When I think of the amount of work the secret police have put into this project in the pursuit of bringing criminals to justice, all this political manoevering makes us look like a bunch of dummys.'

'Margaret Kinnear had a call girl relationship with ToninoVera and he was so smitten he started treating her as his mistress. He spent money on her, paid her daughter's university fees and kept her exclusively for himself. However, Margaret Kinnear is no bimbo, she's strong minded and wasn't keen on playing second fiddle, or being the property of Mr.Tonino Vera. She refused to move into the luxury flat he'd offered her, preferring her Housing Association flat in New Horizons where she could be more independent. Tonino still had feelings for her but stopped giving her money. This created problems for Magaret and to maintain her standard of living she began dealing in drugs, using Mafia connections to raise her profile in the criminal underworld. Margaret's daughter Kelly knows more about this than she's prepared to admit and after questioning, she left university to join her mother in Italy where Tonino has agreed to pay for her continued studies in Naples.'

'Lucky her, And Margaret?'

'As I said, Tonino's solved the Kinnear problem for us.'

'He's just bloody marvellous this Tonino. I can't think how we ever managed without him. So what's he pulled this time?'

'Tonino says he's always loved Margaret and now that he's lost his wife, he's going to marry her and the whole family will settle in Italy.

The Commissioner shook his head. Events had completely overtaken his enquiries and he could see no reason to be further envolved in Operation Retiarious.

'As a matter of interest, what's happening about the Mackay boy?'

The chief was beginning to find the Police Commissioner's remarks a little tiresome. She turned to the Cambridge man, 'Perhaps you will explain to the Police Commissioner,' she said.

' The last communication we received from Lititia contained information about a certain sailing ship which makes regular drug runs to Lampedusa in the Med. the ship is owned by a charity which provides sail training experience for young offenders and the disabled. The ship is named the Nuvola Distante and is much admired for her splendid service. However, as you are aware, she's also used for drug smuggling and we all know that Ben Mackay was on board the vessel for her latest run. Ben Mackay had no contacts other than a mobile link with Letitia and we can only assume that he knew something was wrong and that his cover had been rumbled. We decided to put an agent on Lampedusa to check out the situation. Mysteriously, the Novola Distante has put to sea with a shipment of cocaine and yet the whole crew is ashore, also a body has been found floating in the harbour.

The Commissioner was stunned, 'What the hell is going on?'

'We can only assume that the body is that of a hitman, a crew member who tried to kill Mackay and that our Asbo informer turned the tables on him. We believe that Mackay has taken the ship and is making for Malta. It seems incredible but there can be no other explanation.'

'Sounds like we should give him a medal.'

'There's a gale warning in the area and obviously Mackay cannot handle the vessel alone. Before conditions deteriorate, we've already scrambled a helicopter to put an agent on board. His instructions are to scuttle the ship. He'll place a small charge in the ship's bilge and she'll be sent to the bottom. The ship will be reported as having foundered in high seas and Ben Mackay will be reported missing, presumed drowned.'

The threat of being murdered, of having to be constantly on guard, the nightmares, the sleepless nights, had worn Ben down. Then finally, when his life had been on the line, when his will to resist had reached its lowest ebb, in a rush of adrenalin he had taken the initiative. The crisis had passed, leaving him exhausted and desperate for sleep. At the helm of the Nuvola Distante he battled to stay awake, trying to assess the situation, trying to understand what exactly was now required of him in order to survive. He still felt pleased with himself, he had been tested in the most fearful manner and had triumphed over a sinister adversary, a killer who had made him face a life or death situation. At a time when he'd never been more afraid, never felt so weak, he'd found courage and determination.

When we have never been tested, where there is no self knowledge, searching questions often cast doubt on our character and Ben had answered those questions. The killing of another human being in these circumstances weighed little on his conscience. Now he was alone, alone with a ship which demanded the skills of a full crew under sail, alone with the sea and the sky but this new self knowledge was so positive, a new spring of confidence welled within him and he felt no threat, only the enormous challenge which now lay ahead.

He navigated out of the harbour and along the coastline in darkness, keeping a safe distance from the lights ashore. He switched on the navigation lights, but his compass course was way off, having failed to apply variation or deviation and having no idea of the effects of leeway. Although ignorant of these nautical adjustments he felt confident that he would make a landfall and that later in the day, Malta would appear on the horizon. Fighting exhaution and the need for sleep, he tried to concentrate on the swinging compass card which became more erratic as the night dragged on. Dawn finally arrived and visibility increased as the ship's features, stretching at an alarming length before him, emerged from the darkness. The wind sighed through the rigging, but in the wheelhouse, sheltered from the elements, Ben heard nothing of this early warning, and feeling bone weary, hardly noticed a change in the ship's motion. The whisper struck a higher note and the Nuvola Distante heeled, causing Ben to brace himself at the wheel.

The ship ploughed on and the comforting throb of her diesel engine lulled Ben into a sense of security. Daylight continued to filter through the lowering cloud denying any warmth from the sun and in every direction Ben could see nothing but mournful grey. With no land in the sight, the ship's bow rose and fell into each wave, climbing higher and higher as the wind increased. An intense craving for sleep tortured his red rimmed eyes, screamed at his aching limbs while the engine continued to pound a message of monotonous reliability. Ben was losing grip of his senses, he would have to sleep, have to regain his strength. If he could steady the bow, lash the helm, get his head down for an hour, surely the engine would look after the ship. In the engine room that gleaming chunk of vibrating iron would maintain it's revolutions, keeping him safe. His eyes closed gratefully at the thought. Again he fought off sleep, forcing them open, he must first lash the helm, keep the ship heading in the right direction, then he could sleep, then he could rest, just for a few moments, just for an hour. The engine would take responsibility, give him some respite from the sea. He finally summoned up enough strength to leave the increasing demands of the helm, the only means he understood of staying in control. He dropped to his knees, fumbling through a locker in search of a suitable length of rope. He staggered back to the wheel, brought the ship back on course, began securing the helm, when suddenly, with shocking finality, the engine cut out.

Giovanni had always maintained the engine to a very high standard. Its needs, it's demands, it's workings, were more familiar to him than those of his own anatomy. When storage tanks were low on the islands, bunkering services often delivered traces of sludge in the fuel and Giovanni cleaned the fuel filters on a regular basis especially before the ship put to sea. This was not a difficult job, there being no need to bleed the fuel system even when the ship was under way, but the procedure was beyond Ben's experience and his knowledge of marine diesels went no further than the throttle.

When the engine failed, the need for sleep evaporated and instead a whole new set of problems reared before him. Unable to think clearly about a course of action, Ben continued to steer the ship, his knuckles showing white against the dark varnish of the helm. The ship lost steerage and began to yaw, her bow coming up into the wind then paying off. Ben wrestled with the helm and realising that it was impossible to sail an easterly course, instinctively tried to keep the ship heading into the wind. An hour passed, the strain became intense, until, overwhelmed by impossible odds, his mind and body surrendered to exhaustion.

Ben collapsed on the floor of the wheelhouse. He was beyond caring. He had been without sleep for over thirty six hours and in that time he had pushed himself, physically and mentally to extremes. Single handed without the engine, he was unable to manage the workings of the Nuvola Distante, but the ship was sound, her timbers were sturdy and in his troubled dreams, this belief was a comfort to him. The wind increased, the sea responded, tubulent and angry, as white crests bore down on the vessel in menacing columns. The ship settled heavily, beam on to the waves, rolling violently. Her tackle worked loose, pulley blocks crashed back and forth, her main sheet slackened causing the boom to crash from side to side. An occasional wave crashed over the bow, sluicing through scuppers which could hardly cope with the volume of water. The wind now screeched through the rigging while in the wheelhouse, Ben's torso wrapped itself around the compass binacle. The helm, unchecked, continued to spin like a roulette wheel.

Ben lay half awake, conscious of the fierce wind raging outside, hanging on to every precious hour of disengagement, willing himself to find deeper levels of relaxation, closing his eyes, his ears, his mind, shutting out the mayhem which cruelly denied him an escape into slumber. Even more desperate were his survival instincts which remained strong, demanding that he stay awake and after a few hours, he dragged himself off the floor to take stock of the situation. The desert wind had reached gale force and yet it remained a warm wind having no chill factor, even so Ben shivered. Certain that the ship had sustained serious damage, fear and nausea sapped his strength and yet as far as he could see, miraculously, his situation had remained unchanged. With her sails held firmly in gaskets, hatches well battened,the ship seemed to be handling herself against the onslaught. With visible relief, Ben recognised how seaworthy the schooner had proved herself and his old confidence was partially restored. He staggered below to get his wet weather gear, then making for the galley, raided the fridge, gulping down a carton of milk before grabbing a hunk of bread a huge slice of cheese. The ship's ready made store of provisions helped to further restore his confidence and his vigour. He made his way back to the wheelhouse with thoughts of survival uppermost in his mind.

The weather system had moved on, the wind had eased, backing further until it blew northerly. The rolling motion became less violent. Ben wrestled with the free wheeling helm and found that he now had more control over the ship's head, but having no way, she tended to broach, returning to her former position, sliding beam on to the following seas. Ben decided to set some sail. It would be one hell of a struggle but the inner jib was relatively small and could be handled on the foredeck. He decided to have a go. He lashed the helm, left the wheelhouse and staggered forward. Buffeted in the wind, thrown back and forth, doused in in sheets of water, he exerted every ounce of energy on the hallyard winch, until finally he managed to hoist the sail. He had successfully hanked the sail to it's stay but had neglected to fasten on the sheets. The sail flogged forward of its stay, threatening to tear itself into shreds. Ben lowered the sail, attached the sheets and went through the whole process again.

Inside the wheelhouse, having used up his reserves of energy, he felt light headed. His efforts though were rewarded, he found he could now steer the ship in an easterly direction. All he had to do was to determine his position and set a new course for Malta. He switched on the satelite navigational system and began fiddling with the instruments. A different sound rose above the wind and waves, the unmistakable chop, chop, chop of a helicopter diverted his attention. Reluctant to leave the helm, he continued to watch the compass while trying to make sense of global positioning. The helicopter was now directly above him and Ben realised that he was not alone, he was under surveillance, his escape from Lampedusa had been easy to follow and now he could expect reprisals, a rocket attack maybe. With one hand on the wheel, he craned his neck in every direction. There was nothing, only a circle of the waves subdued in the powerful down draught filled his line of vision. The helicopter had approached over the stern and was now stationed over the wheelhouse, thundering like a huge beast about to devour it's prey.

The door to the wheelhouse burst open and a man in a black, wet suit stood framed against the opening. The wind howled through the breech, dispelling any sense of sanctuary or safety, leaving Ben paralysed with shock, unable to speak or move. When the man spoke Ben's fearful misgivings evaporated. 'You ok Ben? Nice day for sailing,' he grinned. 'Her majesty's government has decided you can stand down. For you old son, clean sheets, warm bed and a long rest. You've earned it Ben, we're very pleased with your performance.'

'You mean I'm to be rescued?' Ben stammered. 'This must be Lertitia's doing.'

'Well it is I suppose, but I'm afraid the old girl's dead, sad business. Look, I've got to get you on board the chopper. Grab your life jacket, we're going for a swim. It'll be easier to air lift you in the briny, too dodgy from the deck in these conditions. I slammed into the boom getting here, lucky not to break something. First job though, is to scuttle the ship. Is there an easy access to the bilge?'

'You mean you're goin to sink the Nuvola Distante?'

'Yep, it's Davy Jones for her my friend, now lets get going, we're running out of time.'

'Hang on! You can't sink this ship, not the Nuvola Distante. You've got to understand, I love this ship, she saved my life, she's beautiful, she's strong, she's dependable, she's absolutely brilliant. The two of us could could sail her into port, to Malta, I know we could, and what about all the coke on board, it's a huge haul, all the evidence you need?'

'I know how you feel, there's something special about sailing ships. I do a bit of sailing myself and I can see she's a fine ship, but there's a lot more to this than you know about and orders is orders.' As he spoke his hands went to the sealed container clipped to his belt. He removed it smiling sympathetically at Ben.

'What's this?' Ben queried with a worried look, 'First aid or somthin, iron rations maybe? We've got stacks of food on board.'

'No, these are explosives, designed to blow a hole through the ship's hull.'

Ben fixed his eyes on the cylindrical container. It represented everthing that all his efforts had sought to avoid. He wanted to save himself and the ship. Acting on impulse he sprang into action. He lunged for the open doors, snatching the canister as he went and threw it as far as he could out to sea. 'I'm not lettin you sink this ship,' he gasped.

There was little reaction from the man in the wet suit. 'Ok Ben, take it easy. We'll take a look at your idea, consider our options. You reckon we can handle this ship, bring her into port?' He moved across to the Sat Nav. 'Ok then, let's find our exact position.' He noted the information, transferring longitude and latitude to the chart. 'We're here Ben, take a look on the chart, we're heading in the wrong direction. Malta's over there.' He pointed through the window. 'We need to set more sail, alter course to starboard. If we're ok for fuel we could use the engine.'

267

The helicopter continued to circle overhead. Ben leaned over the chart, 'The engine packed up on me,' he began. A sharp blow behind the ear sent a bolt of lightning into his brain. White hot pain followed, everything began to spin, his mind refused to function, his legs refused to support any weight, he crumpled in a heap on the floor. After that, oblivion.

'Sorry old boy, but if you're going to work for us you've got to learn to carry out orders.' The MI5 agent went below opening every sea cock he could find, on the toilets, on the waste systems, on the cooling circuit. He found an axe in the engine compartment and methodically severed each pipe leading from a valve. Jets of water streamed into the hull. In a final act of vandalism the fate of the Nuvola Distante was sealed.

Ben came round, trussed in a harness, unable to move, swinging on the end of a line, dripping like a fisherman's trawl. He was being air lifted into the helicopter. On board the aircraft, he received immediate attention, dry clothing, blankets, a hot drink, words of encouragement. The MI5 agent patted him on the shoulder. 'Sorry about that old son, but you're working for us now. You can't afford the luxury of opinions, considering the rights and wrongs, you're here to simply carry out orders and if you want to enjoy the scenery I suggest you do just that.'

Ben looked down on the Nuvola Distante. She was already low in the water, wallowing in her death throes. A tear streamed down his cheek. He always seemed to end up losing everything, everyone, he'd ever grown to love. There was his mother, his family. Why had he deserted them? There had been divided loyalties, too much compromise and his relationship with those nearest to him had fallen appart. There had been Skeet, his mate, his friend, someone he naturally looked out for and yet he'd encouraged him in the use of drugs, the very thing that had killed him. There was Meg, a woman who had used him. Her love had been driven by greed and there had been more lust than love. The affair left him feeling empty. There was his love for Kelly. He'd only seen what he wanted to see, heard what he wanted to hear and she had rejected him. And then Letitia whom he'd loved like a mother who had died trying to help him. There were others,

Mike and Josh whom he'd let down. Now there was this ship, something beautiful, something created with strength, care and skill and of which he'd become a part. Now he had to witness its wanton destruction. Why had his life turned out like this? Why had he always come out a loser? Had he at last changed tracks? It didn't seem that way. He'd lost his freedom, he'd lost his identity, he'd lost his innocence, and at that moment he felt he'd lost his soul.

Chapter 17 The Asbo Effect

Blooded and bewildered, Mike felt he'd crossed swords with the Devil, a force beyond his knowledge, beyond his control, a force determined to destroy him and all those he held dear. The psychological effect was worse than terrorism where lives are lost at random, more devestating than war, where conflict is of a less personal nature. His love for Karen had thus far survived the adverse circumstances surrounding their relationship, it had endured against the odds, but now events threatened to finally overwhelm them. Everything he'd worked for, everything he stood for was now on the line, and all because his love for Karen had taken him into the underworld of so called anti social behaviour, a name tag for a multitude of sins, a convenient reference for making reports, for tapping into a computor, for keeping office files in good order, for minimalising it's news impact on society.

Mike had wanted to champion the cause of the underprivileged in his own inimitable, hands on, realistic way, only to find that things weren't so simple. Now life was becoming even more difficult. His immediate priority was to move in with Karen, to give her and her family added security and hopefully reunite her with her eldest son. For practical considerations, it meant he would have to relocate in ghastly new Horizons Park, a voluntary come down, which for a man of his standing might have caused some embarrassment. It was a situation he'd rather have avoided but he had no hesitation in making the decision. It was only a temporary measure until he'd found their ideal home in the countryside, away from the city, away from it's murky subculture. The sale of his luxury flat together with savings would provide him with the capital he needed to go up market in his search for a new home, a new life for his new family, for Karen, for Katrina for Matt and hopefully for Ben, Karen's prodigal son. Mike had always inclined towards altruism, having a genuine concern for the welfare of others. His love for Karen was profound, his love for his family was unwavering and now he'd grown to care for Karen's family, he loved them all. Little did he realise that such devotion would thwart his search for happiness, presenting him with a soul searching dilemma.

Josh had phoned his Dad asking for an urgent meeting at their joinery works and as Mike drove through the industrial estate, he noticed that Euro Express Car Parts and the body shop were up for sale. Josh was busy on the phone but when his father came into the office, he put the phone down saying that he had an urgent business meeting and that he'd call back later. He bounced out of the chair to greet his father, beaming with smiles, happy at last, after the shattering experience his Dad had suffered on the canals, to have the opportunity of delivering good news. 'Sorry Dad, I forgot about your hand,' he apologised after Mike avoided the handshake. 'Getting anywhere with the police enquiries? Dad, I'm determined to get involved, I'm not standing by, letting you handle this alone, I've already written a letter to our MP.'

'Hang on Josh, there's been some developments, a need for caution, and I've been told to keep a low profile. It appears I've had a brush with the Mafia and it's a matter of national security, being dealt with at the highest level. It seems Ben's got himself involved in some serious drug trafficking.'

'The Mafia! Are you serious? This sounds grim, but how come you've been targeted?'

'The head of the Manchester drugs squad says it's because I've been asking too many questions. Got myself involved without knowing it. Anyway, I've been assured there'll be no further threats, it's all been taken care of.'

'How can you be so sure?' Josh countered, looking worried, baffled and then relieved.

'I really haven't any choice. I can't say more, I've been sworn to secrecy and I simply have to trust them and what they say and Josh, you must listen to me, please don't get involved, for your own family's sake. Please keep right out of it. I understand your concern and I'm proud of the way you want to stand up for me, but honestly, the whole thing is right over our heads.' Mike slumped into a chair and Josh thought he'd never seen his father looking so defeated.

Josh remained standing. He took a heavy bill of quantities from the desk and passed it over to Mike, uncertain of how to begin. 'Dad, while you were away there's been some developments. You know I've always thought we could manage a much bigger operation and how recently I've been pricing larger contracts, well, I think we've hit the jackpot. We both know we have the knowledge and the skills to set up a modern production line and architects are showing more interest in our ability to deliver. I priced this big joinery contract with a view to expanding our business. Thing is Dad, I'm thinking more about the future and now's the time to move on, I mean, let's be honest, there's less demand for our kind of work and now suddenly everything's fallen into place. This job's bigger than anything we've ever tackled and now we're more competetive with our estimates, we've pulled it off. Yesterday we received a letter from the architects saying we've been awarded the contract.'

Mike read the front cover. It referred to the joinery section of a proposed new Children's Hospital. The final estimate was a figure which Mike had to read several times before it sank in. 'How on earth can we handle this sort of contract?'

'That's not all Dad, I've got orders for stairs, doors and built in cupboards on a huge housing estate.'

'Josh I'm I'm absolutely gobsmacked! I don't know what to say, I always knew you had the ability, but this, this really is ambitious. You don't think it's a step too far? I mean we'd need bigger premises, more machines, more staff, more transport, more management and a hell of a lot more money.' Mike scratched his balding head, certain that such a proposal would never get off the ground. Now he looked positively bewildered, but he could see by Josh's enthusiasm that he'd already given these problems a great deal of thought. 'Ok, let's hear the rest of it.'

'I know it seems too good to be true, but Euro Express Car Parts and the body shop have moved and the premises are up for sale at a very reasonable price, less than £6 per square foot. I've been over the place with the estate agent and it's absolutely perfect. They've re-vamped the interior and made a separate canteen and toilet space in the body shop. It's a huge opportunity for us and right on our doorstep.' He handed Mike a complete cost assessment for all their requirements, including the machinery together with a projected analysis of staged income from the two contracts. It was all very convincing.

For Karen, each day brought a clearer understanding of what had happened on the canals. The realisation that Ben had dragged Mike and her family into a cesspit of unbelievable violence and terror seemed to cancel out any chance of normality, any expectations of happiness. She had always been brave when dealing with the setbacks in her life, the crushing intimidation of domestic abuse, the emotional traumas of raising a young family on her own and more recently, the outrage of violence on the streets, but now she had the jitters and New Horizons Park offered little comfort. New Horizons was not fit for living, a mile high slum harbouring a contageous disease, the modern equivalent of a leper colony, or at least that is how it registered with Karen. In New Horizons, every chance of happiness, any hope of a fresh start, usually ended in despair and now living there seemed like a life sentence. A new life with Mike had offered a fairytale avenue of escape, and yet even this precious relationship was now threatened by her wayward son and his decent into organised crime. It had all started with the Anti-Social Behaviour Order. Instead of making him a social outcast, it had given him street 'cred'. Instead of bringing shame, it had brought him respect. For those who were law abiding, it had scandalised his behaviour but for the criminal element, it had made him an attractive proposition. Karen blamed all her misfortune, all her heartache, on this single imposition. It was no substitute for properly organised sport in schools, for real opportunities to learn skills in trade and industry, for family moral support. It was simply another form of administration. It had given bureaucracy mountains of paper work, while helping to encourage crime. Karen had seen the results, the shooting of a school master by Pitbull Patterson, the tragic death of Marvin Cooney, a beautiful young man whose mind had been deranged by drug abuse and now her own son in mortal danger, emotionally unstable, having an affair with an older woman, running with Mafia hoodlums, taking appalling risks. Guilt was never far away and there was nothing she could do or say in order to alleviate the pain. In Karen's mind, the escalation of crime and calamity had resulted from Ben's Anti-Social Behaviour Order. The thought did little to apportion blame or ease her conscience. It had labelled the family, damaging everything that was good. It had been a blight which had brought shame, anxiety and fear. It had been the Asbo effect.

Karen was close to losing those virtues which had sustained her in times of adversity, her dignity and her self respect, and recently she had been given another blow which threatened to further undermine her stability. She had received a redundancy notice from the mini supermarket to which she had given faithful service for more than five years and last week it had opened its doors for the last time. There was talk of company plans for a giant, new store on the outskirts of the city but in the face of a creeping recession everything remained under wraps and job security was far from certain.

It was Monday morning again, the beginning of another day, another day of apprehension in the face of an impending crisis. Matt and Katrina were at school, Mike had left earlier for his meeting with Josh and Karen anxiously awaited his return. His decision to move in with her had given her the strength to carry on and having him near had transformed the flat, making it a sanctuary from the world outside. He was her rock, her comfort and her only joy.

The door bell rang and Karen rushed to answer the door, hoping Mike had returned with some good news. She opened the door and to her dismay a policeman and a policewoman stood on the balcony. In New Horizons, police were rarely seen knocking on doors and for Karen, blue uniforms mean't serious trouble. In a curious way she welcomed an official visit, perhaps it had been decided to bring the matter concerning Ben into the open, to let her know that he had been arrested and offer her their support. However, on this occasion they stood well back with an air of sympathy and some discomfort and Karen immediately knew she was about to hear something dreadful. 'Mrs Mackay? Mrs Karen Mackay?' The policewoman asked as if enquiring into someone's health.

'Er, yes, yes I'm Mrs Mackay,' she answered nervously. 'This is about Ben isn't it, my eldest son. Oh my God, whatever's happened to him?'

'Mrs Mackay I'm afraid we have some bad news, I think we'd better step inside, if we may,' the policewoman continued.

The words knifed into her. 'He's dead isn't he?'

'We don't know that for sure Mrs Mackay, but he has been reported missing. Look, we understand this must come as a great shock and perhaps we should talk inside. We can bring you up to date with all the details, explain everything, if that's alright with you Mrs Mackay.'

Karen had lived in fear of this very moment, half hoping it would never arrive, yet half knowing that it would. 'Yes of course,' she whispered.

Karen tried to focus on the thought that Ben was missing and the chances of his survival but as the story unfolded hope gave way to despair. The facts seemed strangely distant, remote from her every day existance, disconected from her own reality, having no relevance to the rest of her family. She listened to the words, an unfolding drama of short sentences, delivered with genuine sympathy and the utmost sincerity.

'Mrs Mackay, were you aware that Ben was involved with a much older woman? A Margeret Kinnear?'

'I knew he was seeing someone but he was just playing the field. It was a phase he was going through and I was sure he'd grow out of it. He never had a serious girl friend that I know of.'

The policeman, who had said nothing thus far, acting as though he had first hand information, continued, 'Margaret Kinnear is the head of a major drug dealing operation here in Manchester and has direct links with the Mafia in Naples. She is a very dangerous woman and for some time our undercover agents have been keeping a close eye on her. We were closing in on her organisation and were ready to make an arrest when she gave us the slip and flew out to Naples. She took your son with her.'

'But you say he's gone missing. Do you mean missing in Italy? How do you know he's missing?' Karen probed.

'The policeman was warming to his task. 'The Italian police have also been watching Margaret Kinnear and Ben is known to have been on board a sailing ship making a regular Mafia drugs run to an island off the coast of Tunisia. On its return voyage, the ship foundered in a severe gale. I'm afraid Mrs Mackay it appears that all hands were lost. For obvious reasons, the ship failed to report its position and although there's been an extensive search and rescue sweep, no bodies have been discovered. I'm really sorry having to report this, we're both very, very sorry.'

'But if you knew Ben was mixed up with Margaret Kinnear, why didn't you tell me about it. I had a right to know. I might have been able to stop him leaving. I'd have thought you had a duty to inform me as his mother?' Karen struck back in a forlorn hope of not having to face the truth.

The policeman continued with his plausable explanation, having no reason to believe that he wasn't telling the truth, 'Your son has an Anti-Social Behaviour Order and of course we were keeping an eye on him, but he'd stopped drug dealing, running with street gangs and causing trouble and he'd taken a regular job with a reputable company. In fact we were impressed. We had no idea he was infatuated with Margaret Kinnear or that she had so much influence over him. Like you say, we thought he was playing the field, just a young man's sexual adventure and in any case he's an adult and his love affair with her was a private matter and no concern of ours. I'm surprised you weren't aware of it'

'But surely they must have had life rafts or something. Surely there must be some hope of survivors?' Karen began to falter, there was a catch in her voice. The awful realisation that she had most probably lost Ben, her eldest son, for ever, was presenting itself like a poisoned chalice.

'Please don't give up hope Mrs Mackay, not yet. We shall continue our search for survivors and will keep you closely informed.' The policewoman softly intervened, offering comfort while showing real concern. She herself was a mother and had suffered the loss of her first child at birth. She understood a mother's pain and grief.

In the days that followed, each dawn held faint expectations, each evening left Karen feeling empty. Slowly and remorselessly the days became weeks, the weeks became months until finally she gave up hope. To her, nothing seemed to matter any more. Only her love for Mike endured.

With typical disregard for his own aspirations, Mike had invested his savings and the proceeds from the sale of his flat in the new business venture. The capital was readily available. Contracts pending and the opportunity to buy Euro Express meant that quick decisions had to be made. He had absolute faith in Josh's ability and still believed the political will of the country celebrated risk taking and that the bank would offer generous support. In order to buy new machinery, set up the manufacturing process and improve administration, a considerable bank loan was required and this had been negotiated. The bank, however, required the deeds of the small unit they already owned and the two new, larger units as collateral.

Mike planned to sell the small terraced house, take out a mortgage and move the whole family into a new home away from the city. The forthcoming marriage had been put on hold until property transactions were completed but there had been no buyers for the terraced house. Mike and Karen were now living together in the New Horizons flat. It was a fresh experience for both of them, facing up to the demands of family life and the daily round of domestic chores. These familiar pressures were easily shared, their love having been tested in the most dire situations, but life in New Horizons had a way of corroding the will. Drug abuse, domestic violence, juvenile crime, vandalism and verbal obscenities crowded around their home in every direction. The fabric of their lives, like the concrete structure which surrounded them, was threatened with erosion. Surrender and apathy hung in the air like a dead weight. Only the young screamed their agonised graffiti from the walls.

With few resources Karen had fought against the burgeoning squalour of this notorious estate, she had tried to maintain standards, to set a good example for her children but now she felt exhausted and on the point of giving up. Mike, showing much concern over this, decided that something was needed to represent their making a stand, a formal statement of their love, a symbol of underlying strength and unity, a marker in their lives which stood for something that could easily be recognised. He proposed they should be married at the earliest opportunity, inspite of their situation. Not the grand wedding he'd hoped for but in a registry office followed by a quiet family get together. The idea helped Karen focus her thoughts and she readily agreed.

Mike had planned for semi retirement but now he felt obliged to throw his whole weight behind the new business venture. His excursion into the problems of juvenile crime, drugs dealing and street gang mentality had ended with Winston's funeral and his efforts to console Mary, Winston's mother. It had been a harrowing experience leaving him with a sense of failure. Now, in a breathtaking switch, he found himself yet again embroiled in commerce, facing an enormous financial challenge. He thought he'd left these struggles behind years ago, that he'd established financial security and now had no money problems, but no, family pressures had conspired to make further demands. These demands were ambitious, culminating in a precarious enterprise requiring hard work and dedication.

The cost of high powered electrical installations and an efficient extraction system for the removal of sawdust went way over budget. A shortage of skilled joiners and wood machinists meant that Mike and Josh would have to work long hours. However, the first phase of the housing project finally got under way, and after the inevitable teething problems, doors and staircases were coming off the production line. More than ever before in his life, success depended on the political climate and solid support from the bank.

Mike's faith in banking gave way to frustration. The days were long gone when a client could pick up the telephone and speak to a bank manager. Now there were procedures, impersonal procedures, voice recorded instructions, call centres and foreign dialects, not easily understood. Mike's old bank manager, his friend and confidant, had left years ago after a bout of illness brought on by disillusion and stress. A couple of painful foreclosures, the ruthless enterprise of modern banking, its thorough dishonesty and cunning had given him grave concerns about his own integrity. He'd had enough, and after handing in his resignation, he bought a farm, an unction for his troubled mind. These days bank managers were always on the move. They looked the same, they talked the same, greedily preoccupied with money for its own sake while hawking a wide choice of financial products, cleverly devalued in small print.

To day Mike had an appointment with his current bank manager. He felt like a schoolboy summoned to the headmaster's study. He was not in a good mood. His love for Karen had already drawn him into unfamiliar territory and now the fact that Ben was missing had taken the joy out of their lives. After the abrupt and traumatic ending to their holiday on the canals he gave more thought to his own mortality. Every day Karen suffered heartache, fear and outrage and Mike realised how fragile were the expectations of their lives, how readily their dreams might fade. He sensed how easily that which is precious is lost, how casually promises are broken.

He recalled previous meetings, when a bank manager would have invited him directly into the office with a welcoming smile. Today he sat, frustrated and impatient in the waiting room, waiting on the bank manager's pleasure, a softening up process, which Mike felt amounted to an insult. In order to remain objective, he studied the décor. It was a splendid room, a late Victorian tribute to Mike's own craft with fielded oak panels around the walls, sash widows in solid oak, long and slender with delicate glazing bars reaching towards an ornate ceiling The whole building had been sold to a brewery chain for refitting and a new branch was due to open in the same street. It would be less ostentatious, directly functional and more severe.

A whole series of events had led to the meeting with the future of their joinery business very much at stake. The crisis had arisen against a background of life threatening violence from a criminal underworld of which Mike had little knowledge. All he'd ever done was help those he loved and offer a couple of underprivileged kids a fair chance in life. Like a fool, he'd lost his way, stumbling among the emotional clutter which surrounded their families and the problems they faced in their every day lives. With Ben he'd gone even further. He had wanted more than anything to make Karen happy and his energies had been exhausted in a search for her missing son. Dangerous probing had led to an attempt on their lives, a shocking, violent intrusion which had left them dumfounded and in constant fear. They had sought police protection, had considered moving to a different part of the country, only to be promised that there would be no more violence, the problem had been dealt with at the very highest level and that Ben was safe. Ben had got himself envolved with matters of national security and it was in everyone's interest for Mike to stop asking questions. Much time had been spent pursuing these matters, trying to clear a mountain of baggage with a view to marrying the woman he adored while giving her comfort and support. Then came the awful news. The police assurances had been worthless. Ben was not safe, he was missing, presumed dead.

Banks were recording unprecedented losses and many were on the verge of collapse. Manufacturing industries were already feeling the pinch, unemployment was rising and it was not a good time to make huge investments. However, initial prospects for Mike Edwards Joinery had looked good. Vera Motors had given ground on every enquiry and the sale of Euro Express had sailed through. The production of duck boards and work benches had been given priority over bespoke joinery from regular customers and the first phase of kitchen furniture, stair flights and doors for the housing development had been completed ahead of schedule.

At this point everything changed dramatically. High percentage mortgages were no longer readily available and the market for new housing suddenly collapsed. The developers suspended all building operations, hoping that things would improve. Government funding ran dry and the hospital project was shelved for a year, possibly longer. Mike Edwards joinery found itself saddled with enormous debts and very few orders. The financial situation was serious, the livelihood of the Edwards family and their employees was on the line, leaving Mike with the uncomfortable task of disscussing their misfortunes with the bank manager, hoping for a positive response and some possible solutions.

A door leading from the bank manager's office to the waiting area, opened with a flourish, 'Good morning Mr Edwards, do come in, so sorry to keep you waiting, rather chilly outside, no heating on I'm afraid.'

Mike sat facing the manager. This was an important meeting and he wished to make a fresh appraisal of the young man he was dealing with. He needed to engage a friendly face, a sympathetic eye, but on this occasion the manager's eyes were diverted, shooting an occasional glance from one side of his desk to the other. It was a sly, involuntary reaction and Mike was unable to make a connection. He decided to forego the pleasantries and get straight to the point. 'No doubt you're concerned about our overdraft, and so are we. I'll be honest with you. There's every sign of a down turn in the construction industry and circumstances beyond out control have scuppered our immediate plans for expansion. The contracts we discussed at our last meeting have been put on hold and we've been left with a problem. The builders are only committed to phase one of the housing project and payments are getting slower and slower. The hospital starting date was provisional but we were assured that it had been given the government go ahead. I mean, to us, a contract backed with government money is as safe as you can get. Now it seems there's very little chance of the hospital work or the housing contract going ahead, well at least until there's a change in the financial climate and the housing market improves. As you know, on the strength of these contracts, we've invested a great deal of money and now we're relying on your backing to see us through.'

'Mr Edwards, what exactly do you propose?'

'Well, we'll continue our efforts to win new contracts of course, but we need time. We've layed off the extra staff, but obviously we don't want to lose our old employees, they're highly skilled and some have been with us a long time. We've already cancelled remaining orders for machinery and are hoping to let the unit which has the least machinery. We're really asking for an increased overdraft, enough to keep us going until things improve,' he paused for a moment, 'About £100,000 over the next twelve months would give us the leeway we require.'

'Mr Edwards, I'm glad you've taken the initiative by coming to see me, it shows you realise just how serious this is and it put's you in a more favoured light. The bank *is* getting concerned about you're account. We're very much aware of a collapse of the housing market and the change in government policy concerning public spending and believe me, we are as disappointed as you are.' The bank manager flicked the intercom, 'Oh, Miss Townsend, will you please bring me the Edwards file.' He shook his head as though the bank had made a serious misjudgement and had been let down 'This is bad news Mr Edwards, very bad news indeed.'

'Surely it's not that bad. If you go back over the years, you'll see we've always recovered from the occasional downturn.' The manager's face held a blank expression and he appeared to lose interest, only his eyes remained alert, darting back and forth with their examination of the sundry items arranged across his desk. Mike continued, 'Our record speaks for itself, we're a family concern, with a good reputation, we've built up a good business and now more than ever we're geared up to meet the new challenges of modern industry.' Mike suddenly realised he'd forgotten the bank manager's name and instantly regretted it. 'I've banked here since leaving school. You know we're hard working and honest in our dealings.'

The secretary came in, giving Mike a well rehearsed smile. 'Now let's see.' the manager frowned as he quickly went through the file. 'Against your present overdraft, we hold the deeds of your industrial units, perhaps you're able to offer further collateral? The deeds of your homes for example?'

'What! Are you saying you need more security? The value of our work units alone is far in excess of our borrowings, surely you can extend loan facilities against the property you already have?'

'Mr Edwards, in the present financial climate I'm afraid I can't. Property prices are in free fall and the market is saturated with unsold industrial units. It would be imprudent of the bank and we would be failing in our duty to savers and shareholders alike, if we made reckless decisions concerning loans. You must also bear in mind that your business is not a limited company and if you're unable to meet the demands of your creditors, the liquidation of your assets would quite possibly include the sale of your homes. He tapped something into a desk computor waiting for a response. None came. 'Mr Edwards, I'm sure you're aware of our present difficulties?'

Mike sat with his arms folded. He'd already decided he didn't like this self assured, little prig, a weedy individual, who relished giving him a lecture. 'Hmn.'

'If you provide us with additional security, your present overdraft can be extended, but I wouldn't recommend this course of action. To be quite frank, we can see no improvement in the construction industry, at least not in the foreseeable future and I believe further expenditure will only serve to push you deeper in debt. To reduce the damage, I suggest we appoint a Liquidator before the situation becomes less tenable.' There was a brick wall finality in the bank manager's voice, as though he'd diagnosed a terminal illness, and for the first time he looked his customer straight in the eye. Mike's rugged appearance and the mounting tension between them ruffled his confidence.' I suggest this is the best course of action for all concerned.' He cleared his throat, 'In the present circumstances.'

Mike simply stared him down. He was no longer listening and his thoughts were elsewhere. For weeks now he'd been given the run around. All he ever heard from authority was lies, lies and more lies. Karen was close to a nervous breakdown and they had now been forced to live in a slum, the business was now threatened with closure and in every direction he seemed thwarted. Now this, this from a bank that had become a faceless entity, an institution he felt was rotten to the core. 'Hmn,' he grunted.

'Mr Edwards, I'm anxious to hear your response. Are we to have your co-operation?'

'I seem to have forgotten your name,' came the relpy.

The bank manager was beginning to feel decidedly uncomfortable. Was his client dumb, or was he being rude? 'Richard, Richard Dursely- Bywaters.'

'I know you're more used to dealing with my son but we have met on a couple of previous occasions. The reason I've forgotten your name Richard, is that you haven't earned my respect.'

'Oh, really! I suggest it's more to do with your lack of understanding. You seem unable to grasp the trouble you're in.'

'Oh I understand the importance of brass all right, but do you, I wonder? Banking used to be about making sound financial judgements. Money oiled the wheels of agriculture and industry, it promoted more efficiency, encouraged prudence, thrift and innovation, it gave priority to enterprise in the work place, those pursuits which ultimately provide our basic needs. Banking was a form of good husbandry, looking after the nations stock meant that we could enjoy other benefits like education and a National Health Service.'

'Well, Mr Edwards, Isn't that precisely what we're doing?'

'No Richard, that is precisely what the banks are not doing. Did you know Martin, Martin Gough, one of your predecessors who belonged to the old school of banking?'

'Oh yes, poor old Martin. They say he couldn't change with the times, was so out of touch, banking finally left him behind.'

'I don't think so, Mr Dursely-Bywaters, it was the other way round. He left banking behind. Martin had the interests of his clients at heart. He understood their problems and took the trouble to learn the practical implications. He was tough, but his guidance was positive, with an emphasis on maintaining industrial strength. You see Richard, with you it's different, you've no real interest in Edwards Joinery or what we are trying to achieve.'

Richard Dursley- Bywaters was now sitting very upright. 'That's unfair. you're making assumptions, assumptions directed at me personally and I resent your tone.'

Mike ignored the protest, determined now to speak his mind and to hell with the consequences. 'Banking is now plainly driven by greed. Manipulating the loan markets, manoeuvring the flow of money through your accounts, making excessive charges, dealing in money for its own sake. These practices have become your trade mark and you Richard, are very much a part of that new regime. Banks are more than ready to forsake industry, preferring to gamble away the nation's wealth in a race for easy profits and quick returns. You're just a bunch of wheeler dealers.'

'Mr Edwards, you're entitled to your ill informed opinions, but they have nothing to do with the financial mess you've made of your own affairs and your attitude is certainly doing nothing to help the situation.'

'Come on Richard, be honest. We've all read about the mess our banks are in, the banker's gravy train, the obscene salaries, the eye watering bonus schemes, the lavish expense accounts, the extravagant lifestyles. No wonder banks have run the country into debt, encouraging irresponsible loans rather than thinking about the nation's future and *you've* set us all a fine example with your own Mickey Mouse debt levels,. The Bank of England's set the lowest interest rates ever and it's plainly obvious that you no longer function as a bank. You're so preoccupied with your own debt, you're afraid to give out loans. My business is not about wheeler dealing. The results of our labours are all around for everyone to see, a legacy of our craft and skill. Take a good look at your contribution, what have you left? Misery, hardship and broken dreams, that's your legacy, not to mention a tax burden for generations to come. '

The bank manager was beginning to squirm. 'There has to be competition, we have to stay ahead of the game. You're an ex rugby player, surely you can see that.'

'Yes there has to be competition, but in a civilised society we must have standards, trading has to be fair. I played rugby against rugby players, not men like yourself. Exploitation of ignorance, poverty, the underpriviledged and the weak reduces our moral fibre, but then, you wouldn't know anything about that would you?'

The bank manager was speechless. His ego had been shredded. All his endeavours, his studies, his rapid promotion through the banking hierarchy had been trashed. From the outset he'd felt superior and very much in control, setting the boundaries, quoting the terms. He always felt this way, no matter who the client was, but this meeting had broken the rules of engagement. People looking for credit were always on their guard, showing respect for his powers and the impositions he was able to dictate, but this had been different. A few chosen words from this fearless, pugnacious character, whose looks belied his interlect had cut him down to size. The iridescent colours of his carreer, his confidence, his standing, his prestige, had reached giant proportions only to explode like a bubble of soap. Blinkered for most of his career, his sights firmly set on power, privilege and the trappings which money can buy, he now had a vision of those goals, he strained to see the prize and found he was staring into empty space. He was an intelligent man, more sensitive and tougher than he looked.

'Mr Edwards, Mike isn't it, Mike Edwards, I'm at a loss for words. I should feel outraged but instead I find myself in sympathy with you're argument. I know you're angry but I'm not afraid of you, you know. I understand what you're saying and everything you've said is true.'

It was Mike now who found himself speechless. 'Yes it is Mike Edwards. It always used to be Mike, never Mr Edwards. Martin and I were friends.'

'Mike, I'm not holding out much hope, but I'm going to arrange a meeting with our area manager and I promise I'll do everything I can to get you that overdraft. In the meantime I would like to meet both you and Josh as soon as possible and I shall require your most recent balance sheet and a projection of cash flow over the next six months.' He reached for his diary, 'Thursday morning, 10 o clock, ok?'

For the first time in his position as bank manager, he found the courtesy to escort his client to the main entrance. He shook Mike's hand. 'It's been a great pleasure seeing you again Mike, I only wish it had been under different circumstances, but I promise to do the best I can.'

'Now you're beginning to sound like Martin Gough and incidently, I liked the way you took what I said on the chin. Sorry if I got too personal, I realise now I misjudged you and thanks for trying to help. I know it wasn't easy. You may be disillusioned with your profession but don't give up on banking, not like Martin who found he couldn't take any more, stay with it. I think there's every possibility you'll make a good banker.'

Chapter 18 The Ways of a Woman.

In the money before morals world of Tonino Vera, women were
nothing more than objects of desire. Tonino Vera used women, he
craved their bodies, especially when they were young. Tonino
was far from handsome, but acquired wealth and power made him
an attractive proposition for those darlings whose self interest
matched his own. He could have married any one of them, an
empty headed signorina who would give him the son he secretly
yearned for, but to everyone's surprise, he married Meg, the call
girl whose services he had paid for as a young criminale. She was
a hard bitch, not easily impressed or intimidated, intelligent,
brassy and beautiful and Tonino had always loved her. He loved
the way she stood up to him, her zest for life and the way she
enjoyed his wealth without being overawed by it. To her wealth
and poverty were as fickle as the roll of a dice. Tonino and Meg
shared a criminal mind, its perverse honesty and disdain for the
law. She was a woman he could live with and yes he loved her, he
respected her, he could trust her and he was not afraid to confide
in her and more than that, it was an alliance which suited the
Mafia. Predudice and discrimination against women were never
more apparent than among the ranks of the Mafia, but Meg had
earned her own share of notoriety and became the first woman to
join their governing body. Her insight, her ability to manipulate
the criminal mind, her knowledge of English, her Celtic sense of
honour and her striking appearance had won them over.

Her's was the marriage of a pagan queen, solemnly
blessed by a misguided catholic church, followed by the more
appropriate delights of a bacchanalian feast. For Meg it was
nothing more than a deal, she had given her daughter a good start
in life and provided for her further education, she had all the
comforts and security one could ask for and she lived an Italian
lifestyle with its celebration of uninhibited pleasures, the good
life, living in the sun on the bay of Naples. In return she made
love to Tonino with practiced sensuality, leaving him exhausted
after each encounter. The real Meg, in a quiet corner of her mind,
still held the memories of youth with its innocence and purity and
she ached for Ben, the young man who had been her lover.

Tonino had expressed fears concerning Lertitia's familiarity with Ben and the threat they posed to the Mafia's lucrative dealings in cocaine and Meg had understood the situation. Secretly, she was heartbroken and refused to believe that Ben had betrayed her. She'd had her suspicions, his nervous tension, the guarded possession of his mobile and she had her own theories about his being reported missing. There was no disputing the fact that the Nuvola Distante had gone down in a dreadful storm, newspaper headlines confirmed this, but she believed the vessel had been abandoned and Ben had taken the schooner to rendezvous with another boat just off Lampedusa. It had all been pre-arranged by Letitia. British intelligence had promised her that he would be rescued. She guessed Letitia had been murdered but had no idea that Ben had also been targeted.

Tonino was feeling good, jaded passion had been resurrected and this morning, he felt like a young man again. Meg joined him for a light breakfast on the marble balcony which led directly from their bedroom. It overlooked the pool and the landscaped gardens with their statues and water features. The balcony stretched the whole length of the villa, supported on a slender colonnade which rose above the greenery with a flourish of classical architecture. Carlo, the fawning domestic, served the food, a salad panzanella, new bread, roasted and flavoured with ripe tomato juice, fresh bazil and piquant capers. He poured a sparkling wine, one of Italy's best, an ice cool Methode Champeniose from Trento in the north east. He fussed around them, shifting the chairs, adjusting the parasol, examining the flower boxes, removing dead heads from the trailing geraniums, while taking ever opportunity to admire Meg's cleavage and curves, casually flaunted through her see through dressing gown. Tonino enjoyed seeing other men lust after Meg, their envy of the carnal pleasure she so obviously gave him, yet afraid to flatter or flirt with her, but Carlo was drooling and Tonino, mellowed by a night of something more than sweet dreams, wearily dismissed him.

'Tonino, Ah'm curious aboot what might have happened to young Ben Mackay. Have they no found his body yet?' When discussing matters of personal concern, Meg prefered to use her own version of English. With Letitia out of the way, Tonino's English had lapsed more into Italian vernacular.

'Meg, mia amore, you still gotta feelings for your toyboy?'

'Och no! But Ah'll be honest wi you Tonino, Ah didna love him, but you ken ah was very fond o the laddie, he amused me. Ah think you liked him yersel.'

'I loved that boy like a son, I coulda given him everything, but Letitia turned him against me, ruined it for him. Anyways he's finito, drowned, gone with the Nuvola Distante.'

'An Ah wonder who killed mah Jimmy?' Was it yoursel who had him wasted? Ah ken he was a psycho.'

'It musta been Ben. Francesco says they quarrelled and they hated each other's guts. They were on board together when the others went ashore and I think they fell out over something, Jimmy musta pulled a knife and Ben turned the tables on him, killed him with his own knife. That's why he took the Nuvola Distante and did a runner.' Tonino shrugged, 'such a pity, he coulda been a good boy.'

Meg didn't believe him but she appeared to be satisfied with the explanation. They turned their attention to the food and wine, the delicious flavours competing with the natural fragrance of the garden, the honeysuckle, jasmine, bazil and sage. Beyond the treeline the morning sun splashed yellow across the azure blue of the Mediterranean, filtering through the leaves to clothe the villa in spangles of gold.

They said nothing, their bodies absorbing the warmth, but Meg's thoughts were elsewhere. The more she thought about it the more convinced she became. Ben had returned to England, gone back to his mother and her new partner, the man he admired and respected but found difficult to accept. Meg loved Ben so much she wanted a new life for him, a fresh start, away from her own influence and the clutches of Tonino and the Mafia. In this respect she and Letitia had something in common. She prayed that Ben had decided to live a decent life, to find regular work and hoped that he'd taken a job with Edwards Joinery. Tonino read her thoughts, 'You still thinking about Ben? There's no more toy boys for you mia amore, not ever, not now you're Mrs Tonino Vera, capiche? '

'Och no! Ah dinnae want a toy boy, Ah'm quite happy being Mrs Tonino Vera just as long as you dinnae go chasin other lassies an promise you'll always look after me, you'll spoil me, pamper me an tell me that you love me.'

Tonino smiled, this woman was not in the least bit afraid of him. 'You know Meg I love you, you're the only one for me, mia bella donna, mia amante, I love you, I love you, I love you.'

Meg stretched her leg under the table, she ran her toes down the inside of his calf. 'Ah love you too, tough guy but Ah canna understand you.'

Tonino laughed. 'You don't understand me? You mean, I still gotta few tricks up my sleeve.'

'You've got more than tricks Tonino, you're a canny braw operator an there's no mistakin, an Ah'm glad Ah'm on your side. It was a clever deal you made back home, getting the heat off you, closing down Euro Express and then shiftin the operation, keepin you're interests in Britain and then plannin to build casinos an all.' Meg shook her head, wide eyed in admiration.

'It's just good business Meg. Money talks. Strange how things have worked out though. Mike Edward's in bed with Ben's ma and his outfit buying Euro Express. Remember Edwards Joinery? Ben tried working there, thought about going straight before he worked for me. Mike Edwards and Ben's ma ended up on our hit list. He was asking too many questions after Ben, started playing detective, talking to the police, and we decided to take them both out. Now it's no problem, it's all sorted and anyways Edwards Joinery is going bust.'

'Och! I know all about the Joinery works, Ben often talked about his ma havin an affair with Mike Edwards, but ah dinnae ken he'd bought Euro Express. When you were dealin with Mike Edwards, was Ben never seen aboot the premises?'

'Ben? No, there was never any Ben around, Ben's gone Meg, drowned, food for the fishes, finito, like I said.'

'You say they're goin bust but Ah ken they were a good firm, doin high class work in the city an Ah ken they've been around for a long time.'

'Business is bad in Britain, they got no industry worth the mention, a lot of manufacturing jobs depend on foreign money with no real support from the banks. Banks are just one big casino. Look around, the whole country's run like a lottery. So what are we doing? We're giving em what they want, more casinos. Edwards joinery's in deep, they've spent their reserves on tooling for work that no longer exists, they can't get work and they're running out of cash.'

Meg poured herself more wine. She wanted to believe that Ben was ok, he'd get a good life, he'd find happiness, he'd meet a young lassie and have bairns, he'd have a good job, become a partner even. At Edwards Joinery. 'Tonino darlin, these casinos you're plannin, where are you thinkin of buildin them?'

'We'll start in Manchester, the capital of the north. It's a great city, modern, liberale, good bars and restaurants and lotsa money. Then we'll consider other towns, but Manchester for sure.'

'Will you dae somethin for me Tonino? It's just a wee sentiment Ah'm askin. A'h canna explain it, it's just for lang syne, Ah canna say more. It'll make nae sense to you, but if you'll dae this for me, you'll ease mah mind no end.'

Tonino was intrigued. 'What d'you mean Meg, 'lang syne'. What is it you want?'

'It's these casinos. Ah want you to get Edwards Joinery off the hook. Ah want you to give them contracts for all the woodwork and shopfittin. Ah ken they'll dae a good job, an it'll look good for you, the boss of Vera Motors, givin a local firm the sub contract work.'

Tonino leaned forward, lost for a moment in the violet, blue depths of Meg's beautiful eyes. He said nothing. Meg continued, 'Ah feel guilty aboot Ben an his family, Ah've caused them grief, an all for mah own pleasure, mah own needs. Ben was only a boy, he wasnee like you Tonino, you can stop the world batterin me, he could never do that. He fell in love with mah daughter Kelly an Ah trashed his love an Ah would nae let him see her. Ah messed up his heed an took him away from his family an Ah think in some ways it's me that's killed him.'

Tonino was listening, his thoughts diverted at last from those violet eyes, he leaned back in his chair, he very carefully guillotined a Cuban cigar, lit it and took a long draw. The tobacco tasted good, the air was still and whisps of smoke hung around the table. He studied Meg's face, he wanted to please her, he shrugged his shouders, 'Ok Meg, for you I can do this thing.'

A few days later, Meg took herself into the city. She was going on a shopping spree with fashionable clothes in mind. After shopping, she left the chauffeur saying she wanted to walk through the Piazzo Bellini, have a coffee and relax. Her first thought however, was to make a call from a public telephone. 'Is that Edwards joinery? Can Ah speak tae Ben Mackay please, Ah believe he's workin there '

'Yes, this is Edwards Joinery, Josh Edwards the manager speaking, I'm afraid Ben's no longer with us. Tragically he's been reported missing, lost at sea. That was some time ago and hopes have faded, the whole thing's been a mystery and we're all terribly upset. I'm very sorry, but who is this speaking please?'

'Ah mind you're Mike Edward's son an Ah'm truly sorry to hear aboot Ben, but Ah wanted tae gi him some important information.'

'Who is this speaking please?'

'Nae mind aboot that, now listen tae me Josh. You'll have had an invitation to tender for bespoke joinery in two, new Manchester casinos? From a London firm of architects? They're a subsidary of Vera Construction in Italy, the group who owned Euro Express Motors and sold you the premises. Have you nae received these yet?'

'Yes, as a matter of fact I'm going through them now. Actually they've come as a bit of a surprise and we're interested to know who recommended us. Who is this speaking please?'

Meg ignored the question, 'Now Ah want you to listen very carefully. This information is just for Mike an yoursel an if you've any sense in your heeds you'll let it go nae further. When you price the work, don't be afraid to gi yoursel a good profit, you'll definitely get the the contract, there's nae other competition.' Meg replaced the receiver.

The anxiously awaited meeting between Edwards Joinery, Richard Dursley- Bywaters and the area bank manager, was delayed for two weeks. The area manager was otherwise engaged in the pressing need for branch closures and a huge reduction in staff levels. On the day of the meeting there were arkward divisions in the Edward's camp. Corruption spreads like a virus and Josh decided not to tell his father about Meg's phone call. Although he'd never met the New Horizons, femme fatale, he knew about her drug dealing, heard the rumours about her exotic life style and guessed it was Meg who'd offered them much needed work on a plate. He had no idea what her motives were but couldn't help feeling the call was genuine. Keeping this knowledge to himself, he pressed Mike to accept the invitations, pointing out that high class joinery was required with no expense spared. They were geared up to meet these sort of standards and a successful tender would mean a lifeline for Edwards Joinery. The winning of such a lucrative order would assure the immediate survival of their business and the financial security of their families. It would also put them in a stronger position when they presented their case to the area bank manager. Josh went further. There were no other joinery firms in the area capable of handling the job and the fact that they were Manchester based gave them a clear advantage over London firms. He was confident they were in with a good chance and argued that it was just too good an opportunity to miss.

Mike remained suspicious of the Vera group and in any case he hated the idea of helping to construct casinos which in his opinion simply profited from the lure of easy money. Life with Karen had shown him the threadbare fabric of our society and he was more than ever convinced that bureaucracy had weakened our moral fibre. The devastation of agricultiure, technology, craft and industry had deprived our youth of the chance to make something of their lives and in its place bureaucracy had filled the gap with ivory towers of bloated administration. Mike had read only recently that maintaining the benefits system alone had cost the government more than a quarter of it's income. He despised office bound social services, petty health and safety regulations, council red tape, trumped up quangos and all forms of excessive administration. The frustrations, the controls, the time wasting interference of officialdom and the rising burden of tax experienced by those in industry confirmed his opinions. And now, living in the bleak landscape of New Horizons with it's domestic abuse, it's empty beer cans, discarded needles, take away litter and screaming graffiti, the blinkers had been finally removed. Too many people were grass hopping around between benefits and casual work, too many people were unemployed, too may people were in prison, too many people were in serious debt, too many people gambled, too many people lied. Mike was convinced that we were in danger of losing sight of the work ethic, the need for self respect and a sense of pride in personal achievement and these values had been so undermined by a succession of weak governments that we now faced the ultimate paradox. If you avoided work, taking all that you could from the community for free, a vast team of administrators would be on your case making sure you got everything. If you worked and saved all your life, a even bigger team would try to get their hands on your money and make sure you got nothing In Mike's opinion, fail safe welfare encouraged a work shy sub culture where petty theft and gambling supplemented the welfare income. The latest publicity suggested that Britain was gambling for it's prosperity, from it's money institutions at the highest level, who favoured quick returns from equities rather than long term investments, down to scratch cards and a national lottery for the man in the street.

Casinos, Mike was convinced, represented a get rich quick attraction in its most subtle form, vulgarity disguised as something sophisticated and the use of high class joinery was nothing more than a dressing to further the illusion. Josh accepted most of Mike's arguments but disagreed about the casinos. Wasn't life and death a game of chance, evolution, the cosmos? You just had to treat it philosophically, not let it influence the direction of your life. In some respects casinos were no different to sports stadiums or race tracks, they provided entertainment in a game of chance and skill and in both venues a great deal of money was involved. However, Mike felt uncomfortable with the idea and remained sceptical. Mike and his son Josh argued their positions and eventually reached a compromise. If they were unable to acquire increased funding, they would declare their interest in the casinos and test the bank's reaction.

Jack Hudson, the area manager was a jovial character, round faced, heavily jowled and a bit over weight. He'd gone through the balance sheets, the profit and loss account and the cash flow projections several times and had reached a decision. He'd read nothing to suggest that Edwards Joinery had a good future and doubted whether the present set up was even viable. Richard Dursley Bywaters sat close to the desk with the relevant documents spread before him. Jack Hudson sat further back as though he wished to survey the specimens before him from a safe distance. Mike and Josh tried to appear relaxed while practically holding their breath. Richard shuffled the papers, Jack opened the conversation with a broad smile, 'Mike, it's a great pleasure for me, coming face to face with a sporting legend, I've always been a keen fan of rugby league and I've supported the Saints since I was boy. I used to love watching you play, and many's the time I've admired your performance on the field. As a matter of fact, I'm on the Saints' board of directors, as a financial advisor, and I know you're still envolved with the game, Bradford Bulls, especially young players I believe, and I must say any club is very fortunate to have you on board.'

Mike relaxed, the area manager actually recognised him as a celebrity, the banker was a keen rugby fan and seemed altogether agreeable and Mike felt certain he was about to hear some good news. 'Thanks very much for the compliment, and it's a pleasure meeting you too, a Saints' fan from way back. You probably know more about the game than I do, certainly when it comes to club finances.' Mike allowed himself a little laugh, 'These days though, I'm a Bradford Bulls' supporter.'

Jack's grin broadened, 'It's a great pity we've had to meet in such trying circumstances. As I'm sure you're aware, financially speaking, these are very difficult times and I'm afraid, as far as your business is concerned, we can offer very little help.'

'Mike could hardly take in this unexpected and utterly blank refusal to help. It seemed as though Jack Hudson had no wish to give the matter further consideration.

'What are you saying exactly? I take it you've discussed our position with Richard, that he's given you all the facts?'

'Actually Mike, at your last meeting, you made a very great impression on Richard and apparently you gave him a severe ticking off. He tells me you've little respect for we wretched mortals in the banking profession?'

'Well I think you should look after our industries as a matter of priority, instead of just looking after yourselves. Agriculture and manufacturing are central to our very existence, neglect industry and you neglect its citizens and a nation becomes weak.' Mike fired back in defence.

'I know you feel strongly about this Mike and I accept that banks have made some pretty dreadful decisions, but things are not like they were when you were dealing with your old pal Martin Gough. Things have changed and we're all struggling to deal with those changes. Gobalisation has made a terrific impact on the world's economies. In the past, growth was driven by the U S economy. Now, Asian countries are using cheap labour which we in the West are unable to match. China in particular is influencing the markets. China's manufacturing output alone has driven up the price of raw materials to record levels, making it even harder for our industries to compete. Manufacturing depends on demand and demand for British manufacturing is in decline.'

Mike tried to absorb these facts and was beginning to feel out of his depth.

'Well I think British industry has been deprived of investment. With our experience and scientific acumen, we could and should, have competed with the rest of the world. Germany, France and Italy have managed it, why couldn't we? We've taken the easy money option, letting others do our work, and look where it's led us. Anyway, we didn't come here to discuss world ecomomics, we're here to discuss the future of Edwards Joinery and Josh and I are confident that with our new machines, we can compete with anybody in the manufacture of specialised, high classs joinery.'

'That may be true Mike, and Richard is convinced that you have a market, but at this moment in time your order books are near empty. You haven't secured the big contracts you'd hoped for, the work hasn't materialised. You've been too hasty. Think about it, on the strength of these provisional orders you've turned away regular customers and now you're running out of time and money. The world is becoming smarter Mike, computor intelligence is being used more and more in agriculture and in manufacturing processes. Sensors are now planted in every conceivable piece of equipment. Machines are changing all the time and require updating with on going investment. Your resources are limited and we are in the middle of a deep recession. The prognosis is not good.'

At this point, Josh who had listened very carefully to the area manager, spoke up for the first time. 'The government has practically nationalised your bank with a huge bale out of tax payer's money, our money. They've insisted that you pass this on to viable businesses. Why aren't you following their instructions?'

Jack Hudson realised he was facing stubborn opposition. It was going to be difficult sending these two characters away without some form of compromise. 'The government is asking us to be conservative in our lending on one hand and liberal with it on the other. We can't do both. We're not nationalised, we still have shareholders and need to rebuild our balance sheets. Look, I've no wish to dash your hopes or raise your expectations but there is a very slim chance that something may come of this. After your last meeting, Richard sent me a rather brilliant and comprehensive report, which has raised a few eyebrows at higher levels. In it he made a strong case for Edwards Joinery and other firms like yours. He suggested we approach the government asking them to engage on a programme of public works, such as hospitals and schools, to get the economy moving. We believe government funding to banks alone is not enough and we're collectively asking them to put money directly into public works. It would help unemployment and kick start the construction industry. A meeting with Ministry officials and our directors is scheduled for the end of the month. These sort of initiatives usually take a few weeks and there may be a negative or limited response, but everyone generally agrees it's a good idea. If your hospital contract went ahead, then of course, we'd be in a position to extend your present banking facilities, but I can't promise anything at this stage. In the meantime, I suggest you put your staff on a three day week, withdraw your new unit from the letting agency and find enough work to see you over the next month. We shall require the deeds of your houses as collateral against the inevitable rise in your overdraft which Richard will review after each wages and salaries withdrawal. If the government's response is unfavourable, then I'm afraid, we'll have to consider foreclosure.'

Jack Hudson was no longer smiling, Richard Dursley-Bywaters hadn't said a word and seemed to fade into the background. Mike looked at Josh, Josh looked at his father.They were both thinking casinos. They felt disapointed, betrayed by a banking system which seemed so have detached itself from the needs of industry and was more concerned with making money for it's own hierarchy. True to character, Mike found it impossible to back down in the face of adversity. However, he remained in control and after an embarrassing silence, decided that a little vote of thanks would be the best way to express his feelings, and ignoring Jack Hudson, who sat with his arms folded waiting for the answer, he turned to Richard. 'I'd just like to say Richard, how much we appreciate your efforts on our behalf. You've been true to your word and you're the only reason we'll not be shifting our account. We realise we'd probably fare no better elsewhere, but at least you've given us some hope for the future. You're our kind of banker Richard, and we'll stick with you for the time being.'

Josh was keen to endorse these sentiments, 'Yes, yes it's quite true, Richard's been very positive about Edwards Joinery and I know how much trouble he's taken over that report. He's visited the works, seen our new machinery, met the staff and talked to some of our customers. He's been absolutely brilliant and he's done this in the face of negative pressures within the bank.' Before either of the bankers could respond Josh continued, 'We're not in favour of handing over the deeds of our houses because there's one other factor to consider. We've been invited to tender for sub contract work on two separate casino developements in the city. The work's extensive and covers high class, hardwood joinery and shopfitting. I'm almost through pricing work and we could be looking at a total contract value of over half a million. I honestly believe we're competitive and being local, have an advantage over London and foreign firms. There's a good chance we may win the contract. All we need is a few weeks grace. Surely, with the possibility of this work and the hospital, which we already have in principal, you can give us some breathing space.' Josh looked confident, he wasn't begging, and as he let this last minute manoeuvre sink in he could hear Meg's voice drumming through his brain 'You'll definitely get the contract, there's nae other competiton.' 'Surely', he repeated.

Jack Hudson turned to face his branch manager. Here was chance to deflate the younger man's ego. 'You never mentioned the possibility of these contracts Richard, you must have known about them or perhaps your researches didn't go far enough.'

'This is the first I've heard anything about them.' Richard replied, 'It certainly put's a whole new perspective on things, wouldn't you say?'

Jack noisily cleared his throat, 'Well of course it does, but why didn't you set out your full agenda before we began our discussion?' He focused his attention on Josh, genuinely puzzled by this latest revelation, played at the last moment like a trump card.

'That was my fault.' Mike explained. 'I was all in favour of not pricing the contract. I was ready to turn it down!'

'Ready to turn it down! There's been some publicity about these proposed casinos. It's foreign investment, manna from heaven, and it could lead to a lot more work. Is there something Mike, I'm missing here?'

'No, nothing. The contracts are perfectly straight forward. It was me getting a bit high minded I suppose. Anyway, I realise there's another side to it and there's nothing to be gained in preaching, not at the expense of my family. It's just there's something about casinos, the way they treat money.' Mike though about it for a moment, 'and banks are no different are they, fuelled by greed?' His battered features broke into a smile. 'For the time being, I'll just have to swallow my pride,'

Six weeks for Edwards Joinery slowed to a crawl and the lack of activity took the heart out of the staff who were already on a three day week. The financial position had developed into a crisis, Edwards Joinery was on the brink of adminstration, liquidators were hopping about like vultures round a sick animal and all seemed lost, when one morning, the casino contracts suddenly appeared in the post together with an invitation to a pre-site meeting with a view to agreeing a programme of works. In the project office, plans, elevations, detailed sections of wood panelling and classical mouldings lay spread across the planning desk and together Mike and Josh considered how their own production line and shopfitting would fit into the main programme. Quantities were taken off for orders of materials, machines were made operational and all that remained was to formally sign the contracts. The bank gave them it's full backing and everyone felt an enormous relief. Jack Hudson phoned Mike to congratulate him, he was very matey and wondered whether Mike was interested in helping the Saint's defensive coach in an advisory capacity. The job would only require an occasional visit and he would be well paid for his trouble. Mike wondered what planet he was on and declined the offer.

Before signing the contracts, Mike and Josh attended the pre-construction meeting with representitives of the Vera group, the main contractor, architects, surveyors, engineers, nominated sub contractors and suppliers all present. They met in the conference room of a five star hotel and were offered French canapes with buckets of champagne. Tonino Vera made a brief appearance. He had charisma and was impeccably dressed, extending a measured warmth towards each individual and among a gathering of hard headed businessmen, he looked every inch a tiger of industy. He went out of his way to engage Mike and Josh in conversation, congratulating them on winning an important nominated sub-contract and enquiring whether there were any problems with the Euro Express units and if there were, he would have them put right. Mike and Josh shook his hand, here was a man who knew where he was going and was worth studying.

The financial crisis was over, confidence had been restored, the spirit of enterprise reawakened with renewed hope for the future and everyone was happy. Everyone that is, except Karen and when Karen was unhappy, Mike was unhappy. The months went by with no news of Ben and the police concluded that he'd been drowned. The Nuvola Distante had sunk in deep water and the expense of retrieving a wooden vessel in these circumstances far outweighed the value of salvage. The police told Karen it was out of the question, adding that to discover the reason for her loss, a submersible survey, sometime in the future was possible, but highly unlikely. Marine insurance thought there was nothing to be gained and there was no good reason for an enquiry. All search and rescue operations had been called off and the case had been closed. The authorities had drawn a line under the investigation and this official closure served to put Karen's everyday existence on hold. She found it difficult to connect with people, she lost interest in the events which surrounded her, she was unable to grieve, unable to martial her thoughts, unable to love. She thought about the happy times she'd had with Ben, she blamed herself for every angry word, every hurt, every denial and all those confrontations which had pushed him away from her. She forgave him for everything and wanted his forgiveness in return, knowing that peace of mind would never be hers, it was too late, too late for healing recompense. Her eldest son, her first child, whose birth had brought her so much happiness, so much fullfillment as a woman had gone for ever leaving her with nothing but regrets. Unable to grieve, she began to lose interest in life itself.

Mike tried to comfort her. He told her about the casino contracts, how it would change their lives, how it would get them out of New Horizons and how their marriage could go ahead as planned. Mike tried making love to her, showing her much tenderness but she no longer responded and ending up weeping and he realised with a heavy heart that nothing would ever be the same again.

Then something happened which seemed to bring Karen back into his world. Katrina, showing her mother's character and a maturity which had been forced upon her, gave Karen her support by showing that all was not lost with her children. Enthusiasm for Katrina's work at school had waned in the face of the on going drama surrounding her brother, but inspite of this, she made an extra effort and suceeded in getting three good A levels, adding to the success Matt had already achieved in his GCSE's. Katrina had done this against a background of creeping family tension and an atmosphere of despair. She had gained a place at Manchester University and Karen had suddenly recognised her daughter's worth. In order to celebrate the good news, Karen resolved to prepare an evening meal for Mike and her children, a quiet family get together which might help her battle against apathy and increasing despondency. Katrina and Matt offered to prepare the meal, but Karen had found her courage and insisted that it would be her way of thanking her children for making her so proud.

Torrential rain sluiced along the access balconies which ran the length of each New Horizons housing block. Courtesy lights which still worked spluttered in protest. Damp patches reappeared around the windows and the rain intensified as though it meant to pressure hose away the accumulated grime and graffiti. In one of the flats, behind curtains which lifted in the draughts, Mike, Karen, Matt and Katrina were cramped around a small table. On the wall above the table hung a Lowry original. It was the picture Karen had admired when she first visited Mike's luxury flat and after selling the property, Mike had given it to her as a Valantine gift. The meal was simple but wholesome, and beautifully presented with a large candle set in the middle of the table. No one was ready for small talk and with so many issues hanging in the air, conversation stayed clear of what was on everyone's mind. Mike decided at last to get positive and he began boldly. 'Karen love, I've been going through the property ads and there's a couple I think we should look at, the sooner we all get out of this dump the better. It's the casino contracts, they've made all the difference, turned around the whole situation. Things were looking bad for Edwards Joinery and I was begining to think putting money into new units and modern machinery was a big mistake, but thanks to Josh we're back in business. He's been brilliant in winning these contracts, getting us back on track. At least now we can afford a decent place to live.' Mike hoped a financial update and the fact that he'd scanned the housing market with a view to purchasing a property would at least add a little cheer.

Only Katrina and Matt smiled, 'Cool, really cool' they echoed.

Mike tried again, 'How d'you fancy living in the country love?' He poured Karen another glass of wine.

Karen looked dejected and showed no enthusiasm whatsoever. At last she spoke. 'Mike darling, I know it's not just the business. You're doing this for us as well, because you love us, and I should feel happy, over the moon about it, but I can't. I can't share in the money you earn from the casinos, I'd rather stay in New Horizons than have any part of it.'

Mike was shaken to the core. 'Karen love, without these contracts we'd be in real trouble, the bank would liquidate our assets, we'd be finished.'

'Darling, I'm well aware of the pressure you've been under and I'll understand if you decide to go ahead but I'm afraid it will change our relationship. I'll always love you, but I couldn't marry you, not in these circumstances. '

'I don't understand.' Mike whispered in a state of shock.

Tonino Vera's a crook, I just know it, the money's rotten and he's rotten and I'm convinced Ben was tied up with him in some way. We know Meg Kinnear's a drug dealer, at least she was, that boy Winston said as much, and we know Ben was having an affair with her, it all makes sense. He was seeing her when out of the blue he lands a job with Vera Motors, as far as I know he's never, ever applied for a job. One minute he's a hoodie with an Asbo to his name, running the streets out of of control and out of work, messing around with drugs, sleeping with a woman old enough to be his mother and the next, he's got a job in the motor trade, dressed up like a car salesman. Then Meg takes him on holiday to Italy. Tonino Vera goes as well, at the same time and Euro Express is up for sale. You start asking questions and someone tries blowing us to kingdom come. Darling, there's something going on. I know we're supposed to keep out of it but I think the police are lying to us. I've got to know the truth, the truth about Ben. I'm sorry darling but I can't, I just can't have anything to do with Tonino Vera.' Karen broke down in tears.

Mike was lost for words. Katrina and Matt were equally astonished at their mother's outburst and how she'd turned her back on their chance of an escape from New Horizons. 'Have you any proof of this mum?' Matt questioned, leaving the table to put a comforting arm around his mother's shoulders.

'No, no proof, I just know.' Karen said wiping away the tears. 'Mike, I don't care about having a big house or having lots of money, I only care about our love and the love we've got for our families. I love you so much Mike, more than myself, isn't that enough?'

Mike bowed his head. He stared down at the table cloth. 'Yes my love, it's more than enough. I only wanted the best for you Karen, to give our love every chance, a few extra comforts, God knows you deserve them. I didn't want you to have to struggle any more, I wanted to make life easier.' He raised his head, his eyes met hers, he thought how wonderful she was, how beautiful. He reached for her, across the table, taking both her hands in his. 'If you want me to give up the casino contracts I will, but it'll put me in a very difficult position. I can't hold Josh back, he's worked so damned hard for this, he's set his mind on it and what's really worrying is, where's it going to leave Edwards Joinery?' A feeling of melancholy settled over the table.

In an effort to change the subject and raise their spirits, Katrina went into the kitchen, 'Does anyone want syrup with their bread pudding?' She called.

'Please,' answered Matt.

Then suddenly the door bell rang. Matt answered the door. It was Josh. 'Hi everybody, looks like I'm just in time for the bread pudding,' he joked. No one laughed. 'Congratulations on getting such good A levels Katrina, brilliant, absolutely brilliant,' he said, kissing Karen and then Katrina. He noticed Karen had been crying.

'Hope I havn't come at a bad time?'

'Of course not, we're always glad to see you uncle Josh. It's just a bit of a surprise that's all. Would you like some bread pudding?' Katrina offered.

Mike had been wrestling with this latest turn of events and his thoughts now centred on Josh and his family. How on earth could he broach the subject? He'd completely gone off the bread pudding. 'Hello Josh, we weren't expecting you but I'm glad you're here, there's some things we need to discuss.'

Well actually Dad, I'm here for the same reason. There's something important I've got to tell you and should have told you right from the start. It all happened today, the one day you wanted to spend with Karen, it's about the casino contracts. They were fixed.' Josh looked nervous, ashamed even as the words tumbled out.

Karen couldn't resist it, 'I knew it.' She said.

'Fixed?' Mike questioned.

'It's a long story Dad and I'm going to be honest, I wanted those contracts. As far as I was concerned we had no choice in the matter. I'd pushed you into a huge investment and I was afraid of letting you down. You knew what Edwards Joinery mean't to me and you went along with it even though I knew your heart wasn't in it.' Josh studied his father for a reaction. 'You're a great guy Dad, the best, and when the offer for the casino contracts came through, I went for them hook line and sinker. But then you see, I'd had a phone call saying that there was no competition, the job was ours and not to be afraid of quoting a high figure.'

'I can hardly get my mind round this.' Mike interrupted, as shock gave way to intrigue. 'Who made the call?'

'I'm pretty sure it was that Meg woman. She didn't say her name, but she enquired after Ben and had a Scottish accent. She seemed to think Ben might be working for us. It's a mystery I know and at first I didn't take it seriously, but when the contracts arrived I went along with it and slapped on a twenty five percent profit.'

'This Meg seems to have a hell of a lot of influence. But why us? I still don't get it,' Mike said, having fresh thoughts about Tonino Vera.

'She was very concerned about Ben, I could sense it in her voice and I think she thought she was helping him in some way. When you think about it, she knew about you and Karen and Edwards Joinery. I think she's a smart cookie and has some sort of hold over Tonino Vera, who can say, it's totally weird,' Josh reasoned.

'So what are you saying Josh?' Karen broke in, anxious to hear more about Ben.

'I'm saying, if Dad's agreable, that we should ditch the casinos, we haven't signed the contracts.'

'I just can't keep up with you Josh. Sounds as though you've had an attack of conscience. Karen feels the same, she thinks we should pull out because she believes Tonino's a crook and from what you're saying it seems she could be right. But what about the bank, about the business, about our future? Where do we go from here?'

'No Dad it's not a matter of conscience, or the fact I've kept this from you. To be honest, I can't afford that many scruples, not when it comes to survival, not when it comes down to family. I was quite happy to go ahead, more than happy, I was over the moon, my risk taking had been vindicated, I was off the hook.'

'Then why, for God's sake?' Mike said, curiously relieved to find that his dilemma had been solved, but increasing anxious about the fact they had no work.

'For a very good reason. Two bills of quantities arrived in this morning's post, inviting us to price for joinery work in two new primary schools as a nominated sub-contractor.' Josh let the news sink in, 'and this letter,' He produced a letter from his inside pocket. 'Take a look at this,' he passed the letter to Mike. 'It's from Richard at the bank. The hospital contract is going ahead as originally planned.'

A Subaru Forester claiming low emissions, with a two litre diesel engine purred through the back streets on its approach to New Horizons. It was black, lost in the shadows as it cruised between the streetlights, it's threatening form, emerging at intervals. Two men sat in the front of the vehicle, hunched forward, their black raincoats further adding to the overall brooding vision of menace. The SUV slid into the New Horizons car park and both men got out. They moved easily and quickly like athletes, with the taller man leading the way as if he knew where he was heading. They entered the stairwell in one of the blocks and tried the lift. It wasn't working. The taller man, without hesitation, made for the stairs and the heavier guy with an older face and tough looking features chased after him.

On the landing of the third floor they were greeted with a brightly coloured mural which stood out from the rest of the graffiti. In giant lettering, some lovesick moron had sprayed, 'Luv is Magick.' The rain had eased and their pace slackened as they walked the length of the dimly lit balcony. Near the end they stopped outside the door of Karen's flat and the older man caught the arm of the younger one and said, 'Now don't let me down, remember, I'm breaking all the rules here, I could end up losing my pension.'

The taller man rang the door bell, 'I know you are, and you'll never know just how much this means to me but I can't think why you're doing it, why you're taking so much risk, why you're willing to trust me when you hardly know me.'

'All my life I've carried out orders, I'm pissed off with it, I want to do something right for a change, use my own judgement and I know you better than you know yourself, understand you better, perhaps even better than your own ma. '

'I'm never gonna be able to pay you back for this.'

'Just let it be our secret.' The tough guy looked at his watch, 'Ok Ben, I'm giving you thirty minutes, I'll wait in the car.'

End

www.ingramcontent.com/pod-product-compliance
Lightning Source LLC
Chambersburg PA
CBHW021952010726
47494CB00003B/701